In Plain Sight

Rebecca Deel

Copyright © 2017 Rebecca Deel

All rights reserved.

ISBN: 1979817480
ISBN-13: 978-1979817486

DEDICATION

To my amazing husband.

ACKNOWLEDGMENTS

Cover design by Melody Simmons.

CHAPTER ONE

Darcy St. Claire stood in the center of what was supposed to be a large living room. With so much junk everywhere, she couldn't tell the dimensions of the room. Anywhere from the size of a closet to a townhouse. Towers of newspapers, books, and magazines littered the space. Piles of clothes. Box after box of shoes, both men's and women's, which was odd since the lady who'd owned the house had been a widow at the time of her death. Why would she buy that many men's shoes? And Darcy was only ten feet from the front door. What did the rest of this monstrosity hold? She shuddered to think about cleaning out this place. Months of work, especially if she had to do it alone.

She turned to stare at the real estate agent, an older woman with an overly bright candy-apple red smile curving her mouth, her expression hopeful. "I thought you said this was a fixer-upper, Mrs. Watson. It would be simpler to burn the place and start from scratch." This dump had to be a serious fire hazard.

"We're experiencing a housing crisis in Otter Creek. So many people have moved into the area, we don't have much available housing. I could find you some land and introduce you to contractors."

"How long to build a house for me?"

"Six months, at least. Dunlap County is in a building boom. I might be able to find you an apartment to rent in the meantime." From her expression, though, the chances of that were slim.

Six months, provided there were no delays which was an impossibility. Darcy sighed. She didn't have the luxury of waiting that long. Living in an apartment? Not in this lifetime. She was finished living the nomadic lifestyle of the past 20 years, whether she wanted to be or not.

Anger tinged with disappointment boiled inside her. Darcy shoved the dark emotions down into a deep well. Wallowing in self-pity wouldn't change anything except to make those around her miserable. It was no one's fault her health wouldn't allow her to continue on the same career path. Her brother, Trent, didn't need to worry about her when he was on a mission with Fortress Security, and he would if she didn't get her act together and reinvent herself. The last thing she wanted to be was a distraction that might cost her brother his life.

She focused on her surroundings, trying to be objective. The outside would be beautiful once it was painted, the shutters and roof replaced. The inside, though. She blew out a breath. She didn't know what would be required to fix the house. This room was filled with wall-to-wall clutter except for a small path to another part of the house. There might be holes in the walls big enough to drive a semi through. Until all the piles of items were cleared, she wouldn't know if the wallpaper was hideous or if great swaths of wall were missing. The small path through the room revealed scuffed hardwood, bound to be gorgeous once restored. At the moment, the hardwood looked tired and scarred.

Three floors to this Victorian nightmare. Did all the rooms look like this one? If so, how many Dumpsters would be necessary to clear the chaos? Too many to count. Worse, she couldn't tackle this project by herself now. Good thing Trent was here, at least until his next mission. If she took on this project along with the shop on the town square, she'd need his help and wasn't sure she could count on him. His job sent him all over the globe at a moment's notice.

The real estate agent's cell phone rang. She glanced at the screen. "I have to take this, dear. Look around." She scurried through the door into the cold December afternoon.

Darcy scowled. Mrs. Watson couldn't fool her. She was getting out of this place before one of the towering disasters toppled over on her. She continued following the path through the room and emerged into a large kitchen. At least, she thought it was large. Even at five-eight, she couldn't see much. In this room, every available flat surface was covered with glasses, plates, utensils, napkins, napkin rings, and candle holders, including the deep stainless steel sink.

The floor space resembled a mini warehouse of boxed and canned food. Incredulous, she counted. Who needed 25 boxes of crackers, 50 of macaroni and cheese, 30 of rice mixes, 100 of instant mashed potatoes? She lost count of the boxes containing canned food.

Her gaze stopped on the refrigerator. A knot formed in the pit of her stomach. Surely not. With so many items piled in front of it, there couldn't be food in the fridge. If she was wrong, science experiments grew in there, a truly scary thought. Her lips twitched. Perfect job for Trent. Somehow she'd con him into checking the appliance for her while she was out of the house. Just in case she was wrong. He was a tough military man. He could handle a bad odor or two.

She laughed softly. Yep, she was officially a sucker, already making plans for this wreck. Darcy hoped Fortress didn't deploy her brother anytime soon. She couldn't make this hovel livable without help, especially the kind with bulging muscles. That described Trent, bulging biceps and triceps, a broad chest heavy with muscle, handsome. Too bad some awesome lady didn't value him as much as she did.

Hearing Mrs. Watson's laughter spurred Darcy to continue along the path through the house. From room to room she wandered, incredulous at the number of empty pill bottles, cotton balls, Q-tips, toothpaste, toothbrushes, and hair brushes.

She knelt to examine a collection of music boxes in a room on the third floor. One in particular caught her eye. A grand piano. While she examined the music box closer, the floor creaked to the right of her position.

Darcy froze. Had to be the old house settling. Then why did she feel as if someone were watching her? Ridiculous, Darcy, she told herself. No one was up here but her. She focused her attention once again on the miniature piano. Such exquisite handiwork. Maybe the relatives of the former owner would allow her to buy this from them.

Another creak sent chills racing down her spine. The only way to quit spooking herself was to check that side of the room. Her lips curved. If she could find a path over there. As she shifted her weight, preparing to stand, a wall of junk cascaded down on her head.

Darcy gasped, hugging the little piano against her stomach to protect it. While waiting for the flood to stop, she heard someone running away from the room. Oh, man. There had been someone inside this room with her. Mrs. Watson? Though she longed to believe that, she couldn't. The real estate agent was wearing cute spiked heels. The footsteps she heard had been made by something other than heels. Boots, maybe.

She listened for some indication that the intruder was still there, but heard nothing. Maybe it was a kid playing hooky from school.

In any case, she needed to finish the house tour. Music box still in hand, she continued the quick scan, staying in doorways to prevent another cave in. The only room not inundated was on the second floor in what was probably the former owner's bedroom. At least here the floor was clear. Against the walls, though, were stacked hundreds of candles.

She knelt beside the closest stack of candles, chose one with swirls of blue and white. Darcy sniffed, eyebrows rising. Blueberry. Sweet. She wondered how many scents were represented by all the candles. Whatever else the former owner had collected, this stash was one she'd keep. After all, who knew when she might need candles?

On the first floor again, Darcy pushed open the door to the downstairs bathroom and shook her head. Box after box of bath soap, bottles of shampoo, piles of towels and washcloths. A cold wind blew through the room. Was the window broken? Frowning, she picked her way to the window. Not broken, open. Why was the window open on such a blustery day? Maybe the real estate agent wanted to let in fresh air. On tiptoes, she peered through the opening to the backyard. Only one gorgeous tree. At least there wasn't a junk heap in the back. She'd need a bush hog or a herd of hungry goats to take down the forest back there, but thankfully no junk cars or more trash littered the lot.

As she dropped back to her heels, she noticed dirt on the linoleum in the shape of a footprint. Someone had been in the house. Chill bumps surged over her body. After ordering a dozen super-sized Dumpsters, the first order of business would be installing a security system. Wonder if she could train the goats to be guard dogs? Yeah, probably not. She couldn't subject a dog to these conditions, either. No telling what a pet would get into. Nothing good, that was for sure. Besides, she didn't have a handle on her own life right now. She'd like to adopt a dog in the future, though.

"Ms. St. Claire? Where are you?"

"Walking down the hallway toward the living room."

"Oh, good. I'll just wait here for you, then."

Right. It was fine for Darcy to risk life and limb in this place, but not the real estate agent. To be fair, she was several years younger than Mrs. Watson. A fall for Darcy meant trips to the chiropractor. If the agent fell, she could break a bone, not something Darcy wanted on her conscience.

The older woman waited near the front door. Bet she planned for a fast escape if the piles began shifting. Couldn't blame her, not after her experience on the third floor. Darcy eyed some of the more unstable piles as she passed, praying nothing shifted and buried her. "I found a music box that I'd like to have. Do you think the owners would sell it to me?"

"I don't see why not. The family has washed their hands of the house and its contents. Take it with you. Now, this house has good bones, doesn't she? What do you think?"

It would be cheaper to light a match than rehab this place. She knew zip about repairing a house. What was she thinking? "You should cut me an excellent deal. This house will take a lot of money to bring her back to life."

The woman's face lit up. "I think we can come to an agreement." She quoted a figure and waited anxiously for Darcy to respond.

She fought to keep her expression neutral, but the figure was a good deal less than she was expecting. The real estate agent must want to unload this white elephant, which made Darcy suspect something else was wrong with the place that she couldn't see. "I don't know. This place will take months to make into a home, not to mention I'm setting up a new business at the same time. It's a lot to take on."

Mrs. Watson dropped the price by $10,000 and waited.

She could obtain a price lower, but didn't have the heart. Everybody needed to make a living. "Deal. Will you take a check?"

"Yes, of course. Oh, you won't be sorry, my dear."

Darcy had a bad feeling the real estate agent was wrong. She foresaw nothing but sore muscles and sleepless nights in her near future. Grabbing her check book, she filled in the amount, signed it, and handed over the paper. "When will you have the paperwork ready?"

"Tomorrow morning. I'll meet you here at ten and hand over the keys. Congratulations, my dear."

Back in her car, Darcy waved at the agent as she drove away. One last glance at the huge old house had her questioning her own sanity. Taking on a house was a big responsibility. A home as old as this one was sure to be a money pit and require constant maintenance. She knew a hammer from a wrench, but that was as far as her home repair expertise went.

The more she thought about the house, though, the more determined she was to breathe new life into the place. She would reinvent this home much as she now had to reinvent herself.

She hoped her brother saw the house's potential. She wanted this new life to work. Darcy was tired of big cities and could no longer travel ten months a year. Trent recommended Otter Creek, a small town where her new dream could germinate and flourish. From what she'd seen, this town was the perfect place to begin her life over again. Now she wanted to give the rundown house the same opportunity. They both deserved a new life.

A last glance in the rearview mirror. Her thoughts shifted to the muddy footprints in the downstairs bathroom and the mysterious footsteps. Uneasiness twisted in her gut.

She hoped the prints belonged to a curious teenager, not an adult with a hidden agenda.

CHAPTER TWO

Rio Kincaid shook his head at the mess his bodyguard trainees had left behind. His friend and teammate, Quinn Gallagher, had hustled this new class out to the shooting range for a weapons session. This group of trainees was impressive. Fortress Security CEO, Brent Maddox, would be pleased.

Approaching footsteps drew Rio's attention to the far side of the room. He paused in gathering the medical debris from his field medicine training session in Personal Security International's gym and grinned at the fellow Fortress Security operative crossing the large wooden floor in his direction. "Trent St. Claire, what brings you to Otter Creek?"

"My sister, Darcy. She's opening a new shop in town."

His eyebrow rose. "What kind of shop?" He envisioned dresses or a hair place.

"Something with food." Trent shrugged. "Not sure what, to tell you the truth. Darcy loves experimenting in the kitchen when she has time."

Didn't sound as though food service would be a wise career choice, though he hesitated to say anything to his friend. Maybe she'd worked in the food industry at an earlier time. For her sake, he hoped that was true. "You'll have to introduce me to her. I'd love to meet Darcy."

His friend grinned. "She's not bad, for a kid sister."

Rio chuckled. "That sounds like a statement to use for blackmail, St. Claire. I'll be sure to pass that along to her at the most appropriate time. How long are you in town?"

"Not sure." His friend grimaced. "I'm expecting a call from Maddox any time. Zane sent me a text a few minutes ago."

Zane Murphy was Fortress Security's communications and research guru. In Rio's experience, the only person better at communication and research was Navy SEAL Jon Smith, another Fortress operative. "Does she know you'll be deployed soon?"

"I promised her I'd help her settle into a house and open the shop. I'm afraid I'll be breaking that promise."

"Can Maddox send another team?"

"No one else is available and there's a hostage situation in Colombia. Three little kids were taken from their beds. They're the grandkids of a U.S. ambassador."

Rio whistled. Talk about a political hot button. Even without the connection to the ambassador, Trent wouldn't pass on the opportunity to rescue innocent children. He didn't blame his friend. Rio loved kids, too. "How can I help?"

Trent helped him gather discarded medical supplies. He cleared a small area of debris before answering. "Do you know anything about Sjogren's Syndrome?"

He frowned as he tossed trash in a bag he held. "I don't think so. Why?"

"It's an autoimmune disease, one Darcy's been diagnosed with."

Oh, man. Not an easy thing to hear from the doctor. "Hate to hear that, Trent. How's she doing?"

"Holding her own, I guess. I haven't been around much." Guilt clouded his gaze. "Our parents are gone now, so it's just us."

Rio understood. His mother had passed away from cancer the year he entered middle school. Now, it was only him, his three brothers, and his father. Lance Kincaid had called his sons his little men and still did, though Rio and his brothers were each over six feet tall. At five eight, the sons towered over their father.

"What do you need from me, Trent?"

A sigh from the other operative. "I hate to ask since I know you and your teammates are busy."

He shoved the last of the trash in the bag. "Life never slows down and we're friends. I don't consider this an imposition. Ask."

"Be available for Darcy when you're not working or training."

Rio wanted to laugh. That left about five minutes a day for Trent's sister. Guess he'd be keeping some late hours when his friend left. Who needed sleep? "No problem. If she needs more help than I can provide alone, I'll volunteer the rest of Durango." He grinned.

"With friends like you, who needs enemies?" Trent muttered. "Nate's still on his honeymoon, isn't he?"

"Nope. He's been back two days." Though not at work yet, Nate Armstrong, Durango's EOD man, was due in the following day. His beautiful wife, Stella, a former U.S. Marshal, planned to ride along with one of the two Otter Creek police detectives until her broken wrist healed. While Rio couldn't put her to work helping Darcy, he didn't have a problem drafting Nate. "Don't worry, my friend. We'll look after her."

In the meantime, Rio would research her condition. More knowledge about the disease might enable him to help her cope. Sometimes one piece of information could make the difference between comfort and misery. "How long ago was your sister diagnosed with Sjogren's?"

"Six months. It's taken her this long to complete her scheduled concert dates."

"Concert dates? Your sister is a singer?"

A snort. "Her talent doesn't extend to vocal music. Darcy is a concert pianist." He paused, a frown forming. "*Was.*"

"Is she popular in Europe?" That might explain why he'd never heard her name mentioned. Though his teammates razzed him, Rio listened to piano music to bleed off adrenaline. It was either that or work out like a demon. A smile curved his lips. Most of the time he did both.

"She's popular all over the world, man. Performed under the stage name Darcy Melton."

Rio froze in the act of cinching the bag of trash. He swallowed hard. Darcy Melton, the woman who'd kept him sane on deployments in the Army and now on missions for Fortress. Nights when he couldn't sleep, her music kept him company. Her dark hair and chocolate brown eyes starred in his dreams the nights he did sleep. He'd never attended one of her concerts, though he'd tried over the years. Rio had scored tickets to one concert at Carnegie Hall only to be deployed unexpectedly on a Delta mission. He'd never tried again. Now he might not have a chance.

The forced career change must be devastating for her. Rio had zero musical talent, but he loved music enough to read interviews by musicians he favored, including Darcy Melton. She'd practiced the piano six to eight hours a day from the time she was in elementary school. Music had permeated her entire existence.

"I see you have heard of her."

"She's an amazing pianist."

"Yeah, she was a child prodigy. Darcy's been performing all over the world since she was ten years old."

"Now I understand why she announced her retirement a few months ago," Rio said, voice soft. "Her publicist put out the story that she was tired of life on the road. Why didn't they announce the truth? People would have understood." He certainly would have. Instead, there'd been criticism of her playing and complaints about her being a diva, wanting more money to perform than she was offered. Didn't fit with what he knew of her. Then again, he didn't know anything about the real woman, only the stage presence and what little actual information was sprinkled throughout the interviews. The rumors about her diva tendencies might be true. Guess he'd reserve his opinion until after he met her. If she was anything like Trent, he'd bet his original opinion of her was correct.

"My sister is an intensely private person. After living in the spotlight for twenty years, she didn't want to share something this personal and especially didn't want pity from her audience. She decided to step away from the concert life with the story she no longer wanted to tour. The truth is Darcy is tired of that life. She's been talking about leaving the concert stage for two years. She hesitated because it's the only life she knows and she claims this is her sole talent."

For her sake, Rio hoped that wasn't true. Otherwise, her shop wouldn't have many customers. Most people were picky about their meals. If they'd eaten some of the so-called meals he and his Delta teammates had consumed, they would be considerably less critical of anything served to them. He shuddered. Even Nate, who was skilled in the kitchen, couldn't make some things taste decent. "And living in a small town is what she wants as a substitute for traveling around the world?" Hard for Rio to imagine Trent's sister being happy with such a drastic change in her lifestyle. Otter Creek, Tennessee, was a world away from the concert stage and recording contracts. How long would she last before needing the stimulus of a faster pace?

Rio, on the other hand, doubted he would ever live in a large city again. Being a member of a Special Forces team for so many years, he saw danger at every turn and hated being in crowds. Made his skin crawl to have strangers at his back. Living in Otter Creek suited him.

At that moment, Trent's cell phone chirped. His friend closed his eyes and sighed before pulling the instrument from his pocket. "It's Zane. Maddox activated my unit."

"When do you leave?"

"One hour. I have to meet the Fortress jet in Knoxville. My teammates will already be on board."

Rio took a last look around the gymnasium. Everything was shipshape, ready for the close quarters combat class scheduled for the first session in the morning. His lips twitched. After the five-mile run and agility training course. Good thing Chef Nate was back from his honeymoon. A friend had been cooking meals in his place, but she was almost eight months pregnant and had her own personal chef business to run. Her husband, the police chief of Otter Creek, didn't want Serena on her feet that long every day, a sentiment the medic agreed with. After noticing her swollen ankles, Rio had bought a cushioned barstool for her to sit on while she chopped, peeled, stirred, and created mouthwatering meals in PSI's kitchen. None of the bodyguard trainees had complained about Nate's absence, something sure to happen if one of the other instructors cooked. No surprise, though. Serena Blackhawk was as skilled in the kitchen as Nate. "Need a lift?"

"Nah. I have my truck. I'll leave it in the long-term lot at the airport. I'll be back here as soon as I finish this mission. Listen, if you're finished here, would you like to meet Darcy?"

His heart leaped in his chest. Have a chance to meet and talk to the woman responsible for keeping him together over the years? "Absolutely. She'll be more comfortable with me if you introduce us." And it would give Rio a chance to see Darcy and Trent together, watch their interaction.

"She texted me a few minutes ago. She's at her store, checking the layout and meeting the contractor."

Rio slung his gear over his shoulder. "Let's go. I'll follow you, stay around if she needs anything after you leave."

"Thanks, Rio. Darcy means the world to me. I don't want to let her down."

The medic clapped his friend on the shoulder. "She'll understand. Don't worry, Trent. We'll take good care of her while you're gone."

Fifteen minutes later, he parked his SUV beside Trent's truck in front of a vacant storefront. A slender woman with dark brown hair stood inside with her back to the bank of windows. He climbed out of his vehicle and met his friend on the sidewalk. "Want me to give you a minute with your sister?"

"Yeah, might be best." Trent looked troubled.

"Sure. I'll wait out here." And try not to look like he was freezing. What he wouldn't give for a hot meal and a chance to watch a ball game. Four o'clock came early. He and his teammates completed their own physical training before going to PSI to work with the future bodyguards. Wouldn't do to have the trainees be in better shape than Durango. He and his teammates had a reputation to uphold. Besides, to do their jobs with Fortress, they had to be in peak physical condition.

"Why are you standing on the sidewalk?"

The familiar voice had him pivoting. He grinned at the tall woman striding toward him. "Del. You look beautiful, as always."

The wife of his Delta unit leader laughed and kissed his cheek. "You do have a way with women, Mr. Kincaid. So what are you doing out here? It's too cold to be standing around without a purpose."

He inclined his head toward the store where Trent was hugging his sister, talking to her while one hand stroked her long hair.

"Who is that?" Del Cahill frowned as she studied the brother and sister.

"Trent St. Claire, a Fortress operative. The woman is his sister, Darcy. She's opening a restaurant."

"We can use another one. It takes too long to be seated in restaurants now."

"Price of growth."

"Do yourself a favor and don't say that where Josh and his brothers-in-law can hear you."

"I value my life too much to do that. Haven't seen my fearless unit leader today. He working third shift again?"

She nodded. "Says he likes it, that the night shift is busier than the day shifts."

He couldn't imagine a town the size of Otter Creek having an active night shift for law enforcement before moving here. Turned out small, fast growing towns had problems with crime, too. "Going home?"

"I have a dinner date with my husband." Del smiled. "He's taking me to a restaurant in Cherry Hill."

"Nice. Order the most expensive thing on the menu."

"I'll tell him you said that."

"Wouldn't expect otherwise, sugar. See you later." He watched her stride down the street to her SUV. His friend was a very lucky man. Otter Creek residents adored their favorite bookseller, as did Rio and the rest of Durango.

He glanced toward the empty storefront again, saw that his friend had freed his sister from his embrace and was looking over her shoulder to the clipboard she held. Probably safe to go inside now. At least he wouldn't freeze anymore. Rio pulled open the glass door and stepped into the building.

CHAPTER THREE

Cold air rushed into the room. Darcy paused in her explanation of the layout she envisioned for her deli and glanced over her shoulder. Her eyes widened at the sight of the tall, dark-haired man walking into her store. Who was this guy? Her gaze skimmed over him. Wow. This one could make a mint on magazine covers. Military short hair, swarthy complexion, trim waist, muscular thighs, broad chest and shoulders. Good grief.

Trent swung around. "Rio, come meet Darcy."

Should have known, Darcy thought. Another friend of her brother. Wonder if this one worked for Fortress as well?

"Darce, this is my friend, Rio Kincaid. Rio, my sister, Darcy."

A smile curved his mouth as he shook her hand. "Good to meet you, Ms. St. Claire. I've enjoyed working with your brother."

Knew it. Another black ops guy. Why did they all have to be so good looking? They were never home, a fact reinforced by Trent's call back to duty. What was she going to do about that monstrous dump Mrs. Watson was passing off as a house? Guess she would clear one room at a time until he returned. All she needed was one bedroom and bathroom shoveled out. Shouldn't take long to clear the soap and shampoo in the first floor bathroom. The rest could wait. "Please, call me Darcy."

By necessity, her main priority was the store since it would be her main source of income. Half the money she'd earned over the years while touring was still in her various accounts and invested for the future. More was in a separate account to start her business and rehab the house. From the looks of the Victorian house, she might need to transfer more funds. "Are you part of Trent's team?"

"I'm a member of Durango."

She blinked. "Durango?"

"Army grunts," Trent said. "Second rate to the SEALs."

"Yeah?" Rio's eyes twinkled. "Amazing we survived all the terrorists without you frog boys, isn't it?"

"When do you leave, Trent?"

Her brother glanced at his watch. "I have just enough time to swing by the motel and grab my gear."

Darcy bit her bottom lip. Rats. He didn't have enough time to look at the house. Darcy would love a second opinion on whether to rehab the place or just knock it down.

"What is it, Darce?"

"I bought a house."

Trent's mouth gaped. "Already? You looked at it an hour ago. Must have been some house."

An understatement. Maybe it was best her brother didn't see the place until she cleaned it up a little. Okay, cleaned it a lot. Trent wouldn't miss much anyway. His missions were short, but numerous. In truth, he was always gone. She didn't have much room to talk. Until recently, she traveled most of the year as well.

Was Rio away as much as Trent? And why should she care? She'd just met the man. "The house isn't going anywhere." Not unless a tornado blew through here and literally took it off her hands. That would not be a great tragedy. It would certainly save her a ton of money and headaches.

"Which house did you buy?" Rio asked.

Uh oh. He lived here and Otter Creek wasn't a thriving metropolis. He'd recognize the house when she identified the right one. After all, how many Victorian disasters could this place have? Her gaze darted to the Fortress operative. "Um, the Victorian over on Piedmont Drive." She prayed he didn't spill the news about the money pit masquerading as a house. Then again, if he hadn't visited the place, he might not know about the mountains of junk the rooms contained.

He stared at her a moment. His gaze flicked to her brother before shifting back to her. "Big place for one person."

She relaxed. Just like she thought, Rio knew the exact house she'd bought, but for reasons known only to him for the moment, he wasn't going to say anything to Trent. Thank goodness. The last thing she wanted to do was worry her brother. She'd make do until he returned to help haul load after load of trash from her new home. All she needed was a clean bedroom and bathroom. The rest could wait.

And that brought her thoughts full circle to the muddy footprints on the bathroom floor. Yet another reason she was reluctant for her brother to leave town. She couldn't ask a stranger to stay in the house with her and she didn't have friends here yet.

"Rio's agreed to step in for me, Darce. I hope I won't be out of the country for long. In the meantime, call him if you need anything."

Right. Like she'd call an acquaintance of five minutes to come haul trash to Dumpsters. "I'll be fine."

Trent cupped her chin in the palm of his hand. "You need help, Darce. Setting up the shop and moving into a new house is not a job for the faint of heart."

Or those with a disease affecting their joints. At least her brother hadn't blurted the details of her situation to Rio. Her eyes narrowed. Or had he? "You told him, didn't you?"

Her big, tough, older brother looked uncomfortable at first, then that stubborn streak of the St. Claire clan showed itself. "You need help. I trust Rio to do whatever you need."

She scowled. "I don't want to impose. I just need some muscle. I'll wait for your return."

"I have muscles," Rio said with a quick grin. "I'll be glad to do the heavy lifting, Darcy."

No point in making the man miserable for offering to help. She might as well kick her pride to the curb. This wouldn't be the only time she'd have to ask for a favor, no matter how much it galled her. Still made her mad it was necessary. "I appreciate the offer, although I hate needing it."

"Understandable."

Looking relieved to be out of the doghouse, Trent swept her into a gentle hug.

"Trent."

"Hmm."

"I want a real hug. I won't break."

Immediately, his bear hug tightened. "Love you, sis." His voice sounded thick.

"I love you, too. Come back to me safe."

He pressed a kiss to the top of her head and released her. Trent held out his hand to Rio. "Thanks, man. I owe you."

"No debt between friends, buddy. Watch your six."

"Copy that."

Darcy blinked away the mist in her eyes as her brother climbed into his truck and drove away. Suck it up, Darcy.

Trent would be fine. He might come home banged up a little, but he'd be home.

"Trent's team is one of the best," his friend said, his voice soft. "They're as tight as family and watch each other's backs."

"Is your team the same?" Darcy turned toward Rio, curious. "You watch out for each other?"

"Oh, yeah. We've been through some rough patches. I trust them with my life."

Rough patches, huh? Bet those patches involved gunfire and bombs. Darcy could not relate. The worst thing that happened to her for the last two decades included her piano not arriving at the concert hall on time or missing her connecting flight. Guess that made her a powderpuff. "How long have you been working together?"

A grin curved his mouth. "Fifteen years and counting. We survived basic training together, were assigned to the same unit, volunteered for Ranger training, and then Delta. We separated from the Army at the same time, then joined Fortress and started PSI."

Delta? Holy cow. And Trent had razzed him for not being a SEAL? The cowboys of the military were tough and found a way to accomplish their mission, no matter what obstacles they had to climb over, go around, or blow up. "Did you work with my brother while you were in the military?"

"We crossed paths." He nodded at the clipboard. "Do you have what you need?"

"I do. The contractor was a great help. I should be able to open in a month or so. Depends on whether I can get the interior ready in time." A job for Trent she might have to farm out to the contractor.

She sighed. With Trent gone for an unknown stretch, she'd use the time to start clearing the house.

"My teammates and I will pitch in, Darcy. We can wield paint brushes as well as guns." He paused a moment, his gaze on her face. "You look tired. Are you finished here for now?"

Guess she hadn't hidden the fatigue. "I can't do anything else tonight. I'm meeting the contractor tomorrow. He and his crew will start in the morning."

"Have you eaten dinner?"

She shook her head. "I planned to eat with Trent." Darcy hadn't paid attention to the food choices near the motel or eaten anything since that morning. Probably explained why she felt like curling up on the floor and taking a nap.

"There's a great hamburger place not far from here. Come eat dinner with me. I'd love to hear about your store and your plans for the house."

Darcy studied him a moment. "Have you been inside the place?"

"Nope, but I've heard rumors around town. You have a lot of work ahead of you if half of what's being said is true."

"Whatever the grapevine is saying isn't as bad as the reality. Thanks for keeping my secret. I didn't want Trent distracted while he's deployed."

"Thought that might be the case. So, may I treat you to the best hamburger and fries around?"

The knot in her stomach loosened. No one would ever know it, but she hated eating alone in a strange place. Stupid problem. It's why she had taken most of her meals in her hotel suite when she traveled. "I'd like that. I haven't eaten for a while."

His eyes narrowed. "How long?"

She shrugged, not wanting to admit it had been almost twelve hours. Trent would have had a fit if he knew.

"Too long, then. Where is your car?"

"Right outside the door."

"Drive to the motel and park your car. I'll follow you and take you to Burger Heaven. It's the most popular restaurant in town."

She smiled. "Sounds like Heaven to me."

Rio laughed. "Come on. If you ask nicely, I'll spring for a milkshake, too."

"Deal." She could do nice for the price of a shake. A strawberry delight was calling her name. Darcy grabbed her purse from the corner and turned off the lights. Rio waited for her to lock up and opened the driver's door of her car.

"I'll be right behind you." He climbed into the SUV parked two spaces over and cranked the engine.

She backed into the town square and drove five blocks to the motel. Not exactly the Ritz, she mused. But it was clean. Her room had two double beds covered in autumn-colored bedspreads. The two chairs in the room were standard issue with minimal cushioning, the material gold. A double sink. Small bathroom. Her lips curved. Definitely not the standard she was used to, but it wasn't a dump, either. She flinched. Unlike her new house.

At the motel, Rio parked next to her car and came around to open his passenger door for her. Grateful the SUV had running boards, she stepped up and settled into the leather seat. Oh, man. The leather smelled great and the thick padding felt good to her joints.

When he climbed behind the steering wheel, Darcy took the opportunity to study his profile from the corner of her eye. Yep, this guy was seriously good looking. More than that, Rio Kincaid was nice. From what little time she'd spent in conversation with him, he seemed to have a good sense of humor. Hard to beat that combination.

A couple minutes later, he turned into a crowded parking lot.

"Wow. You weren't kidding about this place being popular." Every space but three were filled with cars, trucks, and SUVs.

"The burgers here taste like my grandmother used to make, and the fries rival those of the major fast food chains."

Burger Heaven was competition of sorts. No hamburgers and fries in her restaurant. She hoped Otter Creek would like more food choices. She needed her idea to work. Who knew reinventing herself would test her self-confidence?

Walking into the bustling burger joint, Rio's hand settled at the small of her back, his touch light. Many people greeted him as they made their way to the counter to order. Amusement curved her lips as more than one pair of female eyes followed the Fortress operative's progress across the floor.

After placing her order, she found a table at the back corner of the restaurant. Figuring Rio was like her brother, Darcy left the seat against the wall for him. Unlike law enforcement and military, she liked having her back to the crowd.

Rio placed a filled tray on the table and slid onto the bench across from her. "Cheeseburger with fries, soft drink, and strawberry shake, as promised."

Darcy eyed the food remaining on the tray. He'd ordered twice as much food as she had. "Do you eat like that all the time?"

His laughter caused heads all over the restaurant to turn in their direction.

"Sorry," she murmured. "I didn't mean to imply you eat too much. You don't have an ounce of fat on you." And she really needed to shut up. She basically admitted she'd been ogling him. She'd been spending way too much time in the company of her piano. How pathetic was that?

Darcy sighed and unwrapped her hamburger. Maybe if she kept her mouth filled she wouldn't make any more social gaffes. In the end, she needn't have worried. Rio was popular in Otter Creek and several people stopped by the booth to chat for a minute. He took the time to introduce her to each one. By the time the stream of visitors slowed to a trickle, she'd polished off her meal and finished the strawberry milkshake.

As Rio swallowed the last bite of his meal, he gathered the trash. "Sorry about that."

"Why were they asking you medical questions? Are you a doctor?"

He shook his head. "Medic. Ready to go?"

"Thank you for bringing me here, Rio. This was fun."

"I wish I'd had the chance to learn more about your shop and the house."

She laughed softly. "Don't worry. If Trent's gone for long, you'll learn more than you want about both." She paused, her foot on the running board of his vehicle. "Would you like to see the house? Mrs. Watson assured me the electricity was on."

"You have a key?"

"There's an extra under the welcome mat."

Rio scowled. "You've got to be kidding."

"Afraid not. After I sign the papers tomorrow, there won't be a key there."

"Good. I'd love to see the place."

"Hope your medical insurance is up to date. You'll be taking your life in your hands stepping inside."

"Now you've stirred my curiosity." He rounded the hood and slid behind the wheel. Within a couple minutes, they were driving down Piedmont.

Rio parked in the driveway. "Beautiful place. Good bones."

"I heard that from the real estate agent." She didn't know if she believed either of them. Darcy reached for the door handle.

"Wait." The medic wrapped his long fingers around her arm, his gaze fixed on the front window of the house.

"What is it?" She turned. What did he see? At first she saw only darkness through the glass. Seconds later, a small circle of light appeared, sweeping from one side of the window to the other.

Her hand tightened on the handle. Someone was inside her house.

CHAPTER FOUR

Rio unlatched his seatbelt. "Wait here."

A small hand grasped his, grip surprisingly strong. "Where are you going?"

"To have a chat with whoever is in your house."

"He could have a gun."

He turned, eyebrow raised. "So do I."

"Right. What was I thinking?"

Amused at her sarcasm, he tapped the end of her nose. "I'll be fine. It's probably kids looking around. This place has quite a reputation in town. It's supposed to be haunted, you know."

She grimaced. "Great. So not only do I have mountains of debris to toss, I'll have to evict the current resident. Is ghost busting part of your muscle service?"

"There's an extra fee for that."

"Free meals for a month once my store is open if you'll get rid of Casper."

"Deal." It would give him more opportunities to spend time with the intriguing Darcy St. Claire. Definitely not a hardship. "I'll return in a bit."

He slid to the driveway and closed his door with a quiet snick. He'd already disabled the dome light when he purchased the vehicle so the intruder wouldn't be alerted by an odd light shining through the window.

Rio considered drawing his weapon, decided against it. Staying in the shadows, he stepped to the side of the picture frame window. He frowned. What was blocking his view? Aggravated that he couldn't see into the house from his position, he went to his next option.

In silence, he climbed the stairs to the porch. As he approached the front door to try the knob, he stepped on a board that gave a loud creak. Inside the house, something crashed.

A quick check of the knob revealed the door was locked. The intruder must have come in from the back door or maybe a window not in view of the street. Rio leaped off the porch, dashed around the side of the house and almost plowed into a fence. He vaulted over the gate. In the backyard, nothing moved.

Was the intruder still in the house? That creak had been loud enough to alert anyone in the place of his presence. A short distance away, something metal crashed. A man shouted, dogs howled and barked.

He ran to the back fence, scrambled over it, and raced down the street in the direction of the ruckus, leaping over the metal trashcan resting on its side. Seconds later, an engine cranked. Tires squealed and a vehicle sped away. Before Rio covered the remaining distance to the intersection so he could catch a glimpse of the vehicle or driver, his quarry was gone.

He retraced his steps to the Victorian house and hopped the fence into the backyard again. Sounded like the intruder had made good on his escape, but he'd have to check in the house to be sure. He started toward the back of the house, paused. Rio didn't want to leave Darcy in the SUV by herself longer than he already had. Otter Creek was a safe place to live, but there were questionable people anywhere, as evidenced by the escape artist. Trent had left Darcy in his care. He didn't take that responsibility lightly.

He jogged across the yard, cleared the gate, and circled to the front of the house. Darcy stood beside his SUV, worry clear on her face. Should have known she wouldn't wait inside the vehicle. He supposed he should be grateful she hadn't followed him into the backyard or down the street in pursuit of the nighttime disturbance.

Her gaze skimmed over him. Checking for injuries? "Did you see anyone?"

"Nope. I think the intruder got away, though."

"Is that the racket I heard?"

"That's my guess. I want to check the house. Do you want to wait out here?"

She just stared at him.

A small smile curved his lips. "That's what I figured. Anything I should know before we go inside?"

"If we breathe wrong or brush a pile, we'll be buried alive."

"Comforting thought." He walked with her to the porch and pulled up the mat. He unlocked the door. "Light switch?"

"To the right of the door. Do yourself a favor and slide your hand along the wall."

He blinked. Huh. "That bad?"

"Just wait until you see."

This ought to be good. Had to admit, he looked forward to seeing the place. Rio opened the door and found the switch. A second later, light blazed in the living room. At least he thought it was the living room.

Rio's mouth dropped. Good grief. Mountains of clutter littered the room. He couldn't see the floor at all. "How did you walk around in here today?"

"There's a path." She stepped into the entryway beside him. "Whoa. There was a path through here."

Not anymore. "Avalanche?"

"I guess so." She frowned. "Could the intruder have caused it?"

"Maybe. It's also possible some of the stacks shifted and caused the implosion. Holy cow, Darcy. You need a bulldozer in here."

"Tell me something I don't know. The rest of the house is the same way. Rio, should we call the police?"

"We need the incident on record." He eyed the mess in front of him. "Would you know if anything was missing?"

"Not a chance."

"Didn't think so." Rio pulled out his cell phone and called Nick Santana, his unit leader's brother-in-law. "It's Rio. I want to report a break in. Are you on duty or Rod?"

"I drew the lucky straw for third shift this month. You at home?"

He gave the Victorian's address.

"What are you doing there? The house is empty."

"Not even close, buddy. I'm here with the new owner of the place. We noticed a light going across a darkened window. The intruder escaped out the back."

"Huh. I'll be there in a few minutes. Don't touch anything."

Rio had to smile. If he touched a million things, Nick would never know. He slid his phone into his pocket. "A detective will arrive soon to take a look."

"Good luck with that," Darcy said, disgust evident in her voice.

"Can't wait to see his face when he gets a look at this." He bent over and started clearing a path.

"Should we be doing that? The detective won't want us to mess with the crime scene, right?"

"Nick has to have a way into the place and I don't want you falling."

Darcy grabbed a handful of magazines and started a new stack. "I must have been insane to buy this place," she muttered.

"What caught your interest about the house?" When she didn't answer right away, Rio glanced over his shoulder. "Darcy?"

"You'll laugh."

"Try me."

"You even crack a smile and I'll withdraw my offer of free food. Understood?"

"Got it. Tell me your reasoning. It can't have anything to do with the beauty of the place. It's an ugly duckling."

"I want to turn it into a swan, Rio. This place sheltered a family once. It deserves a second chance, a chance to be reinvented."

He straightened and turned, hands full of women's magazines. "That's how you see yourself, isn't it? You're reinventing yourself as something other than a concert pianist."

The tense stance of her body dissipated. She hadn't anticipated his understanding where she was coming from. From what Rio had seen, Trent didn't get it. Every time her brother looked at her, Rio saw the questions and reservation in his eyes. That had to hurt, as if her only remaining family didn't believe in her.

"I can't sit at home and do nothing. I've been working since I was ten years old."

"Good for you." Rio admired her grit and determination. Many people would have given up after such a devastating diagnosis.

"You don't think it's stupid?"

His thoughts shifted to his cousin, Mason. "No, I don't." Maybe someone would give his cousin a second chance once he was released from prison. "It's going to be an expensive rehab. Did you get a good deal on the place?"

"The price was a lot lower than I anticipated."

"Good thing. You could have a yard sale every weekend for months to recoup some of the costs."

She slanted him an amused glance. "As opposed to the bulldozer you suggested a minute ago?"

"What will you do with all this?"

"Donate the clothes to charity, for starters. Is there a bookstore in town?"

"The owner is a friend of mine. Why?"

"I don't suppose the bookstore has any use for used books."

"Actually, Del has a used book section. If she can't sell them, she'll donate them to the library or one of the retirement homes."

Relief flooded Darcy's face. "I'd love to talk to her about the books."

"I'll arrange for you to meet her. You'll like her. She's married to my unit commander, Josh Cahill."

A car door slammed.

"Sounds like Nick's here." He strode to the door.

Nick Santana, one of three Otter Creek detectives, crossed the threshold and came to a dead stop, whistled. "I can't believe this."

"It's like this all over the house," Darcy said. She held out her hand. "Darcy St. Claire. I own this monstrosity."

"Nick Santana. You are one brave woman to attempt bringing this place back to life." The dark-haired man with medium build turned to Rio. "Good to see you, Rio." He rubbed the back of his neck. "I doubt I'll find much. Tell me what happened."

Rio took him through the events after he parked in the driveway, ending with, "I didn't get a look at the vehicle or the driver."

"Not much to go on. Do you know how the intruder got into the house?"

"Front door was locked. I didn't want to leave Darcy alone any longer, so I didn't check the back door or windows."

"You should look at the downstairs bathroom window," Darcy said.

Both men turned their attention her direction. "Why?" Rio asked.

"Someone was in here this afternoon while I was going through the place and shoved a wall of stuff on me. There was also a muddy footprint in the bathroom."

Rio frowned. "You should have told me about the intruder. As for the footprint, it hasn't rained in a week. There's no telling how long the print has been there."

"Let's take a look. Ms. St. Claire, lead the way."

"Please, it's Darcy." She walked between the stacks with Rio at her back and Nick bringing up the rear. As they went from room to room, she turned on lights, revealing more piles of stuff every place they passed.

This place was huge, three floors of wall-to-wall items. It would take Darcy a long time to clear this place by herself, even if she were in perfect health. Trent would have a fit when he saw this.

Maybe he didn't have to see it. Durango would pitch in and help her clear the house. Trent was a friend and they owed him for helping them with a mission a few weeks earlier. Making a mental note to talk to Josh, Rio followed Darcy into a large bathroom filled with soap, shampoo, razors, shaving cream, stacks of washcloths and towels, toothbrushes and toothpaste. Absolutely mind boggling the amount of things in this room.

"Under the window," Darcy said, pointing at the floor.

Nick slipped by them and knelt by the print. "What size shoe do you wear, Rio?"

"Twelve."

A quick grin from his friend. "Big feet."

"It wasn't Rio," Darcy said, her words clipped.

"Not suggesting it was, Darcy. I want to use his foot for a guesstimate on shoe size."

"Sorry."

Rio fought back a smile. Nice that she felt the need to defend him, though it wasn't necessary. He'd have no reason to break into this place. And if it came down to a matter of life or death, he could pick the locks in under fifteen seconds from the looks of them. Something else Darcy would have to take care of, replacing the locks and adding a security system. Trent would insist even if she didn't see the necessity. No Fortress operative took security lightly. Chances were slim their identities could be compromised, but it was still possible.

"Put your size twelve next to the print, Rio." Nick pulled a small digital camera from his pocket and snapped a picture. "I'll get my kit. Don't expect much, though."

"Whatever you find might help." Darcy closed the commode lid and sat. In the glaring light, she looked pale. Rio wanted to take her back to the motel soon. He also realized she wouldn't go before things here were resolved.

He crouched beside her. "You doing okay?"

"Fine."

He wrapped his hand around hers for a moment. "Darcy."

She sighed. "I'm tired."

Definitely needed to do some research on her autoimmune disease.

Nick returned, carrying a black kit in one hand, thin rubber gloves in the other. "Rio, you have a flashlight on you?"

"In the SUV. What do you need?"

"Check around back. See if we have footprints under the window. Watch your step. Ethan will have my hide if you compromise evidence."

"Copy that." He stood. "Want to stay here and keep an eye on Nick, Darcy, or come with me?"

"I'll go with you. If I sit too long I'll go to sleep."

Yep, he needed to get her out of here soon. "We won't take long." Rio returned to his SUV and opened the hatch.

He dug into his Go bag and found a flashlight. "Let's see what we find."

He led her around the side of the house to the gate. Instead of hopping the structure, he unlocked the gate and opened it for Darcy to walk through. He reached back and wrapped his hand around hers, worried about her falling. The yard wasn't well lit and shadows messed with depth perception at night. The yard also needed mowing.

Instead of reprimanding him for his boldness, she let him help her over the uneven terrain. Rio kept his light trained on the ground searching for footprints as they neared the bathroom window.

Five feet from the wall was a bare patch of ground. He found one good print in the hardened ground. Just eyeballing it, the shoe size and pattern looked the same as the one in the bathroom.

Rio approached the window, avoiding the footprint. He shined the beam of light on the window frame. No scratches or obvious signs of forcing the lock, same as the inside.

Nick unlocked the window and lifted it. "Find anything?"

"Hardened footprint leading to the window. Looks the same as the one inside the bathroom."

"I'll check it."

"Fingerprints?"

"Smudges. Whoever came into the house didn't use this window, Rio. It was still locked."

"I locked it this afternoon," Darcy admitted.

Rio glanced along the wall. "Another window, then?"

"We'll check." Nick's eyes twinkled. "If we can get to them."

"If we can't, I'd say the intruder couldn't get through them, either."

"What about the back door?" Darcy asked. "Maybe the intruder came in through there."

"Do you know if it was unlocked when you were here earlier?" Nick asked.

"I didn't come into the backyard. I stayed on the cow path inside the house. The real estate agent might know. She was here when I arrived to look the place over."

"Who's the agent?"

"Colleen Watson."

He have a short nod. "I'll contact her tomorrow."

"I can ask her. I'm meeting her tomorrow morning to sign the paperwork."

Nick handed a business card to her. "Call me with her answer. I'll meet you at the back door." He frowned. "If I can find it."

"Watch your step in the kitchen. There are boxes of food all over the floor."

The detective shook his head and closed the window.

Rio clasped Darcy's hand again and walked toward the back door. Along the way, he checked two windows, both locked. At the door, he crouched and directed the flashlight's beam at the handle.

His gut tightened. Old hardware. New, fine scratches. This wasn't the work of curious teens. Someone had used lock picks on Darcy's door.

CHAPTER FIVE

"What's wrong?" Darcy knew something wasn't right by the way Rio had gone utterly still.

"Take a look." The medic shifted so she could kneel beside him.

She crouched beside him, hoped she could get back up. Along with losing dexterity in her hands, she'd noticed an annoying weakness in her joints as a whole. Wouldn't be the last time she had to accept a hand up. She might as well get used to it if what the doctors told her was accurate. Shoving that aside for now, Darcy peered at the hardware. Looked like a plain doorknob to her. She hated to sound ignorant, but she didn't see what the fuss was about. "What should I be seeing?"

"Scratches."

She frowned. "It's an old house. Everything has scratches."

"Not this kind. Someone picked the lock."

Goosebumps surged across her skin. These had nothing to do with the cold breeze blowing across her body. "Why? I couldn't find anything of value in there if my life depended on it. I'm not sure anyone could."

"I don't know why someone broke in, but I can tell you it wasn't kids."

"How do you know?"

"Those scratches were made with lock picks, not something kids would have access to. When I use them, they leave marks like that behind."

Were lock picks standard equipment for Fortress operatives? Of course they were. What was she thinking? Her lips curved upward. Darcy would love to see the training regimen for Rio and his fellow operatives. It was bound to be full of skills that were handy if not strictly legal.

A couple of muffled thumps and boxes being shoved aside preceded the door opening. Nick stared down at them, then shifted his attention to the door. "What do we have?"

"Lock was picked." Rio focused the light on the knob.

A soft whistle from the detective. "Let's take a look." He set down his kit and lifted the lid. He pulled out a tin and a brush. After examining the scratches for himself, Nick dusted the knob for prints. "Nothing. Just like the window frame."

Rio stood and reached down to lift Darcy. How did he know she needed help? She grimaced as she straightened. Man, her knees hurt.

"Okay?" he murmured.

"I will be." She wouldn't give in. She'd already figured out if she did, the next attempt hurt worse.

He squeezed her hands and turned to Nick. "I need to take Darcy back to the motel."

"Sure. I can lock up for you." He frowned. "Not that it will do much good if the intruder comes back with the lock picks." The detective glanced back into the kitchen. "Darcy, would you mind if I moved things around a little?"

"Go ahead. I doubt I'd know the difference. Why?"

"I can't prevent another break-in, but I can make it a lot more hazardous to attempt. I'll also have Josh drive by here every thirty minutes or so during the night. I'll drive through the neighborhood as I can. Depends on how busy my night is."

Small town crime was enough to keep a detective hopping during his shift? "I appreciate anything you can do. The idea someone can walk in any time he pleases makes me uneasy. What if I'm here next time he waltzes in?" Just the possibility of that happening made her feel a little sick. She hoped her brother wasn't out of the country long. "There was a key under the welcome mat."

Nick scowled.

"I have it," Rio said. "Do you want the key, Nick?"

"Yeah, if that's okay with you, Darcy. Drop by the station in the morning and pick it up before coming here."

"Thanks, Nick."

"No problem." He stood, handed her a card with his name and cell number on the front. "If you notice anything out of the ordinary or feel uneasy for any reason, call me. Rio, I expect to hear from you as well. Don't go off the reservation to deal with this on your own."

"Would I do that?"

A snort. "You aren't out of the country on an op, buddy. Don't put Josh in an awkward position."

"I hear you."

"Yeah, and you aren't agreeing to anything, are you?"

The medic gave a half smile.

With a shake of his head, Nick turned his attention to Darcy again. "Get some rest, Darcy. I'll be around if you need me."

Darcy studied his expression a moment and came to the conclusion the Otter Creek detective meant what he said. Rio walked her to the SUV and helped her inside. Sitting in the luxurious seat was a tremendous relief. Who knew standing took more energy than she could spare?

On the drive to the motel, Rio kept glancing in the mirrors.

What now? "Problem?"

"Nope. Just making sure I don't create one by leading someone to your room."

Way to make her comfortable being alone in her motel room. "Did you have to say that?"

"Would you rather I lie to you?"

"I know three people in this town. You, Detective Santana, and Mrs. Watson. Why would anyone want to hurt me? I don't have anything valuable with me and I don't carry much cash. My only connection to the break-in is I'm buying the house. I can't be in danger."

"Probably not."

And still he checked the mirrors. Darcy rolled her eyes. She couldn't fault him for being vigilant. Trent would approve. In fact, Rio was far less aggravating in the protection department than her brother. Trent could be overbearing. Since their parents died, he'd taken his role as protector and adviser all too seriously. She loved him despite his heavy handedness.

He parked in the lot beside her car and opened his door.

"Rio, my room is ten feet away. You don't have to get out. You can watch me walk to the door."

He flicked her a glance, walked around the SUV and opened her door.

"Stubborn much, Mr. Kincaid?"

"Makes me good at my job, sweetheart."

Sweetheart? Darcy's gaze locked with his. They'd only known each other for a few hours. He couldn't mean that endearment. Could he? No way, much as the idea appealed to her. He intrigued her. The handsome medic probably called all the women in his life sweet names. She didn't really know anything about him. Rio might have a girlfriend for all she knew. Even as the thought surfaced, she rejected it. No, he'd never two-time a woman that way.

If he did, Trent wouldn't have entrusted her to him. Her brother was a good judge of character.

He reached in, lifted her from the seat, and deposited her on the ground, all as if she were light as a feather. "I always walk my date to her door."

"Date?"

"Dinner and conversation is a date. The excitement at your house was a bonus."

She had to laugh. "Well, our date was fun. Thank you for dinner."

"Give me your cell phone."

Her eyebrow rose. She handed him her phone and watched as the medic tapped her screen and called up her contact list. Rio added his name and number, then used her phone to call his. The first few bars of one of her piano recordings sounded in the night air. Shock rolled through her. "You listen to my music?"

"Been a fan for years." His expression sobered. "I'll talk to you about that sometime. Will you be okay here by yourself?"

Was he serious? "You have a solution if I'm not?"

"Sure. I can sleep in my SUV or stay in the room next door."

Warmth bloomed inside Darcy. Oh, yeah. Rio Kincaid had character in spades. "I believe you would do that."

"What's it going to be, Darcy?"

"I'll be fine tonight. Thanks for offering, though."

"If there's a problem, call me. I don't live far."

"Thank you, Rio." She leaned up and kissed his cheek.

The medic's eyes widened. He slipped his hand behind the back of her neck and brushed her mouth with his. "Good night, Darcy," he murmured and stepped away, motioning for her to go inside the room.

Heart pounding like mad, Darcy closed and locked the heavy door. A minute later, Rio left the lot. Good grief. The man was a force to be reckoned with.

Fatigue washed over her. All she wanted to do was sink down on the bed and rest a minute. Because that's what she wanted, Darcy fought to stay upright. If she sat, Darcy wouldn't get up until morning. She refused to sleep in jeans and a sweatshirt.

She dragged her suitcase to Trent's bed, opened it, and found her pajamas. After completing her bedtime routine, she turned off the lights and crawled beneath the covers.

Finally lying flat, she realized her body ached, not just the joints, but deep in the muscles. Darcy remained still, hoping the warmth of the blankets would ease the aches. When thirty minutes passed with no let-up in the pain, she sat up with a sigh, threw off the covers, and found over-the-counter pain reliever in her bag. After swallowing a couple, she settled in the bed again and prayed the meds took effect fast. She had a feeling the next day was going to be long and tedious.

When Darcy dragged herself out of the bed the next morning, she felt almost as exhausted as she had the night before. That along with the morning stiffness made her grumpy. Maybe a warm shower would help. She grabbed her clothes for the day and took them with her into the bathroom.

An hour later, she drove into the heart of Otter Creek and found a parking spot near her store. The contractor was waiting at the door with a skeleton crew. "Sorry I'm late," she said.

"We just arrived ourselves, Ms. St. Claire." Brian Elliott smiled and lifted his to-go coffee cup. "Have you thought about the plans I outlined with you yesterday?"

"Please, call me Darcy. I did consider the plans." About three o'clock that morning when she couldn't sleep. "Let's do it."

"Great. We should have you up and running in a month, provided there aren't delays. If that happens, our time estimate will be adjusted."

"I understand." Darcy thought about the house as she unlocked the door to the shop. "Can you recommend a place that rents Dumpsters, Brian?"

"I planned to have one delivered at the back of your shop for the scrap material."

"This is for the house I bought yesterday."

"Ah. Give me the address and I'll have one delivered."

She opened the door. "I'll need more than one, the larger the better." She wasn't sure one trash bin would hold the excess items from more than a room or two.

The contractor looked surprised. "How many do you think you'll need?"

"About a million, but I'll start with three."

"That bad, huh?"

"The lady who owned the place was a hoarder."

Brian winced. "Oh, man. I've rehabbed one of those homes. We must have filled fifty large Dumpsters before the place was cleaned out."

"This is a three-story Victorian house. Every room is filled to capacity with junk."

The contractor whistled. "I'll have three delivered by ten. When you fill them up, you can either let me know or you can call yourself to have them switched out for empty ones."

After giving him the address and handing him a duplicate set of keys to the store, she crossed the square to the police station. The desk sergeant glanced up as she crossed the lobby.

A smile curved his mouth. "Can I help you, ma'am?"

"I'm Darcy St. Claire. Detective Santana was supposed to leave a key for me."

"ID, please."

Darcy handed over her driver's license. After glancing at it, the barrel-chested man returned it to her along with her house key.

"Detective Santana said everything was quiet through the night and he'd be in contact with you later today."

"Great. Thank you, Sergeant."

"Have a good day, ma'am."

She didn't know if the day would be good considering what was ahead of her, but it was definitely looking up. Would she hear from Rio today? Her cheeks burned as she walked to her car. With all the drama going on in her life, why would the medic be interested in her?

Darcy glanced at her watch. It was almost time to meet the real estate agent. No time for breakfast, not that she wanted to eat this time of morning anyway. There was a convenience store on the way to the house. If they didn't have something hot to drink, she could always buy a soft drink. Maybe that would hold her until lunch. Her doctor would pitch a fit if he knew she was skipping meals again. After today, she'd make an effort to eat better.

She backed into the square and drove to the convenience store. The coffee pot was empty and she didn't have enough time to wait for a new pot to brew. They did have hot water and packets of herbal tea bags. Wasn't green tea supposed to be good for you? Couldn't hurt. She chose a packet of green tea with lemon and ginseng. Near the checkout counter was a display with fresh fruit. The bananas looked good. She selected two and carried them to the counter along with her to-go cup of hot water and green tea.

Back in her car, she ate one of the bananas before leaving the parking lot, then drove to the house. Mrs. Watson was already parked on the street in front of the house. Probably anxious to unload the place before Darcy came to her senses and changed her mind. She studied the dilapidated exterior of the house in the morning light. No question, this was going to take a lot of work, but she was determined to bring this house back to life and create a home for herself in the process.

Darcy grabbed her green tea and climbed from the car. Mrs. Watson greeted her cheerfully.

"How are you today, my dear? Ready to sign the papers?"

"I'd suggest going inside to sign them, but I doubt we could find a flat surface."

"Why don't we sit here in my car? Use my briefcase for a table."

She grinned. Kept the older woman from having to brave the house again. She didn't blame her. That place was an accident waiting to happen. Well, not for much longer. Once Brian had those Dumpsters delivered, she'd start with the lighter items. She just hoped Trent came back soon. Otherwise, she'd be stuck with the lighter stuff for a long time. "Sounds good."

She got into the passenger side of the car and sipped her tea while Mrs. Watson organized all the papers for Darcy to sign. Thirty minutes later, she was a first-time home owner.

"The paperwork will be finalized in a week. In the meantime, feel free to start the cleaning process."

Remembering her promise to Detective Santana, she asked, "Mrs. Watson, do you know if the back door was locked yesterday when we left the house?"

"I'm sure it was. I always double-check doors before I leave. Why?"

"A friend and I stopped by here last night and saw someone in the house."

The older woman's eyes widened. "Did you call the police?"

"We reported it, but Detective Santana didn't find much." At least not that she knew. Darcy intended to ask him if he'd discovered anything when she saw him today.

"Nick's a good detective. If there was anything to find, believe me, he'd uncover it. He's married to Madison, one of the Cahill sisters. She owns the knitting shop. It's also part of the bookstore."

Her eyebrows rose. "That's an interesting combination."

"It works for her and Del, her sister-in-law."

"Do you know why anyone would want to break into the house, Mrs. Watson?"

"Oh, I imagine it's just kids. Once you move in, I'm sure they'll stay away. This is a very safe neighborhood." She stopped abruptly. "Usually."

"Usually?" That didn't sound good. "Did something happen that's an exception?"

"Oh, well, I guess I neglected to tell you. The previous owner of your house was murdered."

CHAPTER SIX

"Murdered?" Darcy's stomach clenched. "Yeah, you did forget to mention that. When did this happen?"

"Two or three years ago, about three months before Ethan Blackhawk was hired as the police chief."

"Please tell me the police arrested her killer."

Mrs. Watson's expression grew troubled. "I wish I could. The police never discovered who killed Gretchen Bond."

Fantastic. Something else for her and Trent to worry over. She definitely needed an alarm system. Brent Maddox could install the system for her. Perhaps he'd offer a discount. She made a mental note to call him soon. Knowing someone couldn't sneak up on her during the night and soothing her brother's overly protective tendencies made the price of the system well worth the cost.

"Congratulations on your fine purchase. I'm sure you'll have many years of happiness in this genteel beauty."

Right. After she gutted the thing. She needed to clear the place soon. Her piano was in controlled-temperature storage and she missed playing. "Thanks for your help, Mrs. Watson."

"Happy to help, Ms. St. Claire." She handed over the keys and Darcy's copy of the paperwork. "I'm sure I'll see you around town. Have a good day, now."

Darcy climbed from the car, tea and paperwork in hand. The real estate agent waved as she drove away, leaving her standing in front of a disaster of a home. A lot of work lay ahead, but it was all hers. Well, hers and Trent's when he wasn't deployed and wanted to visit. Her brother had his own apartment in Nashville where Fortress Security's headquarters was located.

At that moment, trucks carrying her Dumpsters arrived and the drivers unloaded the large metal bins in her front yard. Brian must have put some serious pressure on the company to have the containers delivered this fast. Time to start shoveling out her house.

Darcy glanced down at her bare hands, sighed. No clearing out garbage without gloves. Who knew what she would be touching? With so much debris piled in the place, there must be whole colonies of spiders in every room. Wearing gloves for hours beat dealing with spider bites and hospital visits. As she cranked her car and turned on the heater, her cell phone rang. She glanced at the screen, smiled. Doesn't mean anything, she cautioned herself. Just a new friend checking on her. "Good morning, Rio."

"How was your night?"

"Uneventful or I would have called."

"Have you started bulldozing the house?"

"Not yet. I need to buy gloves. I was afraid to clean without protection for my hands."

"Smart. You should buy dust masks, too."

Huh. Hadn't thought about that. "Good idea."

"Would you like help?"

"I can buy supplies on my own."

Rio chuckled. "Would you like help clearing the house?"

A surge of excitement swept through Darcy. "If you can spare some time, I'd appreciate an extra pair of hands. My store contractor had three large Dumpsters delivered to my front lawn. I'm afraid my house will be the neighborhood eyesore for a while."

"Fast work with the Dumpsters. Buy a lot of gloves and dust masks. I'm bringing a few friends with me."

Fantastic. The more people who came, the faster this part of the project would be finished and Brian Elliott could start the house rehab. "I don't know how to thank you, Rio."

"We'll meet you at the house in thirty minutes."

She slid her phone into her pocket and drove to the hardware store she'd seen in the town square. She wandered the aisles until she found rubber gloves. After a debate with herself, she chose neoprene gloves, figuring they would be snug enough to make grasping smaller items easier. Darcy also bought dust masks. She didn't want her volunteers to become ill. Not knowing how many people were coming, she bought several boxes of gloves and every dust mask the store stocked, then carried the bags to her car and returned to the house.

As she pulled into the driveway, several SUVs arrived and parked along the street. Men and women climbed from the vehicles. Darcy's mouth gaped. Good grief! She'd been expecting a handful of volunteers.

The man in question walked up the driveway and opened her door. "Great timing. Nate's bringing lunch in a couple hours to feed this crew."

"Rio, who are all these people?"

"Bodyguard trainees from Personal Security International, the business my teammates and I run. We train bodyguards for Fortress and other private contractors. Clearing your house is their physical training today."

Her eyes stung. "How can I ever thank you?"

"By agreeing to a second date." The medic smiled. Seriously? Oh, man. She hoped he didn't realize how thrilled she was at the prospect of spending more time with him. "I would love that." She hadn't had time for many dates over the years. Her concert schedule had prevented a serious dating relationship.

"Hey, a beautiful woman's been in town for one day and you've already staked a claim?" A blond-haired man scowled at Rio, arms folded across his massive chest. "How is that fair?"

Rio turned his head and winked at her. "Darcy, this is one of my teammates, Quinn Gallagher. Quinn, Darcy St. Claire."

"Nice to meet you, Darcy. Dump my former friend and run away with me."

The medic scowled at his friend. "Knock it off."

"Quinn acting out again?" A dark-haired man walked up to them, a half smile on his face.

"I'm misunderstood," Quinn protested.

"Right." The newcomer turned his dark gaze on Darcy. "I'm Alex Morgan, another of Rio's teammates. You must be Darcy."

"You're Durango's sniper."

His face lost all expression. "That's right."

Must be a sensitive subject for him. She imagined the general public might have problems with Alex's job. Not Darcy. She knew from listening to her brother how many lives men like Alex saved every day in battle. "Trent's talked about you. He respects your skills." She smiled. "My brother also mentioned you're a newlywed. Congratulations on your marriage."

Alex's eyes lit. "I'm so blessed to have Ivy in my life."

Maybe someday she'd have a husband who felt that way about her.

"Where are the gloves and masks, Darcy?" Rio asked.

"Back seat. I hope I bought enough supplies."

"If we need more, we'll send someone to the hardware store."

"Not for masks," she muttered. "I bought them out."

Rio chuckled. "We'll send Quinn to Cherry Hill if we need more."

"Let's get moving," Quinn said. "Four people to a room, Darcy?"

"Sounds good." Actually, it sounded like a dream come true. This many people would make a serious dent in the Victorian house.

"Start on the first floor," Rio said. He looked at Darcy. "Any room you don't want them to clear?"

"The master bedroom on the second floor. Can't miss it. The room has hundreds of beautiful candles along the walls that I want to keep." She'd be ready for power outages for years to come.

"Any special instructions for other items?"

Darcy thought about the contents of the house. She hated to throw everything away if something could be used elsewhere. "The clothes and shoes should go to a shelter along with the items in the downstairs bathroom. The books go to the bookstore if your friend wants them. Everything else can be pitched into the bins."

"Easy enough." Quinn whistled to capture the trainees' attention and gave them instructions. Rio and Alex handed out gloves and masks. Within minutes, the recruits were making trips to the Dumpsters.

"Where do you want to start?" Rio asked her.

"Living room. I need space for my piano."

"How much room?"

She smiled, picturing her beautiful seven-foot polished ebony Steinway. "It's a seven-foot grand."

"Let's get to work, then."

They joined four others engaged in gathering piles of magazines, clothes, and shoes. The recruits had already cleared a fifth of the room and begun stacking things to distribute as she'd directed. The stacks grew at an alarming rate. Wouldn't be long before the piles became hazardous towers again. She frowned. There had to be a more efficient way to deal with this. Boxes. That's what she needed for the donated items. Where would she find boxes?

"Rio, I need boxes for the items to give away. Would the grocery store have empty boxes or the hardware store?"

"Josh should be up soon. I'll have him pick up boxes and bring them. When we fill them, he can drop them off. In the meantime, stack the items to give away on the porch. That way the clutter will be outside instead of a tripping hazard."

She eyed the waist-high stacks. "Are you sure the neighbors won't mind?"

"We'll clear the stacks outside at the end of the day."

For the next hour, she and Rio worked side by side. Satisfaction filled her as the clear floor space expanded. Clothes, shoes, and books were relocated to the porch. They found more towels and washcloths. Most of those, however, were in bad shape. One look had Darcy tossing them in the nearest metal bin.

To her astonishment, the Dumpster was nearly full. Incredible what many willing hands could do in a short amount of time. She found the paperwork the truck drivers had given her and called to arrange for new bins the next morning.

As she ended the call, another vehicle parked behind hers. From the porch, Rio said, "Need help unloading, Nate?"

"Yep. Hoagies all around and a salad for Darcy."

A salad? Not that she minded, but why was she singled out for a salad? She turned to look at Rio, her eyebrow raised.

"He brought the salad at my request, Darcy."

"Why?"

"I did some research online last night. Just try the salad. I'll talk to you later about things that might help with your health."

He'd left her at the motel and gone home to research Sjogren's Syndrome? "I thought you were going home to sleep last night."

"I did."

She scowled. "How much? An hour?"

"Four hours. It was enough."

And he was here? "You should be taking a nap, not clearing my house."

He just smiled and introduced her to Nate Armstrong, another member of Durango.

"I can help you carry lunch inside the house."

"Thanks, Darcy. Rio, grab the coolers. I brought enough water and soft drinks to get us through lunch. I'll head to the grocery store and restock afterward."

Darcy's eyes widened. How long were they planning to stay? If they continued pitching at the same rate, the place would be clean within a few days.

The medic reached into the back of the SUV and lifted a large blue and white cooler. "How's Stella?"

"Tanned, relaxed, and all mine. She's doing a ride-along with Rod today. My wife can't wait to return to work. She's looking forward to carrying an OCPD badge."

Rio laughed. "Marriage looks good on you, my friend. How is Stella's wrist?"

"Itching like crazy."

"Normal. Sounds like her break is mending."

Nate grabbed several bags of hoagies and strode into the house with Darcy and Rio at his heels. He glanced around. "Table?"

"Check the kitchen," Darcy said. "I can't guarantee it's clear."

He set his bags on the floor. "Which way?"

"Straight back and turn right."

When he returned, he said, "Table's clear and there's a decent path. Let's set up in there. The recruits can spread out wherever there's a spot to eat."

Five minutes later, the wrapped hoagies were arranged on the table and the coolers were lined up against beautiful cabinets Darcy hadn't noticed earlier.

While Nate strode to the stairway and gave a piercing whistle to call the hungry volunteers to lunch, Rio handed Darcy a chef salad in a plastic container along with plastic utensils.

Wow. Lots of protein, almost no cheese, lightly drizzled with salad dressing. Interesting, but beautiful. "It looks great."

"You're not angry?" he asked, voice soft, worry in his brown eyes.

"I'm touched you would forgo sleep to research ways to help me." She was also aggravated with herself for not thinking to do the same thing. Her only excuse was she'd wrapped up her last concert four weeks ago, and spent the remaining time dealing with her apartment and agent. Allen White was not happy with her retirement decision and fought her for six months, right up until her final concert. He would have accepted the news easier if she'd told him about her diagnosis. She'd refused, knowing her agent would have politicized it. Darcy didn't want pity. Besides, she had been thinking about calling it quits for two years. Her touring schedule was brutal and she wanted a life beyond the spotlight, one with a man who captured her heart.

Relief flooded Rio's face. "Good. I'll tell you what I learned on our second date."

Butterflies took flight in her stomach. "Deal."

The trainees trooped into the kitchen and formed a line. Once they selected a hoagie, a bag of chips, and a drink, they scattered throughout the house. The buzz of laughter and conversation was pleasant to hear in the old house and reminded her of better days in the St. Claire household.

Rio cleared a chair for Darcy and seated her at the table with a bottle of water, then commandeered another chair for himself and unwrapped his sandwich.

Must be something about soft drinks that Rio wanted her to avoid. Wonder if green tea was good for her? She had to admit, she felt better after drinking green tea than following a cup of coffee. The conversation on their second date should be interesting. "Do you know anything about the former owner of this house?"

"Only that Gretchen Bond owned the place and lived by herself for many years. Why?"

"How long have you lived in Otter Creek?"

"A few months."

Darcy sighed. "So you don't know the history of the place."

"Sorry, sweetheart. I can ask around if you want me to. Why are you so curious?"

Her heart melted a little at the endearment. "Mrs. Watson told me Gretchen Bond was murdered."

Rio's hand froze halfway to his mouth. "Who killed her?"

"The police never arrested anyone."

"Josh has lived in this town his whole life. If the information is on the grapevine, he'll know."

"Ask me what?"

The warm male voice had Darcy glancing over her shoulder. Oh, man. Another buff guy with male model good looks. This must be Josh Cahill, Rio's other teammate.

"About Gretchen Bond."

"The best person to ask is my father. He talked about Ms. Bond several times over the years." Hazel eyes turned to Darcy. "I'm Josh Cahill. You must be Trent's sister."

"Darcy St. Claire. Thanks for keeping an eye on my house last night."

One of the trainees walked into the kitchen, tugging off his gloves. "What's with the holes in the floors?"

CHAPTER SEVEN

Rio's hand clenched around his bottle of water. "Holes?" He exchanged a glance with Darcy. From her puzzled expression, she didn't know what Johnson was talking about. He hadn't noticed gaps in the flooring. His lips curled. The chance of seeing the holes was slim as crowded as the rooms were.

"We've cleared two rooms. In both, there are holes in the floors."

"Rotted wood?"

"It looks as if someone pried the wood up with a crowbar. Shame, too. These floors are a beautiful maple. My grandma had floors just like them. She loved them enough to tan our hides if we dragged furniture over the surface."

Rio started to rise when Josh motioned for him to stay seated. "I'll check it out. Finish your lunch." He smirked. "I just had a lunch date with Del."

Normally, the jibe would irritate Rio, reinforcing the lack of female companionship in his life. In truth, no woman had interested him for months. His gaze slid to Trent's sister. Until now. Seemed as if that problem had come to an end. The pianist fascinated him with her mix of softness and steel. With all the major changes in her life, would Darcy be willing to consider dating anyone? If she did, what would Trent say? Yeah, he and Rio were friends. That didn't mean the Fortress operative wanted Rio in his sister's life.

Darcy stabbed another bite of salad with her fork. "Why would someone destroy the floor?"

He dragged his attention back to the conversation. "I wonder how old the demolition work is."

"Maybe the trainee was mistaken about the crowbar. Water damage or termites make more sense. Ms. Bond couldn't have maintained the pest control. No bug man would risk life and limb to spray in here." Some of the color leached from her face. "That makes me wonder what kind of insects have taken up residence in the place. Not good. I need to call the exterminator as soon as the rooms are empty."

"Johnson's right," Josh said, striding into the room, expression grim. "The damage to the floors isn't natural wear and tear. Someone ripped up two or three planks in each room."

"Can you tell how long the holes have been there?" Darcy asked.

"I'm not a carpenter, but the damage looks recent."

"Guess that explains the light last night," Rio said.

"Possibly." Durango's leader frowned. "Must be after something specific to do that kind of damage. This isn't random destruction." He turned to Darcy. "Did you tour every room before you bought this place?"

"I couldn't see much. Your friends have cleared mountains of stuff in the last two hours." She grinned. "You also have several inches on me. The only thing I saw was walls of items to pitch."

"The whole town knew Ms. Bond was eccentric. For obvious reasons, we couldn't see in through the windows and she never invited anyone over. This house is going to take a lot of work, Darcy, but she'll be a showstopper. Are you doing the work yourself?"

Rio wanted to protest, realized he couldn't. He and the lady were acquaintances. She also had a stubborn streak as wide as his own. To his relief, Darcy laughed at Josh's question.

"Fat chance of that. I'm good with my hands." She stopped, grimaced. "Well, I used to be. But my skill set doesn't lean toward carpentry work."

Josh tilted his head. "What is your skill set?"

"I'm a pianist, but I'm opening my own restaurant in town. I've already rented a storefront on the square and the contractor started work this morning."

"You should talk to Nate," Rio said. "He's a professionally trained chef."

"What kind of restaurant, Darcy?" Josh asked.

"One that specializes in wraps."

"Wraps?"

"Wraps for breakfast and lunch."

Rio's eyebrows rose. "No offense, sweetheart, but when have you had time to cook over the last twenty years?"

Darcy folded her arms across her chest. "When I wasn't touring and any time I convinced my agent to rent a place with a kitchen instead of a hotel suite. The recipes have been handed down in our family. Trent and I love all of these wraps plus I enjoy experimenting. And if you keep doubting my cooking ability, I don't see why I should feed you for a month."

Josh looked amused. "Does she know how much you eat in a day, Kincaid?"

After a scowl at his unit leader, he turned back to Darcy. "What kind of wraps are we talking about?"

"Trent's favorite breakfast wraps are egg, cheese, and either bacon or sausage. Lunch includes the standards such as ham, turkey, roast beef, and chicken. I've made specialty wraps like turkey and dressing or turkey, cream cheese, and a cranberry spread in the month of November. The menu will also include ham salad, chicken salad, and egg salad on a regular basis."

"Sounds tasty," Rio admitted. "When will you open for business?"

"Hopefully in about six weeks. I've already ordered the sign."

"Yeah? What's the name?"

"That's A Wrap."

"Clever," Josh said. "So, what do you need me to do?"

"Grab some gloves and a dust mask, Major," Rio said. "At the end of the day, we need to transport boxes to the shelter. If Del stops by to look at the books, she'll have first dibs for the store. Otherwise, Darcy can donate them as well."

He nodded, then shifted his gaze to Darcy. "Sorting instructions?"

She repeated the instructions given to the trainees. When he left, Rio nudged the salad closer. "Better eat. Sounds like the others are gearing up for round two. Can't have them showing us up."

Darcy grabbed her fork and finished the rest of her lunch along with polishing off the water.

"Pay attention to how you feel this afternoon."

"Besides the fatigue?"

"I'm interested in the body aches."

As they worked through the afternoon, he kept tabs on her energy level. When she flagged, he encouraged Darcy to rest a few minutes, and gave her nuts he'd asked Nate to bring from PSI along with more water.

She fared better than he thought she might. While playing the piano, she sat for hours. Emptying the three-story house required standing, bending, and walking. At four o'clock, he and Nate loaded the back of Josh's truck and the cargo areas of the SUVs. By the time the PSI trainees stopped for the day, the porch was cleared and the vehicles loaded with donations. He and Darcy watched the caravan leave the neighborhood from the front porch. She shivered in the cold wind. Hoping he wouldn't be rebuffed, Rio slid his arm around her shoulders, drawing her against his side to share his warmth. "Did you see the Dumpsters?" he murmured.

"Not since lunch. Why?"

"Come on. You'll be pleased." He walked with her to the bins, grinned when her jaw dropped.

"We filled all three." Delight filled her face. "It's good I called before lunch to have empty bins delivered tomorrow. Rio, this is amazing. How can I ever repay you for this?"

"A third date."

She burst into laughter. "We haven't had the second one yet."

"Have dinner with me tonight. We'll count that as the second date."

"I'm filthy and probably look a fright."

"Sorry, sweetheart, you're wrong. You look gorgeous with dust on your nose and hair. I know you're tired, but you have to eat. Delaney's is on the town square. We'll fit in with the after work crowd."

"You knew I was going to skip dinner, didn't you? I'm too tired to do justice to a meal tonight and will be lousy company."

He tapped her nose gently. "No skipping meals. Your body doesn't process food right so you can't afford to skip any. You probably need an enzyme to help you digest whatever you do eat."

"Are you sure you slept at all last night, Rio?"

"I'm a medic, Darcy. Researching Sjogren's was interesting."

She wrinkled her nose. "Can't imagine that being true."

He stilled. "You haven't looked into it?"

"Not yet." Her cheeks turned red.

"You should. We need to learn how your body best functions."

She tilted her head. "We?"

He was coming on kind of strong, but he prayed she wouldn't tell him to back off. Aside from his attraction to her, Darcy had made such a difference in his life with her music that he wanted to return the favor. "I'd like to help, if you'll let me."

"The autoimmune disease doesn't bother you?"

"Everybody has to deal with something."

"You are an amazing man, Rio Kincaid."

He grimaced. "I don't know about that. Let's check the windows and doors, make sure they're locked before we go to Delaney's. After we eat, I'll follow you to the motel. I'll feel better if I'm sure you're safe in your room. I need sleep tonight, after all."

"That was not my fault. You're the one who researched a weird disease instead of sleeping."

Together, they toured the house, checking windows and doors. Rio was astonished at how much progress had been made. Sure, they had a lot further to go, but you could walk into most of the first floor rooms without fear of being buried alive by Ms. Bond's belongings.

"What will you do with the furniture?" He glanced at the heavy wood four-poster bed in a downstairs bedroom. Didn't seem like the kind of furniture Darcy would buy for herself.

"Donate it. I want to buy my own. I'm a little afraid to consider what might be lurking in the upholstery or mattresses."

"Don't you have furniture where you live now?"

"Some. The apartment is pretty small. I spent most of my time sitting at the Steinway than anywhere else."

Darcy crouched beside one of the holes. She ran her fingers lightly over the jagged edge. "Johnson was right. This floor is gorgeous. Do you think the contractor can fix the floors?"

"After he replaces the planks, new stain will help all the wood appear the same." He drew Darcy to her feet. "Come on. You worked me hard today and I'm starving."

At the diner, he encouraged her to order food that wasn't processed, then in the interest of being fair, ordered the same for himself. The meal took longer to eat than he wanted because many townspeople stopped by their table to talk and introduce themselves to Darcy. By the time she finished eating, his dinner date was visibly drooping.

As promised, Rio followed her to the motel and walked her to her door. "Sleep well, sweetheart." He leaned down and brushed her lips with a light kiss. "I'll see you tomorrow morning."

"Will the trainees be back tomorrow?"

"That's the plan. We'd like to clear the house before Trent returns."

"What about their training?"

"We'll double up the sessions for two weeks. They'll be fine."

Darcy squeezed his hand. "Promise you'll go to bed soon, Rio."

His heart turned over in his chest. "You have my word. Call me if you need anything."

With a nod, she unlocked her room door and went inside.

Rio waited until he heard the locks engage before returning to his SUV and driving home. He dropped his grungy clothes in the hamper and indulged in a long, hot shower, grateful to wash away dirt and ease aches. He couldn't imagine how Darcy felt.

Twenty minutes later, he crawled into his bed and shut off the light.

At three o'clock, his cell phone rang.

CHAPTER EIGHT

Darcy jerked awake at the ringing of her cell phone. She squinted at the clock. A few minutes after three. Sitting up, she lunged for the phone on the nightstand. Maybe it was Trent.

She glanced at the screen, frowned. "Kind of early for a wakeup call, Kincaid."

"Sweetheart, you need to pack a small bag with enough clothes for a few days."

Oh, no. No, no, no. "Trent?"

"He's been injured. Pack the bag, Darcy. I'll pick you up in fifteen minutes. Don't forget your meds." And then he was gone.

She threw back the covers. Fifteen minutes. Her brain was fogged and she was stiff, again. Shower. The warmth would help the joints. Maybe there was someplace open where she could buy coffee or green tea. She needed caffeine.

Darcy grabbed clothes and hurried through a quick shower. Dressed in jeans and a purple sweater, she tied her running shoes and threw her clothes and supplies into a bag. She checked her purse for her meds, breathed a sigh of relief she wouldn't have to search for them. By the time

Rio's knock sounded on her door, her hands were shaking and her teeth chattering.

It took her a couple tries to unlatch the locks. "How bad is he?"

"I'll tell you everything I know on the way to Knoxville."

"All set?" Josh Cahill stepped inside the room, dressed in his OCPD uniform.

Darcy stared at him, surprised at his appearance. "Are you driving us to Knoxville?"

He chuckled. "I met Rio here for the extra house key. Trent will need a place to recover and he'll be happier in a house than a motel room."

"I don't have furniture for him. I need to get rid of everything in that house, including the appliances."

"We'll take care of the basics from our own houses. Nate will deal with the appliances. You can settle with him later, then purchase the other things you want when Trent is back on his feet."

Some of the knots in her stomach eased. One less thing to worry over. At least she'd have a place to nurse her brother back to health. "Thank you."

He reached over and squeezed her shoulder. "He'll be fine. Your brother is a tough soldier."

She grinned. "Don't let him hear you say that."

"And here I thought SEALs had thick skin."

"We need to go, sweetheart." Rio lifted her bag. He glanced at Josh. "I'll call you as soon as I know anything. Contact Donnelly. Tell him to cover the first aid class until I return."

"You got it." He turned to Darcy. "Take care of yourself, sugar. That's the best thing you can do for your brother."

Rio's SUV was parked beside her car. He opened the passenger door, stowed her bag behind her seat, and lifted her into the vehicle. He had to feel her whole body shaking.

His face softened. "Trent's getting the best care available." With that statement, he hurried around the front of the SUV and climbed behind the wheel. "One of the Fortress jets will be waiting for us."

"Tell me about Trent. Wait. Before that, why were you notified instead of me?" As his only relative, shouldn't she have been notified first?

"Trent asked Maddox to call me before he was taken into surgery. Your brother is a big man. You'll need help caring for him."

"You're going with me?"

He glanced at her. "Will that be a problem?"

"Of course not. Where are we going?"

"Little place called Bayside, Texas."

She frowned. "Doesn't sound as though it has a state-of-the-art trauma center."

"You'd be surprised. Trent took a bullet to the leg and a couple knife wounds to the torso. He'll recover, Darcy, but will take a while to heal."

That sounded so good, but she was afraid he might be placating her. "You promise?"

"If his prognosis was bad, I'd tell you."

And still her teeth chattered.

Another glance her way and the medic reached behind the seat, grabbed a blanket, and dropped it on her lap. "Cover up with this. You're in shock and dealing with adrenaline dump."

Darcy wrapped the blanket around her as Rio turned up the heat. Before long, the shakes stopped, but she was exhausted and convinced she was a complete wuss.

"Think you can sleep?" he asked.

"Too wound up."

"We'll have four hours on the plane. Maybe you can nap then."

She'd never been good about taking naps as a kid. Her mother had complained everything stimulated her.

Forty minutes later, they boarded a Lear jet. The inside was as luxurious as any private plane she'd ever been on. "This is what you guys use to fly around the globe? Maybe I've been in the wrong line of work."

"Fortress has a fleet of five jets now. We use them all the time, sometimes for long hours. Brent didn't see the necessity of skimping on comfort."

"How long before Trent is released?"

"That's a question we'll have to ask the doc." He waved her toward a seat. "As soon as we're strapped in, Gardner will take off."

Darcy dropped into the nearest seat and fastened her seatbelt. As soon as Rio was settled beside her, he activated the intercom system and informed the pilot they were ready.

Once they were airborne, Rio ran the back of his fingers over her cheek, his touch gentle. "You need rest, Darcy. The next few days will be tough on you physically."

"Trent's the one who's injured."

"You're the one who will do a lot of sitting and waiting. You won't sleep or eat much. The stress will take a huge toll on your body. It would be tough on someone without a physical challenge."

"Even you?"

"When my teammates are injured, I'm the one who pulls the most bedside shifts."

She closed her eyes for a moment. Rio didn't deserve her attitude. It wasn't his fault she was scared to death she would lose her brother in spite of his assurances to the contrary. She wouldn't feel better until she saw her brother breathing for herself. "Sorry."

"What do you do when you're hurting physically? How do you alleviate the aches?"

"Heat, usually a warm shower."

"We have a shower in the back. You could try that."

"Or?"

"Or you could let me hold you a few minutes. Body heat might help your muscles relax so you can rest. Want to try?"

She didn't say anything, couldn't. He was offering to hold her? No one had done that in more years than she wanted to count. No one except Trent. Not since her parents died.

Apparently deciding he'd waited long enough for her answer, he slid his arm around her shoulders. "Trust me, Darcy." He settled deeper into the seat, moved the armrest, and eased her against his chest.

By degrees, her muscles loosened and she finally rested her head against his shoulder.

"Sleep," he whispered. "If I hear anything about Trent, I'll wake you."

It seemed only minutes until Rio was rubbing her back with soft motions.

"We're in the final approach, Darcy. An SUV is waiting to take us to the clinic."

She eased away from him, regretting the loss of warmth. Then his words hit her. "Clinic? Why isn't Trent in a hospital?"

"Gunshot wounds have to be reported. We can't explain how the injuries occurred. Ted Sorenson is the surgeon who worked on Trent. He was a top-flight trauma surgeon until he decided he'd had enough of that kind of excitement. Now he's one of the best vets in the country."

Darcy's jaw dropped. "Trent's in a vet clinic?"

The landing gear dropped and within minutes the Lear taxied to a stop. On the tarmac, a black SUV waited, the driver, a big, burly guy with dark hair touching his shoulders and a scar running down the right side of his face, leaned against the vehicle. Oh, man. That injury must have hurt. She wondered why he hadn't had plastic surgery to lessen the appearance of the scar. Then again, in his line of work, the fierce, dangerous look probably came in handy for intimidation purposes. Darcy wouldn't want to meet him in a dark alley. Talk about giving her a heart attack.

Then he smiled. Wow, what a difference a smile made. "Rio, good to see you again. How are your teammates?"

"Doing well. Nate's married now."

"To the hot marshal?"

"That's the one. She's now an Otter Creek police detective. Carlos, this is Darcy, Trent's sister."

The driver opened the back door of the SUV for her. "Doc Sorenson was wrapping up the surgery when I left to come here."

"Do you know how he is?"

He shook his head. "Sorry."

Rio placed their bags on the seat beside her. "We're only ten minutes from the clinic." He climbed into the shotgun seat and Carlos took off the minute Rio closed his door.

The morning sun warmed her face as they drove to the vet facility. Carlos parked behind the back of a long, one-story building and ushered them inside. "Trent should be in the room by now." With murmured thanks, Rio walked down the hall with Darcy and stopped in front of a closed door. He turned the knob.

Inside, a hospital bed occupied the center space. Her brother lay elevated, an IV delivering medication into his arm. Darcy hurried to Trent's side. He was breathing easy, his color good. She brushed the hair away from his brow.

A warm hand rested on her shoulder. "He looks good, sweetheart."

"How long before he wakes up?"

"Not for at least another hour. He'll be in a pretty foul mood when he does awaken. You should be prepared."

Footsteps drew Darcy's attention to the doorway. A tall, muscular man walked in.

"You must be Darcy." At her nod, he said, "Ted Sorenson. Your brother is fine. He'll be off the job for a few weeks. You'll want him to go back long before he's ready."

"When can I take him home?"

"Three or four days. I want to keep an eye on those gut wounds."

"Complications?" Rio asked.

"Usual. His attacker didn't sterilize the knife before using it on Trent." He nodded toward the IV stand. "Antibiotics and pain meds. He's still going to be a handful. Can't let him move around on his own until the wounds have a chance to heal. I don't want to redo my handiwork. You staying, Rio?"

"That's right."

"Good. You can ride herd on him. I'll return later."

Darcy stared at the now empty doorway. "Kind of brusque, isn't he?"

"That's how you know you'll make it. If he's gentle and kind, you're in trouble." He placed a chair close to Trent's bedside. "I'll get our bags."

She sank onto the chair and clasped her brother's hand. "Did you hear, Trent? Your doctor is grumpy, so you're going to make it." He slept on. She could handle her brother's grumpiness, just not planning another funeral.

Rio returned and put their bags across the room near a door she hadn't noticed. "Bathroom's through there when you want to freshen up. Are you hungry?"

Her stomach rolled at the thought of trying to eat anything. She never had been much of a breakfast eater. "I don't want to leave Trent."

"That's not what I asked, sweetheart. Will you eat something if I bring it to you?"

She shook her head. "I'd like a drink, though."

The medic studied her face a moment. "You don't eat in the mornings, do you?"

Darcy scowled. "Do I have a sign on my forehead or something?"

"Trent isn't the only grumpy one. I'll see what I can find you to drink." With that, he turned and left.

Now she officially felt like a shrew. Looked as if she owed Rio another apology. She sighed, laid her cheek on her brother's hand, and settled in to wait.

CHAPTER NINE

Rio grabbed the bags in the SUV's passenger seat. Darcy might not think she was hungry, but her body needed fuel. If she couldn't eat food this early, maybe she'd drink it. He hoped she liked chocolate. If not, he'd try another flavor.

He entered the clinic through the back door and strode down the corridor. At the rear of the clinic, he walked into the small kitchen and deposited the bags on the counter. He pulled out a container of egg white protein powder, dark chocolate cocoa, bananas, and vanilla-flavored almond milk. He dumped some of each ingredient into Sorenson's blender. While the small machine mixed Darcy's breakfast, he nuked hot water in a mug with a green tea bag laced with cranberry and orange.

He poured the protein shake into a tall glass with a lid and a straw. While the tea cooled, Rio returned to the SUV and hauled a 36-count case of water from the back and toted it into the kitchen. Yeah, he was here to help her care for Trent, but he was determined to keep her as healthy as possible. He hadn't earned the right, but he wanted it. Aside from being attracted to her, Rio cared about Darcy and her wellbeing.

After storing water in the refrigerator, he carried her drinks to Trent's room. She raised her head from the bed when he walked in. Had she been sleeping? Too alert for that. Resting, then. Good. She needed every bit of rest she could get over the next few days.

Her gaze dropped from his face to his hands. "What do you have?"

He lifted the mug as he continued toward her. "Green tea." He handed her the shake first. "Breakfast."

She tilted her head as she looked at the contents of the glass. "A chocolate shake?" She smiled. "I can get behind a shake in the mornings. It's every kid's dream come true."

"Try it." He watched as she sipped. Surprise crossed her face. "Like it?"

"This is wonderful, Rio. Where did you get it?"

"I bought the ingredients and mixed it in Sorenson's kitchen. It's a protein shake."

"Will you teach me how to make these?"

He gave himself a mental fist pump of victory. Oh, yeah. Helping the beautiful lady learn to take better care of herself would be fun. "It's easy. Now you can have breakfast without having to eat. When you start working, you can take it with you."

Rio talked to her about the different protein shakes he and his teammates tried over the years, some of which had been gag-worthy disasters. As he talked, he watched her steadily drink the shake. Interesting. Darcy needed someone to talk to her during a meal so she forgot what she was doing. She'd become self-conscious over the many years of eating on the road.

When she finished the last of the shake, Rio handed her the green tea.

"No coffee?"

He glanced up, glad to see her eyes twinkling. "It's better for you not to drink coffee or black tea, Darcy.

They're processed. Your body doesn't react well to processed food or drinks."

She wrinkled her nose. "Guess that includes soft drinks, too. I assume the information is from your research. When we return home, give me a list of the websites."

Trent stirred. Darcy set aside the tea and leaned over her brother. "Trent? It's Darcy. Can you hear me?"

"Darce?" he whispered.

"Right here. The doctor says you're going to be okay."

"Rio?"

"I'm here, buddy."

"Thanks for keeping little sis out of trouble."

"Hey!" Darcy frowned. "I'm not always in trouble."

"He doesn't know you like I do." A small smile crossed his lips. His gaze tracked to Rio. "How long?"

"Two or three days before you can leave the bed without help. If you cooperate, I'll push for two. You'll be off the job for a while, though."

His friend growled.

"You can help Darcy settle into the Victorian house she bought before you return to work." Rio grinned. "You never know. A beautiful woman might catch your attention in Otter Creek. Think of all the sympathy you'll have from the ladies in town."

The other Fortress operative glared.

Sorenson walked in. "Well, Sleeping Beauty is awake."

Trent's glare shifted to the doctor.

"You don't leave the bed without an assist, frog boy. Otherwise, I'll have to redo all my fine needlepoint in your gut. On top of that, you need to keep your weight off that leg for a few days. You hearing me?"

"Yeah, yeah."

"Good. I've got patients who need me." With that, he spun on his heel and strode into the hall.

"Guess I'm going to make it after all."

Rio shared a smile with Darcy before he turned to his friend. "How did the mission go?"

"Rescued the kids. Several of the creeps who took them didn't make it."

"I can see you're torn up about that," Darcy said, tone dry.

"Don't have much sympathy for those who target kids." Trent's eyes were drooping.

"Trent." Rio waited until his friend focused on his face. "Sleep will help you heal faster than anything else. When you're alert, we'll tell you about Darcy's house."

The Fortress operative closed his eyes and slid into sleep.

The next forty-eight hours passed in a blur of activity for Rio. He and Carlos spelled each other, keeping watch so their wounded teammate would sleep and helping Trent move from the bed to the bathroom. Rio had a daybed brought in for Darcy while he and Carlos bunked down on the floor. When Darcy expressed dismay at his sleeping pallet, he shrugged and told her he'd slept in worse conditions than on a clean floor. He didn't figure she needed to know about the nights he'd spent in the mud or perched up in a tree or patching up his teammates under fire.

When Trent progressed enough to walk the hall, Sorenson declared him fit enough to get out of his clinic. "No marathons," the doctor said. "Keep the bandages changed. Rio has your antibiotics. Do exactly what he tells you and don't whine about it. I don't want to see you again, St. Claire." With that, he returned to his furry and feathered patients.

Carlos stepped into the room. "SUV is parked at the back door," he said to Rio. "Will you need help with Trent?"

"Trent can help himself," snapped the grumpy patient.

"Good." The other operative turned his million dollar smile on Darcy. "That means I can help Miss Darcy to the vehicle."

"Hands off," Trent said.

Carlos just laughed and grabbed Darcy's bag in one hand, Rio's in the other. "Yes, Dad," he said as he walked out with her.

"Why isn't he shaking in his combat boots?" Trent complained.

"Maybe because you can't chase him down right now, St. Claire. You couldn't wrestle a wet rag and win today." Rio wrapped his arm around Trent's waist while Trent draped his arm over the medic's shoulders. "Check the attitude at the plane door. Darcy put up with enough crap from you in the last three days."

"I don't know what you're talking about, man."

Anger simmered in Rio's gut. "I listened to you gripe at her for no reason other than you were trapped in that bed and refused to take pain meds. She's handling enough without adding your sniping to the mix."

"You accusing me of mistreating her?"

"She put up with it because she loves you." Rio speared him with a narrowed glare. "I'm not sentimental over hardened military vets and I won't be so accommodating anymore."

"You won't be around to hear anything I say."

"Want to bet? You still need help for a while longer. Darcy can't handle your care. That leaves me to keep your grumpy self in line."

"Bite me," Trent snapped.

"If you keep after Darcy, I'll deck you, injured or not. Am I clear?"

"Shut up and get me out of here." With Rio's support, he limped to the waiting SUV. Carlos had seated Darcy in the third row of seats, leaving the middle for the injured operative.

77

Every mile to the airport, Trent fumed silently in his seat. No amount of gentle prodding by his sister elicited a response. She finally subsided, her expression puzzled.

Her brother's lack of response didn't bother Rio. Silence was better than the constant harping. All operatives hated being confined. Rio got that. He wouldn't tolerate Darcy being on the receiving end of the verbal tirades any longer. Trent could suck it up and deal without tearing into his sister. In some distant corner of his mind, he acknowledged the protective streak kicking in. He tried to tell himself it was the concern of a friend, but he was beginning to suspect there might be more to it than friendship. And wasn't that nuts. He'd only known Darcy for a few days, yet she'd somehow wiggled her way under his armor. Guess he'd have to see how this played out. At this point, he didn't know if she'd consider exploring a relationship with him beyond casual dates. His job made him a risky bet for any woman.

Carlos parked near the plane and assisted Rio with Trent. While Rio helped Trent settle into a seat, Carlos retrieved their bags and deposited them in overhead compartments.

When he left, Rio grabbed a bottle of water and slapped a pain pill on Trent's palm. "Take this."

"I'm fine."

"Shut up and take it, St. Claire. If I have to, I'll make you, but I figure you don't want to be embarrassed in front of your sister."

The other man's fists balled up.

"Trent." Darcy's soft voice drew his attention. "Quit acting like a brat and take your meds."

Rio's eyebrows rose at the steel in her voice. Nice. Guess she'd had enough of her brother's attitude as well.

Trent growled. He swallowed the pill dry. He reclined his seat, grabbed a blanket and pillow Rio had placed on the seat beside him, and closed his eyes.

Stubborn, much? He blew out a breath. Rio figured he'd pick his battles. There would be more to come in the next few days. By the end of the week, Trent should be able to maneuver around the house on his own. That more than anything else would probably go a long way toward fixing the attitude. Highly capable and trained people despised being dependent on anyone other than themselves.

He dropped into the seat beside Darcy and informed the pilot they were ready to roll. A minute later, they were airborne.

Rio twisted in his seat. "How are you, sweetheart?"

"Nothing a night of uninterrupted sleep won't cure."

Right. He knew better. She'd still worry about her brother until she saw major improvements. "I need to stay at your house for a few days."

Her head whipped in his direction. "Why?"

"Trent will need help until the end of the week. You can't physically manhandle him. Do you mind if I stay?" He supposed he could stay at his own place and come if she called him, but he didn't trust Trent's judgment or restraint.

"Of course not. I don't have a bed for you to sleep in, though."

"Doesn't matter. I've spent many nights on the ground. I'll be fine on your floor."

"Wonder if there have been new break-ins?"

"Josh didn't mention that when I called him with updates on Trent." That was another reason for him to stay. Though he didn't plan on mentioning it to Darcy, Rio hadn't been comfortable with her staying in that place by herself, especially with no alarm system. "Have you thought about installing an alarm system?"

"I plan to call Maddox."

"We'll do that as soon as we land." He glanced at her. "Rest for a while. This may be your last chance to do so." Rio grabbed a blanket. "Come here, Darcy." He wrapped his arm around her shoulder and eased her against his chest, much as he had a few days earlier. "Let go for a while. Give yourself a chance to recharge." Her not arguing the point reinforced his suspicions of her exhaustion.

Minutes later, Darcy was asleep. Rio spent the rest of the trip home enjoying the chance to hold her and thinking about the break-ins. Once Trent was on his feet without help, Rio would feel more at ease leaving her in the house. He couldn't figure out why someone kept breaking into the place. Even more important, did the break-ins have anything to do with the previous owner's murder?

CHAPTER TEN

Darcy woke to the deep rumble of male voices. She sat up in a hurry. Who was in her house so early? A glance at her watch had her eyes widening. Nine o'clock? Rats, not early, late. Oh, man. She'd meant to be up before now to check on Trent and spell Rio. She knew without asking that he'd been awake most of the night keeping watch so her brother would sleep.

Would Rio have to work at PSI after being awake all night? She hoped one of his friends stayed with her. Darcy would do her best to help Trent, but he outweighed her by a good eighty pounds and topped her by eight inches. Should her brother go down, she'd have to leave him there until help arrived.

Her lips curved. At least there wasn't much Trent could trip over. The night before, Josh had met them at the house with her key. She'd walked into the place, astonished at the changes since she left to be with her brother. The trainees had cleared the first two floors with the exception of the candles. Rio's teammates had brought over a comfortable recliner, sofa, and three double beds. All the beds were in the first floor bedrooms, a fact Darcy had been grateful for as Trent would have a hard time dealing with the stairs for a while yet. Nate had taken care of the appliances in the kitchen, all top of the line.

As Darcy grabbed her clothes and hurried into the bathroom, she thought about Rio Kincaid and all his care and support for her and her brother. How had any woman let him slip through her fingers? She had to laugh at her herself. She and Rio were in the early stages of friendship. Just because he called her sweetheart didn't mean he thought of her as anything beyond a friend. Some men called every woman in their lives sweet names.

Darcy shoved the circling thoughts to the back of her mind. She had a brother to corral and a house to wrangle into shape. She also needed to check on the progress at the shop. It was a good thing she'd given Brian Elliott her spare key to the storefront. Otherwise, there would have been no progress over the last several days, and that wouldn't do. The deli meant a new beginning for her, one necessary for renewed purpose in her life.

After showering and dressing, Darcy strode into the hall fastening her watch, and ran smack into a broad chest. Hard hands grabbed her before she could fall from the impact. She glanced up into twinkling brown eyes. "Sorry, Nate. What are you doing here?"

"Rio's sleeping. I'm doing the heavy lifting."

"I heard that," her brother called from the other room. "I'm not two, you know. I've been able to get up by myself for years now."

"You tear those stitches loose, you won't be getting up for a long time. You'll be able to maneuver by yourself at the end of the week. By that time, none of us will want to haul you anywhere, frog boy."

"Get me up, grunt."

"Your wish is my command." Nate winked at Darcy. "Your breakfast is in the refrigerator."

"Thanks," she murmured as she followed behind Rio's teammate. Her brother's wild bed hair brought a smile to her face. "How are you, Trent?"

"Sore, hungry, and stir crazy." He glared at Nate. "I want out of this bed. The four walls are closing in on me, man."

"Figured." Nate crossed the room. "Rio suggested the recliner today. At least you'll have company with the PSI trainees coming in and out of the house. You can direct traffic."

"Fabulous. That's why I spent so many years in the SEALs, you know. They taught me great traffic skills."

His barbed comments made her laugh. Though her brother scowled at her, his eyes revealed reluctant humor at his own situation. Progress. She'd take that.

"Glad I can entertain you, Darce." He winced as Nate hauled him up and helped him balance on one leg. Once he was stable, Trent limped with Nate's assistance to the bathroom across the hall.

Some of the tension eased from Darcy's muscles. Looked as if Rio was right again. Her brother was healing at a fast rate.

Nate returned to the hall, closing the bathroom door behind him. "I'll wait here for your brother if you want to drink your breakfast. My wife, Stella, is in the kitchen. There's food if you want it. Otherwise, at least drink the shake."

She grinned. "Rio's orders?"

"Yes, ma'am. None of us disobeys that man's directives, not even Josh."

That made her pause. Interesting comment. "Your medic seems as if he's easy going. Is he that much of a tyrant?"

"When it comes to our physical health, you bet. There's a lot of steel beneath the calm exterior, Darcy. Don't kid yourself. He's as much Special Forces as the rest of us. There's no one tougher and no one I'd rather have at my back. He just hides his true self better."

Huh. Hidden depths to the medic. It made her more curious to learn the real Rio Kincaid. She walked to the kitchen, stopped short when she saw all the food spread out across the counter. "Good grief!"

"Impressive, isn't it?" said the dark-haired woman sitting at the kitchen table, sipping from a cardboard cup.

Impressive wasn't the word Darcy thought of first. "Did you make all this?" Two kinds of breakfast casserole, cinnamon buns, muffins, bagels, cream cheese spreads, a huge coffee pot, and orange juice.

"My greatest cooking feat is popping food in the microwave. The magic chef is Nate. PSI trainees are still working here and his job is to feed them, wherever they're working or training. I'm Stella, Nate's wife." Even as she said those words, the beautiful woman's cheeks reddened.

Newlyweds, Darcy remembered. Sweet. "I'm Darcy, Trent's sister. Congratulations on your marriage."

"Thanks. Come sit with me while you eat."

She turned to the food spread again, flinched. Nope, not happening. "Um, Rio left a protein shake for me in the refrigerator. While the food looks amazing, I don't think I could eat a bite and keep it down this early."

Stella laughed. "Early?"

"Sad, isn't it? I can't tolerate food before noon." Probably came from the weird eating schedule on her concert tours.

"I understand from Nick Santana that you've had some break-ins recently. Why don't you tell me about them?" She held up her left hand which was covered in a cast. "I'm with the Otter Creek police, even though I'm on restricted duty until my wrist heals. I'd like to help if I can."

Darcy retrieved her shake and placed it on the table. The coffee smelled so good. Green tea for her, though. She had no desire to aggravate Rio or cause her body more stress. She saw a couple boxes of flavored green tea bags on the counter. Rio taking care of her again. She selected one with jasmine and orange and nuked the tea bag and water. "What happened to your wrist?"

"Long story short, I was abducted and broke my wrist attempting to escape."

She stared a moment. "Hope your kidnapper is in jail."

"Oh, yeah. He won't be getting out until he's old and gray. Now, tell me what's been going on around here."

In between sips of her shake and green tea, she told Nate's wife what had been happening in the short time she'd been in Otter Creek.

"So you bought this place with the previous owner's possessions still inside?"

"According to the real estate agent, there are very few houses available right now. This was the best she had unless I wanted to stay in a motel or rent an apartment for months while contractors built a house for me. I just didn't want move into an apartment, then into a house if I could avoid it. I'm a creature of habit and I despise moving. Takes me forever to find things and place them where they can be used in an efficient way." Not to mention how difficult it was to move her piano. She couldn't stand the thought of leaving her Steinway in storage for months.

"Nate and I are living out of boxes right now. Frustrating for both of us. Ah, well. One box at a time. Do you have any idea what the break-ins are about?"

Darcy shook her head. "I didn't want to tell Trent yet, but I'm concerned. What if this has something to do with the murder of the previous owner?"

Stella's eyes widened. "The previous owner was murdered?"

"That's what Mrs. Watson told me."

"Do you know anything about the owner or the murder?"

"The woman's name was Gretchen Bond. Her relatives didn't want the house and the items inside. Can't say I blame them. You should have seen this place. If Rio and his friends hadn't helped, I'd still be walking a very narrow path from room to room. Stella, there were so many things in here, I don't know how anyone could look for a specific item."

"If the prize is important enough, people will go to any lengths to get what they want. I'll check into the previous owner's background, see if I can find anything interesting. We'll talk to people around town about her and the house. According to Nate, Otter Creek's grapevine is well developed. Somebody knows something. We have to ask the right person."

"Josh suggested I talk to his father about Ms. Bond since he'd lived here all his life. Mr. Cahill might point us in the right direction."

"Hmm. Isn't Josh's father a banker?"

"I think so."

"Makes sense, then. There's only one bank in town. I imagine the employees know something about everybody."

"The break-ins are strange. Seems as though someone is looking for buried treasure. Who would hide something in the floor?"

Stella tilted her head. "The floor?"

"Oh, yeah. Somebody took a crowbar to the floor in at least two rooms. So now the contractor will have to repair the floors as well as any remodeling I think is necessary."

The other woman glanced at her watch, stood. "Time for me to go to the station. Rod Kelter, the detective I'm shadowing, should be finished with his court appearance by now. I'll do some digging and let you know what I find about Ms. Bond." She paused. "By the way, Nate tells me you're planning to open a deli soon. Will you be hiring workers?"

"One or two people. Why?"

"I have a friend who just moved here. Her name is Leah Conner. She's looking for work."

"Can she cook?"

Stella's lips twitched. "Not a bit. She's really smart, though, and great with people. I don't think you'd have a problem teaching her what she needs to know. She's a hard worker, too. Her husband, Dean, is working for Elliott Construction."

"Brian Elliott is working on my deli and remodeling this place. Tell Leah I'll be glad to talk to her." She gave Stella her cell phone number. "I'll be hard to catch for a while. I have to buy furniture for the house and the deli as well as help out with Trent. I can't leave Rio to do everything."

"He's pretty capable."

"So I've seen. I feel as though I'm taking advantage."

"Believe me, Rio doesn't see it that way. All the guys put themselves out to help each other. I'll have Leah call you. Maybe you two can get together and talk about your plans for the deli. Darcy, there's no pressure to hire her if she won't meet your needs, okay?"

"No problem." She didn't cave to pressure when it didn't suit her. "I'll talk to her and we'll go from there."

"I'm going to track down my husband before I go. Talk to you soon, Darcy."

She finished her shake and green tea. By the time she finished washing her shake cup, the PSI trainees started trickling through the kitchen to grab plates of food.

Nate strolled in a minute later, filled a plate, and poured a cup of coffee. His gaze stopped on her cup now sitting on the counter. "Good. I'll have something you can eat at lunch."

"You don't have to do that," she protested. "You have your hands full feeding the bodyguards plus riding herd on my cantankerous brother."

"It's not a problem, Darcy. I'll just feed the troops the same thing I feed you. They don't care what I place in front of them, as long as it's edible."

"I need to check on progress at the deli." She glanced through the doorway. "I should check the Dumpsters before I leave."

"Empty ones were delivered while you slept. Brian kept an eye on them while you were in Texas."

One less thing to worry about completing today. "Guess I'll go." She hurried to her room, scooped up her purse, stopped. Rats. Her car was at the motel. She needed a ride. Darcy went to the living room. "Nate, could somebody take me to my motel? I need my car."

He smiled. "It's out in the driveway."

Stunned, she glanced out the window. Her black car gleamed in the morning sunshine. "Rio?"

"Uh huh. He had the major stop by and drop him off at the motel."

"I gave him my set of keys, Darce," Trent said. "We knew you'd need wheels today."

The handsome medic thought of everything. Nice. "I'm going to the deli. I'll return soon." She leaned over, kissed her brother on the forehead. "Want anything while I'm out?"

"Books. I need something to occupy my brain."

She blinked. "Any requests?"

"Something recent. I haven't had time to read in months."

That didn't narrow the selection. Her bewilderment must have shown because Nate said, "Drop by Otter Creek Books and ask for Del. She'll have suggestions."

She'd wanted to meet Josh's wife anyway. This was a good excuse. "I'll do that."

Darcy palmed her keys and walked from the house. Her breath caught at the sight of the man leaning against her car.

CHAPTER ELEVEN

Rio tugged on his black t-shirt and laced up his running shoes. He needed a good, hard run after days of sitting by Trent's bedside or sleeping on the floor. Inactivity was driving him crazy. After stretching his muscles, he walked to the living room to see Trent seated in the recliner, scowling out the front window. His recalcitrant patient looked better this morning. Amazing what a decent night's sleep at home could do for morale. "What's up, Trent?"

"There's a strange man talking to Darcy outside." He struggled to get up from the recliner.

"Whoa, whoa." Rio hurried over and restrained him. "Hold on, buddy. What do you need?"

"To find out who that clown is. Darcy's upset."

Rio moved to the window and took in the scene outside at a glance. Trent was right. Darcy didn't look happy. She also didn't seem afraid. Aggravated, maybe. So this guy was an irritation to her. Wonder what that was about? As far as he knew, Darcy didn't know many people in town, and this guy was unknown to him. In Otter Creek, everybody knew each other at least by sight.

Nate strode into the living room with a steaming cup of coffee, frowned. "Anything wrong?"

"Something is up with Darcy. I'll find out what's going on if you keep Humpty Dumpty in the chair."

"Ha ha." Trent sent him a dirty look, but sank deeper into the recliner, apparently satisfied now that someone was checking on his sister. "Send him packing."

Rio saluted and opened the door. A cold breeze slapped him in the face, stealing his breath. Wow. The wind had kicked up in the last hour. He'd need to keep moving on the five-mile run or he'd freeze.

The other man's voice carried on the wind. "Come on, Darcy. Be reasonable. It's too soon to move on. I want you to promise me to think about it. Give me that at least."

Rio's eyes narrowed. What was this about? An old boyfriend, maybe? He was about her age and it was obvious he was from Darcy's life before Otter Creek. This guy talked like he knew her well, not something that made Rio happy.

"You'll never be able to make it without me," the man continued. "This isn't what you want. Only I can give you that. Think of everything you're giving up. Come on, baby. Don't do this to me. We've been together too long to hurt each other this way."

Baby? Something dark and deadly stirred in Rio's gut. What gave this man the right to pressure Darcy to change her mind about anything? He lengthened his stride.

The other man finally looked away from the woman in front of him and noticed Rio bearing down on them. His eyes took in Rio's running attire, one which showcased his muscle-laden chest and arms, and broad shoulders. Didn't hurt that Rio had a good six inches on him, either. The other man swallowed hard.

At his sudden silence and gaze fixed over her shoulder, Darcy spun around. "Rio." She smiled. "You're awake."

He stopped in front of her and cupped her face between his palms. "Good morning, sweetheart." Rio leaned down and kissed her, just a gentle brush of his lips over hers. Not the no-holds-barred kiss he wanted to share, but a definite statement that she was off limits to this stranger. He also knew Trent was watching through the window. He hated to drop a bombshell on his friend, but he was interested in dating Darcy. Trent had trusted her safety to him. Would he trust Rio with her heart?

With a last soft kiss, he dropped his hands, draped his arm across Darcy's shoulders, and faced the man now scowling at both of them. Rio held out his hand. "Rio Kincaid."

"Allen White," came the churlish response.

"Allen was my agent," Darcy said.

Why was he in Otter Creek? He thought back through the part of the conversation he'd overheard. White was trying to pressure Darcy into returning to the stage. A possible relationship aside, this guy wanted her to continue a life which was no longer possible for her. If it was only the fatigue, she could reduce her concert dates, concentrate on studio work. But it wasn't just that. Darcy's problem was the repetitive motion required to be a pianist. How many hours a day would she have to practice to continue in that career? Six, eight? Too many for the joints, tendons, and muscles in her hands and arms.

"I'm still your agent," White muttered. "We haven't scheduled more concerts."

Darcy sighed. "I'm not going back, Allen. You need to accept that and move on to the next virtuoso."

"There is no one like you," he snapped. "Look, if you need to cut back a little, I can work with that. I've been bombarded with calls, begging me to schedule you in different venues. This is the peak of your career, baby.

You're hot and you have to take advantage of the heat while you have the chance."

"I'm not leaving Otter Creek."

"Why not?" His gaze flicked to Rio. "If he's the reason you're reluctant to leave this little berg, bring your boyfriend along. It will give the entertainment reporters something to speculate about."

Darcy drew in a sharp breath, her cheeks flushing. "Rio has a job, one that won't allow him to spend ten months a year away from it."

Interesting. He figured Darcy would tell White right off that Rio wasn't her boyfriend and was pleased she didn't bother to correct her agent's mistaken assumption.

"Many couples have long-distance relationships. You can make it work, Darcy." He tossed a pointed glance at Rio. "Unless he's a Neanderthal and demands every minute of your time."

"He isn't like that," Darcy protested. "I'm not interested in continuing in the same career. I'm transitioning to a different field. I don't want to travel anymore."

"I don't understand you. You're throwing your life away. All those hours of practicing down the drain. You love the attention, the fame you get from performing."

"No, Allen, you love the notoriety of being my manager. I want a real life, one that doesn't include long hours in a practice room by myself, an endless loop of impersonal hotel suites, media interviews, recording studios, and whatever food I can scrape together in the few hours I have. No more. Otter Creek is my home now. You have plenty of clients to keep you busy and now is the time to recruit more."

White blew out a frustrated breath. "I'm not giving up on this, Darcy. You'll never be happy in a small town, not after you've experienced real life in the larger world." He gestured to the neighborhood. "A run-down house, country bumpkin neighbors, a boyfriend who's all brawn and no brains? This isn't what you want. You'll call in a couple weeks and beg me to book another tour for you."

All brawn and no brains, huh? White was lucky Rio was in a good mood this morning. As it was, he was tempted to use those muscles to boot him off Darcy's property. If the agent didn't stop pushing, he'd change his mind about staying neutral and letting her handle the situation herself. One thing for sure, Trent wouldn't have been nearly as patient.

"Don't bet on it." Darcy's voice conveyed her growing annoyance. "I appreciate everything you've done for me in the past few years. Be careful driving home, Allen."

"Not a chance, baby. I'm not leaving until I convince you to change your mind."

The other man's smug arrogance made Rio itch to plow a fist in his face. He glanced at Darcy. She might not want to tell her agent about her health limitation, but that might be the only way for him to accept her decision as final. Unless, of course, she wanted Rio to make him leave her alone, something he'd enjoy.

"Then you are in for a long stay, my friend. I'm headed in another career direction altogether."

"Oh, yeah?" A sneer settled on his face. "What other talents do you have? Music is your life."

"White," Rio said, voice soft. He'd had about enough of this guy, especially since Darcy was starting to shiver from the cold. "You've had your say. It's time for you to leave."

The agent's face reddened. "Keep your nose out of her business. If you want her to keep you in style, she must work."

Did he seriously just say that? This clown thought Rio was interested in Darcy for her money? Darcy's hand wrapped around his wrist. He glanced down at her. Temper glittered in her gaze. That made him pause. Was she angry at him or her abrasive agent?

"Aren't there any decent restaurants in town?" the agent asked, his attention back on Darcy. "I'm sick of Delaney's and I wouldn't be caught dead in that burger place."

Rio's eyes narrowed.

"How long have you been in town?" Darcy asked.

"Five endless days. I couldn't find you. No one knew where you were or they weren't saying."

"You arrived the same day I did? That borders on stalker behavior, Allen."

Yep, it did, behavior that Rio viewed with even more suspicion considering what had been happening in the Victorian house. "What have you been doing all that time, White?"

"Not much," he complained. "Reading, listening to real music, not this country and western garbage so popular in the area, and hunting around town for Darcy and places to eat. I can't believe people live like this."

"How did you find me here?" She leaned closer to Rio.

He'd give this conversation one more minute, then he was kicking the agent into his fancy luxury automobile parked at the curb. Rio turned Darcy more fully into his embrace in order to share his body heat with her.

White snorted. "Your purchase of this broken down wreck is the talk of the town, baby. I didn't have to do anything but listen to the gossip to find this place. This is a waste of your money, you know. You'd be better off bulldozing this place and building something new."

A sentiment Rio agreed with, not that he'd say it to Darcy. She wanted this place to shine and he planned to help her achieve her goal, even if it meant long hours at work, then more hours rehabbing the house. A violent shudder from Darcy had him tightening his arms around her. "Darcy needs to leave. You can call her later or set an appointment to talk to her."

The agent opened his mouth to argue, got a good look at Rio's face, and changed his mind.

Smart man. Rio rubbed his hands up and down Darcy's back as White spun on his heel and stalked to his car. Seconds later, his taillights flashed as he turned the corner, heading into town.

"What's it going to be, sweetheart? Into the car or back to the house to warm up?"

"Car." Her teeth chattered. "I need to check on the deli's progress."

Rio ushered her to the car and helped her inside. Once the engine was cranked, he leaned in and kissed her before closing her door. A small wave and she backed out of the driveway. Shouldn't take long for the temperature to warm up in the vehicle. An hour ago, he'd run her car long enough for the heat to kick on fast.

As he watched her drive down the street in White's wake, his thoughts returned to the agent in question. This guy had been in town for several days. Could he be desperate enough to break into Darcy's house and damage her floors, hoping to scare her back to a career he benefited from?

CHAPTER TWELVE

Darcy's cheeks burned, partly from the cold wind, partly from temper. How dare Allen White breeze into town and try to bully her into returning to the performance stage? He'd never been a bully to her before. Then again, he'd never had reason to be. Until six months ago, Darcy had been content to let him handle the business side of her career. All she'd been concerned about was her music. He was a dogged business manager, a trait she'd valued in him until today. The man was good at his job and he'd worked hard. Along the way, Allen earned a lot of money and she had considered him well worth his exorbitant salary. Now she wondered if all that dedication was for her benefit or his.

Another hard shudder wracked her frame. She held one of her hands over a dashboard vent. The heat felt good to her frozen fingers. She'd only been in the car a couple minutes. The motel was only five minutes from the house, which meant someone had let it run. She knew to her frozen bones that someone was Rio Kincaid with his endearing habit of taking care of little details for her comfort.

She parked in front of the deli. Inside the storefront, she glanced at the busy workers, searching for Brian. She spotted him through the doorway leading into the kitchen. Darcy crossed the open space, skirting workers and equipment. Several of the crew smiled at her or waved as she passed by. "Hey, Brian."

"Darcy, good to see you. How's your brother?"

"Recovering. He'll be fine in a few weeks."

"Accidents are the pits to work through."

Hmm. An accident, huh? Guess the grapevine didn't know about her brother's knife and bullet wounds. That would be pretty hard to explain. So, accident it was, then. "How are things going here?"

"Right on schedule. We're finishing the electrical upgrade for your appliances today and starting the tile work in the front next week. I'll work on your walk-in cooler tomorrow. We're also starting on your refrigerated display cases tomorrow."

"Perfect. Need anything from me?"

"What's the word on your sign for the front?"

"Should be here by the end of next week."

"Excellent. Once we finish the work here, we'll start on your house."

She wrinkled her nose. "You have your work cut out for you."

"Why?"

"Someone took a crowbar to the wood floors in a few rooms."

He winced. "Do you know why?"

"No clue. I hope you have a good carpenter on your crew."

"We have several. Don't worry, Darcy. We'll take care of the floor and any other surprises that pop up."

She hoped there weren't more surprises. At some point, Trent would return to work and that would leave her in the house by herself. Not a comforting thought when weird things were happening. "I'll leave you to it, then."

"Stop in again on Monday. We need to choose paint and take care of the walls before we lay the flooring. I'll have paint samples for you to see."

Minutes later, Darcy crossed the town square to Otter Creek Books. The first things she noticed were heat, scent of coffee, and the kaleidoscope of colors from yarn in bins and books on shelves. She scanned the interior, astonished at the size of the building. She'd never seen that much yarn in one place. Thick, thin, fuzzy, and everything in between. Made her itch to touch everything though she never learned to knit or crochet. There hadn't been time.

Such a huge selection of books boggled her mind. This was a store she would visit frequently. Reading was one of her guilty pleasures. While on the road, she always had a book nearby.

"Welcome to Otter Creek Books. May I help you find anything?" A tall, dark-haired woman approached with a friendly smile on her face. "I'm Del, by the way."

Ah. The bookstore owner and Josh Cahill's wife. "I'm Darcy St. Claire."

Del's smile broadened. "Welcome to Otter Creek. Thank you for donating the books."

"Will you be able to use them?"

"Quite a few. The rest I'll donate to the library or the retirement homes in the area. You look frozen, Darcy. Would you like coffee?"

She inhaled deeply and wished she could indulge. However, she'd already begun to notice a difference in how she felt with the changes to her diet. "No coffee. Do you have tea?"

"Come sit at the counter. We carry a wide variety of herbal and green teas." She slid a laminated list of available tea and coffee across the counter. "What would you like?"

Darcy studied the list and selected cranberry orange green tea. She could use a lift today. Orange flavored things always gave her a boost. "I met your husband earlier in the week. He's been a great help at the house."

The store owner ripped open the packet of tea and dropped the bag in a mug of steaming water. "Josh said the house was in a sorry state."

"A better description is wreck or disaster. I've never seen so many things crammed in one place in my life." She paused. "Did you know Gretchen Bond?"

Del shook her head. "I've only lived here a little over a year myself." She glance up at a portly older gentleman as he walked toward the register. "Professor Cambridge might have known her."

"Known who?" the man prompted, curiosity in his gaze.

"Gretchen Bond. She owned the house Darcy lives in."

The professor's eyes widened. "You bought the Victorian?"

"Yes, sir. I'm Darcy St. Claire."

"Paul Cambridge, history professor at the community college. I'm sorry, Ms. St. Claire, but Ms. Bond and I were only acquaintances. Our main source of conversation was the architecture of her house. I'm fascinated with architecture, you see." He paused. "Would you be willing to let me take photographs of the interior of your house sometime?"

She blinked. "I guess that would be okay."

"Wonderful. Thank you, Ms. St. Claire." He paid for his purchases and left.

A petite blond with a slight limp stepped behind the counter and lifted the glass dome off a plate of brownies. "Time for my chocolate fix." Her bright blue gaze shifted to Darcy. "Would you like a brownie? My sister made them. They are to die for."

Oh, boy, did she ever want one. "I'll stick with hot tea."

"I'm Madison Santana."

"Any relation to Nick Santana?"

Madison's eyes sparkled. "He's my husband."

"I'm Darcy St. Claire. Nick came to my house a few nights ago to investigate a break-in."

"Do you own the Victorian?"

Darcy smiled. "I do."

"I've always wanted to see inside that place. Nick said the lady who owned it before you was a hoarder."

"It's true. You couldn't walk through without taking your life in your hands. It's better now, though. Many people are helping me clear the place."

"So I hear." She smiled at Darcy's puzzled look. "Small town and Josh is my brother. I know the bodyguard trainees are using this as extra physical conditioning."

"I hope the time spent at the house doesn't set them back."

Madison waved her concern aside. "Don't worry. Durango is very good at what they do. They won't let training suffer."

Del grinned. "Josh said the trainees are enjoying the change of pace. Seems they aren't too keen on outside workouts in this weather. At least they're warm in your house and Nate is feeding them well."

"I'll never be able to repay them." Darcy frowned. "Actually, maybe I can once the deli is open."

"Deli?" Madison polished off her brownie and poured herself a mug of coffee. "You're opening a deli?"

"Across the square. I'm opening after the first of the year."

"Fantastic. Something new to chase away the blues of winter. What's the name of your deli?"

"That's A Wrap. All the food will be served in wraps."

"Oh, nice," Del said. "That sounds great. How's your brother?"

"Mending. I'm glad to have him with me for a while. We haven't seen each other much for a few years."

"His job?"

"And mine. It was rare for us to be on the same continent at the same time. I'm looking forward to a couple weeks with him." A smile curved her lips. "I'll be lucky to keep him with me that long. He'll want to go home as soon as he's mobile."

"All the Fortress operatives I've met are the same way. What job kept you traveling so much?" Madison asked.

"Concert pianist."

"No kidding." She leaned on the counter. "Did you record?"

She nodded. "My stage name is Darcy Melton."

"Oh, man. My husband has all your CDs. He loves your music. He doesn't know who you are, does he?"

"Never came up."

She rubbed her hands. "I can't wait to tell him."

Del placed the tea mug in front of Darcy. "Do you listen to classical guitar music?"

"I do. Why?"

She reached under the counter, pulled out a CD, and handed it to her. On the front cover was Nick Santana with his classical guitar. "I didn't realize Detective Santana was this Nick Santana." Darcy sighed. "Sounds stupid since the name isn't exactly common. I love his music, but I never paid attention to what he looks like."

"And you never expected to see him answering a call as law enforcement, either." Madison grinned. "The shine of his stardom is a constant source of embarrassment to Nick. He just loves to play his guitar. Most of the money he makes from sales goes to charity."

"That is nice." She'd done something similar. Now she wouldn't have the income to continue the practice. One thing at a time, she reminded herself. Once her deli was turning a profit, she could resume giving. Right now, though, she was leaking money like a sieve between the house and the deli.

Wind chimes over the door filled the store with sound as a woman with red hair shoved open the glass door and hurried inside. "Good grief, it's cold out there. Sorry I'm late, Del."

"No problem, Annie. Everyone else must think it's too cold to shop for books because it's been slow today." She motioned to Darcy. "Annie, Darcy St. Claire. Annie is one of my store clerks. She also helps Madison in the knitting store."

"Nice to meet you, dear." The older woman patted her on the shoulder. "Are you here visiting a friend or relative?"

"No, ma'am. I'm opening a deli."

"We need a new place to eat around here."

Del looked at her assistant, speculation in her gaze. "Annie, you've lived in Otter Creek a long time, right?"

"Ever since I married my sweet Henry when I was eighteen. I lived in Cherry Hill at the time. Why?"

"Maybe you can tell Darcy about Gretchen Bond."

Red eyebrows winged upward as she returned her attention to Darcy. "Was she a relative of yours?"

"I bought her house."

"You are one brave woman, Darcy St. Claire. Gretchen never liked to throw anything away."

She gave a short laugh. "Believe me, I found that out the hard way. I've had an army of people helping me clear the rooms for several days. What can you tell me about Ms. Bond?"

Del patted Darcy's hand. "I have to go to the community center with a load of books. I'll leave you in Annie's capable hands."

"Take your time, dear," Annie said. "Maybe have lunch with that handsome husband of yours if he's awake."

Del's cheeks flushed. "I might do that. I'll have my cell phone if you need me." She pulled a business card from the pocket of her jeans and slid it to Darcy. "Call me. We'll go to lunch." She smiled. "From the sounds of it, we should do lunch soon. Once you open the deli, you won't have much time for new friends."

With a wave, the bookstore owner left. Another customer walked in the door, this one for Madison. Annie settled on a barstool beside Darcy. "Gretchen and I were friends. She was a school teacher and thrift was part of her DNA. Her father lived through the Great Depression and taught her not to waste anything. When she grew older, Gretchen took that philosophy a dozen steps farther."

She shook her head, humor evident in her eyes. "I tried to convince her to donate all the items in her big old house. After all, who needs fifty pairs of shoes, most of them men's shoes? That made absolutely no sense to me because she was widowed. To be honest, I think she never intended to collect so many things. And once the piles grew, she didn't know what to do with it all. It overwhelmed and paralyzed her. Add to that her lifetime habit of saving everything, and she became a walking example of The Hoarders."

"When were you in her house last?"

Annie frowned. "Oh, I'd say a month or so before she died."

"Do you know what happened to her?"

Sadness filled her eyes. "Such an ugly thing, my dear. Gretchen and I had gone to dinner that night at Delaney's. Oh, we had such fun talking about our school days and her teaching days. Not much had changed. Anyway, I drove her home about eight. Gretchen was an early riser even in retirement. A lifetime habit is hard to break. I found her the next morning."

Darcy reached over and squeezed the other woman's hand. "I'm sorry. I don't mean to bring up bad memories, but I understand she was murdered."

Tears filled Annie's eyes. "It would have been easier to accept her death had it been from natural causes or a fall. But I didn't lose her that way. Someone beat her to death with a hammer."

CHAPTER THIRTEEN

Rio started his run at an easy pace until his muscles warmed, glad to be outdoors in spite of the cold wind cutting through his clothes. At least he didn't have to run on a treadmill. Man, he hated to run on those things. He didn't know anything more boring than running that way. Made him feel like a hamster on a wheel, all that effort getting him nowhere. Outside, he might be running in a much bigger circle, but at least he had new scenery, people, and the occasional dog to outrun. Of course, this time of day, there was a lot more activity than his normal runs at four o'clock. The world was quiet and peaceful that time of morning.

As he ran, he thought about Allen White. The agent was determined to push Darcy back into performing. He had a feeling the business manager wouldn't give up without an explanation. Rio would love to step in and make him back off. He couldn't, though. Darcy wasn't helpless. She was a strong woman who was fully capable of handling White. Unless she asked him to step in or it became obvious she was in danger from the agent, Rio would have to keep his opinions to himself.

For the next mile, he turned his attention to the break-in at Darcy's house. He should touch base with Nick, see if he turned up anything after they flew to Bayside. Maybe he found a usable print on the door frame.

During the third mile on a deserted stretch of road, an engine revved. He'd been aware of a vehicle nearby for the last half mile. Rio glanced over his shoulder. His heart rate spiked as a black SUV raced toward him. The vehicle churned up dirt as it swerved off the blacktop. With seconds to react, Rio leaped from the roadway and raced into a stand of trees. The driver yanked the SUV back on the road and darted away.

Rio scowled, searching for the license plate number. Covered in mud. Bad driver or deliberate act?

The remaining miles passed swiftly as he kicked up the pace another couple notches. When he reached the house, Rio stretched and allowed his breathing to regulate. He tugged off his sweaty t-shirt and opened the front door.

"What do you think you're doing?" Trent snapped.

"Hello to you, too, Sunshine."

"Shut up and answer my question, Kincaid."

"I'm going to take a shower and eat."

"You know what I'm talking about."

"Do I?" Rio asked, his tone mild. The way he felt inside was anything but mild. He liked Trent, respected his skills and his obvious love for his sister. He did not appreciate being questioned as though Rio's morals were spotty.

"I asked you to get rid of the guy pestering my sister. That did not include putting your hands on her."

He was trusted to save a fellow operative's life but not to touch Darcy? Rio's eyes narrowed. "That was her agent, Allen White. He's pressuring her to return to the stage."

Trent scowled. "I'll have a talk with him."

"No, you won't. If Darcy needs help, she'll ask."

"Stay out of my business, Kincaid. How I deal with my sister has nothing to do with you. And that brings me to my other point. Keep your hands off her."

"I care about her, Trent. You should know by now I treat all women with respect. Beyond that, my relationship with Darcy is off limits to you. If she doesn't want me around, I'll abide by her wishes." Much as it would rankle. He liked her and he flat out loved her music. She was the reason he'd survived the aftermath of so many deployments. One day soon, he'd tell her how she'd saved his sanity. "You get a free pass this time because of your injuries. Your sister is an adult. You need to back off."

"She's sick, Rio."

"So what? She's not contagious."

"I don't want her hurt," he growled.

Rio stared, wrenching his fury under control. "You can't wrap her in cotton to protect her, Trent. I would never hurt her in any way." Trent flinched at his soft voice. "We've been on two dates. I want to go on more because I like spending time with her. We might continue to date or not. Whatever we do is not up to you. If you try to interfere, you and I will have a problem."

Silence filled the room. Finally, Trent said, "If you hurt her, you'll have my fist in your face."

"Fair enough." His lips twitched. "You'll have to wait in line, though. Darcy is tough enough to take me on herself if I upset her."

Satisfaction and a little pride lit his friend's face. "That is true. Something I'd like to see myself."

"Thanks a lot, buddy."

"Did you girls kiss and make up?" Nate asked. He leaned one shoulder against the wall as a handful of trainees traipsed to the front door, carting arm loads of towels and old clothes.

"We reached a truce." Trent speared Rio with a meaningful glance. "For now."

Yeah, he got that Darcy's big brother was sending a warning. It was unnecessary. Only time would convince Trent that Rio had honorable intentions. With a salute to his comrade in arms, he walked past his teammate. "Shower time for me."

"Lunch will be ready soon."

Dressed a few minutes later, Rio dodged a trainee carrying a loaded box of toys down the hall. "Sorry," she called back over her shoulder. With a chuckle, he continued to the kitchen. Nate had set up another big spread of food on the counters. Huge bowls of taco salad sat next to bags of tortilla chips. The scratched dining table had three kinds of cookies on platters. Nice. His mouth watered at the sight of fresh baked oatmeal raisin cookies, his favorite. How did Nate find time to cook and bake like this?

"Trent already ate and limped off to take a nap."

"Maybe that will sweeten his attitude," Rio muttered.

"Don't bet on it, Rio. Darcy is his kid sister. He's going to be protective."

"I know. I get it. I was the same way with my younger brothers."

"No, you weren't. It's different with a sister."

And the autoimmune disease only added to his protective instincts. Rio sighed. "I suppose you were the same."

Nate snorted. "Worse. Trent's handling this a lot better than I would have."

Light footsteps sounded, coming toward the kitchen. Rio turned as Darcy crossed the threshold. Immediately, he went to her and cupped the side of her face with his palm, searching her haunted gaze. "What's wrong?"

She bit her lower lip.

"Come sit with me." He clasped her hand and led her to the table. Rio sent a pointed glance toward Nate who promptly left the room without saying a word. "Talk to me, sweetheart. Did you go to the deli?"

"Brian's doing a great job. Everything is progressing on schedule."

Hmm. Not that, then. "Where did you go after that?"

"Otter Creek Books. I met Del and Madison. They're really nice."

So what had upset her so much that she was talking about everything except what he wanted to know? Rio studied her face, noted the pallor. Shock? He crossed to the counter. He grabbed a green tea bag and dumped it in a cup and nuked the water while she continued telling him about the store and the customers she'd seen while sitting at the counter.

When the microwave signaled the end of the heating cycle, he removed the bag and emptied a packet of stevia in it and stirred. He wasn't sure this would take care of it, but he'd try this first. If it didn't, he'd sprinkle a little sugar in it to counteract the shock. As long as he didn't overdo it, a small amount of sugar shouldn't set off any inflammation.

He returned to his seat and set the cup in front of Darcy. "Sip this."

She stopped talking and picked up the cup with shaking hands. "Sorry."

"Hey, it's all right. Even hardened soldiers have to deal with shock." He waited until she drank half the tea before he said, "Let's try this again. What happened, baby?"

"I talked to one of Del's employees, a woman named Annie."

A grandmother to a bunch of rambunctious boys she adored.

"She was friends with Gretchen Bond."

He wrapped his hand around one of hers.

"Annie was the one who found her body. Rio, she was beaten to death with a hammer."

His hand tightened as his mind flashed back to the two occasions on a mission where he and his teammates stumbled across people who'd met an untimely end in a similar manner. Sympathy welled up for Annie. Finding her friend that way would stay with her the rest of her life. "I'm sorry she had to be the one to find her."

"What if the break-in is related to Ms. Bond's murder?"

"It's been a couple years since she was killed."

"But the police never found the murderer."

"It's possible." He frowned. "But why wait this long to break into the house and rip up the floor?"

She sighed. "I don't know. Doesn't make much sense, does it? I guess I got spooked."

Maybe. Rio didn't intend to tell her he'd wondered if the previous owner's death was connected. Too much time had passed without an indication of the killer returning to the scene of the crime. Now that White was in town, Rio was more inclined to think he had something to do with the holes in the floor. What better way to scare Darcy into going back to the life she'd been living than to make this safe haven seem dangerous?

"We can talk to Nick."

"Stella Armstrong was here while you slept. She promised to do some digging on Gretchen Bond."

"She was a U.S. Marshal before she married Nate."

"Wow. How long have they been married?"

"Two weeks."

"She asked me about a job for a friend of hers, Leah Conner."

"Leah and her husband, Dean, moved here about a month ago. Do you have a place for Leah?"

"I'll need at least one helper. According to Stella, I'll have to teach Leah what to do. She doesn't cook."

"Shouldn't be a problem. She's a smart lady."

Darcy tilted her head. "You know her?"

"Talked to her a couple times in town and she and her husband helped move Stella's belongings into Nate's place. She and the Conners have been friends for a while."

"Must be nice to have friends like that."

Rio captured her chin in the palm of his hand. "Sweetheart, you have friends like that."

Her cheeks flushed. "The PSI students don't count."

"Maybe not, but Durango does. You are one of us now." He would have said more, but his cell phone rang at that moment. Rio checked the display screen. His eyebrows shot up. "I need to take this." Rio swiped his thumb across the screen. "Hi, Dad."

"Hope this isn't a bad time, son."

"What's up?"

"I need a favor." A pause. "Well, your Uncle James needs a favor."

"Name it."

"Would you have room at your place for a boarder?"

"As long as it's not one of my brothers who had a fight with his wife, sure." His attempt at levity was met with silence. Uneasiness twisted through his gut. "Dad? It's not one of my siblings, is it?" Man, he hoped not. His brothers were all deliriously happy with their mates and he didn't relish seeing one of their marriages fall apart. He loved his sisters-in-law. They were amazing and perfect matches for his brothers.

"No, son. They're all happy as far as I know."

"Talk to me, Dad."

"Mason is being released from prison tomorrow, Rio. James doesn't want him to come back here. The town's already up in arms about his release and there have been threats made against him. Will you let him stay with you for a while?"

CHAPTER FOURTEEN

Darcy watched with growing concern as Rio's expression went blank. She'd seen that look often on her brother's face when he was upset and didn't want anyone to know. Had something happened to a family member? Not knowing what else to do to offer comfort, she reached over and threaded her fingers through his.

He glanced at her, raised their clasped hands and kissed the back of hers while he listened to his father speak. After a bit, he said, "Do I need to go pick him up?" More silence, then he closed his eyes. "Dad, please," he said, voice choked. "Don't cry. It's going to be okay. He'll be fine. I'll pick him up and bring him here. I assume all the legalities have been taken care of?" He was silent for a moment. "Who does he report to?" Then, "Dad, I don't mind. Yeah, love you, too."

Curiosity soon outpaced the concern. Who would be fine? She squeezed his hand when he ended the call with his father. "Are you okay?"

He placed his phone on the table and wrapped his arms around her. "I'm fine, baby."

"Your family?"

"Safe. My father called about my cousin, Mason." Rio eased her away from him. "He's being released from prison tomorrow."

Her jaw dropped. Prison? Not the explanation she'd been expecting. She recalled the conversation she'd overheard. "Mason wants to stay with you?"

"Uncle James wants him to stay with me instead of going home."

"But why? I would think the only place your cousin would want to be was home."

"He can't go home," he said, his voice flat. "They live in a small town, smaller than Otter Creek. The residents know he's being released and have already made threats against him. Uncle James is afraid for my cousin's safety."

"Why was he in prison?"

"Vehicular manslaughter. He got behind the wheel of a car while drunk and hit a family in another vehicle. A mother and her infant were killed in the wreck."

"Oh, Rio. How tragic for everyone involved." Including his cousin. "How long was he in prison?"

"Thirteen years."

"That's a long time."

"Could have been longer. The judge could have given him up to 60 years. As it was, Judge Hart wanted to make an example of him. I'd say he accomplished that."

"Is he being let out on parole?"

His face hardened. "No. He was denied every time he was eligible for it. The sentencing judge and the victims' family made sure of that. He will be on probation for a good while, though."

"You're picking him up?"

He nodded. "I'll have to leave early tomorrow morning."

"Would you like me to go with you?"

An emotion Darcy couldn't identify glowed in his eyes. "You will never know how much the offer means to me, Darcy. However, the trip will take about 8 hours total plus whatever time we need to spring him. That's a long time in a car for you and Trent still needs assistance."

"And?"

A wry smile curved his lips. "I don't know how Mason will react to seeing me, much less a stranger."

"Bring him back here with you."

"I planned to drop him off at my house."

"Rio, bring him here. He shouldn't feel like he's being abandoned in a strange town, as if you're embarrassed by him."

"Are you sure?"

"Positive." She smiled. "I've got plenty of room." Darcy stopped. "Rats. I have the room, but not a bed. We need to go shopping."

He chuckled. "I'm happy to offer my muscles. First, though, you need to eat."

"As do you."

"True enough." He drew Darcy to her feet. "I'll ask Nate if he can stay longer. I don't trust your brother to be a couch potato without an enforcer present. The PSI trainees are too busy to do that."

She frowned. "Do you think he's that unwise?"

"He's Special Forces, sweetheart. He hates being housebound, will push himself too hard. If he does, Trent could pop stitches and set himself back in recovery time."

Without saying more, Darcy handed him a thick paper plate and chose one for herself. She eyed the taco salad which smelled fantastic. Who knew healthy food could be so appetizing? She scooped out a portion. A glance inside the coolers revealed more soft drinks and bottled water. Guess she was drinking water. She frowned. Come to think of it, she hadn't drunk any water today, a habit she couldn't let continue. While she waited for Annie to help customers, Darcy had surfed the Internet on Sjogren's Syndrome on her phone. One of the things she'd read was the need to drink a lot of water, particularly reverse osmosis water. She needed to ask Brian to install a whole house filtration system with the reverse osmosis in the kitchen. Otherwise, her bottled water bill would be high.

After lunch, she and Rio hunted down Nate who agreed to stay until they returned. An hour later, Darcy was the owner of a queen-size bed. Another stop at the closest department store netted a nice comforter in hunter green, a couple pillows, two sheet sets, and a bed skirt. In a different department, she discovered a sale on towels and washcloths. Perfect. She needed new ones for herself and Trent anyway. She might as well buy them now.

Both of them were loaded with bags returning to his SUV.

"I need to wash everything but the pillows, Rio. Do you know where I can find a laundromat? My washer and dryer are in storage until the house is ready."

"You can use mine. I'll give you my spare key and you can wash whatever you want when you have time."

"I don't want to impose." She had to admit, though, she was curious what made the medic tick. Personal spaces could tell you a lot about the person who lived in them.

"You're doing a favor for my family, Darcy. This is the least I can do to repay you."

She waved his statement aside. "There's no debt owed, Rio. Don't think I haven't noticed how much you've been taking care of me as well as my brother. If anything, I still owe you for staying up several nights so Trent would sleep."

Rio cranked the SUV and turned the heat on high before he turned to her. "Does it bother you?" he asked, his voice soft.

"That you stayed awake all night?"

He simply stared at her.

Ah. Not the staying awake part of the conversation. "Rio, I'm not used to someone taking care of me, but I like it. Trent's never around long enough to do it. So, no, it doesn't bother me."

"I'm glad." He shrugged one shoulder. "It's my job to take care of my teammates."

Her heart sank. "Do you see me as a teammate?" Boy, she hoped not. She sure didn't feel that way about the handsome medic.

Rio leaned over the console, slipped his hand behind her neck, and tugged her toward him. He captured her mouth in a series of deep, drugging kisses. When he finally eased his mouth from hers, his eyes glittered with heat. "Does that answer your question?"

"Rio," Darcy whispered as she brushed his mouth with hers. "Is this real?"

"As real as it gets, baby."

"I don't know what to do with this. I haven't dated much over the years. No time and no interest. Until now."

He smiled. "There's no deadline, Darcy. We take as much time as we need to get to know each other. The only thing I ask is that you're totally honest with me. If our relationship isn't working for you, tell me. Have to be honest, though, in the interest of fairness. I don't want the friends-only speech. I think that might break my heart."

"If you promise to tell me if this isn't what you want."

"No chance, sweetheart. You are a dream come true."

Her heart squeezed at his declaration. "So does this mean we're dating?"

He chuckled. "It does."

"I suppose I need to tell Trent soon."

"He already knows."

"How?"

"He saw me kissing you outside this morning. We had a discussion about it."

Discussion, huh? She could imagine how that went over with Rio. "Was he upset?"

Rio trailed his fingers down her cheek. "He warned me against hurting you."

Darcy's cheeks burned. "I'll talk to him." She loved her brother, but he didn't have the right to interfere in her life. For goodness' sake, she was thirty years old, definitely old enough to know her own mind. If she didn't want to pursue a relationship with Rio, she was capable of telling him so.

"It's not necessary. We reached an understanding. He loves you, Darcy, and you're his younger sister. Now that your parents are gone, he feels an obligation to protect you."

"I don't need protection from you."

"No, baby, you don't. All you have to do is tell me the truth. I can't promise I won't try to change your mind, but I will abide by your wishes." He glanced at the dashboard clock. "We should return to the house. Nate needs to leave soon."

Darcy settled back into her seat and buckled her seatbelt. Minutes later, he parked beside her car in the driveway. Arms loaded, they carried everything to the house.

Trent was in the recliner, glowering at everyone who came and went. His narrowed gaze shifted to Rio.

"Trent." Darcy waited for her brother's gaze to lock with hers. "I love you, but knock it off. I can take care of myself. I don't want to ruin the time we have together fighting. Got it?"

Another glare at Rio before he growled. "Yeah, I got it. Don't like it."

"Too bad, bro. Deal with it."

His attention shifted to the bags in her arms and Rio's. "Did you buy out the store?"

"I needed to pick up more items for our linen closet and another bed."

"Isn't yours comfortable?"

"Mine is in storage. I need another bed for a guest."

"Who?"

"My cousin, Mason," Rio said. "He's going to stay with me for a while. I didn't want to dump him at my house and leave him."

"So, go home, then. I don't need you."

Darcy gasped at the harsh comment from her brother. Rio's hand brushed her lower back. Glancing at him, she caught the slight head shake.

"You won't sleep, Trent, not without someone on watch. During the daytime, you'll have too much traffic through here to sleep much. You want out of this house and back on the job? Let me provide the security you need to rest so I can leave faster. My staying will help Darcy sleep better, too. She needs to rest as much as you."

"Fine," he snapped. "How long will I have a babysitter?"

"Until you don't need one." He turned to Darcy. "Have you told him about the break-in?"

Trent sat up, clamped a hand over his gut, winced. "What are you talking about? What break-in?"

"The night you left, Rio took me to dinner," Darcy said. "On the way back to the motel, we stopped by the house and noticed a light going across the window. Turns out I had a visitor poking around in here."

"Did you catch him?" he asked Rio.

"Had too much head start. The police detective found smudged fingerprints and a shoe print, a size twelve work boot."

"So Houdini is most likely a male. You sure the print didn't belong to one of the hordes of people coming in and out of here?"

"Doubtful. We found it before PSI trainees started helping."

"So this guy was just poking around in here, looking around?"

"We think he was tearing up the floors in a few rooms as well," Darcy chimed in.

Trent scowled. "Simple vandalism? Maybe it's a bored teenager with big feet."

She gave a quick grin at that comment. Good to know her brother hadn't lost his sense of humor despite the wounds and frustration. "We don't know yet. The police are looking into it, including Nate's wife, Stella."

Her brother relaxed deeper into the recliner. "She'll take care of it. Stella's a great cop."

"She is also very hot." This from her husband who walked in the room at that point, a broad smile on his face, joy in his eyes. Oh, yes, definitely a newlywed.

Trent winced. "Please. That is too much information for my innocent mind."

A chuckle from the chef. "You're just envious."

"She's an amazing woman."

Darcy studied her brother, unsure exactly what she'd heard in her brother's voice. Discouragement? Sadness? She was convinced something had happened in recent weeks, something Trent hadn't shared with her. With that comment, she wondered if the trouble concerned a woman. A new resolve formed to convince her sibling to talk to her before he returned to duty. Otherwise, he'd have to shoulder this burden by himself for months. She'd bet he hadn't talked to anyone else about whatever was bugging him. Only their father could penetrate the blank shield Trent projected to the outside world. Dad wasn't here anymore. There was just Darcy. Oh, yeah. She was definitely going to get him to unload before he left. If nothing else, she'd hassle him about it in the car on the way to the Knoxville airport where his truck waited in the long-term parking lot. Maybe there would be an amazing woman here for her brother. He was a good man and deserved someone special in his life. Trent would be a great husband and father.

"We good here?" Nate asked. "It's about time to take the kids back to class."

"Appreciate you spelling me, Nate," Rio said.

"Not a problem." He turned to Trent. "I left you a pan of banana pudding in the fridge, buddy."

"Hey," Rio protested. "He is going to share, right?"

"Get your own," Trent said, a smug smile on his face.

Nate rolled his eyes. "If he ate all that by himself, he'd be sick as a dog, Rio." He strolled to the stairs, put two fingers in his mouth, and let out an ear-splitting whistle.

Within a couple minutes, the PSI trainees began drifting through the living room and outside to the SUVs on the street. One woman stopped when she reached Darcy. "I don't know if anyone told you, but we found more holes on the third floor. Every room up there has at least two holes in the floor. A few more have holes in the walls."

What was going on in her house?

CHAPTER FIFTEEN

Rio dragged a hand over his face. "Every room?"

"Yes, sir." The trainee tucked strands of red hair behind her ear. "Can't figure out what the point of the holes is. Looks like they took a sledge hammer to the walls."

"Do the holes in the walls go all the way through to the outside?" Trent asked.

"No, sir. There's not much insulation up there, though. You'll need to patch the walls pretty fast. Otherwise, the heating bill will be astronomical."

From what Rio had seen so far, Darcy's electric bill was going to be high anyway. He hoped Brian had a few suggestions for her to save some money. Otherwise, she would be pouring money into this Victorian year round. He didn't know anything about her financial situation, but he suspected she wouldn't want to waste unnecessary money in heating bills, especially since she planned to open the deli in a few weeks in addition to remodeling the house.

"I'll have the contractor take a look," Darcy promised. "He'll be here in another week to start the remodel."

"The weather is supposed to grow colder in the next few days," Trent said. A wry smile curved his mouth. "Had nothing better to do this afternoon than watch television. You need to have the contractor check it tomorrow, Darce." His gaze turned toward the stairs. "I can look at the walls for you."

"No." Rio folded his arms across his chest. "Do we need to have this conversation again?"

"Did I ask your opinion, Kincaid?"

"You're getting it anyway. Your leg needs more time to heal before you tackle two flights of rickety stairs."

His friend growled.

"I'll take pictures with my phone so you can see the damage," Darcy said. "You should be able to tell me if Brian needs to come now or if the repairs can wait until next week."

Rio recognized the restlessness and frustration on the other operative's face. He'd witnessed the same many times in his teammates after job-related injuries and in himself as well. Military personnel were notoriously bad patients. "Darcy, if you have the Internet connection hooked up, you can put Trent to work on his laptop doing research."

"What kind of research?" Trent asked.

"Security systems for Darcy's house. For obvious reasons, she needs a top-of-the-line system."

Her brother's surly expression dissolved. "Excellent idea. I'll put together a list of things I want installed in and around your house, Darce. We'll have technicians from Fortress install the system."

"While you're researching, check out safe rooms," Rio said. "We don't have many tornadoes around here, but when one occurs, it does a lot of damage."

"Tornadoes?" Darcy's head whipped his direction, her eyes wide. "You have tornadoes here?"

"Usually fall and spring. Otter Creek is in a relatively flat section of Tennessee, so if a tornado spins up, there aren't many obstacles to slow it down."

She swallowed hard and turned to her brother. "I want the best safe room out there."

Suited Rio as well. He and his teammates weren't sent on missions as much as Trent's team, a choice Durango had made together, but he wanted to know Darcy was safe while he was out of the country. One less thing for him to be concerned over.

Trent gave a short nod. "I'll take care of it."

"Do you have any idea how much this is going to cost me?" Darcy asked.

"Doesn't matter. I'm paying."

"I can handle the price, Trent. I want to know how much to set aside."

"Think of it as a housewarming present."

Darcy frowned. "A toaster is a housewarming gift, not a security system and safe room."

"I'll throw in a toaster if you want one."

"That's not the point."

"Darce, I want to do this for you. It will give me peace of mind when I'm out on a mission."

"You fight dirty, bro. I don't want you distracted. Knock yourself out shopping on the Internet." She checked her watch. "I'll call the telephone company and arrange for the Internet connection."

Quinn jogged down the stairs. "Everybody's out except Red here."

"Excellent." Nate tugged on his leather jacket. "We should get back to PSI in time for a couple sessions before dinner."

Red groaned. "Please tell me it's class work and not PT."

"One session's in the classroom, the other in the gym."

"Come on, Red," Quinn said. "I'll help you to the SUV since you're in such bad shape."

A scowl, then, "I can handle it." She stalked outside.

"Darcy, there are two more rooms to be cleared," Quinn said. "The trainees have sessions in the next few days that can't be rescheduled. I'll bring them back to finish at the beginning of next week."

She shook her head. "That's not necessary. I can't believe how much work you've done. I can handle two rooms."

"I'll help her," Rio said. "And Trent will be more mobile in a few days."

"It's no problem for us to come back, Darcy," Nate said. "Let us know the day before you need us. We'll adjust the schedule."

"I'll be fine, but thank you. Tell your trainees how much I appreciate their help. Once my deli is open, I'll feed you and your colleagues lunch along with your students."

He grinned. "Looking forward to it. Trent's been bragging about your wraps all day."

On the way out the door, Quinn glanced back over his shoulder. "Your Dumpsters are full again, Darcy. Schedule a pickup for tomorrow."

"Quinn, can you help with Trent tomorrow? I'll be gone all day." Rio didn't want Darcy here by herself with her brother in case there was a problem. Not likely, but he'd rather be sure.

"I'll ask Sanders to cover for me."

A minute later, the caravan of SUVs was gone.

"I don't need Quinn," Trent said.

"And if you fall, do you expect your sister to help you up? You want to be stubborn, fine. Do it when the stubbornness won't impact Darcy."

The other operative glared his direction until he saw Darcy's distressed expression. "Check the new holes the trainees found, Darce. We need to see what we're up against."

Darcy grabbed her phone. "We'll return in a minute."

"Take your time," he said, his lips curling upward. "I'm not going anywhere."

Rio accompanied her up two flights of stairs. By the time they reached the last step, Darcy was panting. When she would have proceeded into the closest room, Rio wrapped her in his arms. "Just for a moment," he murmured. "Catch your breath."

Darcy rested against him until her breaths came at a normal pace. "Thanks."

He dropped a quick kiss on her upturned lips, then released her. "Come on. Let's walk through the rooms, see where repairs are needed."

Red wasn't exaggerating. Every room on the third floor had holes in the floors and several in the walls. He frowned. What was the point? If it had been teens, he would have expected spray paint on the walls, crushed beer cans tossed around, and cigarette butts littering the floor. This was more deliberate. Not vandalism, necessarily, though there was destruction. No, this was intentional. The vandal was looking for something, but what? What did Gretchen Bond have that someone wanted badly enough to risk detection to find? More important, was Darcy in danger from the man destroying her house?

CHAPTER SIXTEEN

Rio frowned. How long had the searcher been destroying floors and walls? Bond had been dead for two years and the most recent break-in was less than a week ago. The damage appeared to be recent. Why wait this long to hunt?

"Got it." Darcy waggled the hand holding her cell phone. "Do you know anything about repairs like this?"

"Not as much as Mason. I don't know about now, but while growing up he loved working with his hands. Uncle James is a carpenter."

"I see." She looked thoughtful. "Do you think your cousin would repair the walls and floors for me? I have to pay someone to do it. Why not Mason?"

"Ask him." He'd probably appreciate the freedom to do something he enjoyed. "If Mason agrees, he'll have to do it in the evenings. He needs to find a job soon."

"I understand. We can close the doors until the repairs are completed. In fact, that's probably a wise idea for all the rooms." A wry smile curved her mouth. "At least it will cut down on the drafts."

"The house will be more energy efficient when Brian's finished."

"That will take a miracle, Rio."

They retraced their steps downstairs where Darcy handed her phone to her brother. "Take a look at these."

Trent scrolled through the pictures, blew up a few. "These need to be repaired as soon as possible, Darce."

Darcy glanced at Rio. "We have a solution for that. You're busy with the security system and safe room. Rio's cousin, Mason, might be able to do the repairs."

"Yeah?" His gaze shifted to Rio. "He does this kind of work?"

"He has in the past. It's been a while." He was reluctant to discuss why Mason might not have been doing carpentry for a while. If he was smart, he kept himself busy with any work he could lay his hands on. Would he have had access to that kind of equipment?

"Sounds like a fair trade for staying a few days," Trent said.

She shook her head. "Only if he wants to do this. He's under no obligation, bro. He'll be living in his cousin's house whenever Rio returns home." She held out her hand for the phone. "I'll call the phone company now. Hopefully, they'll come tomorrow."

When she walked into the kitchen to make her call, Rio watched his patient's body language. "How long since you took pain meds?"

A pause, then, "I don't remember."

"Too long. I'll find over-the-counter pain pills."

"Thanks. Look, man, I'm sorry about giving you such a hard time over Darcy. I love her and she's the only family I have left."

"She loves you just as much, buddy, and she's worried about you. The faster you mend, the better she'll be." Rio went to his room for the pain killers in his mike bag. As a medic, he carried a wide variety of drugs to help his injured teammates, including the over-the-counter variety.

After shaking a couple into his palm, Rio swung by the kitchen to grab a bottle of water for Trent and pulled up short when he saw Darcy standing in the middle of the room, staring. "Sweetheart? What is it?"

"Look at this room," she whispered.

He scanned the kitchen, puzzled. What was he supposed to notice? He didn't see anything out of the ordinary. "What are you seeing, Darcy?"

"It's clean."

He blinked. "Okay." That was a good thing, right?

"Rio, you don't understand. I cleaned the counters so it was safe to hold food and utensils, but that's all. Someone scoured this room. The cabinets are gleaming and the counters and floors are spotless. This took hours of work. Who would do this?"

"Nate. He's a fanatic about clean kitchens and workspaces."

"I owe him for this."

With his free hand, Rio cupped her chin and turned Darcy's face toward him. "Baby, there's no debt owed. But if it will make you feel better, invite him and Stella for dinner when you're ready to entertain." He smiled. "Invite me, too, please. I'd love to spend more time with you."

"Deal. The phone company will come tomorrow."

"Good. That will help all of us."

"Trent is kind of pitiful, isn't he? He's never liked being stuck inside, but I think he's become worse over the years."

"I'm not much better," he admitted.

Her brow furrowed. "But you've been content the past few days while my brother has become more surly."

"I was also spending time with you and you fascinate me."

"Why hasn't some woman snapped you up, Rio?" she asked, her cheeks pink.

Where was she going with this? "Why do you ask?"

"Everywhere we go, women seem interested in you. I can't imagine at least one of them hasn't tried to capture your attention."

Rio pressed a soft kiss to her lips. "A discussion for another time. Come on, you should tell Trent when his work begins."

When he would have turned away from her, Darcy stopped him with a soft hand to his cheek. "You will tell me?"

"Not today, but I will answer any questions you have, provided the details aren't classified."

"Fair enough. My brother is restricted on the information he can share from his SEAL days as well. Just don't use the classified information excuse to dodge questions you prefer not to answer."

"I can't very well insist on honesty from you if I don't offer the same. If I can tell you, I will." He hoped she didn't ask questions she couldn't handle the answers to. That was the reason all his relationships in the past hadn't lasted beyond a handful of dates. His work drew a lot of women. The reality of him being called up at any time for a mission that could last weeks soon made him less appealing. He was a bad risk. His work was dangerous and, with him on call for a mission any time, he couldn't be counted on. What woman wanted that?

Trent glanced up as they returned to the living room. "Well?"

"The technician is coming tomorrow at ten to hook up the Internet."

He beamed. "Excellent. Are you going out soon?"

Rio said. "What do you need?"

"More books. Anything except the sappy romance stuff Darcy prefers. If I'm to be housebound for a few more days, I need more to read than my shoe size."

"Books or magazines?"

"Yes."

Rio chuckled. "I'll see what I can find for you. Darcy, do you want to go with me or stay with Trent?"

"Go," her brother said. "I'll watch television, maybe nap."

Darcy leaned over and kissed Trent's cheek. "I'm trusting you to stay right here. We'll pick up dinner from Delaney's and bring it back."

"Nate has been telling me good things about the diner. Hopefully I'll be able to go myself next week. Take your time, Darce. I'm not hungry yet, so there's no hurry on dinner."

Rio bundled Darcy into his SUV and turned the blower on high. Felt like the temperature had dropped a good ten degrees in the last hour. "I hope you have a good winter coat. We get a lot of snow and ice in Otter Creek during the winter months."

"I need to buy one. It wasn't necessary in Florida."

Five minutes later, he parked in front of the bookstore and rounded the SUV. "After we buy reading material for Trent, we should buy you a coat. There's no cloud cover tonight which means the temperature will drop fast."

She shivered as a gust of wind buffeted them. "Good idea."

Inside the store, Nick Santana sat at the coffee bar with his wife while Del rang up a customer's order.

Madison smiled. "Hi, Rio. Darcy, welcome back. How about something hot to drink?"

"Green tea for me," Darcy said. "Rio?"

"Coffee." The woman at his side sighed. He leaned over, brushed her mouth with his. "Sorry, baby," he murmured.

"I won't complain too much since the changes are working, but I miss coffee."

"Here you go." Madison placed Rio's coffee mug in front of the seat beside Nick, who watched him and Darcy with amusement gleaming in his eyes. "Have a seat, Darcy. What kind of tea would you like this time?"

She scanned the menu again. "Green tea with mint."

"Great choice. My sister loves that one. She swears it's the only thing that settles her stomach."

"How is Serena?" Rio sipped the coffee, stopped, stared into the mug. What was in this? He'd expected plain joe and gotten something with flavor. Hazelnut, maybe? He turned to Nick. "You could have warned me," he muttered.

His friend burst into laughter. "Too much fun watching your expression. It's the new flavor this month."

"Do you like it?" Madison asked.

"I'm more of a no-flavor coffee drinker."

She scowled. "You sound like Nick and my brother. Serena is great. No more all-day sickness from the pregnancy and she's pretty cute with her baby belly sticking out." Madison turned to Darcy. "Serena is one of my two sisters. We're identical triplets."

"Sounds like that would have been fun growing up."

"It had its moments."

Over the sound system, classical piano music began to play. Rio recognized it as one of Darcy's recordings. As soon as the music began in earnest, Darcy zoned out. Her eyes closed, her body swayed gently to the rhythm, and on the coffee bar, her fingers subtly moved. Conversation fell silent until that piece concluded and another began.

When she opened her eyes, Darcy noticed the three of them watching her. Her cheeks blazed. "Sorry."

"Don't be," Nick said, understanding in his eyes. "I do the same thing." He held out his hand. "It's nice to formally meet you, Darcy Melton. I love your music."

She grinned. "Nick Santana, your guitar playing is absolutely magic. I've listened to you for years."

He inclined his head as he released her hand. "Quite a compliment coming from a performer who graced the world stage for twenty years. Have things been quiet at your house?"

"No new break-ins. We found holes in the walls and floors after the PSI trainees started clearing rooms."

Nick's eyes narrowed. "Recent?"

"Looks like it," Rio said. "Darcy has a lot of repair work to do before Brian and his crew begin remodeling. Did you find any evidence at the house?"

"Black thread that might belong to the perp. The shoe print is a size twelve Wolverine work boot. No fingerprints or palm prints. In other words, not much." He sounded frustrated.

Madison slid Darcy's mug of steaming green tea in front of her. "Do you need anything besides hot drinks?"

"My brother, Trent, wants more books and magazines to read while he recuperates," Darcy said.

"He's healing well?" Nick asked softly.

She darted a look at Rio, wanting to know how much information to share with a local cop.

"He should be on the job in a few weeks," Rio answered. "Gunshot wound to the leg, knife wounds in the gut."

Nick whistled. "Nasty business. Mission accomplished?"

"Yep. Kids got out safe. Trent and one other teammate were injured. Both will recover."

"Good to hear." He stood, leaned over the counter to kiss his wife. "I'll pick up groceries on the way home, baby. Rio, Darcy, I'll be in touch. I understand Stella is looking into the Bond woman's background. Maybe that will help us figure out why there's interest in the house." He clapped Rio on the shoulder. "Darcy, I'll be on duty again tonight. Call me if you need anything." With a nod, he left.

"Hi, guys." Del stepped behind the coffee counter. "Did you stop in to get warm?"

"And to buy more books and magazines for my brother." Darcy sipped her tea. "Any suggestions for a guy who hates to be cooped up and works with your husband?"

The store owner rolled her eyes. "I have several customers like that, especially since PSI opened. Come with me. I know of several things he might like. Bring your tea. You can sip while you browse."

Rio watched her stride away.

"Like that, is it?"

He turned to Madison. "Like what?"

"Oh, come on, Rio. Anyone can see that you're crazy about her."

He flinched. Oh, man. That wasn't good. "They can, huh?"

"Does she feel the same way?"

"We're in the very early stages of dating, Madison. I like her a lot. I hope she feels the same way about me." He sighed, dragged a hand over his face. "And now I feel like an elementary school kid. Maybe I should put together a simple questionnaire for her, complete with boxes to check if she likes me or not."

Madison laughed. "I'll leave you alone about her. For now. Need a refill on the coffee?"

"Sure, but not that kind, sugar. Just the plain stuff."

"Spoilsport."

Del and Darcy returned to the counter, arms filled with books and magazines. While Del rang up the total, Darcy finished the last of her green tea, once again swaying to the piano music being piped through the store. Lost in the piano concerto, she didn't hear Del give the total.

Amusement surged through Rio as he dug his wallet from his pocket and handed Del his debit card. She swiped the card, bagged the books and magazines, then left to help another customer.

When the music ended, Darcy surfaced. She noted the bags of books, sighed. "How much do I owe you, Rio?"

"Nothing. How long has it been since you played the piano?"

"Two weeks, the longest I've ever gone without touching a keyboard. Why?"

"You need piano time, baby."

"My Steinway's in storage. Do you have a piano I can play?"

He shook his head. "I know where there's a piano for you to play. Let's take care of the coat first, then we'll see about the piano."

While Darcy tried on full-length wool coats, he called Marcus Lang, pastor of Cornerstone Church, the place where he and the rest of Durango attended worship services when they were in town. "This is Rio Kincaid."

"What can I do for you, Rio?"

"Would it be possible for a friend of mine to play the sanctuary piano for a while?"

"Of course. We just had it tuned. I'll be here for a while. The board meets in an hour."

"I don't know how long she'll play. Will we disturb your meeting?"

"We meet in one of the larger Sunday school rooms on the other side of the building. Your friend can play as long as she wants."

He slid his phone into his pocket as Darcy strode into sight clad in a cranberry-colored coat.

"What do you think?"

Rio stood. "It's not as beautiful as you are. Buy that one. It's perfect for you."

Minutes later, they left the store, Darcy wearing her coat. He escorted her to his SUV. "Next stop, a grand piano."

Darcy's face lit. "You were able to arrange it? Thank you, Rio."

He leaned in, stole a quick kiss. "You're welcome, baby."

When he turned into the church parking lot, Darcy's breath caught. "This is great. A nice piano and good acoustics."

Pleased he could offer something to fill her need, Rio walked her into the church. Marcus Lang stood in the foyer, waiting. Rio introduced them.

"Thank you for letting me play," Darcy said. "My piano's in storage for a while longer."

"Any time you want to play, let me know. If I can't be here, I'll have someone meet you." The pastor turned to Rio. "Will I see you and your teammates Sunday?"

"We're not supposed to be deployed for a few weeks." Didn't mean they wouldn't be activated if Brent Maddox needed another team. He glanced at the woman by his side. Rio hoped Fortress wouldn't call them anytime soon, but Maddox was down one team since Trent and his teammate were injured.

"I'll look forward to seeing you for service." He smiled at Darcy. "Enjoy yourself. There's no hurry." He turned and walked to his office.

"This way, sweetheart." Rio clasped her hand and led her through the double doors to the sanctuary. He turned on the lights and walked with her to the stage. While she set aside her purse and coat, he uncovered the piano and raised the lid.

"It's beautiful." Darcy smoothed a hand over the black satin finish. "A Boston. Fantastic."

"It's a good piano?"

"Oh, yes. It's a Steinway design. The sound is rich and full. If I didn't own a Steinway, this would be my next choice." Without saying anything else, she sat on the bench and began to play.

Rio settled on a nearby pew, content to listen as Darcy played through several pieces by Debussy, Mozart, Bach, and Clementi. Into the second hour, she shifted from classical to hymn arrangements, then finally to Christmas music.

When she removed her hands from the keyboard, he stood. "Feel better?"

Her movements as she rose were slow and stiff, but her lips curved into a broad smile. "I feel amazing." She descended the stairs from the platform and threw her arms around his neck. "Thank you, Rio."

He wrapped his arms around her, tugged her close to his chest. "Thank you for sharing your music with me, baby. I love your CDs, but there's something magical about hearing you in person."

"You never attended a concert?"

"I wanted to. Even had tickets once, but an hour before concert time, I was activated for a mission. After that, I was never in the same place you were to try again."

"Ms. St. Claire, that was incredible." Marcus Lang strode up the aisle from the back of the sanctuary. "You have been blessed with an amazing musical gift."

She smiled at the pastor. "Thank you for letting me play so long."

"I know I'm putting you on the spot, but would you consider giving a Christmas concert here at the church? We're raising money to help with the medical expenses of one of our children in the congregation. She's been fighting Leukemia."

"Julia?" Rio asked.

The pastor nodded. "I know it's short notice, Ms. St. Claire. Would you think about it?"

"Please, call me Darcy. I would love doing a benefit concert for Julia." She stepped out of Rio's embrace and scooped up her purse. A moment later, she handed Lang a business card. "My cell phone number's listed. Call me with the date. I'll need access to the church piano unless I can have mine shipped to Otter Creek."

"Absolutely." He glanced at the card, slipped it into his pocket. He looked back at her. "Would you mind if we advertised the concert? The more people who attend, the more we can do for Julia."

"No problem. Use my stage name." She smiled. "Darcy Melton."

Lang's eyes widened. "I attended one of your concerts a couple years ago, but I didn't recognize you." He smiled. "I was also in the very top row of seats in the concert hall. I would have needed opera glasses to see your face."

Darcy laughed. "The beauty of concerts like that is you don't have to see the artist's face to enjoy the music."

His smile faded. "I don't know how much we can pay you."

"No charge. I'm happy to help. Would it be possible for me to meet Julia? I'd like to find out which Christmas songs she likes so I can include her favorites in the list of music I play."

"I'll see what I can work out for you." The pastor checked his watch. "Break time is over for the board meeting. Guess I should go back. I'll be in touch soon, Darcy." He shook Rio's hand. "Later, my friend."

"I'd say Trent is hungry by now." Rio helped Darcy into her coat. "Let's see what Delaney's has on special tonight."

When they returned to the Victorian house, Rio carried three takeout containers inside.

"About time you came," Trent groused. "I'm starving."

"You said you weren't hungry."

"Three hours ago."

Darcy grabbed the top container and uncovered the meat loaf, mashed potatoes, and green beans. "This should make up for the delay."

"Oh, man." Trent ripped the covering off the plastic utensils. "This smells great." A bite later, he moaned. "Okay, you're forgiven." Another bite, then, "What kept you so long?"

"Shopping for your books, a winter coat for me, and a stop at the church for me to play the piano."

Her brother's face softened. "Enjoy it?"

"I've missed playing so much."

"Have Brian stop by tomorrow and check the floor in here." Rio asked. "If he thinks the floor can support your piano without reinforcement, have your piano shipped up here."

"That's a great idea, Darce."

She smiled as she took off her coat and laid it aside along with her purse. "I think I will."

Later that night, Rio walked Darcy to her room. He cupped her face gently between his palms. "Good night, baby. Sleep well."

"You will rest?"

Her concern made his heart turn over. "Your brother should sleep most of the night."

She rose on her tiptoes and kissed him. "I'll see you in morning."

"I need to leave by six."

Another kiss and he nudged her inside her room. He waited until her door shut before returning to the room he'd been sharing with Trent. "Need anything before I turn in?"

"Sleep in the other guest room. You snore, buddy."

Rio laughed. "Liar. You're the one who snores." He sobered. "I'll be on the couch. No one will get past me."

"Thanks."

After completing his own bedtime routines, Rio stretched out on the couch. He figured he'd get a couple hours of sleep between catnaps, enough to make it through the next day. He'd crash hard tomorrow night and would have to ask Quinn to stay here.

The night was quiet until a few minutes after two when the silence was shattered by Darcy's scream.

CHAPTER SEVENTEEN

Rio threw off the blanket, palmed his Sig, and raced to his girlfriend's room. "Darcy!" As he reached for the door, the knob turned and his girl dived into his arms.

"What's wrong, baby?"

"A man, outside the bathroom window."

"Darcy!" Trent bellowed from his room.

"Stay with your brother."

She released him. "Go."

He ran out the back door in time to see a black-clad figure clear the fence. Rio shoved his weapon into his holster and sprinted across the yard. He scrambled over the fence and bolted after the man who terrorized Darcy, determined to capture him this time.

Dogs howled at the passage of the stranger through their territory. Same route, same dogs. Rio's lip curled. Not the same result, buddy. Part of his morning run had included reconnaissance around Darcy's home, particularly between the Victorian house and the intersection.

He cut through the Bradys' backyard, darted across the alley to Dogwood Lane and dashed toward Tulip Grove where he'd spotted tire marks from the previous escape.

Footsteps pounded nearby, coming closer. Rio put on a burst of speed, arrowing for the nondescript sedan parked under a darkened streetlight.

A whip-lean figure dressed in black from head to toe rushed toward the sedan, glancing over his shoulder. He shoved his hand into his pocket.

Weapon?

Keys rattled as the figure aimed a remote at the car.

Not this time. Rio surged forward and took down his opponent as he reached for the driver's door. The man threw back an elbow, caught Rio in the jaw, knocking him to the side. Lights sparked behind his eyes.

The man scrambled to his feet, again reaching for the door.

Rio swept his opponent's feet out from under him and dived on top of the man when he hit the ground. He blocked a roundhouse punch and jerked his head to the side to avoid a head butt.

Enough of this crap. Rio slammed his fist into the man's gut with a rabbit punch. His opponent went limp.

He jerked the man to his feet. "You tried to break into the wrong house, pal. Let's go."

"I don't know what you're talking about. I'll call the cops, have you arrested for assault."

Rio noted the man's bare hands. Unless he'd tossed gloves somewhere on his race from the house, this idiot left behind prints. Easy find for the cops. This jewel didn't have time to hide them well. Hopefully, Darcy would identify this guy as her peeping tom. "Great idea, calling the cops. Move."

The other man tried to bolt. Rio adjusted his hold to a more painful one. "I don't think so," he said, and propelled him down the sidewalk and into Darcy's backyard. He didn't want this guy inside Darcy's house again, figured the cold wouldn't hurt him for the few minutes before law enforcement arrived. He shoved the other man to the ground. "Don't move." Rio drew his weapon, aimed it center mass, and grabbed his cell phone.

#

Hearing a muffled grunt from Trent's room, Darcy hurried to her brother's door. "I'm okay," she said as she stepped into the room. "There was a man at the bathroom window. Rio went after him."

Trent eased his legs over the side of the bed. "Hand me my jeans, Darce. How about some coffee?"

"At this time of morning?" She frowned. Not a chance that she could drink something like that this time of morning. Her brother and his military friends were different, though. They seemed to live on the brew. "A snack, too?"

He shrugged. "Wouldn't be opposed to that."

Right. "Rio wanted me to stay with you until he returned. I'll wait in the hall until you've changed out of your pajamas." A few thumps and growls later, Trent's door opened and he limped out, weapon in his hand. "Let's go. I need that coffee. Is there banana pudding left?"

She had to grin at that. "Half a pan. Should be enough for your snack."

In the kitchen, she turned on the light over the stove and prepped the coffee maker while her brother sat at the table. Though he'd been roused from sleep abruptly, he was moving decently well. Not bad for being a few days out of surgery.

As the coffee dripped into the carafe, Darcy dished a bowl of banana pudding and placed it in front of her brother along with a spoon. It annoyed her to notice that her hand was shaking. Fabulous. Her brother and Rio were steady as rocks. She, on the other hand, felt like her body was shaking apart. How did these men live like this all the time? Adrenaline surges and dumps. Fierce firefights or nothing. Darcy wasn't cut out for that life. The question that worried her now was whether or not she could handle the life as Rio's girlfriend?

Her gaze locked on her brother's. It was one thing to know Trent was in danger on missions. How would she deal with Rio in the same line of work and facing the same kind of danger?

"It will be okay, Darce." Trent covered her hand with his. "We'll figure this out and put a stop to it. By the time I return to work, you'll be safe in this house."

"I know." She kissed the top of his head, secure in the knowledge that he wouldn't return to work unless the danger to her was eliminated. Darcy suspected Rio would be the same. Once the coffee finished, she poured a cup for her brother and decided on tea for herself. Not green, she thought. Something soothing. With the adrenaline racing through her system, the last thing she needed was a shot of caffeine.

Darcy studied the boxes of tea on the counter, happy to find one with a mixture of chamomile and apple. Once the heating cycle finished, she carried the steaming brew to the table and sat beside her brother. "Shouldn't Rio be back by now?"

What if something had happened to him? Her heart clenched. Maybe she should go look for him. And do what? Try to help him? She had to shake her head at her own crazy thoughts. Rio Kincaid didn't need her to bail him out of trouble. He was a trained professional. All she would likely do was get in his way, provided she could even find him. She had no idea where he'd gone.

"He's fine, Darce. No two-bit thief will get the best of Kincaid."

A siren sounded, drawing closer by the second. The sound abruptly cut off. Frowning, Darcy walked to the living room window. Nick Santana climbed out of his car and jogged around the side of her house.

She hurried to the kitchen and to the back door. "The police are here." Darcy opened the door. A blast of cold air rushed into the kitchen. In the backyard, Nick was handcuffing a sullen man. She drew in a deep breath. Thank goodness. That was the man she'd seen at the window. She'd recognize his cold gaze and scarred brow anywhere.

Rio climbed the deck stairs. "Is this the man you saw, baby?"

She nodded. "Are you okay?"

"I'm fine. Go back inside. It's too cold for you to be out here without a coat and shoes."

She glanced down at herself. Oh, brother. She was dressed in winter pajamas and barefoot. Her cheeks heated. "I'll go change." Darcy closed the door and hustled back to her bedroom. Within a couple minutes, she returned to the kitchen, this time fully dressed, including the shoes.

She was surprised to see Josh Cahill in the kitchen with Trent. "Josh. What are you doing here?"

"I was the closest prowl car on duty. I'm taking your visitor to the station."

"Is this the guy who's been breaking in here?" Trent asked.

"We don't know yet," Josh said. "Nick's the best, though. If this is the guy, he'll find the evidence he needs to lock him up." He glanced at Darcy. "You doing okay, little one?"

Her lips curved. Little one? No one had called her that since she was in elementary school. "I'll be better if this is the guy we're looking for. The holes in the floors and walls spooked me."

Josh frowned. "There are holes in walls, too?"

"Big ones," Trent said. "She needs some major repair work done. Maybe we should make this clown do the repairs if he's the one who caused the damage."

"If this man is our culprit, he's been looking for something." Josh folded his arms across his chest. "I don't know that I would give him the opportunity to look more."

"I wish I knew what he wanted," Darcy murmured. "Ms. Bond had so many things in here. Why break in and destroy floors and walls when there were plenty of items to pawn?"

"Let's hope Nick finds the answers for you."

She drew in a deep breath. What if there were others out there who knew what this guy was after and planned to search for themselves? She shuddered. Nope. It wouldn't do any good to spook herself like that. If she allowed herself to dwell on those thoughts, she would never sleep in this house again.

Nick Santana opened the back door and motioned to Josh. "He's all yours. Process him and put him in holding. I'll be here a while."

"Is he talking?" Trent asked.

"Nope. Maybe some time in a cell will loosen his tongue."

A couple minutes after Josh left, Rio returned to the house, blowing on his fingers. He'd run out of the house without his coat. She sprang up and poured a mug of coffee for him.

"Thanks, babe," he murmured before sipping the steaming brew.

"Did he say anything to you?"

"Aside from swearing at me? No. When Nick arrived, he shut down completely."

Her brother finished off his bowl of banana pudding. "Did he give you any trouble?"

Rio sent him a scathing look.

"Figured. See, Darcy. I told you he wouldn't have any problem with this clown."

Nick opened the back door and stepped inside. "Darcy, where did you see this guy?"

"Outside the bathroom window."

"Show me."

"Sure. Would you like coffee? It's fresh." She smiled. "No interesting flavors."

He chuckled. "I wouldn't say no to a cup. It's freezing out there."

She poured him a mug, waited for him to down a quarter of the brew before leading him to her bathroom. "He was peering in this window." She reached for the light switch.

"Wait." Nick crossed the room, pulled out his flashlight, and checked the lock. His eyes narrowed. "It's unlocked."

Cold chills swept over Darcy's body. "That can't be. I checked it before I went to sleep."

"You're sure?"

"Positive," she whispered.

"Okay. Turn the light on now."

The room flooded with light. Darcy blinked against the brightness. She turned to ask Nick a question when she noticed the writing on the mirror. A hard shudder wracked her body. "Nick."

He spun around, scowled. "Come on." The detective gently took her arm and urged her from the room. "I need my kit." He walked with her to the kitchen.

Rio stopped mid-sentence, set down his coffee. "Darcy?"

"He got inside the house." Her voice wobbled.

"How do you know?" Trent demanded.

"He left her a message on the bathroom mirror in lipstick," Nick said. He pulled out a chair next to Rio and gently pressed her to sit.

Didn't take much encouragement. Her legs felt weak. This creep had been ten feet from her.

Rio sandwiched her hand between his warm palms. "What did the message say?"

"Leave or die."

CHAPTER EIGHTEEN

"What woke you, sweetheart?" Rio's hands tightened around her ice-cold one as the shudders increased.

"I was cold." A tight laugh escaped. "Now I know why. I can't believe he was in the bathroom and I didn't even know. He could have…"

"He didn't." A fact that made him very aware of how easily he could have lost her. If this man had intended to hurt her, she would have been dead long before Rio knew anything was wrong. Made him wish he'd hit the guy harder when he ran him to ground. He exchanged a grim glance with Trent.

His friend gave a slight nod. "I'll take care of it."

"Take care of what?" Nick asked, tone sharp. "He's in custody and neither of you are on a mission."

"Take care of the security system I plan to have installed here. I'll put a rush on it. In the meantime, Darcy, you should change rooms."

"I hope you don't expect me to argue. I don't want my own bathroom enough to stay in there until the security system is installed."

"Excellent idea." Nick strode toward the living room. "I'm going to get my kit."

"Are you okay, Darce?" her brother asked, his voice gruff.

"I will be." A ghost of a smile curved her lips. "This guy's pretty bold, isn't he?"

Determined, desperate? Either characterization didn't make Rio happy. The question he wanted answered was what did he want? "He can't hurt you now."

"Maybe this will be the end of it."

He hoped so, but until Rio knew for sure why this man broke into the house, he wouldn't relax his vigilance. He made a mental note to contact Quinn and alert him to the latest episode. He trusted his teammate to watch over Darcy and Trent both, though the injured Fortress operative wouldn't appreciate knowing Rio thought him a liability right now. If it came down to protecting Darcy's life, Trent would do what had to be done. He'd do some damage to himself in the process. Whether his friend admitted it or not, he needed help with security for a few more days.

He checked the time. Great. He had to leave in three hours. "Sweetheart, do you think you can go back to sleep?"

"I can sleep in the recliner if you want to take my bed," her brother offered.

Darcy shook her head. "I'm too wired to sleep."

"When did you plan on washing the towels and sheets at my place?" Rio pressed her still warm tea into her hands.

"After I checked in with Brian." She sipped her drink.

"If you grow tired while the washer and dryer are running, take a nap." In fact, he liked the idea of her taking a nap in his house. He wanted her to view his home as a haven of safety. And what was up with that? Pretty fast emotional leaps for only dating a few days.

"I might do that."

Despite questioning himself, deep satisfaction grew in Rio over Darcy feeling comfortable enough to sleep in his house.

Nick returned, crime scene kit in hand which he placed on the floor in the hall. Retrieving his coffee mug, he sipped, then asked Darcy, "Do you remember if this guy was wearing gloves?"

She frowned. "I don't think he was."

"We'll at least nail him for breaking and entering if that's the case. I'll need the lipstick he used." The detective finished his coffee and set the mug in the sink. "I don't know how long this will take, Darcy. You could sleep in another room."

She waved aside his suggestion. "Don't worry about me. Just find something to use to lock up this guy so I don't worry about waking in the middle of the night with him standing over me."

Everything in Rio rebelled at that thought. This guy was never getting close to Darcy again.

"I'll get started, then." Nick collected his kit and walked to the back.

Rio eyed Trent who yawned broadly. "Why don't you go back to bed, buddy? I'll keep Darcy with me."

"Do you need me, Darce?"

She shook her head. "I'm okay, bro. Get some rest." She smiled. "You can keep watch over me tomorrow while I rest."

"You got it, sis." He maneuvered to his feet and kissed the top of his sister's head. "Come get me if something else happens." With a nod at Rio, he walked out. A minute later, his bedroom door shut.

Rio pulled Darcy to her feet. "You might not be able to sleep, but you can rest. Come sit with me."

He led her to the living room and tugged her down beside him on the couch. Snatching the fleece blanket he'd tossed aside at her scream, he draped the cover over her and wrapped his arm around her shoulders. She settled against his chest with a sigh of contentment much as she had on the plane. Gradually, the shivers stopped and she relaxed.

"Rio?" she murmured.

"What is it, sweetheart?"

"Thanks for staying with me."

He tightened his grip. "I won't be anywhere else, Darcy. Not until I know you're safe."

Within a few minutes, her breathing evened out. Good. He knew a short night's sleep would hit Darcy far harder than it would him or Trent. Fatigue was one of the worst symptoms she battled every day.

An hour later, Nick walked into the living room. His gaze dropped to Darcy's sleeping form, his lips curving. "Got prints this time," he whispered. "I'll let you know what I find out." With a wave, he slipped out the front door and closed it softly.

Rio spent the next hour enjoying the time to hold his girl close. At 5 o'clock, he slowly moved his arm and tried to shift away from Darcy. His intention had been to lay her on the couch, but she stirred and opened those beautiful hazel eyes. "Sorry, baby," he murmured. "I need to leave soon."

She gave him a sleepy smile and wrapped her arms around his neck. "How long?"

"About forty-five minutes."

"Go shower. I'll make breakfast."

"You don't have to do that, Darcy. I'd planned to pick up something on the way to Nashville."

She leaned in and kissed him. Oh, man. He could so get used to this on a regular basis. This was what he'd envied his newly married teammates over. The tenderness, having a woman in his life who cared for him and his needs. Selfish, maybe, but he poured everything he had into his teammates, especially when they were injured. He knew he mattered to them. They would take a bullet for him in a heartbeat, but he wanted someone who was only his, a woman who would pour herself into him as he did for her. Yep, he was an official card-carrying sap.

"Now you can stop for more coffee and a snack instead of breakfast." Another kiss. "Let me do this for you, Rio."

Who was he to argue if his girl wanted to take care of him? "Thank you, sweetheart." He helped her stand and steadied her until she was stable, then retrieved his clothes and shaving kit from the bag stashed in his room.

When he emerged from the bathroom, the scent of fresh coffee greeted him along with something else he couldn't quite identify. He dropped off his gear in the guest room and followed the mouthwatering scents into the kitchen.

Darcy turned at his entrance, smiled. "Breakfast is ready."

His gaze skated to the breakfast bar and the plate and mug waiting for him. "What's this?"

"Breakfast burrito."

"Fast work."

"Nate left several ingredients in the refrigerator. I combined a few things."

He bit into the wrap and closed his eyes at the explosion of flavors. "Darcy, this is incredible. Is this one of the wraps you plan to sell in your deli?"

She nodded.

"If this typical of the rest of what you plan to offer, your deli will be a huge success."

She beamed. "Thank you. I hope the rest of Otter Creek has your food taste."

Before he'd finished with the first wrap, she slid another onto his plate. Once he'd finished eating and polished off the rest of his coffee, Rio carried his dishes to the dishwasher, and wrapped his arms around her. "Take care of yourself today, baby. Rest when you need it."

"You're okay to drive? I can go with you if you're too tired."

Rio's heart melted. "I slept enough to get through the day."

"With coffee?"

"Goes without saying." He captured her lips with his. When she pressed closer to him, Rio deepened the kiss and spent several minutes enjoying the taste and texture of Darcy's mouth. By the time he eased her away, his heart was racing. He knew he was in deep already.

He gently stroked her cheek. "I don't know how late we'll be."

"Doesn't matter. I'll be waiting for you and Mason. His room will be ready for him." She paused. "Where should I put him?"

"He won't care, baby. I think he'd like a room to himself." Rio would if he'd been incarcerated for years with constant cellmates.

"I'll figure something out. Be careful, Rio."

"Call if you need me or want to talk." With a last lingering kiss, he grabbed his jacket and walked out of the house. After fueling his SUV, he took the entrance ramp to Highway 18 and headed to Nashville.

Rio activated his Bluetooth and called his teammate. "I'm leaving Otter Creek."

"Kind of late for you, isn't it?"

"Rough night."

"What happened?"

Rio explained the events of the early morning.

Quinn gave a soft whistle. "Think this is the end of it?"

"I hope so." He heard the doubt in his voice.

"But?"

"I think it's not over."

"What do you need?"

Warmth bloomed in his gut. He hadn't expected anything different from his friend. Rio would have done the same if the situation were reversed. "Keep an eye on Darcy as well as Trent. Make sure she doesn't skip meals."

"Anything else?"

He hesitated, not wanting to divulge something Darcy didn't want out in public. However, the more Quinn knew, the better he'd be able to look out for her, and his friend wasn't one to gossip. "Don't let her become too tired."

"Okay." His friend dragged out the word.

"She has Sjogren's Syndrome, Quinn." Rio summarized the disease and its symptoms. "That's the reason she retired from the concert stage. She can't keep practicing six to eight hours a day and keep up with the touring schedule."

"I'll do what I can to help her."

He ended the call a couple minutes later and settled in for the remainder of the four-hour drive. At ten o'clock, he parked in the lot of the reentry facility on Harding Place. He climbed out of his SUV, circled to the front of the hood, and settled in to wait.

At the five-minute mark, the door to the facility opened and a dark-haired, broad-shouldered man strode from the building. He scanned the lot as he walked, hesitated when his gaze locked on Rio. A resigned expression settled on his face.

Rio straightened as Mason approached. His cousin didn't have anything in his hands. No belongings, then. Of course, whatever he'd owned thirteen years ago probably wouldn't fit. Looked like he'd filled out quite a bit and gained a few inches in height over the years.

"Rio."

He smiled, extended his hand. When his cousin took it, he pulled him into a one-armed hug. "Good to see you, Mason. Ready to get out of here?"

A short nod, then, "Dad's not here?"

Rio unlocked his vehicle and climbed behind wheel before he answered. "He asked me to come get you."

Mason frowned. "You're driving me home?"

He cranked the engine. "Uncle James wants you to stay with me for a while."

His cousin's head whipped his direction. "Why?"

"The townspeople are upset over your release. Some made threats against you. Uncle James wants you safe."

He sighed. "Where am I going?"

"A town called Otter Creek."

"Never heard of it."

Rio chuckled. "You'll like it. Otter Creek is about six thousand people larger than Summerton."

"Is it large enough for me to find work? I have to find a job as part of the terms of my probation."

"There's work for you. Don't worry about that. Right now, we need to make a couple stops."

"You need something?"

"Nope. You do. You need clothes, buddy. You won't fit into anything I own. Once we take care of that, we should eat lunch before we head home. Any particular type of food sound good to you?"

"Mexican."

"I know just the place."

"Rio, I can't pay for any of this right now." His voice sounded choked.

He glanced at his cousin, noted the high color in his cheeks. "Consider this the birthday and Christmas presents I haven't been able to give you over the years."

Rio drove to the Providence shopping center and walked with his cousin into one of the department stores. By the time they'd finished, Mason had plenty of clothes, work boots and running shoes, and a winter coat, gloves, and hat. When his cousin protested at the last purchases, Rio said, "You haven't been through an East Tennessee winter. Trust me. You need all of this."

"How long have you lived in Otter Creek?"

"A few months."

Mason frowned. "Where were you before that? Wait. Dad said you were in the military."

"I was in the Army for several years."

"What was it like?"

"Wonderful and terrible. My teammates are the best. Some of our missions were the stuff of nightmares."

"What was your job?"

"Medic."

"I don't know a lot about what you went through, but I did see some of the news reports."

"The media reported the sanitized version from the military brass."

They stashed the purchases in the back of the SUV and Rio drove them to a small family-run Mexican restaurant he and his teammates enjoyed when they were in Nashville training with Fortress Security. Two hours later, they were headed to Otter Creek. With one stop at Starbucks to get both of them some much needed coffee, the rest of the trip was driven straight through.

At seven, Rio parked in Darcy's driveway.

"This is your house?" Mason asked, staring at the huge Victorian.

"This is my girlfriend's house. We're staying here for a few days. Her brother was injured on a security mission and needs assistance for a few more days."

"Are you sure it's okay for me to be here?" he asked, his voice soft.

"Darcy insisted I bring you here, Mason. You're welcome to stay. When her brother, Trent, doesn't need me, we'll go to my house."

The front door opened and there she was, standing on the porch.

"Is that your Darcy?"

"It is."

"She's beautiful, Rio."

Oh, yeah. She was gorgeous, but that wasn't what attracted him to her. Her piano music was a draw, no question. What attracted him most was her loyalty, her grit and determination, and her heart. He strode toward the house.

Darcy hurried off the porch and into his open arms. "Welcome back." She squeezed his waist, then stepped back and turned to Mason who was slowly walking toward them, as if unsure of his welcome.

His girl smiled, held out a hand to his cousin. "Mason, welcome. I'm so glad you're here."

Rio noted how careful Mason was with her. "Thank you for letting me stay a few days."

"Your room is ready. Can I help you bring anything in?"

Quinn stepped onto the porch. "I'll take care of it, half pint. Get back in the house before you freeze."

Rio dropped a quick kiss on her upturned mouth. "Go on. We'll be inside in a minute."

With an exasperated sigh, she returned to the house.

"Quinn, this is Mason, my cousin. Mason, my teammate, Quinn Gallagher."

The three of them gathered all the bags from the back of the SUV and carried them inside. Trent was seated on the recliner, television remote in his hand. He climbed to his feet. Rio was pleased to note his movements, though slow, were a bit easier than the day before. Progress. He introduced Mason to Trent.

"You interested in some repair work?" Trent asked Mason.

"What kind?"

"Holes in the floors and walls. Some clown broke in here before Darcy bought the place and did some damage."

"Give Mason a chance to put down his bags." Darcy scowled at her brother.

Her brother frowned. "I figured Rio had already asked him about this."

"I didn't have the chance." His cousin had slept most of the way to Otter Creek. From what Rio could tell, it looked as if he hadn't slept much in prison. Probably too busy trying to watch his back. "He can examine the holes tomorrow, see if it's something he wants to tackle."

"Where do I put his stuff, Darcy?" Quinn asked.

"This way." She led the three of them to the bedroom she'd occupied the night before.

When Rio raised his eyebrows, she flushed. "Alex installed a security lock on the window. I thought Mason might like his own room and bathroom."

"I don't want to put you out," Mason said. "Really, I can make do with the floor."

"Absolutely not. It's no trouble. There are several bathrooms in this place. Besides, I haven't chosen a permanent room for myself yet. We set up the bedrooms down here for Trent's sake. I want you to have this room."

With a nod of thanks, he subsided.

While they lined his bags against the wall, Rio's cell phone signaled an incoming text. He checked the display, frowned. Nick, asking Rio to call when he had a chance.

"Excuse me a minute." His gut knotted as he strode into the kitchen to place the call. "It's Rio. What do you have?"

"Break-in artist's name is Troy Sutton. He lawyered up as soon as I took him into the interview room."

"Not surprising."

"Long arrest record, too. He's done time on three occasions."

"For?"

"Theft."

Huh. What would he had wanted to steal in this place? "And you don't know what he was after?"

"Nope. Wouldn't say anything except to recite his lawyer's name and number."

And that said quite a bit about this guy. "Anything else?"

"He always works as part of a crew, Rio. This guy has partners somewhere."

CHAPTER NINETEEN

Darcy entered the kitchen, Quinn and Mason close behind, as Rio slid his phone into this pocket, his expression grim. "Mason, you must be hungry. Does spaghetti sound good?"

"Anything is fine."

She brought noodles and meat sauce from the refrigerator, and set them on the counter. Within minutes, Darcy placed a steaming plate of spaghetti in front of Mason and Rio. Unlike Rio, who carried on a conversation with everyone in the room, Mason kept his head down, his attention on his plate. A holdover from prison? When the men had cleaned their plates, she asked, "Would you like more? Or maybe dessert?"

"Nothing for me," Rio said. "Dinner was great, sweetheart."

"Mason?"

He shook his head. "Thank you, Darcy."

"The kitchen's always open. Get whatever you want at any time."

With a nod, he stood, carried his plate to the sink. "Is there a phone I can borrow? I'd like to call Dad."

"Take mine." Rio swiped his screen a few times. "You're all set. Touch the call button when you're ready."

His cousin murmured his thanks and left the room, phone in hand.

"He'll be all right, Rio," Quinn said, voice soft. "Being out of prison after living behind bars so long is a huge adjustment."

"That's not what's wrong, is it?" Darcy asked. "Who called?"

"Nick."

"Did he have to release the guy who broke in?" Sutton going free was the only thing she could imagine upsetting her boyfriend. Her heart skipped a beat at the term. Hard to believe she was dating this amazing man. Who knew moving to Otter Creek would begin so many good things? Her brother had pressured her to relocate to Otter Creek because of PSI and the Fortress operatives who lived here. If Trent was out of the country, he wanted Darcy to have someone to count on for help. A relationship with Rio was not what her brother had in mind.

Rio shook his head. "He's still in custody, but not talking."

"Lawyered up?" Quinn asked.

"Yeah."

Darcy frowned. "But that's not the problem."

He reached over and clasped her hand. "Troy Sutton has been in and out of the system for years for theft. He always works with a team."

A hard shiver raced over Darcy's body. Sutton wasn't working alone, which meant her house was still a target for his cohorts. "Did Nick find out what he wants?"

Regret filled Rio's gaze. "Sorry, baby."

"Does he work with the same crew for heists?" Quinn finished off his soft drink.

"I wish. Unfortunately, he chooses new people for each job."

"Takes a long time to train with new people."

"They aren't like us, Quinn. They don't train. Each person has his own specialty. They also choose high-value heists that take a while to plan. He's been in prison three times. Sutton doesn't hurt innocents, which explains why he didn't touch Darcy this morning." He cast a troubled look her direction. "His crew, however, isn't so humanitarian."

"We don't know his crew. He might have chosen people like him this time."

"We can't count on that, sweetheart." Rio eyed his friend. "When will the Fortress techs install the security system?"

"Day after tomorrow. That's why Alex and I installed some basic security measures on the first floor. Sutton's crew might still break in, but they'll make a racket doing it."

"Maybe we should move you to the second floor," Rio said to Darcy. "It's more secure. These clowns won't slip past us to reach you."

She smiled, pleased she could alleviate some of his concerns. "Way ahead of you. I already moved my belongings to the second floor. I also had the new bed delivered up there." Trent couldn't handle stairs yet. She thought Mason wouldn't want to be far from Rio. That left her. Suited her fine. She had her own bathroom on that floor and all those wonderful candles. Darcy had spent the day on the sleeping arrangements and laundry. Although tired, creating a peaceful, pleasant place for Mason and Rio made her feel good. She'd arranged a surprise for Rio as well.

He squeezed her hand. "Perfect." Rio eyed Quinn. "You'll stay?"

"Can't miss your beauty sleep. You'll scare your girl."

He snorted. "Right." Rio glanced up as his cousin returned and handed him the cell phone.

"Thanks. Dad says he owes you."

"No hardship on my part. I enjoy your company."

"Join us," Darcy said.

Mason shook his head. "Thanks, but I'm kind of tired." He gave a wry laugh. "Who knew being in the real world was taxing."

"There's no television in there, but Trent has several books you can choose from if you want to read a while."

His eyes lit. "Would he mind?"

"Of course not. Come with me." She led the way into the living room. "Mason needs a couple books to read, Trent."

Her brother gestured at the piles on the floor near the recliner. "Help yourself, man."

After scanning the stacks of books, Mason chose two and retreated to his room, closing the door with a soft snick.

"He's okay?"

Darcy dropped a kiss on her brother's cheek. "So far. Thanks for sharing."

"Acclimating to the outside will take a while."

"I figured as much. I'll encourage Rio to turn in as well." He looked tired after not sleeping much for last several nights and then the round trip to Nashville today. Darcy suspected Rio stayed awake after their intruder. Every time she stirred while on the couch with him, he soothed her back to sleep. He always looked after others in his circle of friends. Who did the same for him?

She returned to the kitchen and caught Rio rubbing his face with his hands. Quinn clapped his friend on the shoulder and left the room. "Mason isn't the only one who needs sleep."

The medic dropped his hands and gave her a sheepish smile. "I wanted to spend time with you. I missed you."

"We'll have time together tomorrow. Breakfast date?"

"Sounds good. Walk me to my door. I need a goodnight kiss."

She grinned, a band of warmth squeezing her chest. "I can do that."

They walked to his room. She stretched to give him a quick kiss, but Rio smiled and nudged her inside his room. With the door almost closed, he wrapped his arms around her and pulled her close. His mouth captured hers in a series of long, deep kisses. He skimmed his lips across her cheek and down her neck, ending with a tiny love bite.

Goosebumps surged over Darcy's body as he set her gently away from him. She stared up at him, dazed. Rio Kincaid was so good at that. "Good night, Rio."

He opened the door and stole another soft kiss. "Sleep well, baby."

She stumbled down the hall to the kitchen where she gathered the remaining dishes and turned on the dishwasher. Despite what she told Rio that morning, Darcy hadn't taken a nap during the day. Too much to do. She and Brian had chosen the paint colors for her deli and then drove to Knoxville to a restaurant supply place where she bought appliances for the kitchen. After a fast lunch, she collected the laundry and carted it to Rio's place. A few hours there had netted her insights into the man who was worming his way into her heart at a rocket pace. No question her boyfriend loved his family, but his teammates held a special place in his life. Rio had photo albums on one of his bookshelves that she'd enjoyed looking through. At first, she'd been hesitant, but Darcy concluded if he didn't want people to look at the pictures, he would have hidden the albums. Rio had been cute as a kid along with his brothers.

After telling her brother and Quinn she was turning in, Darcy climbed to the second floor and got ready for bed. She grabbed her Kindle and settled into the first book of a

Nora Roberts trilogy. She'd just begun the third chapter when her cell phone rang.

"Darcy, it's Stella. I'm meeting Leah tomorrow morning for breakfast at Delaney's. Would you like to eat with us? Gives you a chance to meet her."

"Sounds good. I'll drop by the deli after breakfast. I can show Leah what I'm planning."

"I also researched Gretchen Bond's background."

"And?"

"No surprise to you, she collected a lot of things."

A soft laugh from Darcy. "My Dumpsters are full of those things. Who collects carpet samples or different kinds of tile?"

"I heard she was pretty eccentric her last few months. And she grew more secretive about her purchases."

Darcy frowned. "How so?"

"According to Maeve, Otter Creek's foremost contributor to the grapevine, every time Ms. Bond bought anything, she told everyone she met about her new purchase. That stopped about a year before she was murdered."

"Paranoid?"

"I don't have proof, but I'm afraid whatever she started collecting her last year of life may have led to her death."

CHAPTER TWENTY

Rio opened his eyes, squinted at the bright sunlight filtering through the blinds in his room. He frowned. What time was it? Rolling over, he snagged his cell phone to check the time. His head dropped back on the pillow. Incredible. He'd slept twelve hours straight, something he'd never done even as a teenager. His lips twitched. Not that his mother would have let him or his brothers get by with that. She wouldn't let her sons keep vampire hours by staying up all night and sleeping the day away. Much as he hated that rule growing up, now he appreciated the extra hours he had with his mother before they lost her to cancer.

His hand stroked the iPod Darcy left for him on his pillow. She'd downloaded all her CDs and provided top-quality ear buds. Last night was the first time in years Rio slept through the night without a play-by-play of his Delta missions. Her piano music had kept him grounded in the present instead of mired in the ugly past where he'd lost fellow soldiers despite his every effort to save them.

The worst memories were the ones where he and his teammates arrived too late to save the innocents in a war beyond their control. One simple gesture from his girlfriend had quieted the nightmares. Grateful didn't begin to cover what he felt toward Darcy at this moment.

Rio threw back the covers, grabbed his clothes and shaving kit, and headed for the bathroom across the hall. Twenty minutes later, he emerged, feeling better than he had in over a week. After dropping off his gear in his room, he went in search of Darcy and found her manning the stove. He stood in the doorway a moment, just taking in the sight of her competent hands flipping pancakes. What would it be like to wake every morning with her in his arms? A dream come true. Something to contemplate later. Today's goal was to enjoy his girl. Tomorrow would take care of itself. He crossed the room and laid his hands on her shoulders.

Darcy gasped, dropped the spatula, and spun around. "You move like a ghost. Make some noise next time."

He chuckled, shifted his hands to her waist, and leaned in to give her a tender kiss. "Good morning, sweetheart."

She studied his face a moment, smiled. "You look rested."

"I am. Thank you, baby."

"For?"

"The gift of your music. That's why I slept as well as I did. You kept the nightmares and flashbacks at bay."

She raised on her tiptoes and brushed his mouth with hers. "I'm glad. Do you have many of those?"

He stilled. "Almost every night." Would the remnants of his military life chase her away? Man, he hoped not. He didn't want to lose her.

"Are you hungry?"

The knots in his belly loosened. "Starved."

"Coffee's ready. Pour yourself a mug and sit while I finish breakfast."

"Have you taken care of your own meal?"

"I'm going to breakfast with Stella and Leah."

"Delaney's?"

"Maybe this time I'll finish my meal in an hour. You draw a crowd, Mr. Kincaid."

He poured a mug of coffee and watched poetry in motion. Darcy's movements were graceful, reminding him of her motions at the keyboard. Rio sighed. Yep, he was a total sap. If his brothers or teammates heard him, he'd never live this down. "Anything new happen yesterday?"

Darcy flipped the last pancake from the pan onto a platter which she placed in front of him along with maple syrup. "Brian evaluated the floor in the living room. It has to be reinforced before the piano arrives. He can't do it before the end of next week." She sighed. "I really wanted my own piano to practice for Julia's concert."

"Has Pastor Lang called with a date?"

"Two weeks from tomorrow. A member of the church is in marketing and will spearhead the publicity. Word will leak soon. Allen will track me down to demand his cut of my pay."

"Tell him when I'm around. I want to see his face when he learns you're playing without pay. As for the floor, Mason and I can shore it up for you."

Darcy sat next to him. "Know anything about handyman work?"

"Enough to hold the tools for Mason to work his magic."

She rolled her eyes. "I could do that. If Mason is interested, I'll pay him what I would have paid Brian's crew. Having access to my piano sooner is worth the money."

"Anything else happen?"

She hesitated, her expression troubled.

Rio paused with his fork halfway to his mouth. "Sweetheart?"

"Stella called last night."

"What did she have to say?" Couldn't be good considering Darcy's reluctance to share.

She summarized the conversation, ending with, "What if Ms. Bond stumbled onto something that grabbed the attention of Sutton's crew and one of them killed her?"

Rio considered that as he took another bite. "I wonder if these guys are patient enough to wait three years to tear into the house."

"Same question we had earlier. What sparked the interest after all this time?"

"Did she have relatives?"

"According to Mrs. Watson, the relatives wanted a check for the sale, but they refused to clear the house."

"Can't blame them for avoiding the job. Something else to consider is Sutton isn't violent. I don't think he killed Ms. Bond. Another member of his crew, however, might be a different story."

"Stella thinks because Ms. Bond stopped sharing about her purchases, she stumbled onto something valuable."

Rio finished the last of his pancakes and polished off the final sip of his coffee. "Would Annie know something?"

"I'll stop by the bookstore, see if she's working."

"If not, Del will give you her contact information."

Footsteps in the hall alerted Rio to Mason's approach. Even injured, Trent wouldn't have made any noise. His cousin looked rested.

"Good morning, Mason." Darcy handed him a mug of steaming coffee. "Pancakes for breakfast or you can find something else."

"Pancakes sound great."

He sat beside Rio and sipped, sighed.

"How did you sleep, Mase?"

His cousin glanced at him, his gaze haunted. "Better than I have in thirteen years. It was quiet and safe."

"We have places to go this morning. When you finish eating, we'll leave."

"Mason, I have a job for you if you're interested."

His cousin looked up from his plate. "What do you need?"

"I need my living room floor reinforced to handle the weight my seven-foot grand piano. I'd love to ship the piano here in a couple days. Would you be willing to do the work for me? I'll pay you what the contractor would have charged."

"A seven-foot grand, huh? You must really love music."

"She's a concert pianist, Mason," Rio said. "Music has been her life for twenty years."

His cousin's attention shifted back to Darcy. "I'll do it, but you don't have to pay me, Darcy."

"Of course I do. Brian doesn't have the men to spare right now. You're doing me a favor. I have a concert in two weeks and need my piano here. After reinforcing the floor, I'll pay you to patch the walls and floors, unless you're too busy working."

Mason's face twisted, worry shadowing his features. "If anyone will hire me."

"You might be surprised," Rio said. He had a couple ideas about that, but he'd have to see what panned out for his cousin.

After Darcy left for Delaney's, Trent hobbled into the kitchen, glanced around. "Where's Darce?"

"Breakfast with Nate's wife."

The operative grabbed a plate from the counter and peered at the platter of pancakes. "Looks good. Your work, Rio?"

"Darcy's. Mason and I have errands this morning. You'll be okay for a while?" A scathing look was his reply. Rio grinned. Figured that would be the response. "No stairs, buddy. Internet's up?"

"Yeah. They came about ten yesterday morning."

"Did you decide on a safe room?"

Trent shook his head. "Spent the day making a list for the security system. The safe room is on today's agenda."

Quinn strolled in, rubbing his scruffy jaw. "Please tell me Darcy made enough for me, too."

Rio motioned to the still full platter. "Plenty for both of you. You're off guard duty. Trent's fine for a few hours."

His teammate eyed the Fortress operative. "I don't know. I caught him staring at the stairs a lot yesterday."

"Shut up and get out," Trent said, scowling.

"After I eat. Riding herd on you yesterday stoked my appetite."

After Mason finished, they headed into town. The air had a distinct bite to it, making Rio wonder if they were in for snow.

"Where are we going?"

"First stop is the police station. You have an appointment with Ethan Blackhawk, the police chief. He's your probation officer."

A hard swallow, then, "What should I know about him?"

"He's tough, but fair. Ethan will want you to succeed, so he'll ride you hard to make sure you stay out of trouble. He's fiercely loyal to his family and his officers, a first-class tracker, Army Ranger. He also hates the politics that goes with his job. He's a good man, Mason."

In the station, the desk sergeant called Backhawk's assistant, then waved them through to his office. They crossed the bull pen and Rio knocked on Ethan's door.

The six-four Native American police chief waved them inside. "How's Trent?"

"Mending fast. Won't keep him down much longer. Ethan, this is my cousin, Mason Kincaid. Mase, Ethan Blackhawk."

The police chief shook hands and motioned to a visitor's chair. "Have a seat. You, too, Rio." His gaze returned to Mason. "Unless you'd prefer him to wait in the bull pen."

"It's fine for Rio to stay."

"I've been looking at your file. You must have ticked off the judge, Kincaid. Thirteen years was a pretty stiff sentence. I'm surprised you weren't granted parole since your behavior in prison was exemplary."

"The victims' family is wealthy and well-connected. They showed up for every parole hearing along with many important people from my hometown. The only support I had was my family."

"Did you think that was unfair?"

"I made a poor choice, one which cost a young mother and her infant their lives. I can't rectify what I did. I knew eventually I would be released, but the baby will never have a chance to grow up, marry, have children of her own. The mother won't spend long years with her husband, perhaps have more children. I destroyed that family with one stupid decision." His voice choked off.

Ethan sat in silence a moment, studying Mason's body language. "You have a second chance, Kincaid. Don't screw it up. Here's the plan. You'll check in with me once a week. You need a job, fast. Where will you live?"

"With Rio until I'm on my feet."

The police chief yanked open one of his desk drawers, pulled out a note pad and handed it to Rio. "I need contact information for the record."

Rio dashed off the information. "Mason will have a cell phone by the end of the day. I'll text you the number as soon as I know what it is."

A nod, then, Ethan's attention shifted back to Mason. "A normal citizen would have a little leeway on how they unwind after a hard day of work. You have zero. As part of the terms of your probation, no alcohol, no drugs, no weapons. I'm well aware of what Rio and his Delta unit routinely carry on them and in their vehicles. If we test

Rio's weapons for prints, yours better not be on them. Am I clear?"

"Yes, sir."

"We have one bar in town. Stay away from it and the liquor store. Any job you pursue cannot deal with the elderly or children. As soon as you land a job, I need to know what you're doing and who your employer is. If anything changes, I need to know immediately. This is a small town, Kincaid. I'll see you everywhere and I'm not too busy to do spot checks on you. Otter Creek also has a grapevine that rivals military intelligence. If you think no one will notice what you do, be prepared to spend more time as a guest of the state of Tennessee. Hear me well, Kincaid. One DUI and you'll be behind bars so fast your head will spin. Do you have a vehicle?"

Mason looked faintly ill. "No, sir."

"You'll eventually need one." A hard smile curved Ethan's mouth. "Don't be surprised if you're pulled over routinely. Questions?"

"No, sir."

"If you have issues or concerns, I want to know about it from your lips, not second hand." He turned to Rio. "You have questions?"

"There's a possibility Mason will be working with Elliott Construction. They also rehab houses. The homeowners may be elderly or have children. Will that be a problem?"

"I don't see that as an issue. No daycares, schools, or nursing homes as a regular employee. Kincaid, we'll meet every Friday morning at eight unless there's an emergency on your part. If that happens, I expect a phone call before our appointment. If I'm tied up, the detective on duty will meet with you. That's going to be Rod Kelter, Nick Santana, or Stella Armstrong." He stood, extended his hand. "Good hunting on the job."

"Thank you, sir." His lips gave a ghost of a smile. "Please, call me Mason. Looks like we'll be spending a lot of quality time together."

Ethan chuckled. "See you in a week, Mason."

Outside the station, Rio's cousin glanced his direction as they walked down the station steps. "Were you serious about that construction job?"

"Brian Elliott said he'd be willing to talk to you. He's working in Darcy's deli." They crossed the square and went into the shop. Two workers were painting walls to the beat of country music.

He frowned as he noticed vulgar graffiti on the walls. Darcy hadn't mentioned anything about it and she should have. The messages left on the walls reminded him of the one on her mirror. Could Sutton or one of his crew have struck here in another bid to scare her?

He scanned the faces of the workers. The older of the two men turned, nodded their direction before resuming his task of covering the foul language. No Brian. Rio walked to the back of the shop where Brian was leveling an industrial-size stove.

"Rio. Good to see you, man." He wiped off his hand and extended it. The contractor eyed Mason. "Brian Elliott. You must be Mason. Ever worked construction?"

"My dad's a carpenter. I worked construction during high school and college."

Brian's eyes lit. "What can you do?"

While he and Mason discussed the skills his cousin picked up on the job, Rio wandered back into the main dining room as Darcy walked in the door with a short, dark-haired Leah Conner.

His girlfriend's gaze darted to the walls. Blood drained from her face. So the graffiti was new. Rio had been afraid of that.

"Rio!" Leah smiled.

He kissed her forehead. "How are you, sugar?"

"Fantastic."

"I can see that. Dean must be treating you like a princess."

The young woman blushed. "Absolutely."

Rio chuckled. Had to love newlyweds.

"Why are you here?" Darcy asked.

"Mason's talking to Brian about a job."

"That's great." She wrinkled her nose. "I just hope Brian doesn't keep him so busy he can't reinforce my floor."

"No problem, Darcy," Brian said, striding into the main room with Mason. "He'll do that for you as part of Elliott Construction."

"Congratulations, Mason." Darcy beamed at him. "That didn't take long."

Brian clapped him on the shoulder. "He's a well-rounded worker. If his work ethic is as good as it seems, he'll be a great addition to Elliott Construction." He retrieved the clipboard leaning against the wall and pulled off a few sheets of paper. "Mason, bring these in tomorrow morning. You start work at seven. Your first job is reinforcing Darcy's living room floor. Look at it today. Tell me what you need and if you require assistance." He handed Mason a business card. "My cell number is on the bottom." He extended his hand. "Welcome to Elliott Construction, Mason."

He turned to Darcy. "I see you've noticed the artwork. We found it this morning. This is on me, Darcy. One of my crew forgot to lock the back door before we left last night. I promise you it won't happen again."

"Can't let you take the blame, boss," the older painter said. "I'm Doug Walsh, ma'am. The unlocked door was my fault. Was in too much of a hurry to see my girlfriend."

"You may have made the mistake, but someone took advantage of it," Darcy replied. "Whoever wrote that is doomed to disappointment. I'm not leaving."

After a few last instructions to Mason, Brian returned to the kitchen with Darcy and Leah to show them the progress he'd made. Looked to Rio like Darcy might have found her first employee.

"Rio," Mason murmured. "Did you see the tattoo on Walsh's forearm?"

He scanned the body art, frowned. It looked faded. "Can't make out the design from here. Is it important?"

"I recognize it from prison. He's an ex-con who was affiliated with one of the more vicious gangs in prison."

CHAPTER TWENTY-ONE

In the bookstore, Darcy searched the interior for Annie. Her gaze locked onto the redheaded dynamo as she hustled to the second level of the store with a group of elementary students behind her.

She grinned at the enthusiastic chatter. To have that much energy would be a blessing.

"I wish all my customers were that excited about reading." Del walked behind the counter and set a stack of books beside the register. "Need some hot tea, Darcy? We just unboxed a new shipment of tea. One of them is mint with pieces of real chocolate in it. Interested?"

"That sounds amazing."

"Large cup?"

"Please."

"Did you need anything else? Maybe more reading material for your brother?"

Darcy laughed. "Not yet. I need to talk to Annie, though. Do you know when she'll be free?"

"Fifteen minutes. Can you wait? If not, I can step in for her and send her down."

"That's not necessary. I'll drink my tea while I wait."

The store owner dropped a diffuser filled with mint chocolate tea in hot water. "I hear you're doing a concert in a couple weeks to raise money for Julia Kendall. You're settling in fast."

"Wow. Rio was right. The grapevine around here is amazing."

"It's shocking how fast things get around town. I have a secret source, though. While Josh was on patrol this morning, he talked to Pastor Lang. The law enforcement people are buzzing about it. Julia's father is a cop and they've all taken Julia's illness pretty hard. She's a favorite of everybody in town, but especially the cops."

That explained the fast swell of information. Allen would be cornering her soon. "Does Julia come to your store?"

"All the time. Julia loves to knit and read." Del tilted her head. "Would you like to meet her?"

"I'd love to. I want a list of her favorite Christmas music to include in the concert."

"She's upstairs. I'll introduce you when the kids come down." When the phone rang, she excused herself and grabbed the wireless handset.

Darcy shoved her hand inside her purse, looking for a pen and paper. She hoped Julia liked the popular Christmas songs she already had in her repertoire. Her lips twitched. Otherwise, she would be scouring the Internet for sheet music to purchase and print, then memorizing the pieces.

Behind her, bells announced the entrance of a new customer. Darcy glanced over her shoulder, smiled at her boyfriend and his cousin. A welcome sight that sent her heart rate soaring. "Hi."

Rio brushed her mouth with a light kiss. "How was breakfast?" he asked as he sat next to her. Mason wandered off to browse the book shelves.

"Fun. And, yes, I did manage to eat in a normal span of time."

He chuckled. "Won't be long before you have visitors whether I'm with you or not. People in Otter Creek are friendly and nosy. Their favorite pastime is one upping their friends in the information game."

"Rio, Rio," came a sweet voice. "I haven't seen you in forever."

Darcy turned to see a small girl with a cap of curly black hair beaming up at the medic.

"Well, hello, Tiger Lily." He lifted her into his arms. "How's my girl?"

The child giggled. "I'm out of the hospital."

"I see that. Are you finished with your treatments?"

"Uh huh. I don't have to go back for three whole months."

"Now that's cause for celebration. How about a chocolate chip cookie? My treat."

She bounced up and down in his arms. "I love chocolate chip cookies. Can I have one from here? Serena makes them."

"She makes the best cookies. I say we all get one."

Del returned and tapped the girl's nose. "Hi, beautiful. What can I get you today?"

"Chocolate chip cookie, please. One for Rio and the lady, too."

"You got it." She smiled. "Have you met Darcy yet?"

"Uh uh."

"Julia, the pretty lady is Darcy St. Claire. Darcy, Julia Kendall."

Julia eyed her and leaned against Rio's chest. "Hi," she said, her voice soft.

Darcy smiled. "It's nice to meet you, Julia."

Rio stroked her hair. "Darcy agreed to do a concert at the church in a couple weeks to raise money for your treatments."

"Do you play the guitar like Nick?"

"Piano. What are your favorite Christmas songs, Julia?"

A couple minutes later, Darcy's paper was full of music selections.

"Here you go, sweetie." Del handed her a cookie, then gave one each to Rio and Darcy. Annie returned with her group of students. "One chocolate chip cookie for each of you, compliments of Serena Blackhawk."

A cheer went up and the crowd rushed the coffee bar.

Darcy laughed at the press of small bodies and reaching hands. Within a couple minutes, the cookies had been handed out and the teacher and her assistant bundled the kids in their coats, hats, and scarves. Rio hugged Julia and sent her to join her classmates. When the students left, the silence was as much of a shock as the deafening noise had been.

"Whew! They're a handful." Annie poured herself a mug of coffee and sat beside Rio. "Julia looks good, doesn't she?"

"Like a million bucks considering what she's been through."

"Here's your tea, Darcy." Del slid the tall mug in front of her. "Coffee, Rio?"

"Just what I need with this cookie."

As she poured the steaming brew into a mug, another customer walked into the store. Annie started to stand, but Del waved her off. "I've got it. Darcy needs to talk to you."

"I need more information on Ms. Bond."

"Tell her why, sweetheart."

"Something happened?" Annie set her mug down, alarm on her face.

"Another break-in, this time with us in the house."

"Oh, my. Was anyone hurt?"

"Everyone's fine, sugar." Rio squeezed her hand. "We caught him. He's in jail."

"Did he steal anything?"

"He left a message on my bathroom mirror," Darcy said. Remembering those words scrawled in lipstick still caused a ball of ice to form in her stomach. "He said to leave or die."

Annie scowled. "Why would he say that?"

"My guess is he wanted free access to the house." Rio sipped his coffee. "Do you have any idea what Ms. Bond collected that was worth the risk?"

"Something small," Darcy added. "The holes in the walls and floors aren't big."

"I can't think of anything. I'm sorry. Every time I went over there, her rooms were more cluttered, but nothing looked valuable to me. Of course, I was afraid to examine anything too carefully."

"What about special interests, especially that last year?"

Annie's cheeks flushed. "The only thing she obsessed over was pirates."

Darcy stared at the other woman. "Pirates?"

"Obsessed how, Annie?" Rio asked.

"Costumes, books, treasure maps, movies." She shrugged. "Gretchen had the money and it was a harmless interest."

Darcy exchanged glances with Rio. "Explains the books on pirate history and historical romances we sent Del."

"I shelved those in the book exchange section or boxed them for the retirement home. I think Del sent some of the better history books to the library." Annie wrapped her hands around her coffee mug. "I didn't realize Gretchen bought so many. Your burglar wouldn't have been interested in those." Doubt crept into her eyes. "Would he?"

CHAPTER TWENTY-TWO

When Annie left to help a knitting customer, Rio eyed Darcy's stunned expression. He sympathized. Pirates? He'd left that fantasy life behind when he turned ten. Why would Gretchen find them so fascinating? "What do you think?"

"Is it possible some of the books were rare, like a first edition?"

"If the books were valuable, Del would have asked if you wanted them back." He frowned. "Nick said Sutton and his crew go after high-value items."

"No one would place valuable books in a wall or floor to protect them. If the books were the target, Sutton wouldn't have broken in."

"Unless he didn't know you got rid of them."

"How could he not? Otter Creek's already talking about the concert. The neighbors know what sat on the porch every day. The grapevine is bound to have a bulleted list somewhere." She scowled. "I should have asked if the town has a Facebook page. Somebody must have taken pictures and posted it."

Rio chuckled. "Told you they were nosy."

"Yeah, go ahead and laugh, Kincaid. They're talking about us, too."

"Does that bother you?"

"Everybody is sticking their nose in our lives."

He trailed the back of his finger over her cheek. "Darcy, I hope you don't think I'm going to complain if the word spreads that you're off limits to other single men in town. You've lived in a big fishbowl for twenty years, baby. This is just a smaller one with friends and neighbors who will be customers at your deli. They don't mean any harm." He shrugged one shoulder. "It's an aspect of small-town life you'll have to get used to."

"Your life isn't an open book to them. Why should mine be?" she said crossly.

"Only certain parts of my life are open. There are things I can't even tell you. The townsfolk are used to Josh keeping silent about his missions. They know not to ask too many questions and if they ask one question too many, no one complains when Josh refuses to answer. If they ask me something they shouldn't, I tell them I can't answer."

"I don't have the excuse of national security risks or confidentiality issues."

"Tell them something without giving away everything. The other side of the nosiness is people will go out of their way to help you. You can count on them in a pinch. Watch and see at your concert. Even though it's Christmas and they have presents to buy for their own families and friends, the town will turn out to support Julia and her family."

The mutinous expression on Darcy's face smoothed out into one of wonder. "Really?"

"Don't take this the wrong way, sweetheart, but it doesn't matter that a concert is being performed by the world renowned pianist Darcy Melton. Anybody doing a benefit for Julia will garner support simply because it's for her."

"I've always wanted to live in a place where people cared about each other."

"You got your wish. You'll learn to deal with the extreme interest in your life. Right now you're a hot topic because you're new. In a few months, you'll fade into the woodwork like the rest of us."

The bells over the door chimed and a gust of cold wind blew toward the coffee bar. Rio glanced over his shoulder, narrowed his eyes at the man making a beeline for Darcy. "Incoming," he murmured.

She turned, sighed. "Hello, Allen."

"I've been looking all over town for you. The man at your house wasn't helpful at all. Claimed he didn't know where you were."

"It wasn't a claim. I didn't give him a list of my errands. You have my cell phone number. You could have called."

"The phone is no way to plan your big comeback tour, baby."

Rio stiffened at the endearment. He also didn't like the way Darcy shrank away from her agent. "Back up, White."

"Listen, Ron, this isn't your business. Take a walk or something while Darcy and I discuss a few things."

"Allen," Darcy snapped. "His name is Rio and he's not a dolt."

Rio's eyebrows rose. White thought he was Darcy's arm candy? Unbelievable. "You and I need to take a walk, buddy." He stood.

Darcy grabbed his hand. "Rio."

Her voice told him all he needed to know. She wanted to handle the situation herself. He laced their fingers together and waited.

"Allen, I'm not returning to that life."

White's eyes glittered. "You've been here less than a week and already scheduled for a concert. Admit it. You love the life, Darcy, and you miss it."

"I will never return to that life. I still love to play the piano and I might occasionally do a concert, but those will be few. You're wasting your time trying to convince me to return to the stage, Allen."

"Sweetheart," Rio murmured. "Tell him the truth."

"Tell me what?" White glanced back and forth between them. He cringed. "You're not pregnant, are you?"

Darcy's jaw dropped. "You can't be serious."

"You could have kept a man in your life a secret."

"That's your assessment of my character?" she asked, arms folded across her chest.

"Because if you are pregnant, we'll work around it. In fact, the audience will love it. Everybody loves new mothers."

"I'm not pregnant," Darcy whispered fiercely.

"Then what secret haven't you told me?"

Rio squeezed her fingers gently, gave her a slight nod. It was time to tell her agent. Otherwise, he'd hound her to return to her former life, a life she couldn't continue without compromising her health.

With a sigh, Darcy explained the diagnosis and limitations she faced. "You are not to spread that around anywhere, Allen. I don't want to be the lead on the news cycles."

The agent stared at her a moment, stunned. "Why didn't you say something? I would have understood. Look, you don't have to stop performing. We can set up a few concerts a year and record albums."

"I can't practice for hours every day, Allen. If I can't practice like I should, I'll become sloppy. Audiences have a low tolerance for mistakes when they expect excellence. I'd rather go out on top of my field than continue giving concerts for fewer and fewer people while the critics tear me to shreds."

"We'll work something out if you give me a chance."

"That's enough." Rio glared at the other man. "She told you that part of her life is finished. Accept it and move on."

"Listen up, Ron. You must not have too much between your ears because this doesn't concern you."

Rio raised his and Darcy's clasped hands, kissed the back of hers before untangling their fingers. With a couple swift moves, he spun the agent around and propelled him out of the store into the cold winter day.

"Take your hands off me." The agent's voice came out high and squeaky.

He maneuvered White down the sidewalk and around the back of the building. One shove and the other man's back was pressed tight against the wall. "Darcy's health is at stake, White. The doctor told her she couldn't continue on her career path. Her decision to change her career is not up for debate. Are you so interested in money that you would ruin her health and shorten her life?"

The other man's fists clenched. "We can get other opinions. She has enough money to consult doctors all over the world. There has to be a specialist who can help."

"There is no cure, White. The best Darcy can do is manage the symptoms."

White scowled. "What do you know about medicine?"

"I'm a trained medic. The bottom line is I won't let you badger Darcy into doing something harmful to her health. I also better not hear anything about Darcy's illness on the town grapevine. If I do and she hasn't told people herself, I'll know it was you who talked." He moved in toe to toe with the agent. "I won't be nearly as nice if we have a chat about that. Do you understand what I'm saying?"

"Are you threatening me?"

"Nope, just promising an intense conversation." He didn't specify the conversation would involve physical repercussions on the agent's part. Rio longed to make his point quite forcefully now, but figured Darcy wouldn't be happy. "Look, I know you care about her." At least, he hoped this guy had Darcy's best interests at heart rather than his own. "Don't make this career change harder on her than it already is."

White's lips pressed together in a tight, straight line. "Fine. She wants to do a concert for this hick town? I get a cut of her pay. It's in the contract she signed."

"How long is the contract valid?"

"Another year. Any concert she performs, I get a percentage of the proceeds."

"Whether you set it up or not?" Didn't seem fair.

"It's a standard contract," he said, tone defensive. "It's the price of representing her. I have to make a living, too."

Rio wondered what it would cost to break that contract. Might be worth investigating. White was in for a surprise when he tried to collect his pay for this concert. His lips curled at the corners. Refreshments afterward was a given. If the agent was lucky, his pay would be leftovers.

The women of Cornerstone Church were excellent cooks. He ought to know. More than one of them had tried to snag his attention by feeding him when he first arrived in town with his Delta teammates. He'd appreciated the meals and made friends of the women because none had interested him as anything more than that. Until Darcy.

"Are we done here? I'm freezing."

Rio stepped aside and allowed White to pass. He wasn't sorry for irritating the other man and would do more than that if he didn't stop harassing Darcy.

He followed behind, making sure White didn't return to the store to badger Darcy. Satisfied when the other man stalked toward his expensive sports car, Rio returned to the store where his girl sipped her tea, gaze focused on the door, Mason seated beside her. Relief flooded her face when he stepped inside.

"Everything okay?"

"I think he understands." He'd better if he knew what was good for him.

"Does he need a trip to the hospital?"

"There's not a mark on him." This time. Next time? All bets were off.

"You showed more restraint than Trent would."

"What did he want?" Mason asked.

"For me to return to touring." She stood. "Did you find any good books, Mason?"

A slow nod. "More than I can afford this week."

Del walked up in time to hear his comment. "Did you check the books on the borrow shelves?"

He shook his head.

"Come on. I'll show you. Take as many as you like. Bring them back when you're finished. When you buy a book from me and don't want to add it to your own keeper collection, donate it to the borrow shelf and I'll give you ten percent off your next purchase."

Mason glanced at Rio. "Do I have time?"

"We have a few minutes."

Darcy asked, "You and Mason have other stops to make?"

"Department of Motor Vehicles, the bank, my cell phone carrier. He has to have a bank account in which to deposit his paycheck. To do that, Mason needs a driver's license."

"And the cell phone?"

"I can add him to my account for a minimal fee."

"The cell phone isn't cheap," she murmured.

"He needs the independence and the connection with his dad, sweetheart. Plus, Ethan will want to check on him. Cell phone's an easy way to do that."

"And the clothes and shoes?"

"He came out of prison with nothing and he's bulked up in the last 13 years. He can't borrow my stuff anymore."

"You're not fooling me, Rio Kincaid."

He stilled. "I'm not?"

"No." She wrapped her arms around his neck and pressed a soft kiss to his lips. "You're doing everything possible to ease his transition."

"Maybe."

"Definitely. I like it. I like him, too. He reminds me of you."

Rio's heart turned over in his chest. Oh, man. Darcy St. Claire was something else and fast wrapping silken bonds around his heart. He laid his forehead gently against hers. "What's next for you today?"

"Shopping for dishes for the store and finding furniture for the house."

"Pace yourself, baby. You have time."

"I need to practice tonight. Interested in going with me?"

"I wouldn't miss it."

Del returned with Mason trailing behind, carrying an armload of books. Rio chuckled. "Think you have enough, Mase?"

"I haven't read these and I need something to help me wind down at night after working on Darcy's house."

"You're helping her remodel?" Del asked as she bagged the books.

"I'm starting with Elliott Construction tomorrow. Darcy's house is my first assignment."

"Congratulations on the job, Mason." She handed him the bag. "I'll look for similar books and set them aside for you. We'll swap when you've finished these."

"Thanks, Del."

"I'm always happy to cultivate another reader."

Rio kissed Darcy. "We'll see you at the house. I'll pick up dinner. We can go to the church after we eat."

In the car, his cousin placed the books behind his seat. "What's next?"

"DMV. You need a driver's license to open a bank account."

On the way, Rio activated his Bluetooth and called his friend, Zane Murphy. Zane was a communications guru at Fortress Security. He was also a whiz at research.

"Murphy."

"It's Rio."

"Missed me already? It's only been three weeks, buddy."

He snorted. "Right. I need a favor."

"Name it."

"I need you to do some research for me."

A few clicks of a keyboard sounded in the interior of the SUV. "Go ahead."

"Find out what you can about Allen White. He's Darcy St. Claire's agent."

"Why?" The Navy SEAL's voice hardened. "Is he harassing her?"

"In a way. He's urging her to continue touring and recording. I want to know if he's just looking out for her or if there's more behind him showing up in Otter Creek to talk to her. He's pushing hard, and it's ticking me off."

Zane was silent a few seconds. "Is he raising a red flag in your mind or does this have to do with the woman?"

Rio's cheeks heated. "The woman."

"Fast work, man. You're braver than I am. Trent is a fierce watchdog."

"I know. He's already tried to take a bite out of my hide."

"Anyone else you want me to check on?"

"Troy Sutton. He broke into Darcy's new house and left a threatening message on her mirror. We suspect he ripped up the floor in several rooms and the walls in a few."

"You catch him?"

"He's in custody."

"Any marks on him?"

Rio had to grin at that question. The SEAL knew how to make a guy hurt without leaving telling marks. Delta had taught him the same kind of techniques. "Nothing that shows." But he'd hurt for a while. His knowledge of biology came in handy for more than one reason.

"Good job. Anyone else you want me to run?"

"Check out Doug Walsh. He's working for Darcy's contractor. Also run a lady named Gretchen Bond. She's deceased and the former owner of Darcy's house."

"Will do. Keep me posted on what's happening in Otter Creek. I'll do what I can to help. Darcy's a sweetheart. She sent me books and magazines by the box when I was laid up in the hospital. I want to make sure she's safe."

"I hear you, Z. Thanks for the assistance."

"I'll let you know what I find out."

Rio parked in a space at the DMV.

"Who's Zane Murphy?" Mason asked.

"A friend who works at Fortress Security. My Delta teammates and I also work for them."

"Delta?" Mason's head whipped his direction. "You were Delta?"

"That's right. Zane is in communications. He can find out anything about anybody. I've only met one other guy who's better than he is."

"He was laid up in the hospital?"

"IED in Afghanistan. Left him in a wheelchair."

"Tough break. Was he Delta?"

"Navy SEAL." He unbuckled his seatbelt. "Let's go. Be prepared to wait. The DMV is not known for being fast." He grabbed a book he had stashed in his console. Taking a hint from Rio's actions, Mason selected a book from his bag. An hour later, Mason had a new driver's license.

At the bank, Aaron Cahill greeted them. "Liz has been asking about you, Rio, complaining she hasn't seen you for a while."

"Tell her I'll stop by soon. I want to introduce her to somebody special." Josh's mother had adopted her son's teammates, especially Alex, whose family disowned him when he joined the Army.

Aaron's eyes twinkled. "Would this be the beautiful young woman you've been seen around town with?"

Rio chuckled. "Yes, sir."

"We look forward to meeting her." He turned, held out his hand to Mason. "You must be Mason. Welcome to Otter Creek, son. What can I do for the two of you?"

"I need to open a checking account," Mason said.

Aaron scanned the room, checking on the availability of his people. "Come with me."

To Rio's surprise, Josh's father took them to his office. "We can wait, Aaron. You have more important things to do."

"This won't take long. Don't forget, I started my career here as a teller and worked my way up. I can handle opening an account." He handed Mason papers and a clipboard. "Fill these out for me. I'll begin the preliminaries."

While Aaron filled out the computer forms, he asked Mason questions and drew out the story of his arrest, conviction, and jail time.

"I have a job, sir."

"Good for you, Mason. I need a phone number, son. Do you have one yet?"

"That's our next stop," Rio said. "Use mine until his is activated."

A nod, then, "I recommend a joint account for a few months. You willing to do that, Rio?"

"Absolutely."

"Is that necessary?" Mason asked, his voice soft.

"It's better. You're establishing a new track record here, Mason. Before long, it won't be necessary."

Within minutes, the account was opened and Mason was promised a debit card in the mail within two weeks. Back in the SUV, Mason sighed. "I'm sorry, Rio. I didn't expect your name to be tied to mine like this."

"It's not a problem."

"I won't let you down."

Rio reached over and squeezed his cousin's shoulder. "I never doubted it."

The next stop was Rio's cell phone carrier where he bought a smart phone for Mason and added him to his account. In the SUV, he gave Mason his cell phone number as well as those of his teammates and Ethan Blackhawk. He nodded at the phone. "Text Ethan your number and tell him you're working for Brian."

As Mason figured out how to work his phone, Rio cranked the engine. His Bluetooth chimed an incoming call. He frowned, gut tightening with dread.

CHAPTER TWENTY-THREE

Darcy left the store, pleased with her afternoon's work. The shop's dishes were paid for and in storage until her deli opened. The next item on her list was furniture. Stella had told her about a wonderful store in Cherry Hill. Armed with instructions, Darcy drove onto Highway 18.

About five miles from Otter Creek, she noticed a dark-colored SUV trailing her. Rio? He hadn't mentioned leaving Otter Creek. When the SUV stayed back and her phone remained silent, she put the vehicle from her mind.

In Cherry Hill, she parked in front of The Furniture Gallery, looking forward to the next few minutes. Who didn't want to furnish a whole house? She spent over an hour browsing for comfortable furniture. How much should she buy? One floor at a time, she decided, starting with the first floor. She knew what she wanted on the second floor although she was reluctant to make the purchase. Her lips quirked. Unless, of course, they offered a big discount.

When she told the store employee that she was furnishing an entire house, the woman's face lit. "Show me what you like."

An hour later, Darcy owned furniture for the Victorian's three floors. The saleswoman had offered Darcy a deal she couldn't pass up. The Furniture Gallery agreed to store her furniture until the renovations were complete.

She climbed into her car, laughed at herself. One floor of furniture, huh? She'd had fun, though. Kara, the saleswoman, had great taste and amazing ideas. Darcy hoped Rio liked the furniture.

Her face heated. Making long-term plans already, Darcy? She shoved the question of Rio's response aside. Their relationship was in the early stages, though it didn't feel that way to her. She had traveled a long way down the relationship road in the past few days. The furniture was for her, though. If she and Rio stayed together, they could choose other furniture if he didn't like her choice. He probably wouldn't care as long as the furniture was comfortable and not too fussy. Trent also preferred comfortable, sturdy furniture.

Darcy headed for Otter Creek. Not long after she left Cherry Hill, she glanced into the rearview mirror and spotted a dark-colored SUV several car lengths behind her. She frowned. How many of those things were in the area? Many, considering the guys who worked for PSI and the long line of black SUVs that brought the trainees to her house. SUVs and trucks were the vehicle of choice in and around Otter Creek. Maybe she should trade her car in for an SUV. She'd noticed a problem climbing out of her car in recent months. Perhaps Rio knew a good place to buy her next vehicle.

She returned her full attention to the curvy road, a hazardous proposition when covered with ice and snow. Yet another reason to purchase something to handle this mountainous terrain. She glanced at the edge of the road, grateful for the guardrail. She didn't know how far down the drop went on this mountainside and didn't want to find out. If she slid over the side, her small car would fold up like a fan.

A racing motor drew her attention to the rearview mirror again. Her eyes widened. Oh, man. Was this guy crazy? The dark SUV was careening toward her with no room to pass. What was this guy thinking?

If he insisted on passing, she'd pull as far to the right as possible. She glanced at the edge of the road again and prayed he'd slow down. He sped up, coming close enough Darcy could see the driver, a man with sunglasses, a dark hood pulled over his head.

Darcy's hands clenched around the steering wheel, uneasiness punching her pulse rate up another notch. Another quick glance to the edge of the road. She swallowed hard. Not a good place for aggressive driving.

She pressed down on the accelerator to put distance between her and the SUV. Unfortunately, on this steep incline her four-cylinder engine had the speed of a snail while the SUV actually gained on her.

Her hands tightened on the wheel. She really wanted off this road. Darcy scanned ahead, hoping for a visitor's lookout to get her car off the highway. Nothing but road, trees, and guardrail. Two hundred feet ahead, the shoulder of the road widened enough to move off the pavement and allow the SUV to pass.

As the vehicle edged closer and closer, a cold sweat broke out over Darcy's body. She pressed the accelerator to the floor and, though her vehicle gave all it had, the small engine didn't offer much more power. She was definitely trading in her car. Her beloved vehicle handled this road as though it were a golf cart with a top speed of twenty miles an hour. Time for something bigger with more power. She never wanted to go through this again.

She glanced in the mirror. Her breath stalled in her lungs. A few more seconds and the SUV would catch her. "Go around me, buddy," she muttered.

Darcy prepared to slow to allow the SUV to swing around her. Another check informed her the guy was right on her tail. Instead of darting around her, the black SUV surged forward and slammed into her bumper.

Her scream filled the interior of her car as the big vehicle shoved her car toward the guardrail. Darcy hit her brakes, but only slowed her forward progress. She needed a new plan.

Up ahead, the road was clear with no on-coming traffic. Praying her desperate plan worked, she took her foot off the brake, floored her accelerator, and eased to the left, away from the guardrail. Another hard hit from the SUV. Darcy spun her wheel hard to the left. The SUV hit the rear panel of her car, sending her into a spin. Her vehicle careened toward the mountainside on the other side of the road. Seconds later, metal shrieked and glass shattered. Pain exploded in her head.

CHAPTER TWENTY-FOUR

Rio activated his Bluetooth to answer the unexpected call. "What's up, Nick?"

"Where are you?"

The detective's clipped tone had Rio straightening. "At the bank with Mason."

"Get on Highway 18 and head toward Cherry Hill. Darcy's been in an accident."

A lightning strike of adrenaline flooded his system. He peeled out of the parking lot and raced out of town. "Injuries?"

"Cut to the forehead, bumps, bruises. She refuses to go to the hospital. She needs to go."

"Is the ambulance on scene?"

"In route. We're a few miles from Otter Creek. You should arrive about the same time as the ambulance."

"Did she lose consciousness?"

"Hold on." Nick's voice sounded muffled in the interior of the SUV. "For a few minutes. She's complaining of a headache, but says otherwise, she's fine."

"Don't let her move around. She might have a concussion and internal injuries."

"Copy that."

"Five minutes." He swerved onto the entrance ramp to the highway and zipped past the posted speed limit, hoping none of Nick's buddies in blue were lurking nearby because he wouldn't stop until he reached the accident scene. Just the thought of Darcy being in a wreck made him queasy. He suspected his girl was unconscious longer than she realized. Otherwise, she would have called him.

He frowned. Had she called the police? Is that why Nick was on scene? The idea she called law enforcement without also calling him didn't sit well. Dial it back, Kincaid. He'd talk to her after she'd been checked out. Yeah, their relationship was new. Still, he must be able to trust her to keep him informed. Otherwise, he'd be distracted on missions, a good way to get himself or his teammates killed.

"You okay, Rio?"

He glanced at his cousin. "I will be as soon as I see Darcy is all right." His lips curved. "I'm about to make the lady unhappy. She's going to the hospital, whether she wants to or not. As the hours pass, she'll feel every bump and bruise. I want a doctor to tell me she's fine."

A minute later, he slowed at the sight of the ambulance's flashing lights. "Look at her car." A ball of ice formed in his stomach. From the damage to her vehicle, she was lucky to walk away from the accident.

Mason whistled. "That baby is totaled."

No question his girlfriend needed a new car. Even if the insurance company fixed it, he wouldn't trust the structural integrity of the car. His hands tightened around his steering wheel. He'd prefer she drive something bigger than a tin can. He wanted Darcy to have more metal around her for protection. Was their relationship too new for him to insist she purchase a safer vehicle?

Rio slowed when one of the OCPD officers motioned for him to stop. Sanchez recognized him and waved him on through. He parked behind Nick's red Jeep. Darcy was still seated in Nick's vehicle. An EMT knelt on the ground in front of her, examining her forehead.

"Darcy."

She glanced up, relief flooding her face. "Rio."

One of the two EMTs nodded at him in greeting. Tom Gates and his partner, Ryan Holt, had attended a couple of Rio's field medic classes at PSI. When Rio walked toward her, Gates stood and moved aside.

He crouched in front of her, cupped her beautiful face in his hand. "You okay, baby?"

"I'm fine."

A cursory examination of the cut told him she needed stitches. "You need to go to the hospital, Darcy."

She scowled. "Why? I don't have broken bones."

"The cut on your forehead needs stitches, sweetheart. They'll check you for a concussion and internal injuries. This isn't the time for stubbornness, not with your health at stake."

"Can't you do it? Trent said you take care of stitches and more on missions."

"This isn't a combat situation."

"Please don't make me go." She leaned close and whispered, "I hate hospitals."

He chuckled and tapped her nose. "None of us like them until we need them. Go for me and Trent. We need the assurance you're all right." He needed irrefutable proof so his heart rate would settle into a regular rhythm instead of the current NASCAR pace. "Please."

Her resistance melted before his eyes as her shoulders slumped. "Dirty pool, Kincaid." Her eyes narrowed. "If I agree, I'm allowed the same tactic if you're injured. Deal?"

He couldn't refuse though he wanted to. "Agreed." He'd try not to complain too much when he landed in the hospital because of his job. Rio glanced at Gates, the EMT.

"Let's get the lady out of here before she changes her mind."

Darcy clasped his hand. "You'll go with me?"

He turned to Mason. "You okay to drive home?"

His cousin paled. Jaw flexing, he gave a short nod.

"Rio." Nick motioned him to the wreck.

"Be right back," he said to Darcy. To Gates, "Wait for me."

The EMT exchanged glances with Holt. "Sir, it's against company policy for you to ride with her."

Rio narrowed his eyes. "I'm certified as an EMT in this state, Gates. I'm also friends with the owner of your company. Shall I call George Crenshaw for you to confirm?"

The EMT's jaw flexed. "No, sir."

"Wait."

"Yes, sir."

He glanced at Mason, inclined his head toward Darcy. Although he doubted Gates and Holt were part of Sutton's crew, he wouldn't take chances with her life. His cousin moved to Darcy's side.

Rio jogged to Nick.

"Look at the back of her car."

He walked around to the rear of the vehicle. His blood ran cold. "This wasn't an accident. Another car hit her." He frowned. "From the damage to the back end, a truck or an SUV."

"Very good, Rio. Darcy said it was a black SUV." Nick pointed to the side of Darcy's car. "Paint transfer."

Black SUV? He scowled, wondering if it was the same one which tried to run him down during his run. He'd have to tell the detective about the incident, but not until Darcy had been examined by a doctor. Rio motioned to the wrecked car. "What do you think, Nick?"

"The accident reconstruction team will have to confirm, but I'd say the SUV rammed her from behind, caused her to spin out. Her vehicle hit his at one point. So we'll be looking for a black SUV with damage to the grill and side. Her white paint will have transferred to his vehicle." He stepped closer to Rio. "The skid marks indicate she tried using her brakes to stop him from shoving her car over the side of the mountain."

Cold fury flooded his body. "She saw a man?"

"Not close enough to identify him." Nick squeezed his shoulder. "Go to the hospital with her. I'll be here a while."

"How did you arrive so fast?" Rio murmured.

"Pure chance. I was in Cherry Hill on an errand. I arrived at the scene minutes after the accident. I'll see you at the hospital. Rio, stay with her. Seems Sutton's crew is in town after all."

He returned to Darcy. "Ready, sweetheart. Mase, Trent will want to come to the hospital. Tell him to wait until we know more. Darcy may not be admitted. If you can't convince him to wait, don't let him drive."

"We need to go, sir," Gates said.

Rio helped Darcy stand and walked with her to the ambulance. Once she was situated in the back, he tossed keys to his cousin. A minute later, the ambulance left the scene, leaving Nick and Mason behind.

"Did Nick tell you what happened?" she asked.

He squeezed her hand. "He gave the essentials. We'll talk later." When they didn't have an audience interested in their conversation.

Her gaze flicked to Gates, then returned to Rio. "Can you convince the doctor to let me go home?"

"If it's safe for you, I will." He scanned her body, noting scratches and bruises. "How are your arms and hands?"

She sighed. "They hurt."

When he got his hands on the man who did this to Darcy, he'd be the one hurting. Had this clown been trying to kill Darcy or just scare her? Rio clenched his jaw. Didn't matter. This guy would regret targeting Rio's girlfriend.

The ambulance stopped outside the emergency room doors. Rio escorted Darcy into the hospital where they were shown into an examination room.

Warren Ross strode into the room. His eyebrows rose at seeing Rio at Darcy's bedside, holding her hand. "Hi, Rio. Why are you here?"

He inclined his head toward the woman at his side. "This is Darcy St. Claire, my girlfriend. She was in a car accident and unconscious for a time."

The physician turned his attention to his patient. "I see you need stitches. Any other injuries I should be aware of?"

"Headache, body aches. I don't think I have any broken bones."

"Let's take a look. Rio, wait in the hall, buddy."

Darcy bit her lip. "Can he come back before you do stitches?" She blushed. "I don't like needles."

"Sure. I'll tell you a secret, Ms. St. Claire." Ross smiled. "I don't like needles either. We'll numb the area well before we stitch your cut."

Rio squeezed Darcy's hand before stepping into the hall to wait. Sometime in the last few minutes, the hospital had experienced an influx of new patients. He frowned. Most of them were kids. He stopped one of the nurses. "Sandy, why are so many kids here?"

"School bus accident. No serious injuries, thankfully. A few bruises, couple cuts."

"What happened?"

Sandy dropped her voice to a murmur. "I overheard the bus driver talking. He was cut off by a banged up black SUV on Highway 18. He slammed on his brakes to avoid hitting the vehicle and skidded into a ditch."

A banged up SUV? Rio wondered if it was the same one which caused Darcy's accident and maybe tried to take him out. "Thanks for the information."

"Sure." Sandy's bright blue gaze turned speculative. "I'm off this weekend, Rio. You want to catch a movie?"

"Afraid not. My girlfriend wouldn't appreciate me stepping out on her."

Shock settled on her face. "Girlfriend? When did this happen?"

"It's new."

She smiled. "Must be. I haven't heard anything on the grapevine. Who's the lucky lady?"

"Darcy St. Claire. She's opening a deli on the square next month."

"Nice. Congratulations. Well, my break is over. See you, Rio."

Rio pulled out his phone and called Nick. "The driver of the black SUV has been busy. The hospital is buzzing with reports of a school bus accident on Highway 18. Guess who caused it?"

"Why do you think it's the same vehicle?"

"Bus driver's description was a banged up black SUV. How many of those do you think we have around here?"

"Not enough to be a coincidence. I'll check it out and get back to you."

"You'll need to add another incident to your notes." He described the incident on his run, winced at the dressing down from his friend. "Sorry, Nick. My priority is Darcy, not an SUV I couldn't distinguish from other black SUVs in the area. If you weren't a cop and Madison was a target, would you have reacted any different?"

A sigh. "Probably not. How's Darcy?"

"Don't know yet. Warren kicked me out of the exam room. I'll go back in when he stitches her forehead."

"You get to hold her hand, huh? Does it bother you that someone else is doing the stitches?"

Rio thought about it. "Nope. She hates needles. I'd rather let Warren take the blame for causing her pain while

I rack up good boyfriend points for comforting and distracting her."

A chuckle from the detective.

"Nick, the accident isn't a bad coincidence, is it?"

"Not even close. Your girlfriend is lucky to be alive. After the break-in and writing on the mirror, simple theft was still a slim possibility. That is not the case anymore. If Darcy hadn't used her head, we would have found her at the bottom of the mountain. I don't know who these people are, Rio, but they're not messing around. They tried to kill your girlfriend."

CHAPTER TWENTY-FIVE

Rio assisted Darcy from his SUV. This was lousy, Darcy thought, feeling cross. Everything hurt. She was stiffer than a thousand-year-old woman. How could she play the piano when she had trouble standing much less sitting on a piano bench with no back support?

"As soon as you reassure Trent you'll live, I'll give you something for pain."

"I already turned down high-powered pain killers from the doctor. And you shouldn't have made me fill his prescription. I have a mind of my own." She closed her eyes, sighed. She really needed to shut up. Rio had taken excellent care of her despite the bad-tempered sniping. "Sorry. You didn't deserve that."

"I've heard worse from my teammates, sweetheart," he said, amusement in his tone.

"I'm not normally in such a foul mood."

He stopped, turned her into his arms and settled his hands at her waist. "Baby, don't worry about it. You're entitled to a bout of grumpiness after the day you've had."

Tears stung her eyes. Yep, time to change the subject before she descended into a storm of tears sure to alarm her boyfriend and her brother. "We should go inside before Trent comes out here."

The medic opened the door and walked inside with her.

"Darcy!" Trent struggled to his feet, limped over to embrace her with exaggerated care. "Are you okay?"

"Yes." She patted her brother's back, head resting over his heart. "Stitches in my forehead and soreness." Good thing Trent hadn't seen the car or he wouldn't be so calm.

"What happened? Did you skid?" He scowled. "You don't drive over the speed limit. Was the pavement wet?"

"I need to sit down, bro. I'll tell you everything."

Rio took her coat and purse. "I'll get you a drink to take the pain meds," he murmured.

"Thanks." She lowered herself to the couch beside Trent.

"Talk to me, sis."

Darcy clasped his hand and launched into an explanation of the afternoon's events.

Her brother grilled her for details of the black SUV and driver. "Are you sure you're okay, Darce?"

She squeezed his hand. "Positive. I'll have a headache and soreness for a few days. Other than that, no residual effects."

"Do the police have this creep in custody?"

"Not yet, although Nick is following up on a couple of things," Rio said as he handed Darcy a small soft drink and two smelly brown capsules and two white capsules.

She wrinkled her nose. "What is this?"

"The white pills are an over-the-counter pain reliever. The rank ones are Valerian root, an herb that helps with stiffness and pain. We'll save the heavy duty meds for bedtime."

Trent's eyes twinkled with amusement. "Bet the Valerian is from Sophie Winter."

"Good guess. She keeps the Fortress medics stocked with it." To Darcy, he said, "Sophie owns a vitamin shop and is married to the Fortress logistics coordinator."

With a nod, she swallowed the meds and enjoyed the first soft drink she'd had since she met Rio. "I'm surprised you brought me Coke."

A shrug from the handsome medic. "Dissolves the meds faster. Other than this, we have to stick to your diet. Your main problem right now is inflammation in the soft tissue. Anything processed, like most comfort food, will add to the inflammation."

She scowled. "Did you have to dash my dream of chicken and dumplings?"

"Sorry, sweetheart."

Right. He didn't look the least bit sorry. Her eyes narrowed. In fact, the medic looked a tiny bit smug.

The front door opened and Mason strode in, covered in dirt and cobwebs. His gaze darted straight to Darcy. "How are you, Darcy?"

"Aside from soreness, fifteen stitches, and a bad headache, I'm fine."

His lips curved. "Good to hear. Let me clean up, then we'll talk about your floor." He slipped off his boots and carried them in the direction of the mudroom.

"I'd like to do the same." Darcy finished her drink and capped the empty bottle. She couldn't wait to change out of clothes covered with airbag dust. She hoped changing clothes would alleviate the nagging tickle in her lungs making her cough, an event which wracked her sore body.

Rio lifted Darcy to her feet. "You need to keep the stitches dry, sweetheart. I have a waterproof bandage in my mike bag that should hold you long enough for a shower."

She forced a smile to her lips as she turned to Trent. "I'll be back in a bit."

"Take your time, Darce." Despite the return smile, worry darkened his gaze.

Darcy hated that look. Once he was convinced she'd live, the shadows would be gone from his eyes. Rio laced his fingers with hers and led her to his room. He opened his medic bag and pulled out a bandage. He covered the doctor's bandage with his.

"This should do it unless you let the water run over your forehead for a long time."

"No chance," she murmured. "I'm exhausted."

"Understandable. I'll walk you upstairs and wait for you."

"That's not necessary, Rio."

"Baby, you've had a shock and another adrenaline dump. You might become dizzy and weak. I want to be close in case you run into trouble. I would do the same for my teammates."

Might *become* dizzy and weak? She was already there, not that she'd tell Rio that. "I'm not your teammate."

He cupped her cheek, his touch gentle. "You're my girl and precious to me." He turned her toward the hall. "The longer you're on your feet, the less chance you have of finishing that shower without running into difficulty."

That got her moving. She wanted a shower. In her bedroom, she dropped her purse on the bed as Rio walked into the bathroom, gathered a towel and washcloth, and laid them on the counter.

He came back out, dropped a light kiss on her lips. "Warm water, babe." He slipped into the hall and eased the door almost shut. Darcy figured that was as much of a concession as she would get from him. Aware of her waning strength, she grabbed a change of clothes. By the time she finished her shower, Darcy was trembling. She dragged on her clothes, found a pair of socks, considered pulling them on herself, then thought better of it. Opening the door, she said, "Rio, would you mind helping with my socks and shoes?"

"Of course not." Her boyfriend straightened from the wall. When she sat on the bed, he dropped to his knees in front of her. "Are you hungry?"

"Starving."

After tying on her tennis shoes, he stood and held out a hand. "Let's see what's in the refrigerator. If nothing appeals, I'll run out to Delaney's."

Fortunately, Nate had left enough food to prevent Rio returning to the cold outdoors. Darcy wanted to laugh at herself. The medic had been exposed to much harsher conditions on missions than a couple minutes out in the cold.

Mason and Trent joined them in the kitchen for a meal of chicken salad sandwiches, chips, fruit, and a drink. She had the same, minus chips or bread.

Halfway through the meal, Rio's cell phone chirped. A glance at the screen and he made a call.

"Murphy."

"Zane, it's Rio. You're on speaker. What can you tell me?"

"Troy Sutton is a three-time loser. Spent ten years as a guest of the state. Three convictions on burglary charges. All high-end stuff."

"Must not be top of the food chain if he got caught three times."

"Not even close. His only claim to fame is he attempted to steal the Collinsworth diamonds in Memphis. That attempt landed him behind bars for three years."

"What about Allen White?"

Darcy's fork slipped out of her hand. "Allen? You're investigating my agent?"

"Hello, Darcy," Zane said after a pause. "How are you, sugar?"

"A little worse for wear."

"What happened?"

She gave her friend a condensed version of the afternoon's events. "I'm bruised, but fine."

"Rio?"

Darcy frowned at the cell phone. "Hey, I'm still here. You think I'm lying to you?"

"Nope. Downplaying the seriousness of your injuries like your brother does."

She turned her gaze to Trent. "Is that right? What did you tell him about this round of injuries?"

Her brother shrugged. "That it was just a scratch."

She rolled her eyes. No wonder Zane questioned her honesty.

"She sustained a cut to her forehead which required fifteen stitches," Rio answered. "Other than that, she has a headache, bruises, and soreness that I suspect will take a while to dissipate."

"Just bruises, huh?" Zane's sarcasm came through the phone loud and clear.

"What about White?" the medic prompted.

"In debt up to his ears and desperate for Darcy to go back on the road."

"I don't understand," Darcy said. "He's one of the most sought after agents on the circuit."

"That was before he started representing you five years ago. White spent most of his time on the road with you, leaving a junior agent in charge of the office and all of his other clients. The junior agent didn't pay attention to details or cater to the clients as White did for you. He's down to a handful of clients and his lifestyle can't be sustained by the few he represents as none of them are the powerhouses that you are."

"Were," she corrected.

"Sugar, you've been off the concert stage a few weeks. Trust me, you still have the ability to pack a performance hall."

"How long has White been in Otter Creek?" Rio asked.

"His credit card bill shows he registered at the motel two weeks ago."

Darcy's breath escaped in a whoosh. Allen lied to her. She wondered what other lies he'd told.

"What about Gretchen Bond?" Rio asked.

"Stella's looking into Ms. Bond and the house. Maddox pulled me off your search to support another team."

"When you have time, keep digging into White and Sutton. I want to know if there's any connection between the two. See if you can uncover the identity of Sutton's crew."

"Copy that."

"Did you check into Doug Walsh?"

"He's a real jewel. In and out of prison for theft and assault since he was 18. His name also popped up in a few suspicious deaths in prison, but the officials had no proof he was involved. He also hails from around Otter Creek. Darcy, be careful, sugar. Got a feeling we're only seeing on the surface."

That made two of them. She shivered as goosebumps surged up her spine, hoping no one else would be hurt before they figured out what was worth killing over.

CHAPTER TWENTY-SIX

Once the others were asleep, Rio settled onto the recliner and called his team leader.

"How's Darcy?" were the first words out of Josh's mouth.

"Sleeping off a massive headache. Stitches in her forehead, soft tissue damage."

"I saw what was left of her car. She's lucky to be alive, Rio."

"I know." Just remembering the state of her car sent a fresh surge of fury through his body. His hand clenched around the phone. "You on patrol tonight?"

"I'm on duty in a couple hours. What do you need?"

"Keep an eye on the motel. Darcy's agent lied about how long he's been in town. Makes me wonder if there's something else he's lying about." He summarized Zane's information.

Josh whistled softly. "Gives him motive to encourage your girl to return to the performance stage."

"Even if she agreed, it would only be for a short time."

A pause, then, "Moving fast, aren't you, Rio?"

He frowned, thought through what he'd said. "I didn't mean that like it sounded." Although claiming Darcy for his own permanently appealed more than he'd ever dreamed. "Darcy's health won't allow her to continue in that career."

"Trent didn't say anything about her health."

"He won't until she agrees to share the news. The last thing Darcy wants is publicity on this."

"Her agent isn't as discriminating?"

"Exactly. I warned him about talking to the press, but that's no guarantee he won't capitalize on the publicity."

A snort from his friend. "You and Trent will mop the floor with him if he does."

"White thinks I'm all brawn and no brain."

"Then he's a fool. Don't worry. I'll swing by the motel several times during my shift."

"Thanks. Is it too late to call your father?"

"He'll be up for another hour at least. Mom's a night owl."

He wanted to set an appointment to ask about Gretchen Bond. Though he wanted to learn what he could as soon as possible, Rio was due at PSI in the morning. Trent was mobile enough to care for himself. Plus, Mason had been given the green light to work on shoring up Darcy's floor, which meant he'd be available if they needed help. "Great. I'll call him in a bit. Darcy and I have questions about Ms. Bond."

"He's the man to ask. If he doesn't know, Mom probably does. She might not contribute to the Otter Creek grapevine, but she's plugged into it. You still off tomorrow?"

"Nope. Johnson's wife is scheduled for a C-section tomorrow." A minute later, Rio ended the call and dialed Aaron Cahill's number. Liz answered the phone. "It's Rio. Hope I'm not calling too late."

"Of course not. What can I do for you, Rio?"

"I need to speak to Aaron."

"Sure. And stop by when you have time, son. It's been too long since we've had a chance to visit."

Warmth spread through him. "I'll do that. I want to introduce you to Darcy."

"Come to dinner one night so we'll have time to get acquainted."

"I'll talk to Darcy and get back to you."

"Here's Aaron."

"What do you need, son?"

"A little time with you. My girlfriend and I have questions about Gretchen Bond."

A chuckle from Josh's father. "Girlfriend, huh? You have excellent taste, my friend. She reminds me of Liz when we were dating."

Rio had to grin at that comment. He loved watching Aaron and Liz Cahill. They were obviously in love even after so many years of marriage.

"When is a good time for you and your girl?"

"One evening. I return to work at PSI tomorrow."

"Hold on a minute." After a muffled conversation with Liz, he returned. "Why don't you come to dinner tomorrow night?"

"Darcy's asleep right now. I'll ask her in the morning if that's not too late to confirm with Liz."

"That's fine. Josh tells me an injured teammate is in town. Invite him along with Mason."

"Thank you, sir. Tell Liz Darcy can't eat anything processed."

"I'll do that. So you and Darcy want to know about Ms. Bond. Does this have anything to do with her murder?"

"We're hoping you can help us figure that out. Strange things are happening in connection with the house."

After ending the call to Aaron, Rio stared at his phone a minute, then made one final call.

"Yeah, Elliott."

"It's Rio."

"What's up?"

"Are you sending someone to help Mason tomorrow?"

"Planned on it. Why?"

"Don't send Doug Walsh."

"Why not?"

"He has a record, Brian. I don't want him near Darcy."

"Two things. One, he served his time and deserves a chance, just like your cousin deserves one. Two, Walsh is my employee, not yours. You do not have the right to tell me which employees I send on a job." Rage vibrated in the contractor's voice.

Rio's own temper spiked. "You're a professional, Brian. So am I. Security is my business. Darcy's safety is my top priority. Assign someone else to assist Mason, or PSI will reconsider hiring Elliott Construction for any future projects." A potent threat as PSI had many campus buildings in the planning stages.

"You play hardball," he muttered.

"When it comes to the wellbeing of the woman I care about, count on it."

"All right. I'll keep Walsh at the deli." Elliott ended the call.

Rio checked the locks and security system, then got ready for bed. When he turned out the light, the memory of Darcy's crushed car and blood-streaked face kept him awake long into the night.

When his alarm blared at four in the morning, he growled and turned off the blasted thing before dragging himself out of bed and into his running clothes and shoes. Some days, leading by example hurt more than others. This day was one of those. Of course, it didn't help that he'd tossed and turned until just after one. When he'd fallen asleep, his dreams had been a nasty mixture of Delta missions gone wrong interspersed with Darcy's accident.

Rio yanked on a knit hat and stepped outside. The frigid air slapped him in the face, a sharp wakeup in the quiet hour before dawn. He set a slow pace, allowing his muscles to warm.

Half a mile from Darcy's house, a prowl car slowed to a crawl beside him. He glanced over. "Morning, Major."

Instead of a return greeting, Josh leaned over and opened the passenger door. "Get in."

Rio's eyebrows rose. He recognized an order from his team leader when he heard it. "Yes, sir." What was going on? Josh didn't say anything on the drive to Darcy's.

Nick Santana's vehicle sat in the driveway. He got out of the car as soon as Josh parked.

Not good. A ball of ice formed in his stomach. Something was definitely wrong. He glanced toward the house, noted the lights. "Darcy?"

"Let's go inside," Josh murmured.

He scrambled from the patrol car, ran up the porch stairs, and threw open the front door. Trent climbed to his feet, clad in sleep pants and a t-shirt declaring that the Navy ruled. "Where is she?"

"Kitchen."

He ran, not daring to slow until he'd seen with his own eyes that she was safe. "Darcy."

She spun. "Rio." Darcy drew a deep breath, relief flooding her expression. "I was worried. Nick and Josh wouldn't tell me what they wanted."

He blinked. They were looking for him? Why? He lifted her chin and kissed her. "You're okay? Nothing happened while I was running?"

"We're fine."

"How do you feel?"

"Not bad, considering."

One by one, Rio's muscles relaxed. He turned as Nick and Josh walked into the kitchen. Rio glanced at Nick, but his main attention focused on Josh. His teammate was grim. This wasn't going to be good. "What's wrong?"

"We need to ask you some questions," Nick said. "We can do this here or at the station. Your choice."

"Here, provided I can shower off the sweat before you grill me." There was no doubt in his mind that that was what his friend intended. Did Nick remember that Rio was Special Forces, trained to deal with interrogations? He figured it wouldn't be in his best interests to remind the cop of his training.

The detective gave a curt nod. "Don't take long." He signaled Josh to go with him.

Rio's fists clenched. "That isn't necessary." Did Nick think he had so little honor as to dive out a window and take off rather than face trouble head on? And, yeah, he knew there was trouble. Otherwise, the detective wouldn't be here so early in the morning. No one delivered good news this time of day.

"Stand down," Josh murmured. "It's standard operating procedure. Nick's just doing his job."

"I don't know what you think I've done, Detective, but I'm not a flight risk."

Nick sighed, his expression troubled. "No one said you were. Get moving, Rio. We'll sort everything out when you've cleaned up."

Face burning, Rio yanked off his shirt on the way to his room. He snatched his work clothes. "You camping in the bathroom with me, Major? We both know I could slip out the window and be gone before Santana could sound the alarm." And that was probably why the detective had sent Josh to babysit. Only Josh and a healthy Trent stood a chance of stopping him.

Josh scowled at him. "Hurry up, Kincaid. I have a breakfast date with my wife in a couple hours." He sat in an armchair facing the bathroom door and pulled out his cell phone. Seconds later, his tone softened when his call was answered. "Morning, beautiful." His team leader waved at Rio to proceed.

He knew better than to demand answers from his teammate. On missions, he kept Durango in the information loop because their lives depended on it. In the civilian world, however, Josh answered to others higher in rank, including Nick.

After a quick shower and shave, Rio emerged from the bathroom dressed in black camouflage pants and long-sleeved t-shirt. He laced up his combat boots while Josh finished his call to Del, then strapped on his holster and weapon.

His teammate stood.

"Advice?"

"You need an alibi for the hours between ten last night and two this morning."

"Then I'm out of luck. I don't have much of one except sleep." Well, trying to sleep anyway. Between insomnia and nightmares, his few minutes of sleep was anything but restful. He strode down the hall with Durango's leader close on his heels.

Rio returned to the kitchen where Darcy handed him a mug of steaming coffee. "Thanks, sweetheart." He eyed the detective sitting at the table, holding his own mug of coffee. "What's this about, Nick?"

His friend motioned for him to sit. "Where were you last night and this morning between ten and two?"

"Here. Darcy, Trent, and Mason all went to bed about that time. I called Josh at 10:30, then talked to Aaron and Liz about 10:45. That conversation lasted until around 11:00. Then I called Brian Elliott. After that, I went to bed and got up at 4:00 to run. Your turn, Santana. What is this about?"

"Troy Sutton was murdered last night."

CHAPTER TWENTY-SEVEN

"Murdered?" Rio's stomach knotted. "And you think I did it?" Nice. What happened to trust? Nick should know him well enough by now to offer him the benefit of the doubt. And his teammate, Josh, had been in the trenches of war with him for years. Did he really think Rio would stoop as low as murder? "I thought he was in jail."

"He was released late yesterday afternoon."

He scowled. "And you didn't tell us? Thought you were supposed to protect and serve, Nick."

"Sergeant," Josh snapped.

Nick held up one hand, fending off Josh's dressing down, the other hand clenched around the mug, the only sign of his irritation at Rio's remark. "I'm not on day shift this month, Kincaid," he said, his tone mild. "I was working Darcy's accident and didn't find out Sutton made bail until I identified the body at the crime scene."

Darcy laid her hand on Rio's shoulder as she set a plate with two wraps on it in front of him. She squeezed his shoulder before grabbing more plates for Nick, Trent, Mason, and Josh.

Rio downed one of the wraps before trusting himself to talk. Though he knew the food was good, the turmoil in his gut made the wrap taste as bland as sawdust. "How did Sutton die?"

A glance at Darcy before the detective answered. "He was beaten to death."

Color drained from his girlfriend's face. "Sit down, sweetheart." Rio pulled out the chair next to his for her and rose to nuke some chamomile tea. "My hands don't have injuries, Nick."

"Didn't say anything about the perp using his hands."

He glanced over his shoulder as he closed the microwave door. "Do you know what weapon was used?"

"Hammer."

Darcy buried her face in her hands. "Oh, no."

Nick straightened. "Know something I don't?"

"How long have you lived here, Nick?" Rio asked.

"Almost two years. Why?"

"The previous owner of this house was a homicide victim. Ms. Bond was beaten to death with a hammer."

Nick's gaze darted to Josh. "Any arrests?"

"Nope. It's a cold case. Ms. Bond died a few months before Ethan arrived. Detective Beauchamp worked the case until the trail went cold. By the time Ethan came, the old police chief was gone and Beauchamp had died from a heart attack. Rod brings the case out every few months and looks it over, but hasn't turned up any leads."

Darcy frowned. "Who's Rod?"

"Rod Kelter. He's married to my other sister, Megan. She's the editor of the town newspaper."

"Isn't Sutton's manner of death a coincidence?" Mason asked. "Every wanna-be handyman has a hammer."

Josh's lips curled. "There are no coincidences in law enforcement."

"He's right." Nick grabbed his empty plate and took it to the dishwasher as the microwave signaled the end of the heating cycle for Darcy's tea. "This house is the connection between Sutton and Ms. Bond's murder. He wanted something bad enough to try and scare Darcy into leaving the premises. And now that he's been murdered in the same manner as Bond? No, it's not a coincidence."

"Same perp?" Josh asked.

"I'll pull Bond's file and compare it to Sutton's. I might ask Stella to look at the Bond case, see if she comes up with anything."

"It's all connected, isn't it?" Trent asked, a dark frown on his face. "How much danger is my sister in?"

"I don't know." The detective leaned back against the counter, arms folded across his chest. "Don't go anywhere alone, Darcy."

She gave him a wan smile. "No worries, Nick. I don't have a car now, remember?"

Trent's attention shifted to his sister. "Is your car in a body shop?"

"More likely the junkyard," Mason muttered.

"That bad?"

"I doubt the insurance company will bother repairing it," Darcy said. "Even if they do, I'm getting rid of it. I want an SUV that can handle the mountainous terrain along with snow and ice in the winter."

Satisfaction surged through Rio at her words. "I'll help you find something, baby."

She smiled as he pressed the mug into her hands. "I hoped you might."

"You downplayed the severity of the accident," Trent accused her.

"Would I do that?" she asked, a look of pure innocence on her face.

He scowled.

"Do I need to go to the station, Nick?" Rio asked.

The detective waved that off. "I'll confirm your conversation with Liz, Aaron, and Brian. If I have other questions concerning your whereabouts or any evidence I uncover points to you being at the scene of the crime, I'll track you down and haul you to the station."

"Fair enough."

"Why did you think Rio was responsible for Sutton's death?" Darcy asked. "He wouldn't murder someone."

Rio, Josh, and Trent all stiffened. A twinge of uneasiness rolled through Rio's gut. She knew what Trent did for a living. Rio worked for the same group. Killing someone was not his first choice, but he'd do it without hesitation if his teammates' lives depended on it. He'd do the same thing for Darcy and Mason. Could she handle his job?

"Rio cares about you. Anyone around you two sees it. Do I think he killed Sutton? No. Is he capable? Oh, yeah. The military does a fantastic job training their soldiers. I never served in the military, but I am well aware of the lengths Rio would go to in protecting you. If he thought your life was in jeopardy from Sutton, he'd do whatever was necessary to ensure your safety."

"I don't doubt about that. But cold-blooded murder with a hammer? Absolutely not. If Rio wanted him dead, he wouldn't have needed a hammer. He knows many ways to kill with his bare hands. Sutton could have hurt me the night he broke in. Instead, he left a message in lipstick on my mirror. Rio did not kill him."

"And if Rio believed Sutton was responsible for your accident? Do you think he wouldn't track Sutton and exact revenge?" Nick tilted his head. "If Trent was in better shape, he could have taken out Sutton himself, as could Josh. Durango team has the skills to get away with the crime and the ability to slip in and out without being seen. They're men of integrity, though. If one of them killed Sutton, they would have called the police and surrendered immediately. I suspect your brother has the same integrity. Do I think one of them killed him? No, but I have to follow procedure and eliminate suspects. The nature of the crime and Sutton's previous threat to you led me to Rio. I'll confirm his alibi and move on."

"Why aren't you questioning me?" she asked, temper glittering in her gaze. "I could have used a hammer on him to protect myself or my boyfriend."

Trent flinched at that declaration.

Rio turned her head gently toward him. "Nick's trying to help."

"By blaming you for something you would never do?"

"Don't kid yourself, Darce." Trent placed his empty mug on the table with a solid thump. "Durango's medic might appear as if nothing riles him, but he's just as fierce a fighter on the battlefield as the rest of his unit. He's Delta, sis. That makes him one of the most dangerous men on the planet." He stopped, smirked. "Even if he isn't a SEAL."

Rio snorted, then refocused on the woman seated next to him. "You don't have to defend me, Darcy."

"Nick should question me, too," she insisted. "I could have done it."

"Not possible, baby. First, the pain medicine Doc Ross prescribed knocked you out. I checked on you twice before I turned in. You didn't budge either time. Second, I don't think your joint issues would allow you to beat a man to death with a hammer. Unless you were very lucky on the first strike, Sutton would have overpowered you. Third, I suspect your hands and arms are still sore from the accident. Fourth, you don't have it in you to hurt someone deliberately in cold blood. To defend yourself or someone you love from imminent danger, absolutely. Otherwise, no. That's just not you."

Nick's lips edged up. "In the interest of fairness, I'll get statements from Darcy, Trent, and Mason as well."

Rio wanted to laugh at the satisfaction on his girlfriend's face, but decided it wasn't wise. Their statements would consist of one paragraph, two at the most if Nick stretched it.

His gaze shifted to Trent. The other Fortress operative wasn't taking heavy-duty pain meds anymore. If Rio had left the house to confront Sutton, Trent might have heard him. Moot point, though. He hadn't left the house.

"Rio didn't leave the house," Trent told Nick.

"How do you know? Weren't you asleep?"

A quick grin from the operative. "Not that asleep. I took a couple of over-the-counter pain relievers. I checked all the windows and walked every inch of the first floor yesterday afternoon. The windows creak when you raise them and the floors groan everywhere."

"Rio could have learned which boards squeak and avoided them," Nick pointed out.

"If he had time. He didn't."

A nod from the detective. He pulled out his notebook and pen. "Mason, we'll start with you." Within a few minutes, he had statements from all three of them. "Darcy, do you have a cell phone?"

She nodded.

"Good. Keep it with you, even in the house." A wry smile curved his lips. "Sutton already proved this place isn't all that secure."

"That changes today," Trent said. "Fortress will be installing a security system."

"We both know security systems are only a deterrent. Someone determined to get in here will find a way." Nick shoved the notebook back into his pocket and grabbed his coat from the back of the chair he'd occupied. "Darcy, thanks for feeding me breakfast. I'm looking forward to the opening of your deli. Josh, you're with me."

Amusement lit his eyes. "Yes, sir," he murmured. He rose, leaned down and kissed Darcy's cheek. "Thanks for taking pity on hungry cops." His gaze locked with Rio's.

"Call Murphy," he murmured before following Nick from the house.

"What did he mean by that?" Darcy asked.

"Nick can't tell me what he found at the crime scene and I won't put Josh in a bad place by asking him for information known only to law enforcement. But he must think there's something I need to know or he wouldn't have encouraged me to contact Zane."

"I don't understand," Mason said, a frown on his face. "What does Josh think Zane can do? He's not a cop and he's not here."

Trent grinned. "Zane Murphy is one of the best hackers in the business. I doubt OCPD's computer system will be a challenge. As soon as Nick enters the information in his computer, Z will have access to what Rio needs without compromising Josh."

Rio's cousin whistled softly. "You guys are scary."

"Nope, just good at what we do." Rio rose and cleared his plate and coffee mug. He glanced at the time, grimaced. "I need to go. I have a session in thirty minutes. Mase, keep an eye on things today."

"Count on it."

Trent rose. "Might as well take a shower. The Fortress techs will be here in an hour." He punched Rio lightly in the shoulder as he passed.

"I'll walk you to the door," Darcy said. She followed him to the living room where he'd deposited his mike and Go bags by the door before his run.

He turned and circled her waist with his arms. "Be careful today, sweetheart."

She studied his expression a moment. "You're worried."

"Someone tried to force you off the mountain side yesterday. You bet I'm worried."

"I have Trent and Mason here with me as well as whatever techs Fortress sends. I'll be fine. If anything weird happens, I'll call you."

"Thank you." He leaned down and brushed her lips with his. "I spoke to Aaron and Liz Cahill last night after you went to bed. They invited all of us to dinner tonight."

"The faster we uncover information, the better."

"It's not too soon after your accident?" He trailed the back of his fingers over her cheek. "I don't want to make you hurt more."

"I won't hurt any less by staying here. I'm looking forward to meeting Josh's parents. I've heard good things about them from Del and Madison."

His cheeks burned. "They sort of adopted Durango. Aaron and Liz are like second parents."

"In other words, be prepared for a grilling?"

"They won't be that bad." Maybe. Probably. He blew out a breath. "They'll love you. How could they not?"

"You are a keeper, Rio Kincaid." Darcy tugged his head down for a long, deep kiss. "Text me the time to be ready."

After another kiss, he grabbed his bags and left. While he waited for his SUV to warm up, Rio sent a text to another Delta teammate who now provided special order vehicles. Hopefully, Bear would have the type of vehicle Rio wanted for Darcy. If his relationship with her continued long term, he needed the security of knowing she was as protected as possible when driving.

On the drive to PSI, Rio called Zane. He hoped the tech geek wasn't too busy to do more digging.

CHAPTER TWENTY-EIGHT

Darcy shivered as she closed the door behind Rio. Man, it was frigid outside. She hoped the PSI trainees had sessions indoors today. Otherwise, all the trainers would be outside with them.

She returned to the kitchen to find Mason putting the last of the breakfast dishes in the dishwasher. "Thanks, Mason."

He shrugged. "You cooked. This is the least I could do. Brian is sending another worker over to bring supplies and give me a hand. He should be here by seven."

"This place will be busy today." Darcy's cell phone chirped in her pocket. She glanced at the screen, eyebrows winging upward. What did he want?

"Darcy? Everything okay?"

"It's nothing. Do you know when the floor will be ready? I'd like to schedule the piano delivery."

"Tomorrow night at the latest. I may be finished tonight, but I wanted to allow extra time in case I run into something unexpected."

"Josh Cahill's parents invited us all to dinner tonight."

A ghost of a smile curved his mouth, a mannerism that reminded her so much of Rio. "That would be an unexpected thing. I should finish the floor."

She squeezed his hand. "The invitation included you, and you should go. Mason, this is your new home. You have to make connections in Otter Creek. For that matter, so do I."

He glanced away. "Not many people will accept me."

"Give them a chance. We can't focus on the folks who reject us. This is a new start. We'll make friends and prove ourselves worthy of trust. That's all we can do."

His gaze locked on hers. "I could screw up again."

She regarded him in silence for a moment. "Do you plan on drinking and driving?"

A shudder wracked his body. "No. I don't want to return to prison. The incessant noise, smells, watching my back all the time." He shook his head. "I can't handle that again. More important, I won't ever forget the price of my stupidity. Every time I sleep, I see the faces of that mother and baby."

"Did you know the family, Mason?"

"She was a classmate. That's bad enough. Worse, her family sends me age-progressed pictures of them every year on the anniversary of their deaths." He swallowed hard. "Even if I wanted to forget the consequences of my actions, which I don't, the family won't let me."

Darcy's heart ached for Rio's cousin. She understood the family was devastated by the loss of their loved ones. But he'd paid a heavy price for his mistake. He deserved a second chance. "Is that why you decided to come to Otter Creek instead of going home?"

Hurt darkened his eyes. "The Fitzgeralds stirred my hometown into a feeding frenzy. Dad's received threats, people promising to kill me if I showed my face in town again."

Oh, man. How devastating for Mason and his family to spend so many years apart and still not be able to be together. "So you came to Rio?"

"Dad sent me to him. My guess is he wanted to be sure I stayed out of trouble."

More likely, his father wanted Mason to have protection if the Fitzgeralds came after him. "You and Rio were close growing up?"

"We had fun together. Played on the same ball teams. We lost touch when Rio entered the military and I went to college. He's a good man, Darcy."

She sipped her protein shake. "I know. I've heard nothing but good things about him for months. The Fortress operatives are impressed with his skill."

Mason's cell phone signaled an incoming call. He checked the screen, smiled. "Excuse me. It's my father." He swiped the screen and pressed the phone to his ear. "Hi, Dad." Rio's cousin left the kitchen, heading toward the living room.

Darcy drank her shake before pulling out her own cell phone. She scowled at the second text from her agent. She didn't want to deal with him today, especially this early. For that matter, why was he awake? Allen didn't like seeing the sun rise in the mornings. Beyond that, he'd lied to her about when he arrived in Otter Creek. Could she really trust anything he said?

If she had to deal with him today, at least Trent and Mason would be on hand along with the Fortress techs. Without a vehicle, she couldn't meet him anywhere.

Another text message came in. Allen again? A check of the screen had her smiling. Stella. She placed the call to her friend. "You're up early."

"Nick called and told me Sutton is dead. Nasty business, Darcy."

"Tell me about it. Rio and Trent are both worried. To tell the truth, I'm worried, too. I can't imagine what was so valuable in this house that a group of thieves is killing for it. This house was full of junk."

She'd seen what the PSI trainees carted from the house. While she was in Texas with her brother, Rio's teammates had sent pictures. Just more of the same items. There had been nothing in this place worth keeping except the candles and the miniature piano.

"I saw pictures of your car. These guys think you know something."

"That's ridiculous. All I've done is clean out the house with help from friends and acquaintances. I don't even know what they want."

"I may have some information on that. Is it all right if I stop by?"

"Sure. Fair warning, though. Fortress techs will be here by seven to install a security system."

A soft laugh came through the phone. "At least I don't have to worry about that. Nate already had a top-of-the-line system in place when we married. The grapevine says your car is toast. Do I need to pick up anything for you?"

"The only thing I need is company to keep my mind busy."

"That I can do, at least for a couple hours. See you in a few minutes."

Darcy washed her glass and straw and gulped the rest of her tea. By the time she finished, the doorbell rang, if you could call it that. She cringed at the flat, irritating chime. Definitely time for something new. Maybe it was the musician in her, but she couldn't stand those discordant notes long term. She sighed as she walked to the door. The list of things to replace or repair was growing longer by the day. Her lips curved upward. If she could find a pen and paper, she'd be in business.

"Don't open the door without checking!" Trent yelled from his room.

She scowled toward the hall. Did her brother think she was an idiot? She crossed to the peephole. Stella stood on the porch, two hot drinks in a carrier in her hands. Coffee? Hot chocolate? Contemplating sipping either choice made her mouth water. And Rio wasn't around to know if she cheated. She unlocked the door.

Stella smiled. "Nate thought you would like something hot."

"Wise man, your husband. Come in from the cold." She closed the door behind the detective. "Is he working at PSI today?"

"Oh, yeah. You should have heard him gripe this morning when he left to run his five miles. The trainees will have a couple sessions outdoors today. None of the guys are looking forward to it."

Darcy flinched. "Five miles, huh?"

"Each member of Durango runs that far or more every morning."

She eyed the trim woman walking beside her to the kitchen. "What about you?"

Stella waggled her cast-covered arm. "I get a pass until this thing is off. Five more weeks to go." She set the carrier on breakfast bar and shed her cold weather gear. "After that, I'll have to lace up my running shoes. Wouldn't do for the criminals to outrun me."

Darcy climbed on the barstool beside Stella. "What did you bring? Coffee? Chocolate?"

"Nate sent blueberry green tea. If you like it, he'll bring you a supply to keep here."

She eased a cup from the carrier and sipped. An explosion of blueberry flavor had her closing her eyes in delight. "Tell your husband I want a big supply. This is fabulous."

"Isn't it?" Stella grinned. "He made this for me on our honeymoon. His mother loves tea and thinks it's fun to mix her own. This is one of her blends."

"Tell him to send me a bill and a steady supply." Another sip, then, "What did you find out, Stella?"

Before she answered, Trent limped into the kitchen, dressed, weapon in hand. The detective stiffened at the sight of the weapon. "Forgotten me so soon, Trent?"

He stopped, furrowed his brow before a smile crept across his mouth. "Stella, right? Good to see you again. How's Nate treating you?"

"Like a princess. We just returned from our honeymoon."

"I heard. Congratulations." He slid his weapon into the holster at his mid-back. "He's a good man, for an Army grunt. Any coffee left, Darce?"

She waved toward the coffee pot. "Help yourself." She glanced at Stella. "I'll make vats of the stuff by day's end."

"Durango lives on it, especially when they're on a mission."

"How do you know?"

Stella's face flushed. "I've been involved in two of their missions. That's how I met Nate. The third time, I was the mission."

"Now that sounds like an interesting story. Can you tell me?"

"Some parts of it. Others are still classified. When we have time and no company strolling through, I'll tell you." She paused. "In fact, we should ask Del and Alex's wife, Ivy, to join us. They're part of the story."

"Oh, this will be good. How about a girls night when Sutton's crew is behind bars?"

"I'd rather not wait until we have these guys rounded up. There's always another case to solve or crisis to avert."

"Do you like Mexican food?"

"Love it."

"We'll plan a meal here for us and let Durango have their own guys night at your place. That way we don't have to worry about being interrupted."

Mason walked in, shoving his phone into his pocket. He pulled up short. "Sorry. I didn't mean to interrupt."

Stella smiled. "You must be Mason. I'm Stella Armstrong. My husband, Nate, is a teammate of Rio's."

He shook hands with her. "Nice to meet you, Stella. Darcy, the other man from Elliott Construction will be here in fifteen minutes and we'll start on your floor."

"I can't wait to have my piano shipped here. I've missed playing whenever I want."

"I'm going to change into clothes I don't mind messing up." After he left, Trent also excused himself to wait in the living room for the Fortress techs, full coffee mug in hand.

"Darcy, do you know anything about the history of your house?"

She shook her head. "Mrs. Watson didn't tell me anything except Ms. Bond's family members didn't want to be bothered with the place. After seeing all the stuff piled in this house, I understand their reasoning. Why?"

"Ms. Bond wasn't the only person murdered in this house."

CHAPTER TWENTY-NINE

Darcy's stomach knotted. "You're serious?"

"I'm afraid so." Stella laid her hand on Darcy's forearm and squeezed gently. "There have been two other murders in its 135-year history."

"I'm assuming the other murders were back a ways. Mrs. Watson said Ms. Bond lived here sixty years."

"Charles Rockingham, the man who built the house, found his wife in bed with another man and killed her and her lover. Whatever passed for law enforcement in those days hung Rockingham on the tree in the backyard."

Darcy's stomach pitched and rolled. She glanced out the windows of the French doors to the yard. Only one tree. Since she wouldn't be able to look at the thing without remembering Rockingham dying on it, that tree was coming down as soon as possible. Stupid sentiment, maybe, but she couldn't enjoy this place while seeing that tree and remembering the previous owner. When spring came, she'd see about planting a blue spruce or maybe some maple trees. "Please tell me the town fathers buried him somewhere else."

"He's occupying a plot in the Otter Creek Cemetery."

A breath of relief whooshed out. "And the other death?"

"The house sat empty for a number of years. The town residents believed the house was haunted by the ghosts of Alice Rockingham and James Edwards, her lover. About twenty years after their deaths, a family moved to town who were unaware of the tragic events until after they bought the house and moved in. The Nelsons had two children, ages seven and nine."

"Please tell me the kids lived a long and happy life."

Stella's hand tightened on Darcy's arm. "Elizabeth and William Nelson and their children lived here ten years. One stormy night, a band of thieves broke in and tried to force William to give them a king's ransom in silver dollars. Of course, he didn't know anything about any silver coins, but the thieves didn't believe him. In their desire to force information from the father, they ended up killing him."

"What about his family?"

"They were witnesses, Darcy. The thieves couldn't allow them to live without forfeiting their own lives. The whole family died that night."

"How long was the house empty?"

"Until the Grahams purchased it twenty years later."

"No tragic deaths when they lived here?"

"Not that I could find."

"I'm thankful for that," she murmured. "At least there was some happiness in this house. What about Ms. Bond?"

"She lived here with her husband for many years. Calvin died about twenty-five years ago. They didn't have children. She willed the house to a niece, but she's in her sixties and doesn't want to leave her grandchildren in California. She decided to sell the place and split the money with her two brothers."

"So you're telling me the break-ins and the SUV trying to run me off the side of a mountain stems back to silver dollars?" Skepticism rang in her voice. "That's unbelievable."

"Because we don't obsess over silver coins. Wouldn't you value the first Steinway ever created?"

"Of course." Just the possibility of playing on that piano made her heart beat faster.

"My preference is handguns." The detective smiled. "My collection pales in comparison to Nate's."

Darcy frowned. "How many does he have?"

"Too many to count. He has four full-sized gun safes at capacity."

"Incredible."

Stella sent her a pointed look. "Don't kid yourself, Darcy. Rio is just as well armed."

"I thought he might be. Trent owns a stash that size. So, silver dollars, huh?"

"I scanned newspapers from 1900 when Rockingham killed his wife. He was president of the Otter Creek bank and, according to the reporter, had a treasure trove of Morgan silver dollars."

"Did the article mention how many?"

She shook her head. "Charles was cagey. He never admitted how many he owned. His wife was the one bragging about the coins."

"Wouldn't he place the coins in the bank?"

"Like many in those days, he didn't fully trust the banks. Too many runs on them. Remember, the Federal Reserve wasn't in existence yet. To hedge his bets, he hid part of his wealth in the house."

"How much is a Morgan silver dollar worth?"

"In mint condition, people pay anywhere from $150 to $5,000 for each one, especially if it was never in circulation. Unlike today's coins which are made of cheap metals, the Morgan silver dollars were ninety percent silver."

"Sutton's crew would kill for that?"

"I've known people who killed for less. Trust me, Morgan silver dollars are rare enough to capture Sutton's attention. One of his crew turned on him."

"How did Sutton learn about the coins?"

"That I don't know yet. I'll keep digging, see if I can figure it out. We should ask Del if she's heard anything. Librarians and booksellers hear all kinds of things and they rock at research. I would ask Maeve, the woman who owns the beauty parlor, but according to Josh, she couldn't keep a secret if her life depended on it. If she knows information, it's out on the grapevine within minutes. I don't think it's wise to let Sutton's crew know we're tracking down leads."

What leads? She didn't want to dampen Stella's optimism, but this was conjecture. "How do we know one of the other families didn't find the coins and spend them?"

"We don't. I think there's a written record somewhere, like a diary. It was common practice then, especially for women. Writing letters and keeping journals were an important part of life." She smiled. "They didn't have social media feeds."

The doorbell chimed again. Darcy sighed. "That has to be changed. It's like hearing fingernails scratching a chalkboard."

Stella laughed. "It's pretty bad."

Her brother limped into the kitchen. "Fortress is here, Darce."

"I'll start a new pot of coffee." Within minutes, the scent of the bracing brew drew techs into the kitchen for a cup before they started work. Trent acted more energized than he had for a week. She smiled at him barking out orders to the techs.

Stella glanced at her watch. "I have to report to the station in an hour. I know the bodyguards cleared most of the house. Is there anything I can help with?" She scowled at her cast. "No heavy lifting, obviously."

"I still have three rooms on the third floor to work on. We'll see what's in them. I'm not sure how much I can do today, but I can form a plan for what's left."

"Great." Stella smiled. "Now I have a legitimate excuse to see this beautiful lady."

"Not much to see yet. However, I did buy furniture for the house."

"Are you serious? The whole house?"

Darcy still couldn't believe she bought that much on impulse. "I couldn't resist when the saleswoman offered to cut the price in half if I bought all of it. The furniture store is holding everything until the contractor's finished. Come on. I'll give you a tour."

Minutes later, Darcy walked into the first of the three cluttered bedrooms.

"This place was a fire trap." Stella walked slowly into the slim path. "Ceramic tile?" The detective turned the closest box so she and Darcy could see the tile. "This is gorgeous, Darcy. Italian marble. There must be enough to do at least a couple bathrooms if you like it."

"What's not to like?" The smoky gray tile would be perfect in the guest bathrooms on each floor. She could already picture the accents in the bathrooms. "Including something Ms. Bond collected in the finished product is fitting."

"Do you know if there are holes in these last rooms?"

"The bodyguards didn't say. It doesn't look as if they made it into these rooms."

"I only saw the living room after it was cleared some. Nate took pictures of the untouched rooms, though. We noticed there was an order to the chaos."

Darcy stared at her. "I only saw the potential for a disastrous implosion. What did you see?"

"Piles of books and magazines. Folded clothes. Boxed shoes. Each room had such things, but they were organized. I'm not sure what Ms. Bond intended to do with everything, but I don't believe she intended to stockpile them permanently."

"Maybe her health or energy level prevented her from carrying out her plan. Annie, Del's helper, was her best friend. She said Ms. Bond's father grew up in the 1930s. She learned not to throw anything out."

"That explains the volume. Annie might be able to tell us more. I'll stop by the store during my shift, see if I can catch her."

"Why did you ask if the bodyguards had been in here?" Darcy scanned the room. The contents resembled the same catastrophe she'd noted in the other rooms.

"The piles have been shifted. In the other rooms, books were stacked against the back wall, clothes on the right, shoes on the left, miscellaneous things in the middle. In this one, everything is jumbled."

She took a closer look and realized Stella was correct. The piles were mixed. Clothes were thrown on top of the piles of books and magazines. The lids of several shoe boxes were off. "Do you think the bodyguards were curious about the contents?"

"Nate and his teammates kept the trainees busy. People traipsed in and out of rooms with loads of items. Someone would have said something to one of Durango if a trainee nosed around when he should have been working."

Darcy considered that. "They were all over the place," she conceded. "Rio and I made several trips through the rooms as well, checking on the progress." She turned. "What's the difference between this room and the rest?"

"Although we haven't seen the other two rooms left to clear, I think Sutton's crew was desperate to find whatever they are looking for before you moved in. Slipping inside with Rio, Trent, and Mason present is much harder, will be next to impossible when the security system is operational."

"Unless they have an expert at disarming systems."

"They can find someone as a last resort. It's easier gaining access to the house in the guise of friendship."

CHAPTER THIRTY

"If all else fails, grab duct tape." Rio waited for the laughter to die down. "I admit it sounds pretty funny." He held up the roll of black-colored tape. "Take my word for it. Don't leave home without it. Duct tape has been part of the standard equipment in my mike bag for years and should be in yours. My teammates carry their own supply in their Go bags. If you don't have any, stop by the hardware store in town on the way back to the motel. The owner stocks black tape for PSI and our trainees. Any questions?" After receiving a negative response from the trainees, he dismissed the group to attend Quinn's session. He didn't envy his teammate. Part of the tactical session was outside in Crime Town. At least the sun was up now and the temperature had risen to the mid-forties, a heatwave compared to the temperature this morning during his run.

Halfway through straightening chairs in the classroom, Rio's phone signaled an incoming text. He scanned the message, satisfaction blooming in his gut. He called Bear. "What do you have for me, buddy?"

"Chevy Tahoe decked out like Durango's vehicles. Who is Darcy St. Claire? Any kin to Trent?"

"Sister."

"I'll give her the standard discount. When do you want delivery?"

"As soon as you can get it here."

"I'll knock off another ten percent if you come get it. We're swamped."

Rio calculated the distance and time involved. He didn't have any sessions tomorrow. Maybe Darcy would like to go along. Though Bear was out of the black ops game, he kept up with his Army buddies and the Fortress operatives Maddox sent his way. "Deal. Tomorrow okay?"

"Make it after one."

"You got it."

Rio gathered the rest of his gear and grabbed his bags. In the hallway, he stopped one of the PSI staffers. "Heard from Johnson?"

"He just called. He's the proud father of a strapping ten-pound boy. Named him Harold Oliver."

He winced. "Oh, man. I feel for the kid."

"That's what I said when Harry told me the name. They plan to call him Junior." The staffer grinned. "Hope Junior has a good sense of humor. With a name like that, he needs one."

If the Fortress techs were still swarming Darcy's house, he should pick up dinner for them. Rio called Darcy, smiled when he heard her voice. "Hello, beautiful."

There was a pause, then his girl burst into laughter. "If you could see me now, you wouldn't say that."

"What have you been doing?"

"Cleaning a room on the third floor, making a million pots of coffee, and feeding this army of technicians. Right now, I have dust all over my clothes, cobwebs in my hair, and streaks of dirt on my face. I'm many things at this moment, but beautiful isn't one of them."

"Sweetheart, you could be covered in mud and I'd still consider you beautiful."

"You are seriously biased, Kincaid, but I thank you just the same. Work went well?"

"Oh, yeah. I taught the trainees about duct tape."

More laughter from Darcy. "Wish I could have sat in on that one."

"Are the techs still at the house?"

"They hope to finish by seven, then head back to Nashville."

"Do I need to buy dinner for them?"

"I would appreciate it." Her voice dropped to a murmur. "These guys plowed through every bit of the food Nate dropped off for lunch and I didn't have a vehicle to buy supplies for dinner."

"How many extra people are in the house?"

"Five technicians."

"I'll pick up the day's special at Delaney's. Will you be too tired to play the piano tonight, Darcy?"

"I need to play anyway."

"I'll arrange for Pastor Lang or one of his staff to meet us."

Delaney's was standing room only. Several people called out a greeting as he waded through the crowd to the counter and placed the order. The waitress said, "It will be a few minutes before it's ready, Rio. The high school basketball team is in the playoffs and it looks as if the whole town stopped here before the game."

"No problem, sugar. I'll visit with a few folks while I wait." He turned toward the right side of the diner and smiled at Julia Kendall who was standing on the bench next to her father, waving at him with a beautiful smile on her face. His heart turned over in his chest. That sweet child had been through so much in the last two years. She deserved a long, happy life.

He threaded his way through the crowd, stopping several times to chat a minute with various ones. Finally, he paused at the booth where Julia waited for him with her father. She leaned over Jim Kendall, slender arms reaching for him.

Rio glanced at the policeman for permission before sweeping her into his arms. "Tiger Lily, how is my girl?"

Her arms wrapped around his neck for a tight hug. "Daddy said I can have a milkshake."

"That sounds great."

"Tell him our deal, baby," her father said.

"I have to eat half a hamburger and five French fries."

He glanced at her plate. Not there yet. Her appetite hadn't returned to normal after her chemo treatments and the doctor was concerned. Her worried parents had resorted to bribery. "May I sit with you a few minutes, Julia? I'm waiting for a takeout."

"Yes, yes." She wiggled in his arms. "Sit with me."

"Thank you." He placed her on the empty bench and slid in beside her. He moved her plate across the table and nodded at the food. "Why don't you eat a few more bites of that hamburger while I talk to your dad for a minute."

Once she was chewing a bite, he turned to Jim. "How are Karen and little James? I haven't seen them in a couple weeks."

"They're great." He motioned to the milling crowd. "Karen's worried about the baby getting a cold or the flu."

"Smart. Folks can't resist holding a baby and his immune system is vulnerable because he's so young."

"I hear your friend has agreed to do a concert for Julia's medical fund."

"She's an incredible musician and she loves kids."

His friend's face reddened. "We appreciate her help. The medical bills are tough to handle on a cop's salary."

Rio glanced at his little friend's plate. The fries were gone as was more than half of the hamburger. He chatted a little longer with her father, telling him about his demonstrations earlier in the day with duct tape. By the time he finished the story, Julia's plate was empty. Nice. He reached over and stroked her hair. "Well, looks like you're ready for that shake now."

"Uh huh. Can I have chocolate this time, Daddy?"

"You bet, baby." Jim's voice sounded choked. "Rio, can you sit with her while I get it? Tracie said she would make it as soon as we were ready."

"Sure. Julia will keep me out of trouble, won't you, sugar?"

The girl wrinkled her forehead. "I'll try. But you're bigger than me."

"True enough. Madison told me you're working on a knitting project for your mom. Can you tell me what you're making or is it a secret?"

She motioned him down. Rio bent so his ear was near her mouth. "It's a scarf, a purple one because it's Mommy's favorite color."

"Nice. She'll love it."

"It's hard. I keep dropping stitches and Madison has to fix it."

"I don't know anything about knitting, but I do know the more we practice hard things, the better we become."

She nodded. "That's what Madison says."

"Here you go, baby." Jim placed the child-sized cup with a straw in front of his daughter. "Rio, Tracie said your order was ready."

"Excellent." He leaned over and kissed the top of Julia's head. "Thanks for keeping me out of trouble, Tiger Lily."

"Bye, Rio." Her cheeks hollowed as she sucked hard on the shake, which Rio knew from experience was thick and rich.

"How did you get her to eat?" her father whispered.

Rio's lips curved. "I distracted you. She can tell you're worried about her and it's affecting her appetite. When you relaxed, so did she and her body let her know she was hungry."

Kendall gave him a rueful smile. "I won't forget that. Thanks, Rio."

He clapped the other man on the shoulder, dived back into the crowd, and paid for the meals. Ten minutes later, he strode into the Victorian house with one large bag of takeout dinners. Within thirty minutes, the food had been consumed and the technicians were back at work to finish the last of the installations, the team leader agreeing to text Trent and Rio the code when they left.

"I should finish shoring up the floor," Mason said. "Her piano will be delivered tomorrow afternoon."

Rio unlocked the SUV and helped Darcy in before eyeing his cousin. "Mase, how much work do you have left?" He suspected Mason was trying to avoid the residents of Otter Creek. Rio wasn't going to let him do it. He couldn't see the Cahills holding Mason's past against him, not knowing what their son and the rest of Durango were called upon to do in the course of their work.

Mason sighed. "Not much."

"The Cahills don't bite," he murmured as he passed. "They're a good couple to have on your side."

His cousin looked skeptical, but didn't say anything more.

Liz Cahill greeted Darcy with a gentle hug. She drew back. "Nick told us about your accident, Darcy. I'm so glad you weren't seriously hurt."

"It was a near thing, Mrs. Cahill."

"Please, call me Liz. All of Josh's friends do." She turned to Trent who folded her hand between his big mitts, his cheeks turning red at her inquiry about his recovery. When her attention turned to Mason, Rio thought his cousin would bolt from the house. "You must be Mason." She smiled up at him. "Welcome to our home, son. If you will all give me your coats, you can go to the dining room. Dinner is on the table."

Amusement surged through Rio when he realized Liz had seated Mason next to her. By the time dinner was finished, his cousin was as charmed by her as the rest of Durango. Yep, Liz Cahill was a steamroller. No one stood a chance against her.

"Let's sit in the living room where it's comfortable," Aaron said. "I'll answer what questions I can about Gretchen Bond."

"I'll help Mrs. Cahill clear the table," Darcy said.

Once they were seated, Aaron said, "What did you want to know, Rio?"

"Anything you can tell me about Ms. Bond."

"A very nice woman. She was a great teacher. All our children had her in English. Can't say Josh made the best grades in her class, but he learned a great deal. Gretchen loved being in the classroom."

How could he ask about Ms. Bond's obsession with pirates or treasure without making her seem strange? Even Annie admitted her friend had grown eccentric in the last few years. Did Aaron know the eccentricity included pirates? "What were her interests?"

Aaron laughed. "Books, obviously. She read everything. She said she didn't have enough room in her house for more books, so she borrowed them from the library. She was one of the most well-read people I've ever met."

"Did you have a chance to see the inside of her house?"

"No. Why?"

"She wasn't kidding about not having any room. Darcy filled over a dozen large Dumpsters with junk that was piled up in that house." Rio summarized the contents of the rooms they'd cleared. "Did Nick or Josh tell you about the problems Darcy has had?"

A grim expression settled on the bank president's face. "Liz and I were shocked. You think the events are connected to the house?"

"Darcy hasn't been in town long enough to make enemies, Aaron. And the accident was no accident. Someone tried to shove her car over the side of the mountain with her in it."

"I'm glad she wasn't hurt worse. Bad first impression of her new home. I'll do what I can to help, though it will be precious little. Gretchen lived in Otter Creek about 60 years, came as a newlywed, and settled into teaching immediately. She finished her degree before she married Calvin."

"You said she read a lot. Do you know what she read?"

His brow furrowed. "Everything. Sorry, that's not helpful. I imagine Annie knows specifics. I served with Gretchen on several boards. She was one shrewd lady. She had tact even when she laid you flat."

"We found books dealing with pirates and pirate treasure. Did she ever mention anything to you about it?"

"Oh, sure. Her great-great nephews were obsessed with pirate movies. She collected books about pirates for them. When she had several, she'd mail them to the boys."

Dead end. Frustrated, Rio rubbed the back of his neck as Darcy and Liz laughed about something in the kitchen.

"What do you know about Charles Rockingham?" Mason asked Aaron.

Rio's eyes narrowed. What was this about? He'd never heard of Rockingham.

Aaron's head whipped in his direction. "The original founder of the bank? How do you know about him?"

"Stella researched the history of Darcy's house and discovered Rockingham is the original owner."

"That's news to me. Rockingham is a notorious character around Otter Creek, and not in a good way. He owned the bank and was well known for being tight-fisted with the money. Got to hand it to him, though, the bank never had a run on it. People knew there was money in the place. He was rumored to have several hundred Morgan silver dollars, but no one found them."

Could the thieves be after the Morgan silver dollars? "Do you think there was any truth to the rumors?" Rio asked.

"I wouldn't be surprised, Rio. Those old bankers knew how volatile the banking system was. They might put some money in the vault so they could tell their fellow townspeople they also deposited money in the bank. The truth is several kept money outside the banks as a hedge against a run on the place. Some buried it, others hid it in their houses. Others stashed the money in hollowed out bricks in the hearth of their homes. I wouldn't be surprised if Rockingham had a hiding place in the house." Aaron chuckled. "It's either that or he spent it all on the house or his wife. She was all about money and her standing in society."

Trent snorted. "Right. Until she took a lover."

"Her lover was a U.S. senator, a wealthy one."

Darcy walked in with Liz. "What did you find out?" she asked Rio.

"The pirates are a bust. The silver dollars are the best lead."

"If you think the silver dollars are connected to what's happening," Aaron said, "you should see Bob Schiller. He has an antiques place on Rosewood. If Gretchen consulted anybody about silver dollars, it would be him."

"Is it possible Gretchen found Rockingham's coins?" Liz asked. "It's been over a hundred years since he died. Wouldn't someone have found the money before now?"

"Not if he hid it well enough, honey." His expression darkened. "If Gretchen found it, she may have talked to someone who ultimately killed her."

When Liz and Aaron walked them to the door, Liz said, "Trent, Mason, come back to see us. It was a pleasure to have you."

"You're always welcome," Aaron said. He laid his hand on Mason's shoulder. "Congratulations on the new job."

Minutes later, Rio parked in Darcy's driveway. "We'll be in later. I'm taking Darcy to the church so she can practice."

Trent saluted and limped toward the front door, Mason following behind.

Rio backed out of the driveway and drove his girl to the white brick church. Lights glimmered in the windows of the auditorium.

Pastor Lang waited for them in the vestibule. "Welcome back, Darcy. Good to see you, Rio. Come get me when you're ready to go so I can lock up. Take your time, Darcy. I'm in no hurry."

Rio followed Darcy into the auditorium. "Don't push yourself, sweetheart." He uncovered the piano and lifted the lid for her, then sat on the last pew and settled back to listen.

From his point of view, he couldn't tell a difference in her playing. He knew her well enough by now to realize she wasn't happy with her performance.

Movement to his right drew his attention. Pastor Lang slid into the pew beside him. "Is she okay?" he murmured.

Rio shook his head. "Sore from the accident."

"Do I need to reschedule the concert? People would understand."

He longed to jump on the offer, knew he couldn't. "Not my call. It's her decision." He already knew she wouldn't change the date. The public relations machine was already cranking out notifications about the upcoming event and his girl wouldn't want to disappoint Julia.

Darcy stopped playing in the middle of one of Rio's favorite pieces and just sat there, staring at the keyboard. Concerned, Rio stood, intending to check on her, when she held up a hand to stop his forward motion and shook her head. Curious as to what she was doing, he sank down on the pew and waited. A few minutes later, she placed her hands on the keyboard and picked up the piece where she'd left off, finished it, then slid off the bench and walked to the back of the church. "I need to talk to Nick."

Rio blinked. Okay, not what he'd expected to hear. "He'll be on duty in a couple hours."

"I'll call him after we're home." She smiled at Lang. "Thank you for meeting us here. I hope I didn't inconvenience you."

The preacher waved that aside. "No problem. I love hearing you play."

She grimaced. "You are very kind."

"No ma'am. Honest. Give me a minute to shut down my computer and I'll walk you out."

Rio rubbed Darcy's shoulders a few seconds. Very tight. He wished Darcy had a whirlpool tub in her house. Guess a hot shower would have to do. "I'll take care of the piano." He left her standing in the aisle to close the lid and cover the piano.

Lang turned off lights on the way out as they passed the switches. After setting the alarm, he walked with them out the double doors. "Darcy, we can reschedule the concert if you need a few more days to recover."

She turned.

A shot rang out.

CHAPTER THIRTY-ONE

Rio grabbed Darcy and threw himself to the ground with her on top, then rolled over to cover her, his weapon up and tracking. In the woods off to the left, someone or something crashed through the underbrush. "You okay, baby?" he asked, gaze locked on the wooded area.

"Yes. You?"

Before he could answer, a low groan caught his attention. He turned. Pastor Lang lay sprawled against the double doors of the church, a stain spreading fast on his shirt.

Rio leaped to his feet. "Lang!" He laid the pastor flat on the concrete and eased his shirt away from the wound. Looked like the bullet went all the way through his shoulder. If they were very lucky, the projectile didn't hit anything except muscle. He heard his girl talking to the dispatcher on her phone. Had to appreciate a woman who was smart and kept her head in a crisis.

"Oh, man." Lang grimaced. "I'd forgotten how much getting shot hurts," he said through clenched teeth.

He stilled, glanced into the face of his pastor. "You've been shot before?"

"Forget I said that."

"Sorry, my friend. Some things you can't erase from memory." Marcus Lang had hidden depths behind the calm exterior he presented to the world.

Darcy sank to her knees by his side. "Ambulance and police should be here soon. What can I do to help, Rio?"

"Stay with him. I need my bag." He returned with his mike bag, yanked on gloves, and dug out two compression bandages. Lang was bleeding heavily. The sooner he slowed the bleeding, the better for his pastor.

Sirens sounded in the distance as he ripped Lang's shirt and applied a bandage to each side of the wound. "How are you doing?"

"Peachy," he answered, voice weak. The pastor's eyes closed.

"Marcus, look at me," Rio ordered. Seconds later, a bleary blue gaze locked on his. "Stay with me. You going to tell me about being shot before?"

"Forget it. Mistake."

"Tough. Cat's out of the bag, buddy. Where were you shot before?"

"Gut."

"How long ago?"

"Another lifetime. And that's all you get, Rio."

"Aw, the story's just getting good."

"Shut up," his pastor groused.

Rio grinned. "I'll get it out of you eventually. I'm persistent."

The ambulance arrived, followed by a patrol car. The EMTs approached at a run, bags in hand. Rio rose, helped Darcy to her feet, and they moved aside for the medical personnel to work on Lang. "One gunshot wound to the shoulder, a through and through. Vic's name is Marcus Lang. Tell the ER doc that Lang is diabetic."

"Yes, sir."

The patrol officer spoke to him and Darcy briefly before calling the station, requesting a detective. Minutes later, two OCPD SUVs skidded into the parking lot. One of them was driven by the police chief, the other by Rod Kelter, the detective on this shift.

Ethan stopped the gurney with Lang on board. He reached down, clasped the pastor's hand. "You're going to be all right, Marcus. Just do everything the nurses tell you."

"Like you do?" the preacher snapped.

Rio grinned. Oh, boy. Pastor Lang was a grumpy patient.

Rod chuckled. "No, better than Ethan. We'll see you at the hospital later." He motioned for the EMTs to load Lang and get him to the hospital. No one said anything until the ambulance left the parking lot.

Ethan crossed the distance to Rio and Darcy with those long, ground-eating strides. "What happened?" he said as soon as he reached them.

Rio gave him the details in rapid-fire military fashion.

"Rod, process the scene. Rio, with me."

"Yes, sir." He pulled out his keys and handed them to Darcy. "Two choices, baby. You can either wait for me in the SUV or drive on to your house. Ethan or Rod can drop me off."

"I'll wait." She walked to SUV, climbed in, and cranked the engine.

He glanced at the detective. "Rod, keep an eye on her." A snappy salute was his answer. He shook his head. Smart aleck.

Ethan pulled out his powerful flashlight and set off for the woods, scanning the ground as he went, Rio following close behind, his own flashlight in hand. He'd heard rumors of the police chief's prowess in tracking and was fascinated at the process as Ethan followed bent grass blades, broken limbs, scuffs of dirt, and partial footprints.

"From the kick out, he started running here." The police chief pointed to the print. "Which means he probably took the shot somewhere right around here. Stay here while I search the area."

"How do you know it's a man?"

"Depth of the prints and length of stride. He's around five-ten, over two hundred pounds." Ethan was silent a moment. "Here's where he took the shot. Take a look, Rio."

He strode forward, careful to step where Ethan had walked. The chief pointed out the brass shell casing. Rio blew out a breath. "Rifle, .223."

A nod. "Take me through what happened again, step by step."

He complied, mentally backtracking when Ethan stopped him to ask questions and confirm details. "What are you thinking, Ethan? Was Lang the target?" he asked, his voice soft. His first instinct was a definite no. Knowing what Marcus had let slip, though, told him the preacher had a past he didn't want to be questioned about. Was it possible something in Marcus's past had caused the events of this night?

The police chief's eyes narrowed. "Why would you assume someone was after Lang? Know something I don't?"

Rio debated whether or not to tell Ethan what he'd learned. The preacher hadn't made him promise not to tell about his previous injury, and Ethan needed every bit of information at his disposal to find the guy who took the shot. Besides, honor and integrity were ingrained in Otter Creek's police chief. The previous injury wouldn't make the grapevine if Ethan was convinced it had nothing to do with this incident. "Lang slipped and told me he'd been shot before. Wouldn't give specifics, though. He said it was another lifetime."

Ethan grunted. "That's a surprise. I'll check into it." His friend inclined his head in the direction of the church where Rod had set up bright lights to work the scene. "You walked on Darcy's right. After Lang locked the door, he called her name and asked her a question. She turned. The shot rang out. Lang went down. Visualize it in your mind. What do you think happened?"

Rio took his time recreating the scene in his mind. He frowned, checked the trajectory. A wave of rage rolled over his body. "Darcy was the target. Again. She turned to look at Marcus and moved out of position. The pastor was hit by mistake."

"That's my take on it even with the knowledge of Lang's previous injury." Ethan nodded toward the church doors where Rod was taking pictures. "An easy one hundred yard shot when you have a scope and there are a lot of hunters in this area. I'll check if someone reported a stolen rifle. I'm not holding my breath, though. If we're lucky, the shell casing will have prints."

"Won't do any good if his prints aren't in the system."

"It adds another attempted murder charge when we run him to ground." Ethan's face hardened. "And we will take him down, Rio. Never doubt that. This perp could have killed Lang. A couple inches difference and we would have transported our pastor to the morgue. I'm not going to forget that."

"Do you need anything more from me or Darcy? I want to take her home."

"Stop by the station tomorrow to formally give your statements." A ghost of a smile curved his mouth. "I know where to find you if I need you. How's Mason?"

"Adjusting. We had dinner with Liz and Aaron earlier this evening."

"Yeah?" He chuckled. "I can imagine how that went. Liz is a force to be reckoned with."

"Mase didn't know what hit him. Liz wiggled under his defenses and stole his heart."

"She did that to me, too."

"Same with all of Durango."

Ethan squeezed his shoulder. "Go, take your girl home. I'll see you tomorrow morning. Tell Rod to bring me an evidence marker."

"Yes, sir." Rio trotted back to the church, delivered the message to the detective, and grabbed his mike bag which he stored in the cargo section of his SUV. He climbed into the driver's seat and glanced at Darcy, whose gaze was fixed on the crime scene. "You okay, baby?"

"The bullet was meant for me, wasn't it?"

He thought about lying to her. Couldn't bring himself to do it. Knowledge was power. In this case, the knowledge of yet another attempt to harm her might save her life. "Yes."

"Will your pastor be okay?"

Rio put the vehicle in motion. "He'll need surgery to repair the damage to his shoulder, but he should make a full recovery." He twined his fingers with hers. "It's not your fault, sweetheart. The blame falls on the man who pulled the trigger."

She turned his direction. "Man? Did you see him?"

"I heard him. No visual. Ethan found his tracks in the dirt. No question it was a man."

"Could it have been one of Sutton's crew?"

"It's possible."

She was silent a moment. "What are we going to do?"

"Keep moving ahead, track down leads. Although Nick and Rod are very good at what they do, even the best of us can use a little help now and then."

"I guess we talk to Schiller next."

"That's right." His fingers tightened on hers. "Trent and I have a surprise for you."

"What is it?"

"The guy who provides our armor plating and bullet proof glass has an SUV ready for you."

"Is it like this one?"

He smiled at the excitement in her voice. "A sister to mine and the other members of Durango."

"That's great. When will I have it?"

"Tomorrow afternoon if you want to go with me to pick it up. I know your piano is supposed to arrive. Trent can tell the movers where to place it. We also need to go by the police station tomorrow morning to give our statements."

A couple minutes later, he parked in her driveway. The lights were off in the house except for the living room. Rio checked his phone for the security code in case the alarm had already been set.

Unlocking the front door, he was surprised to find Trent in the recliner and Mason on the couch, both reading books. One look at Darcy's face had Trent setting aside his book and climbing to his feet.

"Darce? What's wrong?"

Rio took her coat and watched as she stepped into her brother's embrace.

"Rio's pastor was shot as we left the church."

Trent's face hardened, his gaze shifting to Rio. "Details."

He summed up the facts, careful not to speculate too much.

"Was Lang the target?"

His lip curled. Leave it to the other Fortress operative to get to the point. "Not likely."

Trent's dark gaze glittered as he set his sister away from him. "Get packed, Darce."

"Why?"

"I'm sending you to Nashville. You can stay in my apartment while Rio and I flush these guys out. When it's safe, you can come home."

Rio stiffened. He objected to his friend ordering Darcy to leave though he understood the drive to get her out of harm's way. Still, Trent should know better than to issue an order to a woman with a mind of her own.

The woman in question folded her arms across her chest. "Are you planning to leave Otter Creek until it's safe?"

Her brother scowled. "I can take care of myself."

Darcy's gaze dropped to his stomach, then to his leg. "Is that right? Sorry, bro, but you haven't been doing a good job of that lately."

"You're fighting a losing battle, Trent," Mason said.

"He's right." Darcy jabbed her index finger into her brother's pectoral muscle. "Sutton's crew is not making me turn tail and run, Trent. This is my house. My new career is on the line and I already committed to Julia's concert. I'm staying."

"You can practice in Nashville and come back for the concert," her brother argued. "It's not safe for you here."

"Look at me, Trent. I'm not leaving. I trust you, Rio, and Mason to keep me safe while we hunt for these guys."

"They're getting desperate if they took a shot at you. You could have been killed," Trent yelled. "How do you think that would have affected me?"

"Don't go there," Darcy snapped. "I feel that way every time you leave on a mission, yet I don't pitch a fit to get you to stay home where it's safe. All I can do is take precautions. I can't carry a gun, I don't know any self-defense techniques, and I refuse to hire a bodyguard like a celebrity. But I will promise to use my brain and not take chances. That will have to be good enough, bro. The rest will be up to you three."

"Do you have to be so stubborn?"

"Looked in the mirror lately, Trent?"

He growled in frustration, his expression acknowledging he'd lost this battle. "You watch your back, Darcy. Promise me."

She stood on her tiptoes and kissed her brother's cheek. "I promise. You do the same."

Mason stood. "Unless you need me to stand watch or something, I'd better go to bed. I need to finish up the floor in the morning." He said goodnight and left the room.

"That reminds me, Trent. Bear called. He has an SUV for Darcy."

Satisfaction gleamed in his eyes. "Excellent."

"I'm taking her with me to pick it up tomorrow afternoon."

"Even better. The sooner she has a reinforced ride, the better for my peace of mind."

His, too, though he was smart enough not to voice the words out loud. When her cheeks flushed a bright red, he said, "Didn't you say you wanted to call Nick?"

"Hope he won't be an overbearing lout like my brother." She stalked off toward the kitchen.

Rio whistled softly. "Buddy, you need to learn tact."

"You can't tell me you feel any better about her staying here than I do."

He dropped his voice. "Of course not. I don't know her as well as you, but I do recognize that stubbornness of yours in her and a tendency to do exactly the opposite of what she's told."

"Hey," Trent protested.

"Truth hurts, doesn't it? Bet you've been contemplating telling Maddox you're ready for duty in the next week or two." The other operative clamped his mouth shut and refused to answer. He didn't have to. Rio already knew the truth. None of the Special Forces operatives he worked with liked the length of the healing process. "Darcy's smart. She won't take chances with her life." He stepped closer to Trent. "And neither will I. We'll all watch over her. One of Sutton's crew could follow her to Nashville and get rid of her permanently. At least this way we'll be close if they come after her again."

His friend glanced toward the kitchen, expression softening at the sound of his sister's quiet laugh. "You might be right." He turned, limped toward the hall. "I'm going to bed before I stick my foot in my mouth one time too many."

And that clued Rio in to the fact that Trent wasn't as healed as he wanted to be. Normally, the other operative was an avowed night owl. With Darcy still in deep conversation on the phone, he returned to his SUV, grabbed his bags, and dumped them in his room. He dug out the Valerian root. She had to be exhausted after clearing one of the rooms today and she still hurt from the accident. Maybe the combination of Valerian, over-the-counter pain meds, and a warm bath or shower would help her rest.

He found her in the kitchen as she ended her call to the detective. "Everything okay?"

"As good as it can be under the circumstances. I'm not sure I'll be able to play everything I had planned for Julia's concert. Something I've learned over the last few months is how to adjust my expectations."

Rio sat on the stool next to hers. "What does Nick have to do with this?"

"Madison told me how much Julia loves Nick and his music. Did you know she has all his CDs?"

"He's going to help you with the concert."

She nodded. "I'll play a few pieces alone. Nick will play, then we'll play together on the fun pieces Julia asked for. Having Nick play alone in the middle section of the concert will give my hands a break."

"A win-win for everybody. That's brilliant, Darcy, and sure to make Julia happy." He placed the Valerian root and pain meds in front of her. "For the body aches." He stilled. "Did I hurt you earlier when I took you to the ground?"

"Better another bruise than a bullet, Rio." She smiled. "What's one more bruise among the scores I already have?" She swallowed the pills with water.

"Wish you had a Jacuzzi or whirlpool tub in this place."

"Me, too. I think I'll ask Brian about installing one in my bathroom." She leaned into Rio and kissed him, a long, lingering kiss full of heat and promise, one that had his heart rate soaring by the time she drew back. "Goodnight, Rio."

He secured the front door and set the alarm before completing his own preparations for bed. He'd just turned out the light when his cell phone signaled an incoming text.

Rio piled the pillows against the headboard and settled against them. Zane. He called his friend. "What do you have for me?"

"Santana filed his report on Sutton's murder."

"What did you find out?"

"Otter Creek's computer security is at least ten years out of date."

A snort. "Besides that."

"Santana questioned you about Sutton's murder, didn't he?"

Rio stilled. "How did you know?"

"Easy. He made a note in his file about your relationship with Darcy. Fast work, by the way. Be good to her or you'll answer to me."

"You know that's not even a question. What pointed Nick my direction?"

"He found blueprints of Darcy's house at the crime scene along with pictures of her around town. Several of those pictures feature both of you. Sutton was watching her, cataloging her moves. A few of the pictures had a red X across her face. No question Darcy is a target of these clowns. I don't know what they want from her, but they're determined to get it, even if they have to get rid of her and you to accomplish the goal."

CHAPTER THIRTY-TWO

Darcy tugged her Dallas Cowboys sweatshirt over her white turtleneck and lifted her hair free of the collar. Some of her muscles protested. Overall, she was pleased with her improvement. Her lips twisted. The SUV driver had done nothing more than cost her a car she'd been thinking about getting rid of anyway. A last glance in the mirror and she turned away to grab her shoulder bag, also sporting the Cowboys' logo. A girl's accessories had to match, after all.

In the kitchen, Rio was waiting for her, screwing the lid on a travel mug as she walked into the room. "How did you sleep?"

"Okay." When she could sleep, Darcy kept seeing Marcus Lang fall against the church doors, blood pouring from his shoulder. And there was that nausea which had been plaguing her for hours. She refused to give in. Rio and Trent dealt with this all the time without barfing. So could she. Maybe. The churning in her stomach grew worse.

"Liar."

She wrinkled her nose at him. "Do I look that bad?"

"Never. Just tired." He leaned down and took her mouth in a gentle kiss. "Do you want your shake before we leave?"

Just contemplating it made her stomach lurch. "I don't think that's wise."

He lifted his free hand and trailed the back of his fingers down her cheek with a feather-light touch. "I thought that might be the case. I made you some chamomile and mint tea this time. Serena Blackhawk swears this mixture is the cure for upset stomachs. If you're up to it, we'll go to the police station and take care of the statements before we tackle anything else."

Oh, joy. Recount the night's events another time. Maybe writing down what happened would help her process it. Her sense of humor surfaced. If the tea didn't do the trick, she'd have grounds to ask for a soft drink.

In Rio's SUV, she asked, "How is your pastor?"

"Surgery was successful. He'll make a full recovery." He sent her a wicked grin. "And all the single ladies in town will be stocking his freezer with casseroles and baking desserts he's not supposed to eat to aid him in his recovery."

Darcy laughed. "Oh, my. Poor man."

"Yep, but it's fun to laugh at his plight."

She turned, speculation growing. "You've been the recipient of these ladies, haven't you?"

He grinned. "Maybe."

"How many of their hearts have you broken?"

The medic sobered. "None, baby."

"You weren't interested in any of them?" She had a hard time believing that. He seemed to make friends easily, a characteristic she envied.

He shook his head. "They weren't you."

With that statement, Darcy fell a little bit more in love with Rio Kincaid. Butterflies flew in bomber formation in her stomach. Whew! How could any woman resist him? "Rio," she murmured. "I don't know what to say."

"Tell me you'll give us a real chance, Darcy. That's all I want to hear."

"I don't know where this relationship is going, but I can't wait to find out."

He raised her hand and kissed the back of it. A minute later, he parked in front of the police station.

Nick was waiting for them at his desk. He stood as Darcy approached, his dark eyes studying her face. "How are you, Darcy?"

"Fine." When one of his eyebrows rose, his skepticism obvious, she added, "I will be."

He pulled out a chair for her. "Tell me if you need to talk to someone. We have a counselor we recommend for trauma victims. There's no shame in seeking counsel, Darcy. I've been on the receiving end of it several times."

She set her bag at her feet. "In relation to your police work?"

"That and when I lost my family to murder while I was away at college."

"Oh, Nick. I'm so sorry for your loss." She didn't remember reading about his tragic past. The classical guitarist had done a great job keeping it from being bandied about in the media.

"Me, too. I still miss them. The point is I needed help to get past it." He reached into his desk drawer, grabbed a business card, and handed it to her. "Dr. McMillan is very good." He smiled. "She's also notorious for not being able to cook so she'll be a customer of yours. If you decide to consult her, tell her I sent you."

She glanced at the card, then slipped it into her pocket. "Thanks for the recommendation, Nick. I also appreciate your willingness to play in Julia's benefit concert at the last minute."

"My wife and I love that little girl. I'm glad to help. Rod typed out your statements before he went home to catch some sleep." He slid two pieces of paper across the desk, one for her, one for Rio. "Read through them. If you need to make changes, I'll take care of it before you leave." The detective stood, stretched. "Do you want any coffee? It's Serena's specialty blend."

"I'll take some," Rio said absently as he read the paper in his hand.

Darcy sighed. Man, she so wanted a mug of the steaming brew. She missed the caffeine hit of coffee.

The detective crossed the room and filled two mugs. "Here you go," he murmured, handing one to Rio. "Black, right?"

"Yep. We don't have access to cream and sugar on ops." He sipped, moaned. "For a woman who hates to drink it, Serena makes the best coffee I've ever tasted."

"I agree." The deep voice of the police chief easily carried from his office doorway, a mug in his own hand. His gaze shifted to Darcy. "Did you get much sleep, Darcy?"

She scowled. "Do I have a sign on my forehead that says I didn't sleep well? You're the third person who's asked me that today."

He grinned. "I'll take that as a no. Rio, have you checked on Lang?"

"Called as soon as I woke up and talked to a friend on the nursing staff."

Darcy's eyes narrowed as she wondered if the "friend" was a female. Come to think of it, most of the people who stopped to chat with him were women. The same ones who provided casseroles and dessert to capture his attention?

"And?"

"He'll make a full recovery. Darcy and I plan to stop by there after we visit with Bob Schiller."

Ethan's mug stopped halfway to his mouth. "At the antique shop? Talk to me, Rio."

"There's a chance the attempts on Darcy's life are connected to Morgan silver dollars."

"Explain."

"I should have thought of that," Nick muttered. "Stella told me about the coins. Ethan, the original owner of Darcy's house, Charles Rockingham, was the founder of the Otter Creek bank. He owned many silver dollars when he was hung for murder. No one ever found the money."

Ethan frowned. "He wouldn't have put the money in his own bank?"

"Aaron says those old bankers were known for hiding money instead of risking it all in the banks," Rio said. "There were a lot of runs on them in those days."

"No proof?" the police chief asked.

"Nope. The speculation makes sense. I'm still not convinced there are silver coins left, but I think someone believes they still exist."

"And they're willing to kill to get them." Ethan turned to Darcy. "It might be in your best interest to leave the house until we find out who is doing this and put them behind bars."

Her cheeks burned. What was it with these big military men that they thought women were helpless? And, yeah, she was positive Blackhawk was military. She recognized the demeanor and the air of authority he wore like a second skin. "I've heard that before, too. I'll give you the same answer I gave my brother. No. These creeps aren't chasing me out of my house. I'll take precautions, but I'm not running."

Ethan's lips curved upward. "Sounds like several other women I know, starting with my wife. All right. I can't deny that we're short-handed. Anything you and Rio learn, I want to know."

The knots in her muscles slowly disappeared when she realized he wasn't going to force her to leave. He wouldn't be any more successful than her brother. "Deal."

"Remember these guys are serious. They've already killed one of their own. They won't hesitate to kill you or those you care about to achieve their objectives. Under no circumstances are you to take chances or confront them on your own. Stay with someone at all times, Darcy. If I find out you're putting yourself at risk, I'll pack you up and move you out of that house myself. Am I clear?"

Where would he move her to? Probably the motel. She didn't want to go there again if she could help it. Darcy enjoyed being in the kitchen too much to tolerate a sterile motel room for long. Besides, her agent was staying there. Allen would drive her crazy, wanting her to return to the concert stage. "Yes, sir."

"Please, call me Ethan." Amusement lit his gaze. "Got a feeling we'll get to know each other well in the coming months."

She smiled, turned to Nick, and waggled her statement. "Where do I sign this?"

Nick handed her a pen. "At the bottom."

Once she and Rio signed, they left the bull pen. In the lobby, Rio placed a hand on her arm to stop her from heading outside. "Are you hungry or do you want to see Schiller first?"

"Food first." She'd rather visit the antique dealer. Most shops, however, opened at 9 or 10. It was too early for Schiller to be in the store.

"Delaney's okay?" He smiled. "Until That's A Wrap is open, there aren't other options aside from fast food at the gas station."

Darcy rolled her eyes. "Lovely. I'll pass on the fast food. Delaney's it is."

As she anticipated, the place was buzzing about Marcus Lang's shooting and the patrons wanted details from Rio. She admired his careful answers which didn't give details that weren't already on the town's grapevine. What impressed her was the obvious love the citizens of Otter Creek had for Lang.

As they finished breakfast, the crowd began to thin. "Do you think Nate's mother would supply her blueberry tea blend for my store?"

"I imagine she would, especially if you give her free advertising for the tea. In fact, you should talk to her about the different flavors she's come up with. She probably has a website set up for online orders. I'll ask Nate for her number."

Rio drove them from the town square and turned right on Rosewood Lane. Halfway down the street, he parked in front of Schiller Antiques. Inside the store, Darcy wandered the aisles, examining different items before continuing on. The murmur of male voices drew her attention to the front of the shop. Rio was deep in conversation with an older gentleman. The overhead lighting gleamed off his bald head, his genial expression reminding Darcy of her grandfather. Roland St. Claire had loved talking to people, much as this man seemed to. She crossed to Rio's side.

He circled her waist with his arm. "Bob, this is Darcy St. Claire. She'll be opening a deli on the square in a few weeks."

The old man's eyes brightened. "Is that right? Congratulations, my dear."

"Thank you. I noticed you had several hurricane lamps in stock. Do you have more in your inventory?"

"Let me check. I picked them up at an estate sale a few months back. No one's been interested in them."

"However many you have, I'll take them. They're perfect to decorate the tables in my deli." Especially with all those candles Gretchen Bond had collected. Wonder where she found them? Darcy would love to have more. Each one was unique and called to something in her soul.

They were sure to be a hit with her female customers. Maybe Annie would know where Gretchen bought them.

When Bob left to check his inventory, Darcy turned to Rio. "What did you find out?"

"Nothing yet. He wanted to know about Pastor Lang's condition and the name of the beautiful woman who walked in with me."

She smiled. "He's quite a charmer."

"See anything interesting besides the hurricane lamps?"

She mentioned a few of the items she was thinking of buying for the house.

The medic chuckled. "You'll make his day if you ask him to hold those things for you."

"Why? His stock is amazing. He should have many customers begging him to set aside items."

"Not everyone is as appreciative as you."

"Their loss."

They turned as he returned to the main floor, a large box in his arms.

Rio crossed the room in a few strides. "Here, let me take that for you. How many did you find?"

"A dozen more. Are you sure you need that many, my dear?" he asked Darcy.

"Positive. There are also a few other things I'd like for my house, but I don't have a place to put them yet. The contractor will need to do some work before I'll be ready for them. Will you hold them for me?"

"Absolutely. Show me what you're interested in." He pulled out a tattered notebook from his pocket and a stubby pencil as he followed her around the store. He attached sold tags to each, then directed Rio to carry them into the back.

When Rio returned to the counter, Darcy was paying for her purchases. "Mr. Schiller, do you know anything about Morgan silver dollars?"

He frowned as he handed her a receipt. "Morgan silver dollars? What's with all the interest in those?"

"Someone else has asked about them?"

"That young man who was murdered the other day for one."

Finally, a connection she and Rio could give to Nick and Ethan. "Who else?"

"Someone else in the last few months, but I can't remember who that might have been right now. My memory isn't what it used to be." He paused a moment, a thoughtful expression on his face. "Gretchen Bond also came in here not too long before she died, asking about the silver dollars. In fact, she showed me one she had in her possession."

CHAPTER THIRTY-THREE

Darcy jerked beside Rio. He twined their fingers together and gave her hand a squeeze. When she glanced his way, he gave a slight head shake. He didn't want Bob to know too much information. The last thing he wanted was for this good man to become the target of Sutton's crew. "That's interesting. What did she want to know?"

A snort from the old man. "Same as everyone else, what they're worth."

"And that is?"

"Anywhere from $150 up to $6,000, depending on the condition and whether the dollar was in circulation."

"Did Ms. Bond say where she got the silver dollar?"

He rolled his eyes. "Crazy old woman claimed to have inherited a pirate's treasure. Then she just laughed like a loon. Personally, I think she'd been reading too much historical romance." He glanced at Darcy, a flush staining his cheeks. "No offense, my dear."

Wonder how much information Sutton learned from Schiller? "What did you tell the man who was murdered?"

"Not nearly as much as he wanted to know." A smile curved his mouth. "Didn't like the look of him. Just told him the history of the silver dollars and range of value." He snapped his fingers. "The history teacher up at the community college, Paul Cambridge. That's the other person who asked me about Morgan silver dollars. Of course, that's been several months ago. Said he was preparing a lecture for one of his classes and thought I could add to whatever he already knew. Nice man, Cambridge. Wish I'd had a teacher like him when I was in school. Might have finished my degree instead of quitting to seek my fortune in the world. Met my sweet wife, Mary Elizabeth, at my first job, though." Sorrow shadowed his gaze. "I still miss her."

"How long were you married?" Darcy asked.

"Sixty glorious years."

"That's incredible, Mr. Schiller. You're a very blessed man."

He nodded, his face softening with memory. "Now, tell me, young lady, why are you and Rio interested in Morgan silver dollars?"

"Darcy bought Ms. Bond's house."

"Used to be quite a showplace. What are your plans for the old girl?"

Darcy smiled. "To bring it back to life—hopefully a much happier life. I understand that Victorian has seen a lot of heartbreak."

"Indeed. I hope you are successful. Do you want me to inquire about Morgan silver dollars for you?"

Tension vibrated through their handhold. "No, sir. My curiosity is satisfied. I'm really more interested in things for the house. Will you keep an eye out for items that would fit well in a Victorian home?"

"I will, indeed." He looked pleased to be given the task. "How should I contact you if I find anything of interest?"

Darcy handed him a business card. "I don't have a card for the deli yet. My cell phone number is on the bottom."

He glanced at the print, stopped, read more carefully. "Darcy Melton, the classical pianist?"

"Yes, sir."

"My wife loved your music. She would have been so thrilled to make your acquaintance."

She grinned. "Did you and Mrs. Schiller attend a concert?"

"I'm sorry to say we never managed to do that."

"Nick Santana and I are giving a concert with all the proceeds going to Julia Kendall's medical expenses. How would you like a front row seat?"

Schiller beamed. "I would enjoy that."

"I'll make sure your seat is reserved. The attendants at the door will escort you down front."

Outside, a blast of cold air cut like a knife through Rio's coat. "I think you made his day, sweetheart."

Rio unlocked his SUV and opened the passenger door. Once Darcy was safely inside, he climbed into the driver's seat. "We have a couple hours before we need to be in Summerton. How about a stop at the community college? Maybe we'll catch Cambridge in his office."

Minutes later, he parked in one of the visitor spaces at Otter Creek Community College. Students and faculty hurried around campus, eager to get out of the wind. "Come on," he said. "I have someone I'd like you to meet before we track down Cambridge."

He escorted Darcy across the open grass to the Arts building and up the stairs to the second floor. He steered her around the clusters of students in the hall and knocked on Ivy's open door.

"Come on in." The small, dark-haired woman glanced up from her laptop. A delighted smile curved her mouth. "Rio! What are you doing here?"

"How are you, sugar?"

"Better now that I've seen you." Her curious gaze shifted to Darcy.

"Ivy Morgan, meet Darcy St. Claire, Trent's sister. Darcy, this is Alex's wife."

After Darcy and Ivy spent a few minutes getting acquainted, Rio asked, "Where is Paul Cambridge's office?"

"Third floor. His office is right above mine." Ivy glanced at her watch. "If you hurry, you can catch him before his 11:00 class."

Rio's eyebrows rose. "You know his schedule?"

"Sound carries in these offices. Paul's office chair has a piercing squeak when he moves around in it." She turned to Darcy. "Stella tells me we're planning a ladies-only Mexican food night. When were you thinking about doing this?"

"Sweetheart, why don't you talk to Ivy a minute? I won't be long." Rio was smart enough not to admit he'd rather she didn't talk to Cambridge in connection to the silver dollars. The fewer people who knew she was asking questions about them, the better for his peace of mind. If word spread that he was asking, well, so much the better. He'd rather be a target than for the killer to continue pursuing Darcy. Her sharp glance told him he hadn't fooled her one bit. Yep, he'd no doubt pay for that later.

Rio slipped out of the office and climbed the stairs to the third floor. A large class must have just let out because he felt like a salmon swimming upstream through the flood of students coming down the stairs. He located the right office and knocked on the door.

"Come in, but make it fast," came the response.

He opened the door and stepped inside. "Paul Cambridge?"

"That's right."

"Rio Kincaid."

"What can I do for you? If our discussion is going to take a while, we'll have to reschedule for another time. I have a class in five minutes."

"I'm interested in old coins. I understand you're the man to ask about historical significance."

"What kind of old coins?"

"Anything from the 1930s and earlier, specifically the ones cast in precious metal. American coins only."

"That covers a lot of territory, Mr. Kincaid. Any coins in particular of interest to you?"

"Morgan silver dollars."

Cambridge slid a yellow legal pad and pen across the desk. "Write down your email address. I'll send you the information I use for my lectures. Will that do?"

"Sounds great," he said as he wrote his PSI email address. "Thank you."

The history professor scanned the address, frowned. "You're part of the bodyguard school?"

"That's right. I'm a medic. I teach first aid to trainees." Among other things. He'd found it best to downplay his role in the training.

"I see." He stood, grabbed his suit coat off the back of his chair. "I'll get that information to you in the next day or two."

"I appreciate it." He strolled out of the office and down the hall, conscious of the hairs on the back of his neck rising. His lips curved. Guess the good professor didn't know what to make of the medic.

He returned to Ivy's office. "Did you decide when to have your ladies night?"

"Tomorrow night. Darcy's agreed to practice with us as an audience. I can't wait to hear her play."

"Don't expect much," Darcy warned. "The piano won't be in tune because of the move and I'm still dealing with soreness from the wreck."

"Anything you do will trump my efforts. My mother gave up on me learning to play after a year of piano lessons. The music teacher declared me hopeless."

"If you decide to try again, I could teach you."

Ivy laughed. "Don't hold your breath. I'd rather paint any day than practice scales. Maybe when Alex and I have children old enough to take lessons, you could teach them." She asked Rio, "Did you talk to Paul?"

"He's sending information to my email. We're going to lunch before we pick up a vehicle for Darcy. Would you like to join us?"

"I wish I could. I have a class which starts in half an hour. Rain check?"

"Any time, sugar." He ruffled her hair. "See you later."

Back in the SUV with Darcy, he cranked the engine and turned the blower on high. "How hungry are you?"

"I can wait a while. Why?"

"There's a great cafe in Summerton you'll like. The drive will take an hour. The good news is Summerton is also where we're picking up your SUV."

When they walked into Kate's Cafe, Darcy's eyes widened. "Look at this place," she murmured as she scanned the walls. Music memorabilia covered every available surface. Posters, CDs, pictures of famous musicians.

Rio nudged her shoulder and nodded toward the register. Darcy's beautiful face graced an arrangement of her CD covers on the wall to the right.

A wry smile curved her mouth. "The magic of makeup and retouched photos."

He squeezed her hand. "I'd rather have the real thing."

"Rio!" Across the room, a green-eyed redhead waved at him from behind the counter.

"Another one of your conquests?"

He glanced at his companion, relieved to find an amused twinkle in her eye. "She's a happily married mother of two toddlers. Her husband was in one of my units in the Sand Box." Before he and the rest of Durango had gone to Ranger school. He led Darcy to the counter. "How's it going, Kate?"

"Busy, I'm happy to say. Who's your friend?" She turned her gaze on Darcy. Within seconds, shock came over her face. "Darcy Melton?"

Darcy grinned. "It's St. Claire. Melton is my stage name. It's nice to meet you, Kate."

"Oh, man, my husband is going to be so disappointed that he missed meeting you."

"I'm surprised you recognized me. Classical musicians don't have the same media exposure as other artists in different genres of music."

"Blame Rio. He got my husband, Tony, hooked on your music while they were serving together overseas."

"Is he still working with Bear?" Rio asked.

Kate nodded. "Tony loves his job. Says it's not as high voltage as being in war-torn countries, but he gets satisfaction from providing protection for those who need it most."

"We'll see him in a few minutes, then. Bear has an SUV for Darcy."

The cafe owner grinned. "I wish I could see his face. What can I get for you two?"

While they waited for their order, Kate showed them the latest pictures of her sons and the new house she and her husband had purchased.

After a meal of beef vegetable soup and salad, Rio drove to Bear's workshop. He glanced at Darcy to gauge her reaction to the building and chuckled. Exactly the reaction he'd expected. "Doesn't look like much, does it?"

"It's a dump!"

Bear hadn't bothered to do anything with the outside. A metal building with a rusty exterior hid a state-of-the-art operation inside. In true paranoid fashion, the walls were reinforced concrete with several escape routes from the building, including a top-of-the-line bunker complete with stores to last his whole crew a month in case of a siege. His friend didn't take safety for granted, not after surviving some of the most dangerous missions overseas, including one in which he'd been captured by terrorists. Bear still bore the scars from captivity.

"Don't let the appearance deceive you."

She looked skeptical. Couldn't say he blamed her. It did look pretty bad. The parking area was littered with potholes. A few trash barrels were set up in various places in what seemed a random pattern. All of it was designed to prevent someone from hitting the place and making a fast getaway.

He parked near the entrance and, at the door, slid in his Fortress ID. After a visual confirmation of his identity, the door unlocked and he escorted Darcy inside. As soon as they cleared the threshold, the door closed and locked behind them. Within minutes, Darcy finished signing the paperwork and Bear presented the keys.

"Gas mileage won't be as good as the manufacturer claims," Bear said. "You've got extra weight in this baby."

"I don't care," Darcy said. "I just want to be safe."

"Got you covered, little lady. How's Trent?"

"Bad tempered and ready to go back to work."

A chuckle from the mountain of a man. "Sounds like him. You have any mechanical problems, Darcy, you bring this baby back to me. We'll take care of it."

After spending a few minutes with a starstruck Tony Edgerton, Rio drove behind Darcy's SUV. By the time they parked in her driveway an hour later, she was grinning. "Like it, sweetheart?"

"I love it. I'll never go back to a car. I can see everything and I love the feel of the extra weight. It's like my vehicle hugs the road."

"When it snows, I'll take you to an empty parking lot. Driving rear-push on snow and ice is different than driving front-wheel."

"Come on. I want to see if my piano was delivered in one piece."

The rest of the afternoon and evening passed without incident, but somehow Rio felt as if the other shoe would drop soon.

CHAPTER THIRTY-FOUR

Darcy yanked the towel off her damp hair and grabbed her cell phone. She frowned. Allen again. And early for him, too, at a little past six in the morning. With a knot forming in her stomach, she swiped her screen. "Good morning, Allen."

"Finally! I've been trying to get in touch with you for two days, Darcy."

"Sorry. I've been busy." Dodging bullets, SUVs, and persistent agents. And she'd been afraid life in a small town would be boring. Ha! "What's up?"

"I was going to ask you that question. Are you all right? I heard about the accident and the shooting."

"I'm fine. Thanks for checking on me."

"We spent many years together. I care about you."

She sat on the side of the bed. "I know you do. I'm okay, Allen. I already have another vehicle and the soreness is fading." Not fast enough to suit her, but it was leaving.

"And the shooting?"

"Rio protected me and the preacher is recovering." Lang had been in a good mood last night when she and Rio finally made it to the hospital, Darcy was thankful the pastor didn't blame her for his injury.

"Look, Darcy, I don't know what's going on, but you're not safe in this town. Maybe you should go home for a while until the cops figure out who is doing this."

"I am home and I'm not leaving."

"I wish you would reconsider. I don't want to lose you."

Chills swept over her body and she couldn't say whether they were from the cold air seeping through the old window or from Allen's statement. Was she simply being paranoid or was there an implied threat?

She sighed, annoyed. Was she suspicious of her friends now? Stella's statement about the enemy coming into her home under the guise of friendship surfaced in her mind and she decided the time for diplomacy was over. How would she learn anything that might help unravel this dangerous puzzle if she didn't ask questions outright? "Allen, you've been in town longer than a week, haven't you?"

Silence met her statement. "How did you know? Did your boyfriend check up on me?" He sounded outraged.

"It's a small town. People talk," she said. "You arrived before I did. Why?"

"I can't go on a vacation?"

Darcy laughed. "Your idea of a vacation is someplace warm with sandy beaches and women dressed in bikinis. Otter Creek is a long way from that."

"It's a long way from civilization, too," he muttered.

"So why did you come here?"

A sigh. "Honey, you know why. I wanted to see what you were letting yourself in for. I never dreamed you were putting your life in danger or that you chose a town the size of a postage stamp. This isn't the life for you, Darcy. You'll be begging to go back to your real life inside six months."

"I'm not changing my mind. I can't." Twenty years on the concert circuit was enough. She wanted to put down roots. Her face heated. Maybe start a family with a husband she was crazy about. Rio's face popped into her mind. Perhaps someone like Rio Kincaid.

"At least think about recording one or two CDs a year. You already have a loyal audience. I did some research on your condition and I realize now you can't continue the old schedule of practicing and performing. If we record your music a couple songs at a time, we can give you long breaks between recording sessions."

"Let me think about it for a while. Right now, my focus is on the concert next week and preparing the deli to open next month."

"You'll call me when you make a decision?"

"I'll let you know."

She ended the call a moment later and retraced her steps to the bathroom to finish getting ready for the day. In the kitchen, she breathed deep and almost moaned. Coffee. Oh, man. What she wouldn't give to drink a mug of the brew in the carafe.

"Morning, Darce." Trent strode into the kitchen and made a beeline for the coffee. Not much of a limp, she noted. "When are you returning to work?"

He eyed her over the top of his mug as he sipped. "Why?"

"You're stir crazy."

His face took on a mulish expression. "Not until the cops lock up whoever is threatening you."

"Might be a while. Look, bro, I'll be fine. I have Mason and Rio here. The rest of Durango is close and the cops are on alert. When the doctor clears you, go."

"You sure?"

"Absolutely. I love having you here, Trent, but I know you would rather be in the field if you're able."

A nod. "I'll stick around a few more days. Hopefully these clowns will make a mistake before I leave."

Darcy hoped so. She had too much to do to keep looking over her shoulder for the next disaster.

Rio walked into the room dressed in what she'd begun to think of as his work uniform of black camouflage pants, black long-sleeved t-shirt, and at least one weapon. Knowing these military guys, he probably had more than one on him. He brushed her mouth with his, causing Trent to growl. "Good morning, sweetheart."

"Can't you at least hold off until I'm in another room?" her brother groused. "You're giving me nightmares."

"Envious, St. Claire?"

"Shut up, Kincaid."

Rio returned his attention to Darcy. "What's on your agenda for the day?"

"Check on the progress at the deli and track down Annie. I wanted to ask her about the candles Ms. Bond collected. I'd love to buy more if she can tell me where they were purchased. Also a grocery store run to buy supplies for tonight's ladies only dinner. What about your schedule?"

"Full day at PSI and dinner with Durango." He grinned. "Nate's cooking for us."

"Oh, man," Trent said. "What is he cooking?"

A shrug. "Doesn't matter. He can make anything taste good. Nate's cooking enough to feed you and Mason, too."

Her brother's face brightened. "Excellent." He paused. "Maybe I should stay here. I know Stella's a cop, but she's not one hundred percent."

Darcy's lips twitched. Neither was her brother, though she was loathe to point that out. "You'll have to stay in the living room. We're taking over the kitchen and dining room."

"You will feed me a few scraps, right?"

"A chip or two."

"Thanks a lot, sis. Don't know what I'd do without you."

"Darcy, if you're ready to go, I'll follow you to the deli before I go on to PSI. I'd like to see how much progress Brian has made." Rio opened the refrigerator. "I made your shake earlier."

"Hey," Trent protested. "What about me and Mase?"

"You can make your own protein shake if you want one. If not, Josh dropped off one of Serena's breakfast casseroles after you went to bed last night. Foolproof directions are on the lid."

"All right!" Her brother rubbed his hands together as he brushed past Rio and retrieved the casserole container from the refrigerator shelf. "I've heard Cahill brag for years about his sister's cooking."

"You're in for a treat." He handed Darcy her travel container with a straw. "Ready, Darcy?"

"As soon as I get my bag and coat."

"I need to tell Mason the plan for tonight. I'll meet you by the front door."

Minutes later, they were on their way to her deli. She loved her new vehicle, especially the heated seats. When they parked in front of the shop, she was pleased to see they arrived before Brian's crew. She could look at the new changes without getting in anyone's way. One day soon this place would be filled with customers. She just wished her parents could have been here to see it.

She slid to the pavement and searched for her shop key. Finding the right one, she met Rio at the door and unlocked it. As soon as she stepped inside, the scent of rotten eggs made her gag.

CHAPTER THIRTY-FIVE

"Out, now!" Rio hustled Darcy back out to the sidewalk. Thankful a strong wind was blowing this morning, he made sure the door was closed before urging his girl back into her SUV. "There's a gas leak in the deli. We need to move our vehicles, then call the fire department."

"Is it safe to crank the engines?" she said between coughs.

"We have a strong wind blowing the gas away from the door and the door is closed, but we'll wait another minute. Are you okay, sweetheart?" He watched her carefully until the coughing slowed down and finally stopped.

"Whew! I think so. That smell took my breath away."

"Not surprising. Sjogren's Syndrome affects your lungs."

She made a face. "Nice."

He dropped a quick kiss on her lips and stepped back. "Park across the square. We'll call the police and fire department from there."

He waited until she cranked the engine and backed out of the slot before climbing into his own vehicle. He shuddered to think what would have happened if Darcy had flipped on a light.

Once they were safely away from the building, he called 911 and reported the gas leak, then put in a call to Brian. "Darcy and I are at the deli. You and your crew need to stay out of there."

"Why?"

"Gas leak."

"I'll be there in five."

Just as Brian parked beside Darcy, the fire department rolled up. Ethan and Nick strode from the police station, spotted Rio and Darcy, and changed direction.

Rio, Darcy, and Brian met the policemen on the sidewalk. "Gas leak," Rio said.

Ethan scowled, his gaze shifting to the scene unfolding in front of the deli.

"I checked the connections last night before I left," Brian said. "Everything was in perfect working order."

"We'll let the fire department and the gas company do their thing, then we'll check the store," Nick said, zipping his coat higher. "I'll be interested in knowing if someone monkeyed with the locks and broke in."

Brian frowned. "I've had my fair share of equipment stolen off job sites and graffiti like we had earlier, but never something like this. One spark and the whole place would have blown sky high."

"Ethan," Rio said, "what are the chances the leak is an accident?"

"Zero."

Somehow, the remnants of Sutton's crew got access to Darcy's deli and set a trap which might have ended their problem with her for good. Anyone else caught in the explosion would have been collateral damage.

Darcy shivered. "How soon will we know anything?" she asked Ethan.

"The gas company will be here in a few minutes. Once they shut off the valve to your store, the fire department will shut off the electricity and air out the place. When they determine it's safe, I'll take a look at the doors, see if the locks have been jimmied. Brian can go with me to see if anything has been tampered with inside the building. A couple hours from now we'll have some answers."

Del unlocked the doors to her bookstore and stepped out on the sidewalk. "Hey, what's going on?"

"Gas leak in my store," Darcy said.

"Oh, no. Why don't you wait in the bookstore? At least it's warm in there." She wrapped her arms tighter around her body. "It's too cold to stand around out here."

"She's right, baby." Rio sandwiched one of Darcy's hands between his. "Take your protein shake with you. I'll tell you when I hear anything."

"Don't you have to be at PSI soon?"

"My first aid session is at nine. I have some time." He grinned. "My teammates can handle this morning's PT with the trainees without me."

Del's eyes twinkled with merriment. "Aren't they supposed to run outside first thing?"

"Yep. Sorry to miss that."

Ethan chuckled. "Sure you are."

"Come on, Darcy. I'll make some hot tea to warm us up."

"Go on, sweetheart." Rio nudged her toward the bookstore. "I'll bring in your shake and bag."

Brian sighed as he watched the activity across the square. "I need to call my crew, tell them to take the morning off."

"Might be longer, depending on what we find," Nick warned.

With a nod, he grabbed his cell phone and walk a distance away to start his phone calls.

"Rio, these guys are becoming reckless," Ethan said, voice low. "You need to keep close tabs on Darcy."

"Yes, sir."

"I don't have the manpower to put people on her 24/7."

"I understand. Trent and Mason are at the house with her while I'm at PSI."

"What about when she's driving around town?" Nick murmured.

"I can't forbid her to leave the house. She'd tear me into little strips and feed me to Alex's dog, Spenser. The only other place I know that she's going today is the grocery store. Darcy's hosting a girls night at the house this evening. I also know she'll be spending some time on her music."

Ethan folded his arms across his chest.

If the situation weren't so serious, Rio would laugh. The police chief had superior officer intimidation down to a science. "I'll ask her to take Trent with her to the store."

A nod.

Rio retrieved Darcy's shake. Inside, he set her drink on the coffee bar. "Ask Trent to go with you on your errands today."

She winced. "Great. He'll love that. My brother hates going to the grocery store. It's why his cupboards are always bare."

"He'd rather go with you than worry about your safety, especially after this incident."

She stared out the front windows toward her store. "You're sure it's not a coincidence?"

"I'm not betting your life on it." He glanced at Del. "Why are you here so early, sugar?"

"It's book club day. Serena should be delivering food for them in a few minutes."

Darcy straightened. "Oh, good. I've been wanting to meet her. I'd love to set a time to talk to her about her business."

"Stick around for a bit and you'll have your chance. She usually drinks a cup of tea with me before she heads off to her first cooking job."

Nick walked into the store, rubbing his hands. "Please tell me you have plain coffee brewed."

Del glanced at the carafe. "You're in luck. The coffee just finished and there's nothing in there but plain old joe." She poured him a mug. "Aren't you supposed to be off shift?"

"Would have been except Rod has court this morning. Stella will be on hand soon if I need assistance. In the meantime, I appreciate the help staying awake."

Darcy wrapped her hand around Rio's. "Why don't you go on to work? I'm safe. There are people everywhere. When I leave here, I'll go straight to the house for Trent."

"I'm not leaving you unprotected. There might be a lot of people milling around, but none of them are focused on your protection."

"I can't leave the area," Nick said. "But I can stay here with Darcy if you want to run to her house and bring her brother here. I suspect he'll want to be here to keep an eye on things and find out firsthand what happened at the store."

"He's right." Darcy squeezed his hand gently. "I don't want to interfere with your job, Rio."

Though reluctant to trust her safety to anyone else, he recognized her need to take care of him in her own way. Her brother might not be able to run down a perp, but he didn't have to run to pull his weapon to defend his sister. "All right. I'll be back in a few minutes." He kissed her and forced himself to leave.

When he walked into the living room, Trent looked up from his book and frowned. "What are you doing here?"

"Darcy's store had a gas leak."

The Fortress operative scowled. "She okay?"

Rio nodded. "I left her with Nick in the bookstore. She needs to run errands today and I don't want her to go by herself. You up for bodyguard duty?"

"Oh, yeah. Let me grab my coat."

Mason walked into the room, a tape measure and clipboard in his hand. "Hey, I thought you were going to PSI this morning."

"Gas leak at Darcy's store. You sticking around here today?"

He nodded. "Brian wants me to measure every room in the place, so I'll be cleaning out the last two rooms on the third floor. Do you think Darcy will mind if I go into her room to get the dimensions?"

"I doubt it, but I'll ask her. Keep an eye on the house today, Mase."

"The gas leak wasn't an accident?"

"We don't know for sure yet. Brian insists he checked the gas connections yesterday evening before he left."

"Ready." Trent shrugged into his coat, weapon in a holster at his side. "Watch your back, Mason."

A wry smile curved his mouth. "I learned to do that well in prison."

At the bookstore, Rio walked inside with Trent to see Darcy talking to Serena Blackhawk. "Serena, you look more beautiful every time I see you."

She grinned, eyes sparkling. "That's what my husband says, but he's biased."

"He's being honest, sugar." He introduced Trent, then asked Nick, "Any word from Ethan?"

"Gas is off as is the electricity. Windows and doors are open. The fire department says it should be safe to inspect the store in another hour."

Rio stroked Darcy's back. "You staying here until there's word?"

"I want to know what happened. Besides, it will give Trent a chance to do book shopping while he's waiting for me."

Her folded his arms across his chest. "I'm on duty, Darce. I'm not leaving your side."

"The bookstore isn't open for business." Nick drained his mug and circled to the other side of the counter. "Go explore for a few minutes. I'll let you know when I leave."

Trent headed for the men's adventure section.

Rio turned back to Serena. "Where are you headed this morning?"

"Grocery store, then the Andersons. They're having an open house and asked me to prepare the food. Susan couldn't find a caterer with an opening for tonight."

"The guests are in for a treat."

"I'm hoping to pick up another client or two. One of my families moved to North Carolina." She smiled at Darcy. "I'm looking forward to your deli opening, Darcy. We've been needing something quick around here that's better quality than the gas station's offerings. I think That's A Wrap will be very popular."

"I hope you're right."

"If you want to talk more, I'll be happy to help. Sounds like you're on the right track, though."

The door to the shop opened and a gust of cold wind followed Ethan into the store. "Please tell me Del has coffee ready."

Nick grabbed another mug and poured some for his boss. "Progress?"

"We should be clear to go inside at 9:00." He sipped the coffee, sighed, smiled at his wife. "You made this pot, didn't you?"

"Del's on the phone with one of her suppliers." She slid off the barstool and reached up to kiss Ethan. "Got to go. I have a party to cater."

"Don't overdo it, baby," he murmured.

"Susan will be helping me prepare food. I have everything planned out, including rest breaks." Another kiss, and she left.

"I need to go as well," Rio said. "Quinn called. I have to cover the tactical class this morning while he meets with a dog trainer for search-and-rescue." He kissed Darcy lightly and stepped back. "See you tonight, sweetheart. Save me the leftovers."

"I heard that," Trent called. "Sorry, dude. Nate's cooking for you. I have dibs on Darcy's food."

Rio chuckled as he left. Once he worked around the emergency vehicles clogging the square, he called Zane.

"Good early morning to you, Kincaid," his friend grumbled.

"You okay?"

"Yeah. Had an op go south at one this morning. I've been asleep an hour."

"Oh, man. Sorry, Z. Everybody get out in one piece?"

"Yep. What's going on?"

Rio brought him up to date on Darcy's troubles.

"What do you need from me?" His friend's cold, clipped voice filled the SUV.

"See what you can find out about Charles Rockingham. He's the original owner of Darcy's house. There are rumors floating around that he hid a stash of Morgan silver dollars in that house. Those coins are the key to everything."

"You think Sutton's crew is after the coins."

Uneasiness roiled in his gut. "I do. However, I don't believe they came up with this scheme on their own. I think someone hired them to steal the coins." And until they unmasked the person who hired Sutton, Darcy would never be safe.

295

CHAPTER THIRTY-SIX

A few minutes after nine, Annie burst through the door of the bookstore. "What's going on?" she asked as she unzipped her cotton-candy pink winter gear. "It's a madhouse. I had to park three blocks away."

"Gas leak at my store," Darcy said.

"Oh, dear. Do you know how that happened?"

"Not yet. Ethan and Nick just left with Brian Elliott to check inside the shop." She unwrapped one of the trays Serena had left for the book club ladies. "Del's at the back of the store, getting ready for the reader's group."

"I'll just put away my things and man the register." She glanced to the side as Trent walked up to the counter with an armload of books. She smiled at him. "Well, you chose some excellent books, young man."

Darcy grinned at her brother's reddened cheeks. "Annie, this is my brother, Trent. He's visiting for a few days."

"Nice to meet you, Trent. Excuse me a minute while I hang up my coat." She hurried off and returned a moment later without her heavy coat and large bag. "Are you staying for the book club meeting, Darcy? You would enjoy it." She leaned close and whispered, "The club members are a bunch of older women who love to read murder mysteries, the more gruesome, the better." Annie started scanning Trent's books. "Who would think little old ladies would enjoy tracking murderers through the pages of novels? Not me, my dear. I much prefer a good romance."

Trent flinched at that.

"Sounds like fun," Darcy said. "I can't today, though. I need to run errands."

"Maybe next time, then. They meet once a month." She took Trent's bank card and swiped it through the card reader.

"Annie, do you know anything about the candles in Ms. Bond's house?"

"Beautiful, aren't they? For some reason, Gretchen began making candles a few months before she died."

Disappointment flooded her. "That's too bad. I was hoping to buy more candles similar to those."

"If you want unique candles, you should talk to Kira at Kira's Wicks. She makes most of her stock. If you turn right at Dogwood and drive about a block, you'll see her shop on the right." Del's assistant gave Trent his card and handed him a large bag of books. "Enjoy them, Trent. Now, if you don't want to keep these once you're finished, bring them back in and swap them for some of the used stock."

Several older women walked in the front door and straight to the back table. That was her cue to deliver the trays Serena had left. She set a wide selection of muffins in the center of the table, then returned with another filled with cut fruit. So pretty. Annie brought a platter of cookies. Trent brought up the rear with a tray of mugs, some filled with coffee, others with tea.

Returning to the front of the store, she watched Nick stride from the deli toward the bookstore. "Maybe we'll finally hear something now." She grasped her shake container and finished the last of her drink.

The detective blew on his hands as he approached the counter. "The gas leak was not an accident."

Beside her, Trent stiffened. "You're sure?"

"Positive. The gas pipe to the stove was broken and the stove itself was crooked and off balance. When Brian left yesterday it was level and straight, and the pipe is brand new."

"Maybe he's lying. Wouldn't be the first time someone tried to cover shoddy workmanship."

"Doesn't make sense, bro." Darcy glared at him. "Why would he intentionally mess up his own work? He showed me how the stove worked the morning before the car accident."

"Adding work pads his bill."

"Could have blown himself up along with his crew," Nick said. "I can't see him doing that."

"Did someone break in, Nick?"

He shook his head. "No evidence to support that conclusion."

"Was the lock picked, like at Darcy's house?" Trent asked.

Another head shake in response.

"So it was an inside job." Trent folded his arms across his chest. "I guess Elliott could have sabotaged the stove after all."

"He has an alibi, St. Claire. I've already verified it." He turned to Darcy. "How many people have a key to the deli?"

"I have one and so does Brian. I'm sure the landlord has one as well. Other than that, I don't know of anyone else."

"Who's the landlord?" When she gave him the name, he said, "I'll check with him, see if there are other keys floating around. In the meantime, you should have him change the locks. Might be safer for everybody."

"Won't make a difference if Elliott's involved," Trent muttered.

She leaned close to her brother. "Those coins aren't worth as much as he'd make on his building projects."

"And it's too risky," Nick added. "There's no proof the coins still exist, either."

"Somebody wants something from Darcy bad enough they're willing to kill to get it, and I guarantee it's not her Steinway." He turned to Darcy. "You ready, sis?"

She nodded. "See you later, Nick. Keep me posted."

"I'll tell you what I can, Darcy."

Trent snorted, helped her into her coat, and grabbed his bag of books. "Later, Detective."

The hairs on the back of her neck stood up as she and her brother left the store. Outside, she dug out her remote and said, "Could you have antagonized him any more, Trent? He's not just a cop to me. He's my friend and Josh's brother-in-law."

Her brother pulled up short, his expression growing sheepish. "I didn't realize he was that Nick."

Right. Like the name Nick Santana was so commonplace. She climbed behind the wheel, maneuvered out of the square, and turned right.

"Where are we going?"

"Candle shop and your favorite place, the grocery store."

Trent groaned and slid lower in the seat. "Great. Just what I need to make my morning complete."

"Quit complaining. Look at it this way. You'll get to choose your own junk food."

Darcy turned on Dogwood and located Kira's Wicks. "Want to stay here?"

He just stared at her. She rolled her eyes. There might be a killer in there waiting to waylay her. They exited the SUV and went into the shop.

"Oh, man." Her brother sighed. "If I breathe wrong or turn too fast, I'll bring the place down on my head."

Taking pity on him, she left him standing by the entrance, found Kira and described what she was looking for. When she left the shop ten minutes later, Trent carried another bag, this one full of carefully wrapped handmade candles. Darcy couldn't wait to see them in the hurricane lamps she'd bought from Bob Schiller.

Inside the vehicle, Trent said, his voice filled with hope, "Grocery store, then home, right?"

"That's the plan. I want to help Mason clean out the last two rooms on the third floor. He has to measure each room today."

By noon, they returned to the Victorian and unloaded their purchases. Trent's limp had grown worse in the grocery aisles so she was glad to see him head for the recliner as soon as he hung up his coat. After putting the food for her dinner party in the refrigerator, she climbed to the third floor and found Mason gathering items to cart to the Dumpster. "Not much to keep?"

"Not so far."

"Have you eaten lunch?"

"I was going to eat after I dumped this load and washed up."

"Give me fifteen minutes and I'll have grilled cheese sandwiches and hot tomato soup ready for you and Trent." She wrinkled her nose. "I'll have to come up with something else for me." Maybe tomato soup and leftover chicken for her meal.

"Thanks, Darcy."

After lunch, she and Mason cleared the rest of the room. Darcy stood back as he measured the empty space. She shook her head at the new holes they had uncovered in the floor and walls. More work for Mason and his fellow workmen. "Did you measure the rest of the house?"

He glanced her direction before writing down the measurements on his clipboard. "Including your room. I hope you don't mind. Rio said he would ask."

"He did. It's fine, Mason."

"While I was measuring, I noticed there's a stone loose on your hearth. I can fix that for you. I spent a couple summers during my school years doing concrete and masonry work."

"A loose stone?" She furrowed her brow. "Show me."

She and Mason traipsed down to her second-floor bedroom.

"Right here." He crossed the room and knelt in front of her hearth. The stone was at the edge, near the wall. Sure enough, when Mason touched it, the stone rocked. "It should be easy to fix."

"Mason, you don't think…" She stopped, not daring to put what she thought into words. Could this be Charles Rockingham's hiding place for his money? Or was the loose stone just the product of time on crumbling mortar?

His gaze dropped to the rock. "Only one way to find out." He grasped the rock, wiggled it back and forth, working it out of position until he grabbed hold of it and pulled it free. The rock had covered a deep cubbyhole.

Not enough light to see into the depths of the hole. "Do you have a flashlight?" she asked.

"Yep. I'll be back." When he returned, Mason had a large flashlight in his hand. He aimed it at the cubbyhole and clicked on the light.

Darcy peered inside. She gasped. "There's a velvet bag at the bottom."

"The silver dollars?"

"I don't think so. The bag looks empty." She reached inside and wrapped her fingers around the soft cloth. Darcy frowned as she pulled the bag out of the hole. "There's something in here." She loosened the drawstring and turned the bag upside down.

A silver coin dropped onto her palm.

CHAPTER THIRTY-SEVEN

Rio pressed the cell phone to his ear as he reached Nate's porch. "How's it going, sweetheart?" The feminine laughter drifting through the speaker made him grin. Sounded like the ladies were having a good time.

"Terrific. This is loads of fun, Rio. The taco dip is almost ready. We've already eaten the mini-tacos Nate sent with Stella along with queso dip and chips. Ivy's tossing salad as we speak, and Del is removing the chicken burritos from the oven right now. It smells like a Mexican restaurant in here."

"Sounds fabulous." His stomach agreed. "Tell me you have a Mexican wrap on the menu for your deli."

"Absolutely. Want me to save a sample of dinner for you?"

"If you have enough." He'd invited both to Nate's, but with the latest incident at Darcy's store, neither wanted to leave the women without extra protection.

"Don't worry. I made plenty."

"Enjoy your dinner, Darcy. I'll see you in a few hours."

He walked into Nate's place and realized his teammate had cooked a similar menu. On the large television played a pre-recorded football game, one Durango had missed seeing while out of the country on a mission.

Nate walked into the living room, drying his hands on a kitchen towel. "Soft drink, tea, or water, Rio?"

"Tea if it's green or water."

Durango's explosives expert studied him for a moment. "You're adopting Darcy's diet."

He shrugged one shoulder. "It's a healthy one."

"Yeah, but that's not why you're doing it. Does she know?"

His face burned as Josh, Alex, and Quinn shifted their attention from the pre-game show to him. "Know what?"

"That you're in love with her."

Was it that obvious? He'd barely dared acknowledge his feelings to himself much less the woman who had captured his heart. "It's too soon," he hedged. But his friend was right. Rio was head-over-heels in love with Darcy St. Claire, and before long she would figure it out if he didn't tell her outright.

"Not if she's the right one," Alex said, his voice soft. "I knew the moment I saw Ivy she was meant for me."

"And sometimes love grows over a period of time," Josh added. "Took me a year to realize I loved Del."

"The point is you changed your diet to match your girlfriend's," Nate said. "You don't make a radical change like that unless the woman is very special."

"I've never met anyone like her," he admitted.

"Take your coat off and get your drink," Quinn said. "The Cowboys are getting ready to kick off."

Rio draped his coat around the back of a kitchen chair, knowing he and his teammates would end up eating in the living room while they watched the game.

"Does Trent know?" Nate asked as he opened the refrigerator and grabbed a pitcher of green tea.

"I'm still alive, aren't I?"

"I'll take that as a no." He handed Rio a filled glass. "And, yeah, it's green tea. I keep some in the refrigerator for Stella."

"I need your mother's cell phone number. Darcy wants to talk to her about supplying tea for her deli."

"No problem. She supplies it for the restaurant." He sent Rio a text with the number. "Go watch the game. I'll bring the appetizers in a minute."

He retraced his steps and dropped onto the couch beside Quinn. When the Eagles fielded the ball and ran it all the way back for a touchdown, they all groaned.

Nate brought in two trays of mini tacos, then plates. "Dig in, boys. Looks like the Cowboys will need a lot of support to win this game."

"Does anyone know who won the game?" Quinn asked.

"I do," Josh said. "Dad forgot I hadn't seen it yet. He said it was a great game."

"Don't say anything more." Alex loaded his plate. "I've been looking forward to seeing this game for a couple weeks."

In the next hour, Rio and his teammates demolished the mini-tacos plus queso dip and chips. With five minutes left in the half, Nate pulled enchilada casserole out of the oven and refilled drinks.

Josh's cell phone rang. He checked the screen, frowned. "Ethan, what's up?" He listened a moment, his face losing all expression.

Quinn grabbed the remote and paused the game.

"We'll be there in five." Durango's leader ended the call and stood. "Let's roll. Hostage situation at the bank. Three gunmen, twelve hostages, including Dad and Serena. We'll gear up on site. Quinn, ride with Nate. Alex, Rio, with me."

Within a minute, Go bags and Rio's mike bag had been transferred and they were on the move. Otter Creek police officers had blockaded the roads leading into the town square, but one moved his patrol car so the two SUVs could slip through. As soon as the vehicles came to a stop, the members of Durango dived out, grabbed their bags and geared up.

Ethan trotted over, barking out an order for one of the officers to move the civilians beyond the square. "I don't want anyone in the line of fire."

"Yes, sir."

He turned. "I need a special weapons and tactics team. You in?"

"Oh, yeah," Josh said, face grim. "Sit rep."

"Four men armed with handguns. Twelve hostages, seven women, five men. Thankfully, no children are in there." His voice choked off a moment.

No children except for his unborn child. Rio tugged his bulletproof vest down and yanked his shirt on to cover it. "What do they want? Money?"

"They want access to the safety deposit boxes, specifically Gretchen Bond's box."

He froze. "Why?"

"They won't say."

"Why doesn't Aaron open the box for them?"

Ethan glanced at Josh. "He can't. The idiots pistol whipped him and he's unconscious. The manager is out with pneumonia. The assistant manager left for a doctor's appointment ten minutes before the perps stormed the place."

The muscle in Josh's jaw twitched as he slid his Ka-Bar into the sheath on his leg.

"They need to drill the box," Quinn said. "If you're looking for volunteers, I'll do it."

"They brought their own." The police chief glanced at Rio. "I need a medic for Aaron. These guys are skittish enough and I don't want the EMTs in there. They can't handle the pressure. I also want someone who can take down a perp if it's necessary."

"Yes, sir."

"You shouldn't be heading this op, Ethan," Josh said, worry in his gaze. "The feds have jurisdiction in bank robberies."

A sharp look from his boss. "One of them has a gun to my wife's head, Cahill. No one is taking control of this operation but me. Clear?"

"Yes, sir." He reached into his Go bag. "You'll need this." Josh handed Ethan one of the spare comm systems he always carried on missions.

"Thanks." Once the gear was in place, he said, "I never thought I'd say this, Josh, but I want you and Nate to break into the back of the bank. The door is wired with an alarm. Disable it. Alex, you and Quinn find high ground. The best line of sight is probably on top of Del's store. Two of the men are in the main part of the bank; the other two are getting ready to drill Bond's lock box. The loan officer has been stalling as much as she can, but the perps are growing antsy."

He turned to Quinn. "You as good a shot as Alex?"

"Close."

"I want your scope on the second perp." He turned to Alex. "You take the one holding my wife. I'm trusting you with safety of the woman I love." A nod from the sniper. "Neither of you take a shot unless I give the command. Clear?"

"Yes, sir."

Josh dug into his pocket and handed his keys to Alex. "The one with the blue covering."

Durango's sniper and his spotter grabbed their rifles and Go bags and ran across the square to Otter Creek Books.

Ethan yanked a notebook and pen from his pocket, sketched a rough diagram of the bank. "There are security cameras here and here at the back. We don't want them to see you breaking in. The camera shots feed into a computer in Aaron's office. If the perps go into the office, they'll see activity at the door. Any chance Fortress has someone who can create a loop, fast?"

"Zane can do it," Josh said. "You have the IP address?"

Ethan grabbed his phone, punched in a code, and scrolled until he found what he was looking for. "Right here. Aaron gave it to me when I moved here in case something like this happened."

"Text it to me. I'll send it to Z." A minute later, his text tone signaled. With a few keystrokes, Josh sent the information to Zane.

Alex's voice came over the comm system. "In position, Ethan."

"Wait for my command. I want to talk these clowns into surrendering, but my first priority is the safety of the hostages."

"Copy that."

Rod jogged to their group. "Ethan, the perps are demanding to talk to you or they'll execute the hostages, starting with Aaron."

CHAPTER THIRTY-EIGHT

Darcy held her aching sides. "So, then what happened?"

"Spenser gave Alex that 'who me, I'm innocent,' look and my tough Delta husband melted." Ivy sighed while the other women laughed. "Now I need to make another trip to the store for new slippers and this time buy a pair that doesn't resemble cats. Spenser ripped the head off of each one and tore them apart. I'm still finding bits of stuffing in our bedroom."

The doorbell rang. "I've got it," Trent called.

"Nice to have your own butler to answer the door," Stella said. "I don't know about the rest of you, but I can't eat another bite. I say we clean up and go into the living room. Maybe Darcy will play for us."

"Do you feel up to it, Darcy?" Del asked. "If not, we can wait until the concert."

"But we really want a preview," Ivy added with a smile.

"I need to practice anyway."

Trent came into the room. "Darce, there's a Paul Cambridge here. He says you gave him permission to take pictures of the house."

She blinked. "I didn't expect him to come tonight. It's fine to let him inside."

"Do you know anything about him?"

"He's a history professor at the college," Ivy said. "He's fascinated with architecture. The faculty Christmas party was at his house. Where most people have paintings, he has pictures of famous structures."

"I don't care who he is. He's not getting free reign in the house."

"I'll go with him as a tour guide," Stella said.

"Ivy and I will help Darcy clean up." Del started stacking dishes and carried them to the sink. "We'll join you in a few minutes, Trent."

With a nod, he returned to the door to let the professor inside the house. Darcy shook her head slightly. Yeah, she knew her brother had kept the other man locked out on the porch. No one could say her brother wasn't careful.

"Where's Mason?" Ivy asked as she rinsed the first plate.

"He mentioned talking to his father. To be honest, I think we overwhelmed him."

"Must be hard to adjust after so many years out of the general population."

"I guess Rio told his teammates."

Del distributed the silverware in the dishwasher's utensil compartments. "You might as well get used to it. Durango doesn't keep too many secrets from each other."

Stella led Paul Cambridge into the kitchen, a camera in his hand. "Thought we'd start here."

"Hello, ladies. I apologize for intruding, Ms. St. Claire. I was passing by here on the way home and decided to stop in and see if you minded me taking pictures before the renovation began. I had no idea you were hosting a party. I won't take long."

"Most of the rooms are clear so you should have an easy time taking pictures of the structure."

"I'll be out of your way soon." He quickly pulled up his camera and started snapping shots of the room.

Darcy noticed the other women made sure their images weren't captured in any of the shots. Having their pictures taken was a security issue? When he turned to photograph her side of the room, she moved out of camera range. Once he'd finished and moved on to another room, Darcy, Del, and Ivy finished the kitchen.

They traipsed into the living room to wait for Stella. Trent glanced at the three of them and promptly turned the television station to another channel.

"You don't think we'd be interested in boxing?" Ivy asked, amusement lighting her eyes.

His head whipped their direction. "Are you?"

Del grinned. "Not really, but it's fine for you to watch the fight until Stella finishes tour guide duty. Darcy agreed to play for us."

"As long as the sound is off, it's fine for you to watch the fight while I'm playing, bro."

He rubbed his hands together briskly. "Fantastic. You rock, Darce." Trent turned back to the station covering the boxing match. "This is the fight of the century."

She and the other two women exchanged grins. Darcy couldn't remember how many times she'd heard those exact words from her brother. How many fights of the century could there be?

Finally, Stella returned with Cambridge. "I'm so glad you didn't start without me," she said. "I don't want to miss a minute. I can't wait to tell Nate I had a chance to hear you play before he did."

Del's eyebrows rose. "Doesn't he like head-banging rock?"

"When he's working out."

"Same with Alex," Ivy said.

"Before you start to play, Ms. St. Claire, would it be all right if I helped myself to a glass of water?"

"The glasses are in the cabinet to the left of the sink."

"I'll get it for you," Del said. "We put together a tray of soft drinks for everybody anyway."

"Just relax. I'll bring the tray in for you." When he returned, he brought a tray of glasses filled with iced soft drinks. "When I listen to music I enjoy having a drink in my hand."

Darcy suspected the drink he was talking about was a lot different than the ones he was handing to those in the room. When he brought her drink, she smiled and thanked him, not having the heart to tell him she couldn't drink it.

"I'd like to take pictures of the wraparound porch at the back of the house if you don't mind. Then I'll be on my way."

"Sure, Mr. Cambridge."

As soon as he left the room, Ivy sipped her drink and said, "Do you want to drink that now or wait until later?"

"Later." Once everyone was gone, she would pour it down the drain.

Trent muted the sound on the television and Darcy began to play. Like always, the power of the music swept her away. She chose a suite by Debussy, a particular favorite of hers, the dreamy music perfect for a cold evening with a crackling fire in the stone fireplace. When the last notes died away, she glanced at her silent audience to ask if they wanted to hear more.

Her eyes widened as she looked at each of them in turn. Stella, Del, and Ivy were asleep. Darcy turned to her brother with a grin, sure he'd be enjoying the fact she'd put her new friends to sleep with her music. She stilled. He was asleep as well.

Swallowing hard, she hurried to her brother's side. Something was definitely wrong. He would never go to sleep while on guard duty. "Trent." She knelt beside the recliner, shook him. "Trent."

Nothing. Not good. Even if he was exhausted and had fallen asleep, the military trained him to wake up, fully alert at the slightest sound or touch. It was as if he and the others had been drugged.

Her gaze fell on Trent's empty glass. She turned, saw the rest of the glasses were also empty. Paul Cambridge? Why? Darcy stood. Was Mason drugged as well? She took two steps and skidded to a halt.

The history professor stepped into the room with a gun in his hand.

CHAPTER THIRTY-NINE

Ethan glanced at Rio. "Ready?"
Knife secured in a sheath under his pant leg. Backup weapon on his other ankle. He hitched the mike bag over his shoulder and nodded.
"Josh, go. Alex, Quinn, stand by." After his orders were acknowledged, Ethan motioned for Rio to follow him.
They stopped next to Rod who handed Ethan the bullhorn.
"This is Blackhawk. You wanted to talk. I'm coming inside with a medic."
"You stay out there."
"I want my people safe. I'm willing to listen to what you want."
"We want safe passage out of here," came the shouted response.
"We need to talk about how we can make that happen. You want safe passage, I'm coming inside so we can talk."
"Just you, then. And no weapon."
Rio snorted. These guys were fooling themselves if they thought the police chief was harmless without a gun in

his hand. His close quarters combat skills were lethal, but his best weapon was his brain.

"There's a civilian down in the bank. He needs medical help. I know you don't want his death on your conscience. The medic comes in with me or you get nothing."

"We're holding all the cards here, Blackhawk."

"I'm coming inside now." He shoved the bullhorn into Rod's hands. "If one of them takes me down, Josh has control of this operation." He held his hand up when Rod started to protest. "This is a hostage situation, Rod, something Fortress specializes in. I need you out here. If they get past all of us, you do not let these clowns out of Dunlap County."

"You better not get hurt. Sir."

"I'm not planning on it. I have a son or daughter I want to hold in a couple months." A glance at Rio and he strode toward the bank's front door, hands clearly visible. "Stay behind me, Rio."

"Only until we're inside the bank."

"In," Josh murmured over the comm.

"Copy."

Ethan opened the door and walked inside. As soon as Rio cleared the door, he moved away from Ethan. If these guys wanted to shoot him and Ethan, he wasn't going to make it easy for them by lining up like ducks in a shooting gallery.

Aaron lay on the floor in front of teller row. Except for Serena, the other hostages were lying, faces down, near the back wall. The men looked angry. Several of the women were crying. To the right of Aaron stood the gunman pressing the muzzle of a 9 mm weapon against Serena's head. Lava boiled in his gut. Doug Walsh.

The guy guarding the other hostages turned. Rio frowned. Tom Gates, the EMT he'd taught in his medic classes.

"What's he doing in here?" Gates demanded of his crew mate. "He's with the bodyguard school outside of town."

Walsh pressed the weapon harder into Serena's temple, causing her to flinch. "You trying to pull something, Blackhawk?"

He inclined his head toward Aaron. "He needs a medic. Kincaid is an excellent medic."

Down the short hallway, a drill started up. Rio eased the mike bag from his shoulder and crossed the lobby to crouch by Aaron's side. Walsh dragged Serena a couple feet further away, a sneer on his face.

"Locked on," Alex murmured. "Clear shot."

"Secondary target acquired," Quinn said. "No visual on the other targets."

Which meant Josh and Nate were going in blind. Rio unzipped his bag. If the other two men noticed his Durango teammates before Josh and Nate took them down, they would raise the alarm. A single misstep would cost Serena her life and that of her unborn child.

He glanced at Ethan who gave a slight nod. Rio turned his attention to Aaron. His friend was still unconscious. There were two gashes on the side and one on the back of his head, all needing stitches. He ripped open a package of gauze, tried to stem the bleeding from the worst cut, but the blood continued to flow freely.

Rio turned to Serena who was carefully not looking at her father. He'd forgotten about her aversion to blood. "Serena, is Aaron taking blood thinner?"

She gave a slight nod.

Not what he wanted to hear. "Ethan, Aaron needs to be in a hospital right now. If he doesn't get treatment, he could die."

"Oh, man," Gates moaned. "I didn't sign on for this. You said no one else would get hurt."

No one else? Was he talking about Sutton? Maybe Walsh killed the other man.

"Shut up, Tommy," Walsh snapped. "You're the super medic, Kincaid. Treat him."

"He needs meds to help his blood clot. There's also a very good chance he has a subdural hematoma." He shoved his hand into his bag for a packet of QuickClot and poured the contents in the cuts and covered the wounds. This would at least control the external bleeding. If Aaron had internal bleeding like Rio suspected, only a doctor could save his friend.

"All right, Walsh," Ethan said. "You're the one in control. What do you want in exchange for Aaron's release?"

Satisfaction bloomed on Walsh's face. "Safe passage out of here, Blackhawk, and you can cart the old geezer to the hospital."

"What do you want in return for the safety of the other hostages?"

"A car, no cops in sight all the way to the county line. You come after me, this pretty blond dies."

"And if I follow your instructions?" Ethan asked, voice soft, inching to the right.

Oh, man. Rio's gaze shifted to Gates while the police chief engaged Walsh in conversation. He caught the EMTs attention and whispered, "Don't do this, Tom. You're throwing your life away for nothing."

The other man swallowed hard. "You don't understand."

"Then make me understand."

"He's my uncle. I owe him."

"You owe him your life? Because that is what's at stake. You have a choice to make, one which determines your future." If he made the wrong one, Gates wouldn't have a future and Rio couldn't find it in his heart to feel sorry for him.

317

The other man's face hardened. "Then I choose blood. I'm tired of barely making a living."

So be it. Gates was no longer Rio's priority. If things went south, the EMT belonged to Quinn. He shifted his attention to Serena. She was pale and her hands were shaking. "Serena, look at me, sugar." Her gaze locked with his. "Stay with me."

Walsh glared at him. "Shut up, Kincaid." He raised his voice. "Springer, what's taking so long? Did you get them or not?"

Rio shifted his weight as Gates moved closer to the hallway leading to the lock boxes.

"No shot," Quinn murmured.

A glance told Rio the EMT had moved far enough that the concrete column blocked Quinn's line of sight. Guess they were going with the alternate plan. He pulled his mike bag out of the way with his right hand, giving himself clear path to Serena. A slight nod at Ethan.

The police chief eased his right hand behind his back. "You want safe passage, Walsh? I'll give it to you. But the only hostage you walk out of here with is me."

Serena's lips trembled. When she opened her mouth, Rio shook his head. She didn't need to draw attention to herself. She subsided as tears trickled down her cheeks.

The other man gave a bark of laughter. "Guess you have a death wish, Chief. You're too much trouble to keep around for long."

"Something is wrong, Uncle Doug," Gates said. "Adam and Ryan should have been here by now." He swung around, aiming his weapon at Rio, his voice rising steadily higher with each statement. "You're not just a medic, are you? Where are your friends? I bet they hurt Adam and his brother. You're a dead man, Rio." His finger tightened on the trigger of his weapon.

"Now," Ethan said, pulling his weapon and firing on Gates. The EMT flew backward and fell spread-eagled on his back less than a foot from the hostages.

Weapon fire sounded from down the hall. Walsh roared in anger at Ethan for shooting his nephew and shifted his gun toward the police chief. The window at the front of the bank shattered. A large hole opened in Walsh's forehead.

At the same time, Rio sprang for Serena as screams from the other female hostages filled the bank. He caught her just before she hit the ground, Walsh's body dead weight against her back. Rio wrapped her in his arms as he eased her to the floor, keeping his body between her and the carnage in the bank. "Do me a favor and don't look, sugar. I like these boots."

A light swat on his back was his response.

"You okay?"

"I think so."

Ethan kicked Gates' gun away from his limp hand. "Rio?"

"She's fine. Not a scratch on her." His next concern was the baby.

Otter Creek officers swarmed the bank as Josh ran from the hall to his father's side. "Rod," he snapped. "Get those EMTs in here."

The detective motioned for the medics and pointed them at Aaron, then directed one of the officers to the room with the lock boxes.

Rio eased back enough from Serena to look her in the eye. "Go to the hospital to make sure you and your baby are all right, sugar."

Her eyes welled. "Rio, the baby hasn't moved."

His heart clenched. "Any injuries to your stomach? Did you fall or did they hit you?"

She shook her head.

Ethan dropped to his knees beside her. He wrapped his arms around her, his gaze spearing Rio. "Talk to me."

"Take your wife to the hospital."

"I thought you said she wasn't injured."

"It's just a precaution. The doc will want to monitor her and the baby for a while, do an ultrasound."

The police chief paled. "Is the baby all right?"

"Not moving at the moment."

Ethan scooped Serena into his arms and stood. "Rod, you have the scene. Call in Nick to help you process. I'm taking Serena to the hospital."

"Yes, sir."

The EMTs rolled the stretcher with Aaron out the door, followed by Ethan carrying his wife.

Rio grabbed his mike bag. He spared a glance for Gates, then hiked his bag over his shoulder as Nate strode to his side. At that moment, his cell phone vibrated in his pocket.

He pulled it out, glanced at the screen. "It's Zane. He knows who's behind the attacks on Darcy."

"Who is it?"

"He wants me to call him."

"Outside. It's a madhouse in here. You won't be able to hear anything."

He and his teammate returned to the sidewalk a short distance from the first responders. Rio called Zane. "Who?"

"Paul Cambridge, the history professor at the community college."

He frowned. "What's his connection to Darcy?"

"The house. He's a direct descendant of Charles Rockingham."

"You sure?"

"Please. Of course I'm sure. He's researched Morgan silver dollars and Darcy's house for the past six months. There's a trail of emails between him and Troy Sutton, including a contentious discussion of payment once the job is complete. Cambridge is the man behind the attacks on Trent's sister."

"Thanks, Z. I owe you one." He ended the call and relayed the information to Nate.

"Let's go have a talk with Cambridge." A cold smile crossed his friend's face. "I'll persuade him to talk."

Rio found his team leader on the sidewalk, frown on his face, phone in his hand. "What's wrong?"

"Del's not answering her phone."

Ice poured through his veins. He called Darcy, then Mason. No answer from either one. He glanced at Nate, who had his phone pressed to his ear. A grim expression settled on his face as he shook his head. Rio activated his mic. "Alex?"

"I called Ivy. Nothing. We're coming down."

He turned to Josh. "Zane said Paul Cambridge is a descendant of Charles Rockingham."

"He's after the silver dollars."

Alex and Quinn ran across the square and met the rest of Durango at the SUVs. "Trent?" Quinn asked.

"No answer," Nate said.

Trent was down. They loaded their gear in the vehicles and sped toward the Victorian. Rio just prayed they weren't too late.

CHAPTER FORTY

"What did you do to them, Professor Cambridge?" Darcy gaze dropped to the black weapon in the history teacher's hand before refocusing on his face.

"I drugged them. They'll be fine. You won't be so lucky. You've been nothing but trouble since the moment you arrived in town."

She glanced at Stella, who was the closest to her. Her breathing seemed untroubled and deep. Cambridge could be lying. He didn't have an incentive to be honest. He'd made it plain he planned to kill her. She had to help the others. What about Mason? Had he been drugged, too?

"What do you want, Professor?"

"Don't play the innocent with me, Ms. St. Claire. You know exactly what I want."

Fury flooded her body, giving her much needed courage. "The silver dollars." She wished she'd never heard of those things or bought the house. The lives of her brother and friends meant more to her than any treasure or house.

"Hand them over and I'll make sure your death is painless."

Nice. Some incentive to cooperate. Die a painful death or die an easy death. Too bad for him she wasn't choosing either option. "You're behind all the accidents and break-ins. Why? It's just money." And not that much if what she and Mason found in the hearth was the remnant of Rockingham's coins.

"On the contrary. Those coins are my legacy."

Darcy frowned. "I don't understand."

"Charles Rockingham was my great grandfather."

Heat seared her cheeks. "Why didn't you buy the house? It sat empty for three years."

"I didn't know about Rockingham or his treasure until I researched my genealogy during the summer. You can't imagine the thrill of discovering my connection to this amazing house and Otter Creek's history." He scowled. "The Bond woman's family rejected my offer. They wanted too much money."

Footsteps in the hallway, then, "Darcy, why did you stop playing? Your music was beautiful."

"Mason, run!"

Cambridge grabbed her arm and yanked her in front of him, gun pressed to her side. "If you do, she dies."

Mason raised his hands. "What's this about?"

"The silver dollars." When she tried to free herself, the hold on her arm tightened like a vise. She flinched.

"Don't hurt her." Rio's cousin took two steps forward. "Let Darcy go and I'll give you what you want."

"You have the coins?" Suspicion rang in his voice.

"I know where Rockingham hid them." He extended one of his hands. "Give her to me and I'll show you."

A hard shove sent her careening into Mason. He steadied her. "The others?" he murmured in her ear.

"Drugged."

"Show me the coins. Now." Cambridge aimed his weapon at them. "Otherwise, I'll kill you both and search for the coins myself."

She glared at him. "You broke in here several times and found nothing."

A snort. "Who could find anything in this firetrap? That old lady had more garbage in here than a landfill. The search will be easy now."

What were they going to do? If Cambridge killed her and Mason, what prevented him from killing the others? They would remember him taking pictures. If Cambridge let the others live, Ethan would be after him in a heartbeat. Grim determination filled her. She couldn't let him murder everyone in this house.

The professor waggled his gun. "Move."

Mason released Darcy's arms and nudged her ahead of him, placing his body between her and the gun. Her eyes stung at his attempt to protect her from Cambridge. She walked toward the stairs as slow as she dared. She didn't want to give him an excuse for shooting Mason in the back. What she wouldn't give for a weapon right now.

Since that wasn't an option, she needed to use something in her bedroom. Most of her belongings were still in storage. She had a lot of candles, a few clothes, flat shoes, hairbrush, a handheld mirror, nothing that might save their lives. Near the top of the stairs, Darcy's cell phone rang.

"Don't answer it," Cambridge said.

A minute later, the phone in Mason's pocket rang. Darcy's heart leaped in her chest. Very few people had Mason's number. His father, Rio, maybe the police chief, his boss. The successive phone calls gave her hope the caller was Rio. If he didn't get an answer from either of them, he would arrive within minutes and walk into a trap. Think, Darcy. There must be some way to turn the tide. She didn't want to lose Rio.

She and Mason trudged to her bedroom. She cleared the doorway and scanned the room. Her gaze fell on the box of hurricane lamps she from Schiller's store. The glass was too thin to be much of a defense. One of the wooden bases might work provided she got her hands on one.

"Where are they?" Cambridge demanded.

Mason gestured to the fireplace. "Under a stone in the hearth." He crossed the room with Darcy and knelt in front of the stones.

"Not you. Her."

Rats. Cambridge would've been distracted watching Mason, giving her the chance to grab a lamp base. "I'm not sure I can move the stone without help."

"You'll manage if you want your friend to live a few minutes longer."

She scowled at the professor over her shoulder, then sat on the hearth. Hand on the stone, she rocked it back and forth, gradually moving it off the hiding place.

Cambridge inched closer, attention fixed on the stone in her hand. "Hurry."

Darcy slid her hand into the opening, cradled the stone in both hands, and shifted it to the floor. "In here."

"Bring the coins to me."

The professor expected more than one coin. What would he do when he realized there weren't any more? She reached into the hole where Mason had returned the bag. Wrapping her fingers around the fabric, she pulled the nearly empty bag from its hiding place. Mason stood and helped Darcy to her feet.

"Give them to me."

She started toward him when Mason stopped her with an arm across her stomach.

"Toss it," he said.

The other man scowled.

Mason shifted so his body blocked her from moving closer. Stubborn like his cousin. Darcy balled the bag in her fist and tossed it toward Cambridge.

He grabbed it in mid-air. Shock, then rage filled his face. "Where are the rest of them? My great grandfather had three hundred silver dollars hidden when he died."

"How do you know the exact number of silver dollars?"

"I found the journal where he recorded the amount. Now, where are they?"

Rio's cousin moved so he was standing squarely in front of Darcy. She'd never have a better chance. She reached behind her into the box and grabbed a wooden base. Pitiful defense against a bullet, but it was all she had.

She straightened, shifted enough to see Cambridge. "That's all we found. There aren't anymore."

"I don't believe you." Cambridge's voice rose. "You stole them from me. The whole town is talking about how much money you're spending here and at the store. You're spending my inheritance." He aimed at the weapon at Darcy.

"No!" Mason stepped in front of her.

The weapon discharged.

CHAPTER FORTY-ONE

Rio and his teammates parked two houses down, bailed from the SUVs, and approached the house in total silence. Weapons in hand, Josh signaled the others to circle around to the back, for Rio to follow him.

He longed to storm the place, knew he couldn't. Moving in haste could cost Darcy and the others their lives. If they weren't already dead. Pain speared his heart at that thought, followed quickly by resolve to exact revenge if Cambridge had taken away the woman he wanted to spend the rest of his life with.

He and Josh worked their way toward the porch, moving from one shadow to another. They flanked the large picture window. Josh reached up and unscrewed the light bulb, then nodded for Rio to look inside the living room. Darcy had pulled back the curtains at some point, allowing him to see into the house.

Breath stalled in his lungs. "Trent, Del, Ivy, and Stella are down. No visible injuries," he murmured. "No one else in sight." Where were Darcy and Mason? Fear threatened to paralyze him. He forced his rioting emotions inside a mental box to deal with later. Right now, he had a job to do and inattention would kill them all.

"Alex?" Josh murmured.

"Kitchen's empty," he replied, his voice tight. "Josh." Alex's voice cracked.

Rio tried the front door. His eyebrows rose. Unlocked. He glanced at Josh, shook his head.

Durango's leader motioned for him to open the door. "Alex, go."

They swept into the living room, weapons quartering the room. Knowing his teammate would be distracted until he knew if his wife was alive, Rio checked Del's pulse. Relief rolled through him at the steady throbbing in her neck. "Alive." He tapped her cheek, got no response. "Drugged."

Nate, Alex, and Quinn moved into the room while he checked the others. "Same as Del. Get them out of here, Major." Then he would find Darcy and Mason. If Cambridge had hurt them, he was a dead man.

Josh, Alex, and Nate carried their wives from the house, while Rio helped Quinn with Trent. His gut screamed at him to find Darcy, but Trent was a big man. Quinn couldn't carry him unless it was over his shoulder, a position which wasn't possible with the other operative's recent surgery. After Josh laid Del in the SUV, he ran to help Quinn, freeing Rio to search for Darcy.

He sprinted to the house and began clearing rooms, one at a time. Nothing. He approached the stairs. His eyes narrowed at the murmur of voices. The closer he came, the more distinctive the words.

"You're spending my inheritance," Cambridge yelled.

Rio raced up the stairs two at a time, praying he reached them in time.

"No!" Mason. A gunshot, followed by a screech from Darcy, and a loud thump. A roar of fury from Cambridge.

Rio raced to Darcy's room, weapon in his hand. He took in the situation at a glance. Mason lay on the ground, clutching his right thigh, blood seeping between his fingers. Cambridge was on all fours, blood pouring from a head wound. Darcy held a piece of wood in her hands.

Holstering his Sig, Rio crossed the room in three strides as she slammed the wood down on Cambridge's hand which was still grasping a weapon. The professor screamed.

When Darcy raised her hands to whack him again, Rio said, "He's finished, baby," and tossed the wood aside. He gave a passing thought to letting her give him another shot or two, decided it would put Josh in an awkward position. Rio grasped Cambridge's weapon and yanked it from his hand to the accompaniment of the professor's shout of pain.

Relief spread across Darcy's face. "I'm glad you're here."

"Why?" His lips twitched. "You have it under control."

"He drugged the others and shot Mason."

A brush of fabric against the wall made him reach for his weapon. When Josh strode through the door, Rio relaxed. "Got your cuffs?"

"You bet. Do you know what he gave Del and the others?"

"Give me a minute. I'll find out."

"Don't do something you'll regret."

"This creep planned to kill my girlfriend. I will regret nothing." Rio turned to his cousin. "How bad, Mase?"

"Bad enough I want to barf."

He grinned at the ill-tempered comment as Nate strode into the room. "Help Josh take Mason downstairs." His friend looked as if he wanted to argue, but a hand signal from Durango's leader and he subsided, leaning down to assist Josh in raising the injured man to his feet. With Mason between them, Josh and Nate served as crutches.

Rio turned to Darcy. "Sweetheart, an ice pack would help with Mason's nausea." His girl hurried from the room.

Josh tossed Rio his handcuffs, then he and Nate maneuvered Mason from the room. Rio jerked the other man's arms behind his back and slapped cuffs on his wrists amid shrieks of pain.

"Stop whining, Cambridge. You and I are going to have a chat."

The professor sneered. "You slap bandages on people. You don't scare me."

Rio tilted his head. "Let's find out." He raised his pant leg and drew his Ka-Bar from the sheath in his combat boot. The black blade seemed to absorb the light as he turned toward the teacher.

"What are you doing?" Cambridge's voice rose, his gaze locked onto Rio's combat knife. "There's a cop downstairs."

"You think he's going to stop me? You poisoned his wife. No one will care if you don't survive the next five minutes."

The other man swallowed hard. "You're insane."

"Nope. Furious. You'll tell me what I want to know. The question is how much you'll hurt before you talk."

His gaze shifted to the open doorway as if measuring the distance.

"You won't make it." Rio's voice was just over a whisper.

"I'll scream."

"You already have and no one lifted a finger to help you." Rio moved behind the seated man, knelt, and set aside his knife. He clamped a hand over the other man's mouth and yanked his head back.

He grabbed Cambridge's injured hand and squeezed. The teacher's body bowed, his scream muffled. Rio needed answers fast, but he didn't want to upset Darcy more than she was already.

Once the screams had dissolved into sobs, Rio eased his hold on the injured hand. "What drug did you use, Cambridge?"

"I want a lawyer."

"Too bad for you I'm not a cop." Another round of muffled screams. "Last chance, Professor. Next time will be worse. Much worse. Do you know how much damage a Ka-Bar can do?"

"The cops will put you in jail."

A shrug. "I'll tell them you fought me for the knife. Think they'll take the word of a murderer?" He shifted enough so his knee pressed against the injured hand, a reminder to Cambridge of the pain he'd already suffered. "What drug?" he whispered in the man's ear.

His captive shuddered, moaned, said, "Rohypnol."

"Anything else?"

A quick head shake.

He'd have the doctor check his friends for the drug as well as other things. The professor might have lied. Probably not, though. Pain was a powerful motivator, and Rohypnol was easy to find and effective.

"If I find out you lied to me, you'll die a long, painful death." He stood, yanked Cambridge to his feet. "Let's go."

Downstairs, Rio's mike bag lay beside the recliner. Josh and Nate had led Mason to the couch. "On your side, Mase. I need to see what we're dealing with." His cousin hissed as he rolled to his left side. Though he sympathized with Mason's pain, he said, "You're tough. You can handle it."

"Shut up, Rio."

He shoved Cambridge to Josh. "Rohypnol."

Rio used his Ka-Bar to cut the fabric away from Mason's wound. A through-and-through. He found two more compression bandages in his bag. "You might miss your first parole meeting with Ethan."

"Great," his cousin groused. "Hope he doesn't mind a Skype check-in."

Darcy walked in with a gallon-size bag half filled with ice, carrying a kitchen towel in the other hand. "Will this work?"

"Drape that across his neck, sweetheart." He glanced at Josh. "Cambridge needs medical attention, too, Major."

"He'll get it. Nick will be here in a minute to take him off my hands."

At that moment, an Otter Creek PD SUV pulled into the driveway, lights flashing. Nick climbed from the SUV and strode to the house. "I've got this clown." He grasped Cambridge's arm. "Go to the hospital, Josh. Aaron's in surgery and Liz needs you. How are the others?"

"Still unconscious. Rohypnol."

The detective's expression darkened. "Get everybody checked out. Cambridge and I will be taking the scenic route."

Josh left the house at a run.

"Give me the short version," Nick said.

Darcy summarized while Rio and Nate helped Mason hobble to her SUV. His lips curved, wondering what she'd say when she realized he had a remote to her vehicle. By the time he returned for her, she was wrapping up her statement.

Nick glared at the sullen professor. "Legacy, huh? Guess you'll be thinking about that in the state penitentiary. Let's go, Cambridge." He led the other man to his department vehicle.

Darcy grabbed her purse and they drove Mason to the emergency room. Once his cousin was prepped for surgery, Rio returned to the waiting room. Darcy was sitting on a couch by herself at the back of the room, arms wrapped tightly around her middle, head down.

Rio wanted to take her away, spend time holding and kissing her. He'd never been so afraid in his life as when he realized Cambridge had her. The situation could have turned out so different. He'd been a heartbeat away from losing her forever. He longed to tell her he loved her, but this wasn't the time or place.

He sat beside her. Though she didn't look up, Darcy turned her face into his neck. Moisture hit his skin. Rio wrapped one arm around her waist while the other cupped the back of her head. He said nothing as Darcy's stress washed away in a flood of silent tears.

The room filled with friends of the Cahills. Madison sat on one side of her mother, her sister, Megan, on the other. The newspaper editor's mood appeared lethal. Might be better if Nick took Cambridge to some other hospital for treatment. And what about Serena and her baby?

With a shudder, Darcy sat up and wiped tears from her cheeks. "Will they let me see Trent soon?" she asked with a husky voice.

"We brought in several patients for them to evaluate, baby. Might be a while."

Ethan stepped into the waiting room. All eyes turned toward him. "Serena is fine." He smiled. "So is the baby."

Some of the knots in Rio's stomach loosened. The police chief motioned for Rio to follow him. He released Darcy. "I'll be back in a minute," he murmured, signaled Quinn to watch over her, and followed Ethan into the hall out of earshot of the people waiting for word on Aaron.

"Sit rep."

Rio told him what happened at Darcy's house, ending with, "We brought Del, Ivy, Stella, and Trent here to be tested for the drug. Mason should be in surgery now."

"Cambridge's target?"

"Darcy. Mason stepped in front of her as the professor pulled the trigger."

Ethan frowned. "He shot your cousin in the leg."

"Bad control." Mason had filled him in on the way to the hospital.

"Where is Cambridge now?"

"Nick's bringing him here for treatment."

"Sounds like your girlfriend did a number on the professor."

Rio shrugged one shoulder.

A ghost of a smile from the police chief. "Durango did exactly what needed to be done in the bank. The feds will hit town before long to investigate."

"They'll have to wait for interviews. Josh, Alex, and Nate won't leave their wives, and I'm not leaving Darcy's side."

Amusement twinkled in Ethan's eyes. "All of us will be unreachable. I'm not leaving Serena. For once, I hope the fed assigned to this case is Craig Jordan, our least favorite FBI agent. I'd take great pleasure in antagonizing the man."

Brian Elliott rounded the corner and trudged toward them. The contractor stopped a short distance away, shoulders hunched. Brian looked miserable.

Ethan glanced up, nodded, then turned again to Rio. "How bad is Mason's injury?"

"Depends on what the doc finds, but I think he'll be fine. Might need physical therapy."

A grimace from the police chief.

Yeah, Rio got that. Therapy was not fun, but it did the job.

"Any word on Aaron?"

"In surgery."

"Keep me posted. I'm going back to my wife."

Once Ethan left, Brian moved closer. "You were right, Rio. I'm sorry."

"Darcy wouldn't have stood a chance against Walsh. As it is, Cambridge tried to kill her and shot Mason when he protected her."

His jaw clenched. "Will Mason recover?"

He nodded. "He'll be out of work a few weeks."

"His job is secure. So what happens now?" he asked, resignation growing in his gaze.

"You tell me."

"I'll drop off the dorm plans at PSI for the new contractor."

Rio's eyebrows shot up. "Who said anything about finding a new contractor?"

"You're in the security business and I blew off your advice."

"Makes you unwise, not an offense worthy of firing."

The other man swallowed hard. "Thanks. I believe in giving second chances, Rio. I thought Walsh had reformed."

"Would you have allowed Walsh to work in your girlfriend's house?"

A grimace from the contractor. "Probably not. Is there anything you need from me?"

"This is not about guilt or favors, Brian. If you really want to help, finish Darcy's store and get a crew on her house."

"Count on it."

An hour later, Aaron's surgeon walked into the waiting room and spoke to Liz. "Aaron's fine. We drilled a burr hole and suctioned the blood from the subdural hematoma. He'll be good as new, Liz." The doc turned his attention to Rio. "Young man, your quick diagnosis probably saved Aaron's life. You should consider going to medical school."

His lips curved. "I'll think about it." Maybe when he retired from Fortress. His missions made it hard to be enrolled in school and Durango needed his skills.

Rio's gaze sought Darcy's. Could she handle his job? He wanted to laugh at himself. Darcy had taken down an armed man with a piece of wood. Yeah, his girl could handle the Fortress missions.

335

She slid her hand into his. "What is it?" she asked, voice low.

"You're amazing, sweetheart."

"Why?"

"You saved Mason and yourself."

She shrugged. "Desperation. Believe me, I wanted a gun to even the odds."

"Do you have one?"

A head shake.

"I'll buy you one if that's what you want. You'll need to attend a class and obtain your permit."

Darcy watched him a moment. "You're serious."

"I want you to feel safe, baby. If you need a weapon to do that, we'll choose one that fits your hand."

Alex strode into the waiting room, a broad smile on his face. "They're awake. Trent's asking for you, Darcy."

She hopped up and tugged on Rio's hand. "Come with me."

As soon as she saw her brother, she raced across the remaining space and threw her arms around his neck.

"You okay, Darce?"

"Me?" She released him and eased away. "You're the one who was drugged."

He winced. "Yeah, that's pretty embarrassing. I hear you took the pipsqueak professor out yourself."

"He would have killed us all. I didn't have a choice."

"You did good, sis."

"When is the doc springing you?" Rio asked.

"A drop-dead gorgeous nurse is processing the paperwork now."

Darcy laughed. "Guess you are feeling better."

"The only thing I want besides a date with Grace is my own bed."

"I'll have Quinn drive you to Darcy's. Mason is still in surgery."

"Will he be okay?"

"Should be. We'll see what the surgeon says."

A snort from the Fortress operative. "I'll take your word over a doctor any day."

Minutes later, Grace returned. Rio smiled. "Hello, Grace."

"What are you doing here, Rio?"

"Visiting Trent and waiting for word on my cousin. He's in surgery."

She handed the discharge papers to Trent. "Do you have someone to take you home, Trent?"

"You offering a ride?"

Color flooded Grace's face. "I'm off shift in a few minutes."

"I accept. Thank you, Grace."

She beamed. "I'll swing by the waiting room when I clock out."

After the nurse left, Darcy folded her arms, gaze fixed on Rio. "You know her. Was she part of the casserole brigade?"

His lips curved.

"That's what I thought."

Trent's eyes narrowed. "You and Grace were an item?"

"No. She and a bazillion other single women in town brought me and the rest of Durango meals to welcome us to Otter Creek in the summer."

"Didn't know people still did things like that."

"Welcome to small town life. Come on. Let's go to the waiting room so you don't miss your ride."

Not long after the operative left with Grace, Mason's surgeon reported that his cousin was in recovery and doing well. "What's his prognosis, doc?" Rio asked.

"Full recovery. You can see him now if you would like to visit with him. He's still pretty groggy."

Following his directions, Rio and Darcy found Mason. "Mase."

His cousin stirred, raised his eyelids. "Hey."

"Doc says you're going to be fine."

A slight nod. "Dad?"

"He'll be here in an hour."

Mason looked at Darcy. "You okay?"

She kissed his forehead. "I'm fine, thanks to you."

"Good. Rio, take her home."

"Once you're settled in a room."

"Dad will be here soon and Darcy's tired." He sighed, closed his eyes. "Don't need you to watch me nap."

He squeezed his cousin's shoulder. "Get some rest. I'll check on you tomorrow." He held out his hand to Darcy. "Let's go home, baby."

CHAPTER FORTY-TWO

On the drive home, Darcy's energy level plummeted. All she wanted was to crawl in bed and yank the covers over her head. When Rio parked in her driveway, she forced herself to move. She didn't want the medic to carry her into the house or take her back to the hospital, this time for the doctors to check on her.

He unlocked the door, deactivated the alarm, and ushered her inside. She walked to the kitchen for a bottle of water, skidding to a stop as she crossed the threshold. Oh, goodness. Cambridge must have searched in here for the coins while she played the piano. Drawers and cabinets had been emptied, the pantry shelves cleared. Anger burned hot and bright at the history professor.

"What's wrong, Darcy?" Rio stepped into the room behind her and whistled. "I'm assuming you ladies didn't leave the kitchen like this."

She shook her head, fury burning in her gut. If she'd known about this mess, she would have whacked Cambridge a couple more times. Jerk.

"Darcy, after a really bad day, what do you do to unwind?"

Yep, that's what this day was, all right. Colossally bad. "Light candles and take a hot bath." She opened the refrigerator and selected a bottle of water.

"Come on. I'll walk you upstairs. While you take a bath, I'll clean down here."

She shouldn't let him do this, but Darcy was too tired to argue.

Rio curled his hand around hers and led her upstairs. She expected him to leave her at her door, but he nudged her inside, followed her and closed the door. Next, he took the bottle from her hand and placed it on the floor.

Between one breath and the next, he had her backed up against the wall, his mouth covering hers. For several minutes, he took her mouth in series of long, deep kisses. By the time he drew back, her legs would have given out had he not been holding her so tight against his chest.

"I've never been so afraid in my life as I was when you didn't answer your phone." Rio rested his forehead against hers. "I was terrified I wouldn't reach you in time."

"I was afraid Cambridge would kill you the minute you showed up. You were walking into a trap, Rio."

He raised his head, cupped her cheek with his palm, and stared deep into her eyes. "You know what upset me the most?"

She shook her head.

"That I could lose you before I had a chance to tell you I love you more than my own life."

"Rio." Tears burned her eyes. She never thought she'd hear those precious words from this Delta warrior. He acted laid back, but she wasn't fooled. Like Trent, Rio never talked about his feelings. Laying them out like this was a huge risk for him and made her heart melt all the more.

"I know this is fast, baby, but my heart is yours. It belongs to you for all time. There is no one else for me, Darcy. I couldn't have asked for a more perfect gift than you."

Even as the tears fell, she smiled and pressed her lips to his. "I love you, too," she whispered.

He threaded his fingers through her hair and crowded in for another kiss before easing her away from him, his face devoid of expression. "Enough that you can handle my job?"

"You save lives, Rio. How can I ask you to stop doing what you love for your brothers-in-arms? I could be selfish and beg you to stop, but I love you enough not to. You being here with me might mean Josh, Nate, and Alex don't come home to their wives. I can't do that to my friends."

Hope sparked in his gaze. "Durango doesn't take as many missions as Trent's team, Darcy. Our primary assignment with Fortress is the bodyguard school."

"How often do you go on a mission?"

"Maybe once a month and the missions are short."

"Even if your team was like Trent's, I love you enough to take the risk. I'll treasure every moment we have together, Rio."

He wrapped his arms around Darcy, his heart racing beneath her ear. "You won't regret it, baby." A moment later, he released her and stepped toward the door. "Take your time with the bath. Relax. I'll make you a cup of tea while I clean the kitchen." With a blinding smile, he opened the door and walked out.

She pressed her hand to her stomach, hardly daring to believe she was blessed to have this amazing man in her life. The one thing she regretted was not being able to introduce him to her parents. Her mother would have loved Rio.

Darcy gathered what she needed for her bath, then returned to the collection of candles against the wall. She perused the selection, chose one in a mix of lavender and white.

Reaching for her selection, she knocked over another candle. This one rolled a short distance away from her.

When she crouched to retrieve it, she noticed metal on the bottom of the candle. She frowned and picked up the candle, turned it over to examine the metal.

Shock rolled through her. It couldn't be. Could it? Darcy hunted around for something to help free the metal. The only thing she had was a letter opener and she didn't want to scratch anything.

She turned each candle over. Every one had metal on the bottom. Grabbing one of them, she walked downstairs to the kitchen. Maybe Rio had an instrument in his medic bag to free the metal from the wax.

Rio swung around as she crossed the threshold. "Something wrong?"

"Look at the bottom of this." She handed over the candle.

He flipped the votive candle over. His eyes widened. "That looks like the back of a silver dollar."

"Do you have something we can use to extract the metal?"

"Be right back." He returned with forceps. In a couple deft moves, the metal was free. He whistled softly. "A Morgan silver dollar. Know what that means?"

"Ms. Bond hid the coins in plain sight. Every candle has coins on the bottom. But why would she do that? Why not put the coins in a safe deposit box?" She rolled her eyes at her own statement. "Never mind. We saw how secure the safe deposit boxes were. If you and your teammates hadn't been in town, Walsh and the rest of Sutton's crew would have gotten away with the coins."

"What are you going to do with them?"

Darcy frowned. "Ms. Bond meant them for her family. Do you think Mrs. Watson would give me the family's contact information?"

"Stella can help with that." He leaned back against the counter. "You know the coins are technically yours, sweetheart. They sold you the house along with everything inside it."

"They would never have signed away the contents had they known about the coins. I can't keep them, Rio. It wouldn't be right."

"Contact Stella tomorrow. I think she'll enjoy closing this part of the case. It's not often she delivers good news." He brushed her mouth with his. "Still want that bath?"

She wrinkled her nose. "I'm too revved up."

"Sit down and keep me company while I finish cleaning." He slid a mug of tea to her.

Darcy thought she'd feel guilty for sitting while Rio worked, but he didn't seemed to mind and she enjoyed watching him. Crazy as it might seem to someone else, the medic had a rhythm to his movements, almost like music. Right. Trent moved the same way and he didn't have any musical talent. More likely, they both were using what the military taught them. Smooth movements were less apt to catch a terrorist's eye than jerky ones.

Before long, the kitchen was in order and she had finished her tea.

"Sit with me for a while." Rio asked. "I'm not ready to turn in yet." When she nodded, he entwined their fingers and drew her into the living room. Once there, he turned the television on with the sound low and turned the lamp off, plunging the room into darkness. "Preferences?"

"A mystery."

He flipped channels until he found an episode of an older television series, then settled on the couch beside her. He wrapped his arm around her and encouraged Darcy to rest her head against his chest, much as she had on the plane.

The next thing she knew, Rio was laying her on her bed and slipping off her shoes. "Rio?"

"Shh. Sleep well, baby. I love you." A soft kiss and he was gone.

She thought about getting up to change into her pajamas, decided it was too much trouble. With a sigh, she rolled over and snuggled into the pillow to dream of the man she loved.

CHAPTER FORTY-THREE

Rio stood at the back of the church, exchanging greetings with various residents of Otter Creek who streamed into Cornerstone Church.

Marcus Lang stopped beside him, arm in a sling and a huge grin on his face. "This place is packed."

He chuckled. "Bet you wish our worship services were this well attended."

"You're right about that. I'm hoping all these folks will be generous for Julia's sake."

"I don't think you need to worry. That little elf is the town sweetheart."

"I heard Darcy and Nick practicing earlier."

"She wouldn't let me stay around for their rehearsals. Are they good?" He couldn't imagine their collaboration being anything other than spectacular. Both of them were gifted musicians.

"They should record an album together. They'd bring joy to many through their talent."

Rio's lips curved. They'd also make a bundle of money, he thought, watching Allen White strut around the auditorium. Though he still didn't like the man much,

Darcy's agent had taken care of the stage decorations, set aside the tickets she asked to be reserved for Schiller and the Edgertons as well as doing sound checks and arranging makeshift dressing rooms for Darcy and Nick. The detective had rolled his eyes at all the fuss from White.

Nick strode toward him at that moment, dressed in a tuxedo. Rio grinned. "Nice monkey suit, Nick."

His friend scowled and tugged on the collar. "I hate these things. How are you, Marcus?"

"Good. Doc says I'm healing fast." One of the church members motioned for his attention, so he excused himself and stepped away.

"Did you find out why Sutton's crew was at the bank instead of Darcy's house?" Rio murmured.

"Red herring. The professor got them out of the way while he went to the house to find the coins." Nick's face darkened. "He was going to force Darcy to tell where they were."

"At the time, she didn't know."

"Then it's good your lady is smart enough to defend herself with something simple. After he retrieved the money, he planned to leave the country." He glanced over at Marcus Lang. "Cambridge is the one who shot Marcus. Ethan was right. He intended to kill Darcy that night. He was also responsible for her car wreck and the attempt to run you over."

Rio was silent a moment. "Cambridge is lucky to be in jail," he said, voice barely above a whisper.

"Ethan and the rest of your teammates say the same. We also closed Gretchen Bond's case. Walsh killed her. He'd also heard about the coins. She wouldn't tell him where they were. When Stella checked into his record, she found out Walsh was arrested for burglary two days after Gretchen died and was sent to prison for violating his parole." Nick checked his watch. "Gotta go. See you later."

He walked to the front of the church and sat on the first pew.

The lights dimmed and people still standing moved to find seats as the pastor welcomed everyone and introduced Darcy. By the time he left the stage, Rio was seated in the front row beside Julia and her family. The moment she stepped on stage, Rio's heart turned over in his chest. He marveled that she loved him. He didn't deserve her, but he would never take Darcy St. Claire for granted. She was a treasure beyond price, one he planned to cherish for the rest of their days.

Pastor Lang was right. Darcy and Nick were incredible separate and together. Rio caught sight of White's face as they played together and knew the agent would propose a collaborative project for the two musicians. If Julia was any indication of how the album would be received, Darcy and Nick were destined to be a hit as a duet in the classical music world. His little friend was literally bouncing in her seat.

At the end of the concert, Nick called Julia to the stage. Her pixie face glowed as she climbed the stairs.

"Julia, would you like to play with us?" Nick asked.

She nodded her head. "What will we play?"

"How about *Silent Night?*"

The longer she played, the more amazed Rio became at her talent. His Tiger Lily was surprisingly good for someone who'd been playing for a few months.

After they finished their song, Rio handed a small bouquet of pink roses to Nick for Julia, then presented a dozen red roses to Darcy. Her eyes sparkled as he leaned down and kissed her. When applause filled the auditorium, she stepped back, laughing, her cheeks flushed.

Ushers stood at the back, collecting donations from the audience as they left. Forty minutes later, the church was empty save for a few people. Darcy sat on the stage stairs beside Julia. "Well, Julia, what did you think?"

"You're good."

"And Nick?"

She beamed. "He's terrific."

The detective's face burned a bright red.

"You're right." Darcy smiled. "He is terrific."

Marcus Lang walked down the aisle, a broad smile on his face. "Jim, the treasurer wrote you a check." He handed over the folded piece of paper to Julia's father.

The policeman scanned the amount, stopped, looked more closely. "I can't believe this." His voice sounded choked. He turned the check around so his wife could see. She buried her face in her hands, shoulders shaking.

Darcy looked at Rio, alarm growing in her eyes. "What's wrong?" she whispered.

From Jim and Karen's expression, Rio suspected that maybe everything was right. He turned to the pastor. "How much did we raise?"

"All of it. We collected enough money to pay off the medical bills in total."

"How can we ever repay you, Darcy? You, too, Nick." Jim stared at the check in wonder.

"I know the perfect way to do that," Darcy said and turned to Julia. "How about a hug?"

The little girl threw her arms around Darcy's neck and squeezed. Just watching Darcy with her made Rio long for a family of his own, a family with the woman who had captured his heart, the woman whose birthday was three months and four days away.

Rio smiled. He had already bought her gift. The small velvet jewelry box was locked away. He was ready to place the diamond on her finger, but he wanted Darcy to be sure. And when the time was right, perhaps they would have their own son or daughter to love.

Julia released Darcy and raced to Nick to share a hug.

Rio drew Darcy to her feet. He cupped her cheek, his thumb stroking the velvet skin. "Let's go home, baby." And he knew he spoke the truth. Home was wherever Darcy happened to be.

In Plain Sight

ABOUT THE AUTHOR

Rebecca Deel is a preacher's kid with a black belt in karate. She teaches business classes at a private four-year college in Nashville, Tennessee. She plays the piano at church, writes freelance articles, and runs interference for the family Westies. She's been married to her amazing husband for more than 20 years and is the proud mom of two grown sons. She delivers monthly devotions to the women's group at her church and conducts seminars in personal safety, money management, and writing. Her articles have been published in *ONE Magazine*, *Contact*, and *Co-Laborer*, and she was profiled in the June 2010 Williamson edition of *Nashville Christian Family* magazine. Rebecca completed her Doctor of Arts degree in Economics and wears her favorite Dallas Cowboys sweatshirt when life turns ugly.

For more information on Rebecca . . .
Sign up for Rebecca's newsletter: http://eepurl.com/_B6w9
Visit Rebecca's website: www.rebeccadeelbooks.com

Printed in Great Britain
by Amazon